The Striker

Clive Cussler is the author or co-author of a great number of international bestsellers, including the famous Dirk Pitt® Adventures, such as *Arctic Drift*; the NUMA® Files, most recently *Medusa*; the Oregon Files, such as *The Jungle*; the Isaac Bell Adventures, which began with *The Chase*; and the highly successful most recent series, the Fargo Adventures. He lives in Arizona.

Justin Scott is the author of twenty-six novels, including *The Shipkiller* and *Normandie Triangle*; the Ben Abbot detective series; and five modern sea thrillers under his pen name Paul Garrison. He lives in Connecticut.

Find out more about the world of Clive Cussler
by visiting www.clivecussler.co.uk

The Striker

CLIVE CUSSLER
and JUSTIN SCOTT

PENGUIN BOOKS

PENGUIN BOOKS

Published by the Penguin Group
Penguin Books Ltd, 80 Strand, London WC2R ORL, England
Penguin Group (USA) Inc., 375 Hudson Street, New York, New York 10014, USA
Penguin Group (Canada), 90 Eglinton Avenue East, Suite 700, Toronto, Ontario, Canada M4P 2Y3
(a division of Pearson Penguin Canada Inc.)
Penguin Ireland, 25 St Stephen's Green, Dublin 2, Ireland (a division of Penguin Books Ltd)
Penguin Group (Australia), 707 Collins Street, Melbourne, Victoria 3008, Australia
(a division of Pearson Australia Group Pty Ltd)
Penguin Books India Pvt Ltd, 11 Community Centre, Panchsheel Park, New Delhi – 110 017, India
Penguin Group (NZ), 67 Apollo Drive, Rosedale, Auckland 0632, New Zealand
(a division of Pearson New Zealand Ltd)
Penguin Books (South Africa) (Pty) Ltd, Block D, Rosebank Office Park,
181 Jan Smuts Avenue, Parktown North, Gauteng 2193, South Africa

Penguin Books Ltd, Registered Offices: 80 Strand, London WC2R ORL, England

www.penguin.com

First published in the United Stated of America by G. P. Putnam's Sons 2013
First published in Great Britain by Michael Joseph 2013
Published in Penguin Books 2014
001

Set in 12.5/14.75pt Garamond MT Std
Typeset by Jouve (UK), Milton Keynes
Printed in Great Britain by Clays Ltd, St Ives plc

PAPERBACK ISBN: 978–1–405–92506–8
OM PAPERBACK ISBN: 978–1–405–91141–2

www.greenpenguin.co.uk

Prologue

A Smoke-filled Room
1912

The Marmon 32 Speedster parked on Wall Street in a shadow between two lampposts.

Roundsman O'Riordan took notice. It was the dead of night. Orders said let no one bother the bigwig politicians and officeholders who were horse-trading upstairs in the Congdon Building. And the auto had a clear shot at the limousines waiting for them at the curb.

Its side curtains were fogged by the damp rolling off the harbor. O'Riordan had to get close to see inside. The driver was a pleasant surprise, a beautiful lady with straw-blonde hair, and the cop relaxed a little. But all he could see of the gent beside her were steely contours. Still, you couldn't rap your stick on a Marmon 32 and tell the swells to move along like they were bums on the sidewalk, so with his right hand by his pistol, he tapped the side curtain lightly, like touching his glass to the mahogany to signal the bartender of a classy joint he was ready for another but didn't mean to be rushing him.

A big hand with long, nimble fingers slid the curtain open. O'Riordan glimpsed a snow-white cuff, diamond links, and the black sleeve of a dress coat. The hand seized his in a strong grip.

'Paddy O'Riordan. Fancy meeting you here.'

Raked by searching blue eyes, the roundsman recognized the gold mane, the thick flaxen mustache, and the no-nonsense expression that could only belong to Isaac Bell – chief investigator of the Van Dorn Detective Agency.

He touched his stick to his helmet. 'Good evening, Mr Bell. I didn't recognize you in the shadows.'

'What are you doing out so late?' Bell asked.

O'Riordan started to answer before Bell's grin told him it was a joke. Policemen were supposed to be out late.

The detective nodded at the limousines. 'Big doings.'

'Judge Congdon's got a special waiting at Grand Central. Tracks cleared to Chicago. And I'm sorry to tell you I have me orders to clear the street. Straight from the captain.'

Bell did not seem to hear. 'Paddy, I want you to meet my wife – Marion, may I present Roundsman O'Riordan, former scourge of Staten Island pirates back when he was in the Harbor Squad. There wasn't a wharf rat in New York who didn't buy drinks for the house the night Paddy came ashore.'

She reached across her husband with an ungloved hand that seemed to glow like ivory. O'Riordan took it carefully in his enormous fist and bowed low.

'A privilege to meet you, marm. I've known your good husband many years in the line of duty. And may I say, marm, that Mrs O'Riordan and I have greatly enjoyed your moving picture shows.'

She thanked him in a musical voice that would sing in his mind for days.

Chief Inspector Bell said, 'Well, we better not keep you from your rounds.'

O'Riordan touched his stick to his helmet again. If a crack private detective chose to canoodle with his own wife in a dark auto on Wall Street in the middle of the night – orders be damned.

'I'll tell the boys not to disturb you.'

But Bell motioned him closer and whispered, 'I wouldn't mind if they kept an eye out if I have to leave her alone a moment.'

'They'll be drawin' straws for the privilege.'

Backslapping politicians burst from the building and converged on the smaller of the limousines, a seven-passenger Rambler Knickerbocker.

Isaac Bell opened the curtain to hear them.

'Driver! Straight to Grand Central.'

'Don't love handing the vice presidency to a louse like Congdon, but that's politics.'

'Money talks.'

The Rambler Knickerbocker drove off. Senior men emerged next. Moving more slowly, they climbed into the second limousine, an enormous Cunningham Model J, hand-built at great expense to Judge James Congdon's own design. To Bell's ear they sounded less reconciled than resigned.

'Congdon has most of the delegates he needs, and those he doesn't, he'll buy.'

'If only our candidate hadn't died.'

'Always the wrong man.'

Isaac Bell waited for the Cunningham to turn the corner. A police motorcycle escort stationed on Broadway clattered after it. 'If James Congdon captures vice president,' Bell said, 'the president's life won't be worth a plugged nickel.'

He kissed Marion's lips. 'Thank you for making me look harmless to the cops. Are you sure you won't go home?'

'Not this time,' she said firmly, and Bell knew there was no dissuading her. This time was different.

Although he was dressed for the theater, he left his silk topper on the backseat and donned a broad-brimmed hat with a low crown instead.

Marion straightened his tie.

Bell said, 'I've always wondered why you never ask me to be careful.'

'I wouldn't want to slow you down.'

Bell winked. 'Not likely.'

He left his wife with a smile. But as he crossed Wall Street, his expression hardened, and the warmth seeped from his eyes.

Joseph Van Dorn, the large, bearded founder of the agency, was waiting, deep in shadow and still as ice. He stood watch as Bell picked open the lock on the outside door, and followed him in, where Bell picked another lock on a steel door marked *Mechanical Room*. Inside it was warm and damp. An orderly maze of thick pipes passed through rows of steam-conditioning valves. Van Dorn compared the control wheels to an engineer's sketch he unfolded from his inside pocket.

Isaac Bell climbed back up to the street and went around to the front of the building. His evening clothes elicited a respectful nod from the doorman. As the politicians said, Money talked.

'Top floor,' he told the yawning elevator runner.

'I thought they were all done up there.'

'Not quite.'

BOOK ONE

Coal

Gleason Mine No. 1,
Gleasonburg,
West Virginia
1902

I

He was a fresh-faced youth with golden hair. But something about him looked suspicious. A coal cop watching the miners troop down the rails into the mouth of Gleason Mine No. 1 pointed him out to his boss, a Pinkerton detective.

The young miner towered over the foreigners the company imported from Italy and Slovenia, and was even taller than the homegrown West Virginia boys. But it was not his height that looked out of place. Nor was his whipcord frame unusual. The work was hard, and it cost plenty to ship food to remote coalfields. There was no free lunch in the saloons that lined the muddy Main Street.

A miner clomping along on a wooden peg tripped on a crosstie and stumbled into another miner on crutches. The golden-haired youth glided to steady both, moving so effortlessly he seemed to float. Many were maimed digging coal. He stood straight on both legs and still possessed all his fingers.

'Don't look like no poor worker to me,' the coal cop ventured with a contemptuous smirk.

'Watching like a cat, anything that moves,' said the Pinkerton, who wore a bowler hat, a six-gun in his coat, and a blackjack strapped to his wrist.

'You reckon he's a striker?'

'He'll wish he ain't.'

'*Gangway!*'

An electric winch jerked the slack out of a wire between the rails. Miners, laborers and doorboys jumped aside. The wire dragged a train of coal cars out of the mine and up a steep slope to the tipple, where the coal was sorted and dumped into river barges that towboats pushed down the Monongahela to Pittsburgh.

The tall young miner exchanged greetings with the derailer-switch operator. If the wire, which was shackled to a chain bridle on the front car, broke, Jim Higgins was supposed to throw the switch to make the train jump the tracks before the hundred-ton runaway plummeted back down into the works.

'The cops are watching you,' Higgins warned.

'I'm no striker.'

'All we're asking,' Higgins answered mildly, 'is to live like human beings, feed our families, and send our kids to school.'

'They'll fire you.'

'They can't fire us all. The coal business is booming and labor is scarce.'

Higgins was a brave man. He had to be to ignore the fact that the mineowners would stop at nothing to keep the union out of West Virginia. Men fired for talking up the union – much less calling a strike – saw their wives and children kicked out of the shanties they rented from the Gleason Consolidated Coal & Coke Company. And when Gleason smoked out labor organizers, the Pinkertons rousted them back to Pennsylvania, beaten bloody.

'Higgins!' shouted a foreman. 'I told you to oil that winch.'

'I'm supposed to watch the derailer when the cars are coming up.'

'Do like I tell you. Oil that winch every hour.'

'Who's going to stop a runaway if the wire breaks?'

'Get up there and oil that winch, damn you!'

Jim Higgins abandoned his post and ran two hundred yards up the steep incline to the winch engine, past the cars of coal climbing heavily to the tipple.

The tall young miner ducked his head to enter the mouth of the mine – a timber-braced portal in the side of the mountain – and descended down a sloping tunnel. He had boned up on mine engineering to prepare for the job. Strictly speaking, this tracked haulageway was not a *tunnel*, which by definition had to pass completely through a mountain, but an *adit*. *Aditus*, he recalled from his boarding school Latin, meant 'access.' Once in, there was no way out but to turn around and go back.

Where he entered a gallery that intersected and split off from the haulageway, he hailed the small boy, who opened a wooden door to channel the air from the ventilators.

'Hey, Sammy. Feller from the telegraph office told me your Pirates beat Brooklyn yesterday. Eight-to-five.'

'Wow! Thanks for telling me, mister.'

Sammy had never been near a major-league ballpark – never been farther than ten miles from this hollow where the Gleason Company struck a rich bed of the Pittsburgh Seam that underlay Pennsylvania, West Virginia, and Ohio. But his father had been a brakeman on the B & O, until he died in a wreck, and used to bring home stories of big-city games that he would illustrate with cigarette baseball cards of famous players.

The young man slipped Sammy a colorful chromo-lithograph of Rochester first baseman Harry O'Hagan. In August, O'Hagan had accomplished a miracle, still on the lips of every man and boy in America – a one-man triple play.

'Bet New York's kicking themselves for trading Harry,' he said, then asked in a lower voice, 'Have you seen Roscoe?'

Roscoe was a Gleason spy disguised as a laborer.

The boy nodded in the same direction the young man was headed.

He followed the gallery, which sloped deeper into the mountain for hundreds of yards, until it stopped at the face of the seam. There he went to work as a helper, shoveling the chunks of coal picked, drilled and dynamited from the seam by the skilled miners. He was paid forty cents for every five-ton car he loaded during twelve-hour shifts six days a week.

The air was thick with coal dust. Swirling black clouds of it dimmed the light cast by electric bulbs. The low ceiling was timbered by props and crosspieces every few feet to support the mountain of rock and soil that pressed down on the coal. The seam creaked ominously, squeezed above and below by pressure from roof and floor.

Here in the side tunnel, off the main rail track, the coal cars were pulled by mules that wore leather bonnets to protect their heads. One of the mules, a mare with the small feet and long ears that the miners believed indicated a stronger animal, suddenly stopped. Eustace McCoy, a big West Virginian who had been groaning about his red-eye hangover, cursed her and jerked her bridle. But she planted her legs and refused to budge, ears flickering at the creaking sound.

Eustace whipped off his belt and swung it to beat her with the buckle end.

The tall blond youth caught it before it traveled six inches.

'Sonny, get out of my way!' Eustace warned him.

'I'll get her moving. It's just something spooked her.'

Eustace, who was nearly as tall and considerably broader, balled his fist and threw a haymaker at the young man's face.

The blow was blocked before it could connect. Eustace cursed and swung again. Two punches sprang back at him. They landed in elegant combination, too quick to follow with the eye and packed with concentrated power. Eustace fell down on the rails, the fight and anger knocked out of him.

The miners exchanged astonished glances.

'Did you see that?'

'Nope.'

'Neither did Eustace McCoy.'

The young man spoke gently to the mule and she pulled the car away. Then he helped the fallen laborer to his feet and offered his hand when Eustace acknowledged with a lopsided grin, 'Ain't been hit that hard since I borrowed my old man's bottle. Whar'd you larn to throw that one-two?'

'Oregon,' the young man lied.

His name was Isaac Bell.

Bell was a Van Dorn Agency private detective under orders to ferret out union saboteurs. This was his first solo case, and he was supposed to be operating in deep disguise. To ensure secrecy, the mineowner hadn't even told the company cops about his investigation. But the awe on the miners' faces told Bell he had just made a bad mistake.

The year was 1902. Van Dorn detectives were earning a reputation as valuable men who knew their business, and the agency motto – We never give up! Never! – had begun to be muttered, remorsefully, inside the nation's penitentiaries. Which meant that young Isaac Bell had to admit that he was very likely the only Van Dorn in the entire outfit so puddingheaded that he would ruin his disguise by showing off fancy boxing tricks.

Roscoe, the Gleason spy, was eyeing him thoughtfully. That might not matter too much. Bell reckoned he could fix that somehow. But any saboteur who caught wind of him championing a poor, dumb mule with a Yale man's mastery of the manly art of self-defense would not stay fooled for long.

'Gangway!'

The exhausted men climbing out of the mine at the end of their shift shuffled off the tracks. The winch jerked the slack out of the wire, and twenty coal cars emerged behind them and trundled up the steep incline to the tipple. The train was almost to the top when the chain bridle that attached the wire to the front car broke with a bang as loud and sharp as a gunshot.

The train stopped abruptly.

One hundred tons of coal hung motionless for a heart-beat.

Then it started rolling backwards toward the mouth of the mine.

Jim Higgins, who was hurrying from the winch engine to his post at the derailer switch, dropped his oilcan and ran as fast as he could. But the train was gathering speed. It rolled ahead of him, and before he could reach the switch, twenty cars hurtled through it straight down the main line.

Isaac Bell charged after it. He spotted a brake lever on the last car and forged alongside, looking for handholds to jump to. The coal train accelerated and pulled ahead of him. As the last car whipped past, he leaped on to its rear coupler and caught his balance by clapping both hands around the brake lever. He threw his weight against the steel bar, slamming curved brake shoes against the spinning wheels.

Metal screeched. The lever bucked in his hands. Sparks fountained skyward. Bell pushed the brake with every sinew in his body. Swift and purposeful action and determined muscle and bone appeared to slow the runaway. Several more quick-thinking men ran alongside in hopes of leaping on the brakes of the other cars.

But the weight of the coal was too great, the momentum too strong.

Suddenly, with a bang almost as explosive as the parting bridle chain, the iron pin connecting the lever to the brake shoes snapped. The lever swung freely. Bell, shoving it with all his might, lost his balance. The rails and crossties blurred under him as the train accelerated. Only lightning reflexes and a powerful grip on the top rim of the coal car saved him from falling.

The car swayed violently as it gained speed. Being the last car, unanchored by any behind it, the same lateral forces that cracked a whip slammed it sideways against the ventilator house that stood close by the tracks. The impact sheared its pillars, and the building collapsed on the giant fan that drove fresh air into the mine. A shattered roof beam jammed its blades.

'Jump!' miners yelled.

Before Bell could choose a direction in which there was room to land, the train stormed through the mouth and into the narrow confines of the haulageway, where to jump would be to smash flesh and blood against timber, stone, steel and coal. Bell swung his feet on to the coupler and attempted to brace for what was going to be a very sudden stop when they hit bottom.

The coal train swayed in wider and wider arcs with the ever-increasing speed of its descent. The rear car to which Bell clung slammed against shoring timbers, splintering them, and crumbled pillars of coal the miners had left standing to support the ceiling. The front end, nineteen cars ahead of Bell, bore down on a wooden air door that Sammy the doorboy had shut behind it moments earlier as it ascended.

Sammy was addled by twelve hours of work in near darkness and terrified by the roar of the juggernaut hurtling toward him. But he stood at his post, desperately trying to open the door to let it pass. Like a tycoon brushing a beggar out of his way with a haughty hand, the train flung him against the wall, smashed the air door to flinders, and gained speed.

2

The swaying coal car Isaac Bell clung to scraped the sides of the tunnel. The screeching, banging impact severed the wires that powered the electric lights, and the train plummeted downward in total darkness.

Bell pressed himself tight against the cold steel to minimize the distance his body would travel at the moment of impact. It could not be much farther to the coal seam at the bottom. Suddenly, the train jumped the tracks. Metal shrieked as it battered the side of the tunnel and threatened to buck him off like a maddened bronco. Instead, it saved the young detective's life. Sideswiping the walls had the effect of slowing the train. When it finally struck the seam with a thunderclap, he was banged hard against the back of the car, but not so hard as to break bones.

The silence that followed was as deep as the darkness.

Bell leaped down and ran in the dark, back up the route the runaway had taken him, sliding his boots along the crossties to stay in the middle of the track, where he was least likely to smash into anything. He ran as fast as he could with his hands stretched ahead of his face in hopes of feeling an obstruction in time to stop.

He had seconds to get out before he died in the black and airless chaos of the wrecked gallery. For dangers far deadlier than collision lurked in the dark. *Damps* – poisonous carbonic acid and explosive methane – were collecting quickly as the demolished ventilator ceased to draw fresh air from the surface and expel lethal vapors. Suffocating *blackdamp*, thick with carbonic acid, would kill him in ten seconds. *Fulminating damp*, 'inflammable air,' marsh gas exuded by the coal, would blow everyone in the mine to Kingdom Come. Thank God, he thought, most of the day shift was out of the mine and the night shift hadn't entered yet. Only the doorboys were still at their posts.

All of a sudden, the dark lifted. Daylight so soon? But it wasn't possible. He could not be that close to the mouth. Then he realized that the light was coming from behind him – orange flickering light – the sparkle of fire as gas and coal at the face of the seam ignited. The sudden light saved him from stumbling over a doorboy crawling along the tracks.

Bell yanked him to his feet.

'Stand up! Chokedamp suffocates you down low. Run!'

He shoved the boy ahead of him, and together they ran from the flames and smoke chasing them up the slope. The smoke would spread *white damp*, odorless carbon monoxide, which would kill them in minutes if they didn't burn to death first.

They stopped abruptly. The haulageway was blocked. The train had sheared off the pillars of coal that the miners had left standing to brace the ceiling. Unsupported, the ceiling had fallen into the haulageway. A two-foot opening was held up by a single groaning timber.

'I can fit through, mister. I'll get help.'

'Hold on,' said Bell. It looked like it would collapse any moment. He crawled into the narrow space, braced the groaning timber with his back, and tried to hold the mountain. 'OK, sonny,' he gasped. 'Slip by.'

The boy scrambled through.

Bell gently released the pressure and slithered on his belly. Just as he pulled his feet out, the timber snapped. The ceiling collapsed with a roar as tons of coal and slate filled the space.

'Let's go.'

But the boy was frozen in place, staring at what had almost killed them.

'Close shave,' Bell said lightly to put him at ease, and when that didn't work he asked, 'Did you see if little Sammy got out?'

'Dead,' said the boy. 'The train got him.'

'Come on. Let's get out of here.'

They ran, climbing the slope, until they were stopped by another fall. This one emitted no light from the other side even though they had to be near the mouth. But, through it, they could hear a faint tapping. Picks digging through the fall. They grabbed rocks and pounded on the fall, alerting those on the other side that they were alive.

The picking sounds doubled, and doubled again. Soon Isaac Bell saw light and heard a cheer. Ten men battered through the fall. The first face Bell saw belonged to Jim Higgins, who had led the rescue.

Cheering men pulled them through the opening and reached for more. The cheers died on their lips.

'That's all?' asked Higgins.

'Little Sammy was killed,' said Bell. 'I didn't see any others. Give me a pick. I'll show you the way.'

Before they could start down, an explosion rocked the

mine from deep within, and the rescuers knew in their hearts that although they would dig all night for more survivors, and dig all the next day, they would never find a living soul.

They started down. Again they were stopped, not by an explosion but by a gang of club-wielding company police led by a Pinkerton, who shouted, 'Jim Higgins!'

'Right here, we're just heading down.'

'Jim Higgins, you're under arrest.'

'For what?'

'For murdering all them poor little doorboys who died in the mine.'

'I didn't –'

'You abandoned your post. You caused the accident by failing to throw the derailer switch that would have stopped the runaway.'

'The foreman ordered me to oil –'

'Tell it to the judge,' said the Pinkerton.

Jim Higgins squared his shoulders. 'You boys set me up,' he said. 'You found out I am a union organizer. You know that beating me up never worked before, so you waited for a chance to take me out of the fight. You put me on the derailer to keep me away from the workers. And now one of your bought-and-paid judges will sentence me to the penitentiary for a crime you all know damned well I never did.'

'No,' a cop snickered. 'No judge is locking you in no penitentiary. You're headed for the hangman.'

They seized his arms and started to drag him away.

Jim Higgins locked gazes with Isaac Bell.

Bell heard him say, 'There's more where I came from.'

3

'That chain bridle was brand-new,' said the winch engin-eer, a huge man squinting through wire-rimmed spectacles. 'I installed it myself. It could not possibly have parted.'

'Like folks say, it only takes one weak link,' said Isaac Bell.

From the winch at the top of the tipple, he could see down the steep tracks to the mouth of the mine where frantic mechanicians were jury-rigging temporary ventila-tor fans. A hundred rescuers were waiting for them to purge Gleason Mine No. 1 of carbonic acid, inflammable air, and deadly white damp. Only then could they enter the deep galleries where the boys were trapped.

The engineer stiffened. 'I don't install weak links, sonny. I inspect every link with my own eye.'

'I wonder,' said Isaac Bell, 'whether it was the wire that broke.'

'You're doing a lot of wondering, mister.'

Bell responded with a friendly smile that tinged his blue eyes a soft shade of violet. 'Since I rode that train to the bottom of the mine, I'm mighty curious what set her loose.'

'Oh, you're the feller that tried to stop her? Let me shake your hand, son. That was a brave thing you tried to do.'

'I wish I could have stopped her,' said Bell. 'But, I was wondering –'

'Nope, the wire's fine and dandy. Here, I'll show you.'

The engineer led Bell to the giant drum around which the inch-thick steel rope was coiled in tight and orderly rows and showed him the loop that formed the end. 'See, this here thimble inside the loop protects the wire from pinching. You see how it's held its shape? And the clamps here have their saddles on the live side of the wire like they're supposed to, and they held tight.'

'I suppose that means a link in the chain busted even though it's not supposed to.'

The engineer shook his head. 'If they ever snake that chain out of that mess down there, I'll bet you even money it'll be strong as the day it was born. Molybdenum alloy steel. You know what that is, son?'

Bell did but a laborer probably would not, so he shook his head. 'Heard it spoke. Can't rightly say I know what it means.'

'Alloy cooked up by French metallurgists. Much stronger than plain steel. Ideal for lifting chain. Molybdenum steel don't fracture.'

'Then what do you reckon broke?' asked Bell.

'Hard to believe it was the shackle.'

'What shackle?'

'The swivel shackle that connects the wire to the bridle. It's so we can hook her up easy, and it swivels to distribute the load. No, that shackle's the culprit. Even money.'

'Do shackles break often?'

'Never! Almost never.'

'Wonder was it too small for the job?'

'No, sir! Installed it myself. Made darn sure its working

load exceeded the chain's and the wire's. Can't imagine how it failed.'

Bell wondered if there was some miraculous way to ask politely enough to keep the engineer talking, whether he thought that the runaway was only a dream. Then a broad-bellied coal cop swaggered out of the tipple, eyeing Bell suspiciously. 'What are you two jawing about?'

The engineer was not cowed. He was a valuable mechanician who knew his place. But Isaac Bell, a lowly laborer, was supposed to kowtow, unless he was man enough to look the cop in the face, at the risk of his job, and tell him to go to hell.

Bell turned his back on him and walked down the steep slope.

'Where the hell you going? I'm talking to you.'

'They fixed the ventilators,' Bell called over his shoulder. 'I'm going down with the rescue boys. You coming?'

The cop, who had no desire to enter a coal mine filled with poisonous and explosive gases, did not reply, and Bell joined the rescuers, who were dragging new lines from the power plant and wielding picks and electric drills to clear the haulageway and galleries to search for the missing doorboys.

When the last small body had been carried out and the exhausted searchers shambled up to the surface, Bell extinguished his headlamp and hid in a gallery. He watched their lights fade up the haulageway. Then he relighted his own lamp and headed deep into the empty mine on the trail of an enigma.

At no point in his investigation had he seen or heard a hint of union sabotage and now he thought he knew the reason why. Having worked weeks underground, and having just survived the mining disaster set off by the runaway, he had to question the very existence of the union saboteurs that the company had hired Van Dorn to arrest.

He did not doubt the existence of sabotage in labor disputes. Violent incidents abounded in a war between workers and owners that stretched back as far as anyone could remember. Miners had shot it out with the Coal and Iron Police before the oldest man in the mine had worked as a doorboy. Many a railroad workers' strike had escalated from fistfights, clubbings and shoot-outs to derailed locomotives and dynamited bridges. Many a steel mill strike had seen furnaces blown up or had their fires drawn, destroying the works when the molten metal turned solid inside the pots and ladles. Towboats and barges were set adrift, factories put to fire, telegraph wires cut, and owners' mansions burned to the ground. Mounted police had charged like cavalry on the battlefield. Gatling guns had raked strikers' tent cities.

But deep *under* the ground in a coal mine, sabotage was tantamount to suicide. Deep underground, the unionists themselves would be crushed when roofs fell. Suffocated when damps displaced air. Burned alive when gases exploded.

But before he could report that there were no union saboteurs to the Boss – Mr Joseph Van Dorn, founder of the detective agency that bore his name – a young detective on his first case had better make absolutely sure that the runaway had been an accident. That demanded evidence.

Trust what you see, not what you're supposed to see — the first lesson of his long apprenticeship drilled into him by veteran Van Dorns like Wish Clarke, and Mack Fulton and Walter Kisley. And repeated often, very often, by Joseph Van Dorn himself.

Bell walked down the slope to the bottom of the haulageway and passed his light over the twisted wreckage of the coal train that had smashed into the yet-to-be-dug seam at the end of the line. The car at the rear, the bucking, swaying last one he had ridden down in, had been the front car on the way up, the one to which the winch wire's chain bridle had been attached. He found the links at either end of the chain bridle fixed to massive rings fastened to the left and right side of the frame. But the bridle, a length of chain twice as long as the width of the car, had parted right in the middle. He found no shackle. And only half of the link that would have been the middle one remained, jammed into its neighbor. When he tried to pull it out, it sliced his finger.

Sucking the blood, he inspected the sharp edge that had cut him. The fracture was in the barrel, one of the long straight sides of the link. He expected a ragged edge. What he saw was a surprise, and a mystery. Where the steel link had fractured was smooth and flat and sharp as a razor.

It looked like a piece had been cut out with a chisel. Using other links to tap it loose, he worked the broken link out of the one it had jammed in and put it in his pocket. Then he searched for the missing shackle. It must have fallen in the crosstie-lined trough between the steel rails of the coal train tracks.

He looked until his light began to run out of oil, but he never found the shackle. Another mystery. Obviously, the shackle had slipped out of the broken link. But how had the shackle separated from the thimble that formed the wire loop he had seen at the winch?

As he continued up the rails, out of the mine, he recalled the cops who'd been watching him. Rather than get caught with the broken link if they made him turn out his pockets, he slipped it into a crack between a prop and the coal seam and noted the spot carefully in his memory — four support props above the lowest side gallery.

He started up. Or was it three? He went back, counted again, touching each. Four. The hairs prickled on the back of his neck. He had a photographic memory. How could he forget a picture so simple as these four ceiling props standing in a row? He noticed a strange silence. Something had changed in the narrow passages. The ventilators had stopped blowing fresh air.

The damps were gathering again. No wonder he felt light-headed. Bell turned and stumbled upward, toward the distant mouth. If it was blackdamp, he hadn't a prayer. The carbonic acid would stop him within seconds. White damp from the extinguished fire? Minutes. Less than ten.

He broke into a shambling run. His head was pounding and his heart hammered in his chest. He imagined the poison gases chasing after him, breaking like a tidal wave, cresting, splashing, clutching his boots, his knees, tugging at his legs, suction pulling him under. He ran harder, his fading light bouncing low shadows from the crossties. Two ties for each step. He made himself stretch for three longer strides, flowing over the floor of the mine faster than the wave crashing after him.

He was pulling ahead when he saw something gleam in his light. It was tucked against the right rail, half obscured by a wooden tie. He slowed, stopped, stared down at it, desperately trying to mine thoughts from a heavy head. The shackle? Did he imagine it? Or did he see a piece of it directly under his feet? Should he try to pick it up? He had the feeling that if he knelt to pick it up, he might never stand again. His head was spinning. But it was important. The saboteur . . . He gathered his strength and dropped to one knee. Before he could reach it, it disappeared in a shadow that moved over it.

Isaac Bell turned his head to see what caused the shadow.

He sensed motion and found himself looking into golden eyes as simultaneously remote and intent as those of a wolf that had fixed on its prey. The jaws between the eyes formed a fist. The white damp had rattled his mind. He had to stand up. He had to run. The fist traveled at his face with the speed and power of a locomotive. Bell's own fists leaped automatically to block and counterpunch. Then he heard an explosion, deep in his head, and then he saw nothing.

Isaac Bell awakened to a current of cool air fanning his face.

He was flat on his back on the ties between two rails. An electric bulb blazed down from the rough-hewn ceiling of coal. His head ached, his jaw was sore, and as he sat up and looked around he recalled the ventilators stopping and him running from the damp. The fans were running again, the air just fresh enough to revive him. He climbed to his feet and started up the sloping haulageway, his mind shambling through dreamlike memories.

He had found the broken link of the bridle chain. He had hidden it in a crack between the tunnel wall and a roof prop. Fourth prop above the deepest gallery. He had looked for the missing shackle. He hadn't found it. Or had he? Thoughts cascaded. He had seen it. He hadn't seen it. He saw amber eyes. He saw a shadow. He saw a ghostly fist. His head ached. So did his jaw. He had fallen hard. And the only thing he knew for sure was that he was very lucky that the fans had started up again before the damps suffocated him.

Ahead, he saw the light of the mouth. He quickened his pace.

'Where the heck did *you* come from?'

Some miners rigging new electrical wires were staring at him.

Bell jerked a thumb in the general direction of the depths of the mountain and said, 'Tell the mechanician boys who fixed them ventilators I'm going to buy 'em a drink.'

Hundreds of men were waiting to enter the mine and go back to work. Bell melted into the crowd, avoiding the company cops, slipped out the gates, and hurried toward the telegraph office. Dodging the goats that roamed Gleasonburg's Main Street, a shanty-lined dirt road rutted by wagon wheels and reeking of sewage, he pondered the telegram that he would send to Joseph Van Dorn.

Who would sabotage a mine? No union man in his

right mind would murder his own people. Certainly not the mild-mannered Jim Higgins who preached moderation. But if not the union saboteurs he had been ordered to hunt – criminals who he was now firmly convinced did not exist – then who? Could they be the owners of the mine? But the owners had everything to lose if they couldn't dig coal. This disaster could have been much worse. Hundreds could have died. The mine could have been blocked for months instead of days.

But if not the union and not the owners, who?

With that unanswered, Bell turned his thoughts to a stranger mystery. It certainly appeared that a saboteur had chiseled the chain apart. But at the moment when the chain had fractured, the coal train had been climbing to the tipple in plain sight of hundreds of miners. Not one of them, Isaac Bell himself included, had seen a black-smith riding the lead coal car, attacking the bridle chain with hammer and chisel.

4

Isaac Bell took two baths upon arriving in Pittsburgh, Pennsylvania, the first at the five-cent lodging house where he had left his bags and scrubbed off enough coal dust to gain admittance to the city's exclusive Duquesne Club – an ornate Romanesque Revival building that dominated the Golden Triangle where the Monongahela joined the Allegheny to form the Ohio River – the second bath at the Duquesne Club before donning an immaculate white suit.

He asked the front-hall porter to escort his lunch guest, Mr Van Dorn, to the bar when he arrived. Then the young detective shouldered into the favorite watering hole of the industrial barons and railroad tycoons who ruled the capital of America's coal and steel empire. Having researched the coal industry meticulously, he recognized many in the enormous room. But the man who captured his attention right off was holding court under an acanthus-leaf-carved mantel topped by life-size mahogany satyrs – John 'Black Jack' Gleason, ruthless owner of the Gleason Consolidated Coal & Coke Company.

If the day before yesterday's runaway train, explosion, and deaths of six doorboys in Mine No. 1 troubled Gleason at all, it did not show. Instead, he was taunting his fellow barons, with a grin like the satyrs': 'When I drive the union out of West Virginia, my mines will sell coal cheaper than every man in this room. I'll take your customers.'

A patrician turned red in the face. 'My grandfather was a founding member of this club, sir, and I do not hesitate to tell you that you are a vulture!'

'Proud of it,' Gleason fired back. 'If you don't stick with me against the union, I'll buy your bones at bankrupts' auction.'

The founder's grandson stormed out. But the others, Bell noticed, murmured compromisingly, and looked relieved when one of their number steered the conversation toward the Pirates' winning streak.

'There you are, Isaac.'

Joseph Van Dorn enveloped Bell's big hand in a manicured ham-size paw and shook it firmly. He was tall, broad in the chest, broader in the belly, and light on his feet, a balding man in his forties who might have passed for a sea captain who had prospered in the China Trade or a blacksmith who had invented a tool that made him rich. He appeared convivial, with a ready smile that could brighten his hooded eyes. Red burnsides cascading to an even redder beard gave the impression of a man more hail-fellow-well-met than the scourge of the underworld, and many a confined criminal was still wondering how he got confused.

The founder and chief investigator of the Van Dorn Detective Agency was not impressed by much, nor easily nonplussed, but, taking in the lavish club and the wealthy members, he asked in a low voice that carried no farther than Isaac Bell's ears, 'How'd you wangle your way in here?'

'My school friend Kenny Bloom's father put in a word.'

'Do they know you're a detective?'

'No, sir. I'm using the Dagget front.'

'Well done. You can learn a lot in a place like this. Now, what's all this "urgent report" about?'

Bell had spoken with the dining room captain and reserved a table in a quiet corner. He hurried Van Dorn to it. But before he could say a word about the unlikely nature of union sabotage, Van Dorn said, 'You won't believe this, Isaac. I just met the President.'

'Black Jack?'

'Not Gleason. The *President*!'

'Beg pardon, sir?'

'*Of the United States!* TR himself. Big as life. Shook my hand – littler fellow than you'd think. But full of fire. Shook my hand, big as life.'

'Well, that's wonderful, sir. Now, what I found in the mine –'

'The Van Dorn Detective Agency has snagged a plum job. Prince Henry's coming. German Prince Henry of Prussia. Coming to visit America. And we're one of the outfits the Secret Service is hiring to help protect him. That's why Teddy asked me to the White House. I'll tell you this, Isaac, long as the Van Dorns keep Prince Henry unscathed by anarchist assassins, we'll be in the catbird seat.'

Bell said, 'Congratulations, sir. That is wonderful news.'

He was fully aware of Van Dorn's dream of expanding the Van Dorn Detective Agency from its Chicago base into a crack transcontinental outfit with field offices in every city and even, one day, the capitals of Europe. The Prince Henry job had come from working at it 'eight days in the week, thirteen months in the year,' and the Boss was understandably excited.

'Report quickly, Isaac. I'm meeting with Pittsburgh's police chief in an hour. They'll be giving Prince Henry a big testimonial dinner right here in this club.'

Bell had to shift Van Dorn's attention to get permission to investigate the accident for the sake of justice even though the agency was originally hired by the coal company. He said, 'The proud Van Dorn motto – We never give up! Never! – is based on principles.'

'Of course it is. We never ignore crime. We never abandon innocents.'

'The first thing you taught me, sir. We were in Chicago, in Jimmy Armstrong's Saloon, and you said, ' "The innocent are sacred and . . ." '

The younger man paused expectantly.

Joseph Van Dorn was obliged to complete the creed he drilled into his detectives: '. . . and it is the duty of the strong to protect them.'

'The boys killed in the mining accident were innocent, sir. The union man Jim Higgins is innocent of the murder charge. And the runaway train was *not* an accident.'

Van Dorn's eyes gleamed, and Bell knew he had his attention. 'Can you pinpoint the saboteurs who caused it?'

'It was not a saboteur.'

'What?'

'Not in the sense you mean. It was not union sabotage.'

'Then who?'

'Not a saboteur. A *provocateur*.'

'What the devil are you talking about? Are you mincing words? Sabotage is sabotage.'

'No it isn't, sir. Not in the way you mean.'

'Stop telling me what I mean and tell me what *you* mean.'

'The broken chain that caused the accident was deliberately fractured, a fracture very likely caused, I believe, by a provocateur.'

'To what purpose?' Van Dorn demanded.

'To perpetrate a larger crime.'

'What larger crime?'

'I don't know,' Bell admitted. 'Although there have been incidents in labor disputes when provocateurs were employed by owners to fabricate excuses to arrest unionists. But I don't think it is that.'

Van Dorn sat back and crossed his arms over his mighty chest. 'I'm relieved to hear your logic. Wrecking his own coal mine is a mighty expensive method for Black Jack Gleason to arrest unionists.'

'I know. Which is why I wonder —'

'Where were *you* when he sabotaged the mine train? Didn't I send you there to prevent such attacks?'

Isaac Bell said, 'I'm sorry I let you down, sir.'

Van Dorn stared hard at him for a full twenty seconds. Finally, he spoke. 'We'll get to that later. What did you see?'

Bell reported what stoked his suspicions: the suicidal effect of underground sabotage; the mysterious chisel mark he found on the broken link; and the fact that by arresting Higgins, the coal company had undercut the union effort.

Joseph Van Dorn stared at Isaac Bell.

Bell met his gaze coolly. The Boss was a very ambitious man, but he was an honest man and a responsible man.

'Against my better judgment,' Van Dorn said at last, 'I will give you permission to investigate this vague idea for one week. One week only.'

'Thank you, sir. May I draw on men to help me?'

'I can't spare anyone to help you. This Prince Henry tour requires every hand. You're on your own.'

There was a sudden ruckus on the far side of the richly decorated dining room. Black Jack Gleason's party were swaggering in and sitting down for lunch. Gleason pounded his fist on the table and vowed in a loud voice, 'I will destroy the mining unions once and for all.'

The older mineowners counseled caution, noting that in Pennsylvania the union was strong: Winter is coming, we can't afford a strike.

'The nation won't put up with millions freezing in their homes.'

'It's already cost the anthracite operators two million to pay, feed, lodge and arm five thousand Coal and Iron Police with revolvers and breech-loading-magazine rifles. Heck, if we increase the miners' pay ten cents a day, it would cost less than five thousand armed policemen.'

Gleason hit the tablecloth again. Silver jumped. Waiters sprang to rescue crystal. 'Gentlemen, I will say it again. I will destroy the mining unions once and for all.'

'But mightn't we do better to give the miners a small raise and nip it in the bud?' asked an owner.

'Before that damned dictator President Roosevelt horns in,' warned another. 'He'll demand we recognize the union.'

Van Dorn said to Bell, 'The fellows around TR told me that he would love nothing more than to settle a strike.'

Black Jack Gleason laughed at compromise. 'If they strike, I'll break their strike like I broke every strike before,' he boasted.

Bell said to Van Dorn, 'I heard him in the bar. He *wants* a strike if it will hurt his competitors.'

'Hard man,' said Van Dorn. 'But very capable.' His manner toward Bell softened slightly. He himself was a hard man, but not the sort to hide his warm feelings for a young employee he admired. Isaac Bell had been his personal apprentice after graduating from Yale and was the immigrant Irishman's favorite protégé.

'Be careful, Isaac. You heard Gleason. Labor and owners are scheming for every advantage in a high-stakes war. They're digging in to fight to the death. Look out you don't get caught between them.'

'I won't, sir.'

'And whatever you do, don't end up choosing sides.'

'I'll be careful, sir. I promise.'

'I don't believe you.'

The young man stiffened. 'Sir, I've given you my word.'

'No,' said Van Dorn. 'You will break that promise and do something reckless the moment you let your better instincts take command.'

'I don't understand.'

'I've watched you operate. You have an eye for the

downtrodden. Unlike most of your privileged class, you notice that they exist. That sets you miles apart, which is commendable probably. But don't get yourself killed trying to upend the natural order of things.'

5

Isaac Bell changed into miner garb in his five-cent lodging house, paid the landlady to store his bags, and hurried back to the coalfields, traveling to Morgantown, West Virginia, in a B & O day coach and the final eight miles up a narrowing valley on the newly laid interurban Gleasonburg line. The trolley's last stop was near the courthouse, a slapped-together wood-frame affair wedged between a steep hillside and the Monongahela River. It stood next to the bigger, more substantial yellow-brick Gleason company store and housed a justice of the peace, who was the highest legal authority in the coal-mining town, his courtroom, and, in a cellar under the building, the Gleasonburg jail.

Bell headed for the jail.

With only a week to prove his theory, or at least make enough of a case to keep the Boss interested, he had decided on the train that his most productive first step would be to persuade the jailers to let him visit Jim Higgins. The union man knew his business. He had laid the groundwork for a strike by learning who to trust among the miners, who to look out for among the police, who to cultivate among the bosses. Bell was anxious to test his theory on the labor organizer and pick his brain as to who the provocateur might be and what he wanted.

A crowd of miners and their wives and children were

gathering around the entrance to the jail, a separate doorway beneath the courthouse steps. Bell glided through them, politely touching his cap to the ladies and sidestepping small fry. They were a somber crowd. Some of the women were red-eyed from weeping. They were the mothers, Bell realized, of the doorboys. How many, he wondered, were widowed like Sammy's mother? How many of the boys had been their family's sole breadwinner?

They spoke in low tones, like a congregation waiting for the service to begin, and as Bell passed among them he heard whispers that seemed to blame Jim Higgins more than the Gleason Company for the doorboys' deaths.

The jail was guarded by company police. They were fat, older men and Bell feared if the mood turned ugly and the crowd swelled into an angry mob, as grieving crowds were wont to do, they were not up to protecting the accused unionist. A Pinkerton usually commanded the company squads, but he saw no detectives there. At the moment, however, the crowd was peaceful, the company police were firmly in charge. They saw him coming and blocked the door.

Bell said, 'I'd like to visit Jim Higgins.'

'No visitors.'

'His priest in Chicago sent me a telegram, asking me to look in on him.'

'Ah don't care if the damned Pope telegraphed. No visitors.'

'Jim's priest wired some money, thinking a little cash might help keep him comfortable until his lawyers get here.'

The company cop wet his lips. He wanted the bribe. Bell reached in his pocket. But the old man shook his head. 'I got orders. No lawyer, no priest, no visitors.'

'I already tried,' said a woman who had come up behind Bell. 'If they won't let his sister see him, they won't let his priest.'

Isaac Bell turned to her musical voice. When he saw her, a certainty steamed through his mind like a runaway loco-motive: *If the cops refused admittance to this gray-eyed, raven-haired beauty, then God Almighty Himself would be cooling His heels.* He swept his cap off his head and extended his hand. 'Isaac Bell,' he introduced himself. 'I was not aware that Jim had a sister.'

'Mary Higgins,' she replied, regarding his hand with a skeptical gaze. 'I was not aware that Jim had a priest.'

'From his parish in Chicago,' Bell said for the benefit of the cop, who was listening with a suspicious expres-sion.

'Jim is an atheist,' she said and walked away.

Bell followed her through the crowd and caught up at the trolley stop.

'Are you an atheist, too?'

'Not yet,' she said. 'And who in hell are you?'

'I met Jim in the mine. He was trying to talk me into joining the union.'

'Why didn't you?'

Bell shrugged. 'Honestly, I was afraid of getting fired.'

'So why are you visiting him in jail?'

'I thought he got a bad deal.'

'Visiting him in jail will get you fired just as fast as join-ing the union. What's up with you, Mr Bell?'

40

Bell had an ear for expressions and recognized 'What's up?' as English or Australian. Perhaps she had lived abroad. Perhaps she read novels. 'While I explain "what's up,"' he answered with a smile, 'would you do me the honor of joining me for tea? I believe they serve it in the company store.'

'I would not spend one penny in a Gleason company store. Or any other company store.'

'I don't know of any other establishment where I could offer you tea.'

'That is the point, Mr Bell, isn't it? The company store has a monopoly. The workers have no choice but to pay the owners' exorbitant prices or do without. They're paid in scrip instead of real money, which they can spend only at the company store. They're no better off than serfs.'

'Or sharecroppers,' said Bell.

'Slaves.'

'It sounds as if your brother is not the only unionist in your family.'

'You're right about that.' The faintest hint of a smile warmed her eyes as they roamed over the features of the handsome young man before her. 'Except that Jim's beliefs are too mild for my taste.'

'Are you sure you won't make a company store exception for one cup of tea?'

'Positively sure,' Mary Higgins fired back. She glanced up and down the row of shabby barracks, lodging houses and shanties that lined the dirt street and fixed on a saloon with a lantern in its one small window. 'There are other ways. Come with me.'

Bell appraised the crowd around the jail, which was

growing larger, then followed her across the street. She walked fast. She was tall and her skirts swayed, he noticed, as if her legs were long. As she stepped up to the wooden sidewalk, her skirt parted, revealing low boots laced around shapely ankles. A dance hall gal's figure, he thought, with a schoolmarm's stern gaze.

As she led Bell in the door the owner rushed up, crying, 'No ladies allowed in here.'

Mary Higgins unleashed another faint smile, looked the barkeep straight in the eye, and said, 'Somewhere behind your bar is your office and in it a pot of hot coffee. I wonder if this gentleman and I might buy a cup we could drink at your desk.'

The barkeep's mouth popped open. 'How did you know?'

'My father owned such an establishment once. He always said if you drink what you sell you'll end up in the poorhouse.'

'He knew his business,' said the owner. 'Come this way.'

Mary Higgins swept ahead, skirts swirling the sawdust strewn upon the floor. In his office, the barkeep apologized, 'I have no milk.'

'Not necessary,' she said with a glance at Isaac Bell, who concurred with a silent nod that black coffee would be perfectly fine.

'I'll leave you two ... alone. Presuming,' he added gruffly, 'we all understand that my office is not a trysting place.'

He saw a sudden dangerous glint in the young coal miner's eye and quickly apologized, 'I did not mean to imply –'

'Thank you,' Mary Higgins dismissed him.

She sat behind the rough-plank desk and indicated Bell should pull up the barrel that served as a side chair. 'Mr Bell, you are a mystery.'

'How is that, Miss Higgins?'

'You're dressed like a coal miner. You speak like a Fifth Avenue swell trying to sound like a coal miner. And you are failing, woefully, to hide the mannerisms of the privileged. Who are you and what do you want?'

Bell hung his head, the picture of embarrassment, if not guilt. She was sharp-eyed and sharp-eared, so he was not exactly astonished that she had picked out flaws in his disguise. She would make a canny detective. But having noticed her probing gaze, he had already prepared a defense, determined to stay in disguise as long as he could. Stick to your story, Wish Clarke had taught him, illustrating the lesson with a sip from his flask. *Show* folks you're a harmless drunkard. Polish the edges, but keep the frame. Nearer the truth, the less to defend.

Bell said, 'I'll start with who I am. Yes, I was born to privilege. You're absolutely right. But my father lost everything in the Panic of '93. My mother died. My father shot himself – out of shame or grief, I know not which. All I've known since are hard times. But I am proud to say that I have made my way, on my own, by the labor of my own hands.'

Mary Higgins cast a sharp look at his hands, and the young detective was glad of the shovel blisters that had hardened to callus.

'*Princes and lords may flourish, or may fade?*' she quoted Goldsmith with an eyebrow raised inquiringly.

'*A breath can make them, as a breath has made,*' Bell quoted back.

'You would have me believe that you were visiting my brother out of the kindness of your heart?'

'That's about all I have to offer him.'

'Something is agley with your story, Mr Bell. Don't try to fool a workman's daughter.'

'I thought he owned a saloon.'

'That was for the benefit of an honest cup of coffee,' she said, revealing an ability equal to Bell's to bend the truth for a good cause. 'Maybe you've lost your mansions, but your environment and your whole life keep you from even seeing, much less understanding, the conflict of the capitalist class and the working class.'

'Not quite my whole life.'

'The war for justice is simply expressed: there can be no peace without justice – no justice without equality.'

'That is eloquently put,' said Bell. 'I never quite thought of it in such terms.'

'I don't intend to be "eloquent," Mr Bell. Eloquence is folderol. Like the gimcrackery that decorated your mansion.'

'Your brother's hopes are more modest. He told me, "All we're asking is to live like human beings, feed our families, and send our kids to school."'

'My brother is a gentle dreamer. He needs to understand that we won't win the war for justice until the working class and the capitalist class become one, and the worker owns the capital he produces.'

'He needs a lawyer first. A smart one who can convince the judge that Jim cannot be blamed for failing to throw the derailer switch. The company assigned him to a second job, oiling the winch engine, which took him too far from his post at the switch to derail the runaway. When they arrested him, he said it was because they learned he was a union organizer and trumped up the charges to sideline him.'

'I'm not surprised. Nor am I surprised my brother couldn't see their scheme. As I say, he's a dreamer.'

The barkeep burst into the office with panic in his eyes. 'You have to leave. I'm shutting down early. All hell's busting loose.'

Outside, the sun had slid behind the mountain, and night was closing in on the hollow. A cold wind blew down from the higher elevations. Damp air and tendrils of fog rose from the river. The courthouse was deep in shadow.

The crowd around it had tripled in size. Where, earlier, people had whispered, now they were calling out loud, and some were shouting. Bell saw mothers dragging children away, as if they had gauged the mood and found it dangerous. Men came running up Main Street, carrying baseball bats and pick handles.

'What are they shouting?' asked Mary, though surely she heard but could not believe.

'*Murderer!*' said Bell. 'Stay here. Let me see what I can do.'

Henry Clay drifted through the crowd on a route seemingly aimless. He was a broad-shouldered man of thirty-five who moved with effortless grace. Though not markedly tall, he was powerfully built, an asset that he concealed with expensive tailoring when in his Wall Street office in

New York City and with a loosely fitted coat and overalls when pretending to be a coal miner. The red bandanna tied at his throat did not necessarily shout from the rooftops that he was a union man, but it could be construed as a sign of where he stood in the conflict between the working class and the capitalist class. The slouch hat that shadowed his face kept the fading daylight from reflecting the golden yellow hue of his amber eyes.

Face-to-face for an instant with a grim-visaged miner, Henry Clay muttered, 'The son of a bitch might as well have taken up a pistol and shot those boys.' As he moved along, the miner shouted 'Murderer!' at the jail, where the Gleason police were looking nervous.

Clay whispered as he passed another man, 'Those poor boys, I just can't bear thinking on them.'

'Murderer!' erupted behind him. It was like pushing an electric doorbell. 'Poor boys' —*'Murderer!'*

Clay stopped in front of two men who were looking dubious. Smart ones, the sort who would be tempted to take a flier on the union. 'Bunch of fellers told me Higgins is a company spy.'

'The hell you say. Who are you? What's your name?'

'Claggart,' Clay replied, extending his hand and reeling them in with a drummer's smile. 'John Claggart.'

'What's this about Higgins being a spy, Claggart? I heard he's a union man.'

'So did I,' said the other.

'That's what the company wants you to believe. Those fellers told me that the minute their pal said yes to the snake, the Pinkertons were all over him like paint. Blackjacked him something awful, bloodied his face, busted his hand.'

'*Spy!*'
'*Murderer!*'
'*Spy!*'

Clay continued toward the back of the mob, casting aspersions calculated to inflame, and stepped up on a horse trough for a better view. Lo and behold, there was Joseph Van Dorn's favorite – young Isaac Bell – springing up the courthouse steps to try to reason with the mob.

6

'Hang him!'

Isaac Bell had vaulted up the steps just as the grieving crowd of the victims' friends and families exploded into a savage lynch mob howling for Jim Higgins's blood.

'Hang him high!'

'Murderer!'

'Spy!'

'Hold it!'

Bell had a big voice, and when he filled his chest and let it thunder, it carried to the farthest man in the mob and echoed off the mountain. He raised both hands high above his head and it seemed to double his height. He spoke slowly, clearly and loudly.

'Jim Higgins is no spy. Jim Higgins is an honest workingman just like every one of us.'

'Spy!'

Bell pointed a big hand at the miner who had shouted.

'Who told you Jim's a spy? Come on, man, tell us. Was it anyone you know? Any man you trust? Who?'

The miners looked at one another and back at Bell.

'Jim Higgins is no more a company man than you or me.'

The men in front were looking confused. But from far in the back, Bell heard shouting. *'Murderer! Murderer!'*

He could not see who was shouting in the failing light. A shadowy figure in a slouch hat flitted behind the mob. A dozen throats picked up the cry *'Murderer! Murderer!'* and from where Bell stood on the steps he could see a wave-like ripple of motion, and hundreds began to surge closer.

The company police guarding the jailhouse door edged aside.

'Stand fast, you men!' Bell shouted down from the steps.

'Murderer!'

The cops broke and ran. Some fled straight into the crowd, some around it, and when they had gone nothing stood between the lynch mob and the union organizer but a young Van Dorn detective on his first case.

Isaac Bell drew a single-action Colt Army from his coat and leveled it at the crowd. Then he delivered a cold promise.

'I will shoot the first man who steps near.'

Those in the front row, close enough to see his eyes, believed him.

They hesitated and started to fall back.

Joe, you self-righteous son of a bitch! Henry Clay shouted in the confines of his mind, taunting Joseph Van Dorn as if the great detective was glaring across his desk. Or down a gunsight. *Goodness fetches goodness. Fools fetch fools.*

He reached inside his voluminous coat.

Fool or not, young Bell cut a brave figure. The mob, teetering moments before on the cusp of violence, had been sidetracked by his commanding voice. Clay had fired up the back ranks again. But now the young detective had a gun in his hand and it was time to stop Bell before he ruined everything.

The marksman's weapon in Clay's shoulder holster was a top-notch Colt Bisley .45 single-action revolver smithed to a fare-thee-well. In the right hands, at this range, it was as deadly as a rifle. And Henry Clay, who had been trained by a master gunfighter and had drilled with the Bisley as religiously as he had with shotgun, rifle, knife and fists, had no doubt that his were the right hands.

Isaac Bell saw someone come pushing through the mob even as the front ranks hesitated.

It was Mary Higgins, shoving through them and racing up the steps to stand shoulder to shoulder with him.

'If you brought a gun,' said Bell, 'give it to me and get out of here while the getting is good.'

'I don't need a gun.'

'If you believe that, you're dreaming worse than your brother – *Down!*' He saw the blur of a gun barrel swinging their way. He kicked Mary's skirts out from under her and swept her off her feet. A shot pealed from the back of the mob. The bullet stormed so close to Bell's head it knocked his cap off. He could not see who had fired or whether he was leveling a second shot. He was. The shot came with no warning, slamming Bell sideways as it ripped through his coat and burned a bloody track across his ribs.

Bell caught his footing and aimed his Army. He raked the crowd, trying to locate the man who shot him. He still could not see him. He was somewhere behind them. Then he saw that the second shot emboldened the angry miners.

Pushed by those behind, the men in front surged straight at him.

Isaac Bell triggered his weapon, held it firmly at his waist, and fanned the revolver's hammer spur repeatedly with his left hand. Four shots roared out of the barrel so fast that the individual reports combined into one long, loud explosion.

The rapid fire sent a blizzard of bullets inches above the mob. Heads ducked, men scattered for cover. Spanish War veterans familiar with field cannon flung themselves face-first in the mud. Their mad scramble lasted just long enough for Bell and Mary to dive down the steps and into the jailhouse – a small, low-ceilinged cellar that smelled of river dampness and the kerosene lamps that lighted it. It was furnished with a crude wooden desk, a gun rack, two cells, and a dark hall that Bell hoped led to a back way out. He bolted the door.

Jim Higgins was watching from his cell, gripping the bars. Bell spotted keys on the rack and a double-barreled shotgun. He unlocked the cell and shoved the shotgun into Higgins's hands. Higgins stared at the weapon as if Bell had passed him a snake.

'Don't worry about hitting anything. The noise 'll scatter them.'

'Are you all right, Isaac? There's blood all over your coat.'

'Tip-top,' said Bell. His ribs felt like he had just fought ten rounds with a strong man who specialized in body blows. But he could breathe, a good sign that no ribs had splintered.

'Here they come!' cried Mary. She grabbed a lantern off the desk and looked down the hall.

51

The mob was beating at the door. Bell took back the shotgun. Mary returned. 'There's a door and a ladder down to the riverbank.'

'How many are out there?'

'No one. It's too steep. It's right on the bank.'

'Take your brother.'

Mary grabbed Jim's arm and lighted the way. Bell took up the rear. The mob battered at the door. Bell fired the right barrel. The shotgun bellowed. The pounding stopped, but only for an instant. Jim Higgins lowered the ladder. 'Go,' said Bell. 'I'll cover.' He had one cartridge left in the shotgun and one in his revolver. Jim Higgins started down the ladder. The front door splintered as the fence post they were using for a battering ram thrust through a panel.

Bell loosed the second barrel of the shotgun, and the fence post fell into the room as if the men wielding it had let go and run for their lives. 'Go,' he said to Mary. 'That made believers out of them.'

But instead of starting down the ladder, Mary ran to the front room and threw the lamp. It landed on the jailer's desk. Glass shattered and kerosene oil caught fire, spreading flame across the desk and igniting the second lamp. She paused in the hallway, and Bell saw her profiled by the leaping orange firelight. She looked startlingly beautiful, with a smile of satisfaction shining on her face.

The burning jailhouse, which should have distracted the mob, proved Bell's, Jim's and Mary's undoing. No sooner had they climbed down the ladder and begun picking their way along the steep riverbank than the fire rose to the courthouse above it. The wood burned fiercely.

Flames leaped to the sky and dissolved the darkness of night.

'There they are!'

'Git 'em!'

The mob raced among the shanties along the top of the bank. Bell, Mary and Jim Higgins slid to the bottom and splashed along the water's edge. Bell saw ahead of them the barge dock where empties were parked overnight, waiting for steam tugs to push them to the tipple. The street above connected with Dock Street, which sloped down to it. At that point, he realized, the mob would stream down Dock Street and intercept them at the barge dock.

'We're done for,' said Jim Higgins. 'I'm the one they want. I'll stop here. You two get in the water. Try and swim for it.'

The current was swift, the river over five hundred feet wide and pitch-dark beyond the firelight. Bell was a strong swimmer, he could make it across with a little luck. The expression on Mary's face was brave but doubtful that she could swim that far.

'Both of you, stop here,' he commanded in a voice that allowed no argument. He found them a hiding place behind a stone breakwater. 'I'll be right back.'

He ran, leaping obstacles lit by the fire, and climbed up on the dock. At the end of the string of barges was a little yard tug that would do the shuttling. Bell jumped on to the first barge and ran along its gunnel, fighting to keep his footing on the narrow timber shelf. Slip to the right, he would fall in the water; slip to his left, break his neck in the empty hold.

'There he is!'

Bell leaped the space between the first and second barge and ran faster. He barely heard the howls behind him, his eyes fixed on the next barge, and the next, and the single light burning on the steam tug. He jumped from the last barge on to the tug and cast off its lines. The current took it immediately and dragged it downriver swiftly into the dark, beyond the mob, but away from the breakwater where Jim and Mary were hiding.

7

'Mister, what in tarnation are you up to?'

The little tug was a simple flatboat with its boiler and smokestack standing on deck between the helm and a coal bin. Isaac Bell had just grabbed a fireman's scoop and was reaching to open the furnace door when an elderly night watchman with a long white Civil War beard rose, yawning, from a sleeping nest of coiled rope and canvas.

He saw the dark silhouette of the tall detective loom against the burning courthouse, and he pawed a six-gun from his waistband.

Bell snatched it away.

'Sir, I'm only going to borrow your boat for a short ride. Can you let me do that?'

'No, sir. She's not your boat. She belongs to the Gleason Coal Company. I cain't let you steal her.'

'Don't make me throw you overboard,' Bell snapped, praying the old fellow would believe he meant it because, if he didn't believe him, Isaac Bell had no idea what he would do next.

The old man blinked, looked down at the black water, and said, 'Don't hanker to go swimming, just now.'

'Does she have steam up?'

'A mite. I threw some coal on a while back.'

'Throw some more on.'

'Well, all right. It's not like I'm helping you steal her, is it? I mean, I cain't just let her drift into the rocks. Which she's about to do.'

Bell opened the quadrant, sluicing steam into the piston, felt the propeller engage, and spun the spoked wheel. The little tug stopped drifting and headed upstream into the current. He steered for the now distant breakwater and tried to coax more power out of her. The steam gauge showed that with her furnace banked for the night, she had barely enough pressure to make headway.

The old man scooped some coal into the firebox and banged the door shut. 'Son, you a river pilot?'

'No, sir.'

'Looks like you run steamers before.'

'Only yachts.'

'Yachts? Mr Gleason's got a yacht. Named *Monongahela*, after the river – see that courthouse burn? I declare, it will ignite the company store next.'

Mary Higgins, thought Bell, was probably cheering from the bank.

He steered past the barges and the dock to the breakwater where he had left them. They were gone. Searching the bank, he spotted them, running back toward the courthouse. Three men were hot on their trail. Bell swung the tug toward them.

One of the pursuers pulled ahead of the pack, waving a baseball bat. Two yards behind Mary, he raised the bat high in the air. Bell let go the wheel, drew his Colt, took careful aim, and fired his last bullet. The man dropped his bat and fell. His friends tumbled over him.

'Fine shooting,' said the old man. 'That'll larn him.'

Bell rammed the tug's nose into the soft mudbank.

'*Jump!*'

Mary scrambled on and reached back for her brother. Jim swung aboard. Bell reversed his quadrant, backed into the current, spun the helm in a blur of spokes, and steamed for the far shore.

Isaac Bell drove the tug across the Monongahela River and slowly downstream, looking for a place to land. The old man recognized Jim Higgins. 'You're that union fellow, ain't you?'

'Yes, I am. Do you favor the union?'

'Cain't say I do. Cain't say I favor the company neither. They treat folks mighty hard.'

'Would you back a strike?'

'Might. Or might not.'

'I feel the same way,' Higgins said, settling into a conversation that Bell would not have expected to hear in the midst of the night on a stolen tugboat. 'We don't necessarily have to strike. A fair settlement of the miners' and owners' demands could ensure a generation of no strikes and steady work. Cool heads on both sides know that the nation needs coal. It will be to everyone's benefit that we can earn a decent living digging it. Unless the hotheads inflame the miners' imaginations, we can settle this for the good of all, miner and owner.'

Mary Higgins laughed in disbelief. 'Cool heads threw you in jail and sent a lynch mob to hang you.'

'Peace for twenty years,' Higgins replied mildly, 'if cool heads bargain. Massacres if they don't.'

'Brother, if it weren't for Mr Bell, you'd be dancing on air.'

Isaac Bell listened admiringly as Jim Higgins stood firmly by his beliefs, addressing his sister and the old man as if he was trying to coax them into a union hall. 'If hotheads won't give an inch, labor and owner will go to war. Innocents die in labor wars. Innocents were massacred at Haymarket, and Homestead, and Pullman. Innocents will be massacred again.'

Steering along in the dark, eyes peeled for a landing, Bell decided that Jim Higgins was not a dreamer – and certainly no fool – but a thinker with an overarching strategy to end the labor wars and a healthy fear of the violence the wars would spawn.

Ahead, Bell saw a yellow glow.

The old watchman nudged him. 'Sonny, if you intend to keep running – and I reckon, based on events I've observed tonight, you ought to – you might be interested to know that 'round the next bend is the Baltimore & Ohio train yard where you might just discover the opportunity to hop a freight and git the hell out of West Virginia.'

'Isaac, I *would* be dancing on air, like Mary said. But may I ask you one more favor?'

'Name it.'

'Would you escort my sister to safety?'

'Of course.'

'I don't need an escort,' said Mary. 'And I don't want one.'

Jim Higgins said, 'Sister, listen for once in your life. I'm the only fugitive from the law. They'll charge me with breaking out of jail. All you and Isaac did was run from a lynch mob, and even the owners can't call that a crime. If you can get past the Gleason company cops, you'll both be safe.'

'What about you?' asked Bell, and Mary said, 'Where are you going?'

'I'm hoping my friends in the Brotherhood of Locomotive Firemen will smuggle me out in a coal tender.'

'Where?'

'Denver, Colorado,' said Jim Higgins. 'The Western Miners are helping the fellows striking the smelting companies. It's an opportunity to all pull together. If we can threaten an enormous general strike that spans the continent, that'll make the owners listen.'

Alongside the rail yard were the trolley barn and last station stop of a branch of the Fairmont & Clarksburg Traction inter-urban railroad. But when they ventured close, they saw coal cops patrolling the platform. They retreated toward the rail yard. Bell and Mary hid in the woods. Jim returned in an hour and pointed out a string of boxcars on a siding. A freight engine was backing up to it.

'The boys said that empty freight is headed back to Pittsburgh. They put a word in with the brakeman. But look out for the yard bulls. Grab that middle car with the open door. Wait 'til she's rolling and run aboard. Good luck.'

'Did *you* get a ride?' Mary asked.

'The boys'll get me out of here, somehow, don't you worry. Take care, Isaac. Thank you for looking out for her.'

They shook hands. Mary hugged her brother fiercely, and when she wheeled away Bell saw her eyes were bright with tears. Keeping to the shadows, they walked out of the freight yard and along the main line and waited, shivering, in a cold wind blowing off the river. An hour later they heard a locomotive whistle blow the double *Ahead* signal and then the heavy chug of steam as it pulled the slack out of its train's couplers and hauled it toward the main line.

Bell and Mary ducked from the blaze of its headlamp and, when the locomotive passed, started running along the railbed.

'Ever hopped a freight before?' he asked her.

'I'm pretending it's a carousel.'

'Careful you don't trip on your skirts.'

'I never trip on my skirts. I hem them four inches short.'

'You first. I'm right behind you.'

They scrambled up the rock-ballast embankment of the railbed, ran alongside the moving train, and jumped into the boxcar.

Bell watched behind the train until he was sure the yard bulls had not spotted them. Then he slid the door shut against the cold, which had little effect on the temperature as the freight picked up speed and an icy wind began whistling through cracks in the walls. His ribs were throbbing and he felt suddenly too weary to stand. The train lurched and, the next thing he knew, he was sprawled on the wooden floor, flat on his back, and Mary was speaking to him as if from across a room.

'I saw your face in the headlight. White as a ghost. Is the bullet inside?'

'No, no, no. Only creased me.'

He closed his eyes and heard cloth ripping. She was tearing a petticoat into strips. 'Let's get your coat off,' she said, peeling it and his shirt away from the wound.

Bell heard the clink of a flask being opened and smelled whiskey. 'What are you doing?'

'Dressing your wound,' she said. 'This will sting, unless you prefer septicemia.'

'Dress away – *Ahh!*' Bell caught his breath. 'You're right, it does sting, just a mite. Where'd you learn to dress wounds?'

'When the strikebreakers retreat and the thugs are done with their pick handles, there's nursing to be done.'

It occurred to Isaac Bell that Mary Higgins spoke sentences as if they were written on posters. But he loved the sound of her voice. Here, in the dark, the beat of iron wheels clattering on steel tracks rang like music. He was dead tired and he ached all over, but at this moment he could not think of anywhere else in the world he would rather be than riding the rails with this girl Mary Higgins.

'You're shivering,' she said. 'Are you in shock?'

'Just a little. But I'm cold. Aren't you?'

'Freezing. I'm concerned that your wound is worse than you think.'

Bell had been shot before – winged once in Wyoming, and rather more seriously in Chicago – and had a very clear concept of the difference between a penetrating wound and a graze. 'No,' he assured her, 'it's just the shock of the impact. I had heard that a heavy slug like that will really floor you just passing by. Seems it's true. But it's cold in here. Maybe you're right, maybe it's shock making me cold. I wish we had blankets to keep warm.'

'Lay close to me,' she said. 'We'll keep each other warm.'

'Good idea,' said Isaac Bell.

8

Bell awakened to a blood-red dawn glinting through splits in the boxcar walls. He thought it was the pain in his side that disturbed his sleep, but it was Mary whimpering in hers. Suddenly, she screamed. Bell held her tighter and gently shook her awake.

'You're OK. You're safe. You're here with me.'

She looked around the boxcar, rubbed her eyes, and laid her head back on his chest. 'I had a nightmare. I'm sorry. Sorry I woke you.'

'No, I was awake.' He felt her trembling. 'Are you all right?'

'Yes.'

'What did you dream?'

'Five years ago, when I was eighteen, I marched with thousands of women. We were seeking bread for their children. We marched all night to Pittsburgh. Before we could enter the city, Coal and Iron Police stopped us with bayonets fixed to their rifles. They had orders from the governor to shoot to kill.'

She fell silent.

Bell asked, 'What happened?'

'We had no choice but to back down. I could see their orders in their eyes. They would do it, Mr Bell. They would pull their triggers. They would shoot us, as they shot us at

Haymarket, at the Pullman strike, at Homestead, at Lattimer.'

Bell had never heard of Lattimer. 'Do you dream it often?'

'Less than at first.'

'Was it harder to march the next time – I presume you did march again?'

'Of course.'

'Was it harder?'

Mary did not answer. Bell listened to the wheels. He could feel her heart beating against his chest, speeding up with remembered fear. 'I used to think Pennsylvania was the worst,' she whispered. 'The richest railroads, coal mines, coke plants, steel mills are all in Pennsylvania. The state legislature wrote laws founding the Coal and Iron Police to protect them from the workers. The companies own the legislature. They can do anything they want and the law is on their side.'

'You *used to* think Pennsylvania was the worst?'

'West Virginia is worse. Gleason and his bunch don't even pretend that murder isn't a weapon in their arsenal. They don't bother with legal niceties. The union hasn't a friend in the state . . . Where was your father's mansion?'

'Boston.' Stick to your story. Polish the edges, keep the frame.

'Where in Boston?'

'The Back Bay,' he lied.

If she was at all familiar with Boston, she would know that the Bells of Louisburg Square founded the American States Bank, which had a long history of flourishing through financial panics like that of 1893. The Back Bay that he named instead – a neighborhood of mansions erected on filled land by newly wealthy likely to lose their money as fast as they made it – would lend credence to his riches-to-rags *Princes and lords may flourish, or may fade* disguise.

'Where did you learn that trick with the gun?'

'Fan shooting?' he asked, buying time to think his way out of this one.

'You fired four bullets as if they were one. Were you in the Spanish War?'

The nearer the truth, the less to defend.

'I ran off with the circus when I was a boy.'

Mary propped herself up on one elbow and looked into his eyes, and Isaac Bell was convinced that she was the most beautiful woman he had ever seen. 'Were you a reckless little boy or a brave little boy?'

'I was an *adventurous* little boy, and circus folk are very, very kind. The acrobats and the lady shootist became my particular friends. They taught me all sorts of wonderful things.'

The locomotive was blowing its whistle more and more frequently as the train steamed through grade crossings, indicating they were nearing a city. Bell shot a look out the door. The smoke of Pittsburgh rose heavily on the horizon, and soon they were trundling between mills and plants. Endless rows of chimney stacks, tall and straight as blackened forests, lined both sides of the Monongahela River, which was twice as wide as where they crossed it at Gleasonburg and crowded with tall stern-wheeled steamboats pushing long tows of coal barges. The coal

64

was heaped everywhere Bell looked, black mountains to burn in glass factories, blast furnaces, open-hearth smelters, coking plants and gashouses, and in hundreds of locomotives pulling thousands of railcars on broadways that were eight, ten, twelve tracks wide.

'How many men own it all?' Mary had joined him at the door. 'Two? Three? How many workers? A hundred thousand? Five hundred thousand? Millions?'

They passed banks of gigantic blast furnaces, the heart of the Homestead Steel Works, which spread over hundreds of acres on both sides of a bend in the river.

'Fort Frick,' Mary said, bitterly. 'That's what the workers called it. Frick built a fence around it to shield his Pinkerton gunmen. We shot it out with the detectives. Dozens were killed. The governor sent militia with Gatling guns. They arrested the entire Strike Committee. Thank God, juries refused to convict. But they broke the union.'

Isaac Bell did know of the Homestead Battle. The whole nation did. Henry Clay Frick, Andrew Carnegie's manager of the Homestead Steel Works, had fought the strikers to a standstill in a long-ago war when Bell was a schoolboy. Mary must have been in school then, too. But she told it as if she had witnessed it yesterday.

'Since then, they've kicked the union out of every steel mill in Pennsylvania.'

They rolled past the Homestead Works. The yards would be coming up soon. Bell said, 'We've got to jump before the yard to avoid the rail dicks. Soon as the engineer slows down. Stick close. They won't go easy on you just because you're a woman.'

Mary didn't hear him. 'Look at that,' she said, gesturing at a huge white sign so new it was not yet stained by soot.

AMALGAMATED COAL TERMINAL

From his research, Bell recognized the giant tipple that loomed over a combined train yard and barge wharf on a point of land that jutted into the river. It was the latest innovation in the transport of coal to market. Mechanical conveyers lifted coal from wooden Monongahela barges up to the tipple. The tipple rained it down in two directions, filling hundred-car trains, headed east to the seaboard cities, and big, modern barges that were steel-reinforced against the western-river rigors of the Ohio and the Mississippi.

Mary was exasperated by its name. '"Amalgamated"? Why can't they just call a combine a *combine*?'

Bell grinned. 'Would you settle for "united"?'

She did not return his grin. But he saw some smile in her eyes when she fired back, 'If you'll settle for "monopoly."'

'Shake on it?' They touched fingertips and stood looking at each other, balanced against the motion of the train, until Bell swept Mary into his arms and kissed her on the mouth.

At length, Mary asked, 'Weren't we supposed to jump?'

They were still rolling too fast to jump, and Bell finally realized that since it was running empty, the freight did not have to slow until shortly before it stopped.

When the air brakes finally hissed, they were in the yard, an enormous sprawl of track in every direction. It was securely fenced. Bell spotted a break in the palings down by the river twenty tracks away.

'Ready?'

'Ready.'

Bell jumped first and landed with a jolt that seared his ribs. He kept his feet and reached for Mary and caught her as she tripped.

'Let's go. We'll get out of here fast as we can.'

They almost made it. They had crossed twenty pairs of rails and were running the last few yards when from behind a derelict caboose pounced a club-wielding railroad dick in a wrinkled sack suit and a dented bowler hat.

'Stop right there, you two!'

'Give us a break,' said Bell. 'We're just leaving.'

'You're leaving all right – straight to the jailhouse. So's your floozy.'

The rail dick reached for Mary's arm.

Bell stepped between them and, when the yard bull raised his club, hit him with a left-right combination similar to the one that floored Eustace McCoy in the mine. The bull went down, holding his jaw. But the attack had been seen. Three more railroad police came running, pawing blackjacks from their coats. If they got past him, Bell knew, Mary would be next. He knelt beside the man he had knocked down and muttered urgently.

Railroad police were at the bottom of the peace-officer heap, despised as dregs, a bare step above brutal criminals. Few would refuse a Van Dorn detective a favor, dreaming that it might one day be returned with an invitation to join the outfit.

'Van Dorn. Pittsburgh field office. Call 'em off before I hurt somebody.'

'Hell, mister. Why didn't you say you was a Van Dorn!' the rail cop blurted. 'Almost broke my jaw.'

'Keep it quiet!'

'Hold on, boys,' the rail dick shouted. 'He's OK. He's a Van Dorn private detective.'

Mary Higgins rounded on Bell. 'What?'

Her eyes flashed. Her cheeks flushed scarlet.

'A Pinkerton!' she yelled, her voice not at all musical, and slapped Bell's face so hard she knocked the tall detective sideways. 'You're a Pinkerton?'

His disguise in shreds, Isaac Bell tried to explain, 'No, Mary, I'm not a Pinkerton. I'm a Van Dorn.'

'What in hell is the difference? You're all the same strikebreakers to me!'

She slapped him again and stalked toward the hole in the fence.

'You want we should stop her?'

'There aren't enough of you,' said Bell. 'Let her go.'

'What line are you in, son?'

'Insurance. Dagget, Staples & Hitchcock.'

Bell had cleaned up at his lodging house and run with his bags to the train station, which was under construction and surrounded by an obstacle course of cursing carriage drivers and maddened horses, and had bought an extra-fare ticket on the Pennsylvania Special just as the express train pulled in from Chicago. Now, as the special's locomotive accelerated smoothly out of Pittsburgh, he was sipping an excellent cup of coffee in the dining car,

68

sharing a table with three well-dressed commission sales-men, and wondering what Mary Higgins was finding for breakfast.

'Where you headed?'

'New York.'

Mr Van Dorn was there, and Bell was determined to convince the Boss that the gunman he had glimpsed inflaming the lynch mob and then shooting off his hat and holing his coat proved that a provocateur was intent on starting a war in the coalfields. Somehow, he had to per-suade Mr Van Dorn to give him more time to pursue the case. More important, he knew he could not pursue it alone. He needed help, a lot of help. Somehow, he had to convince the Boss to assign to him, for the first time, his own squad of detectives.

9

'Welcome back, Mr Clay.'

The provocateur who shot at Isaac Bell from the back of the lynch mob marched into his elegant Wall Street office, where he was received with great deference, and no little fear, as the proprietor and chief investigator of the exclusive Henry Clay Investigations Agency of New York City. Clay's manager, and secretary, and researcher, and telegrapher all stood respectfully at their desks, while the thugs ready to do his strong-arm work lined up in the back hall. Clay was a cultured man – his clothing exquisite, his taste sublime. The famous author Henry James had been known to converse with him companionably, utterly unaware – deserted, curiously, by his customary sound judgment – that Clay was also as ferociously ambitious as a hungry anaconda.

He had been raised in bohemian poverty by his mother, a struggling portrait painter who had named him after the man she claimed was his father – the ruthless coal, steel and railroad baron Henry Clay Frick, Andrew Carnegie's man of all work.

Henry Clay was thirty-five. He was well educated thanks to his mother's gentlemen friends and clients who had staked him to excellent boarding schools in his youth. But the stints at school were as brief as his mother's friend-ships, and he remained always the outsider – the day student at Choate, Phillips Andover, Exeter, Deerfield Academy, and St Paul's – brushing shoulders, fleetingly, with heirs to the great American fortunes that he hungered to possess himself.

At fifteen, Clay ran away from home and became a Pinkerton spy in the labor unions. At eighteen, in Chicago, he lied about his Pinkerton service and was hired on as the first employee of the great detective of the age, Joseph Van Dorn. Van Dorn had recognized Clay's extraordinary natural aptitude – his striking wit, his astonishing physical strength – and had held high hopes that his first apprentice would help him build his detective agency.

Van Dorn, a child of the Irish revolutions, which he had turned his back on when he saw them descend into criminality, had personally honed the boxing skills Henry Clay learned in school and trained him to fight with guns and knives. And while making Clay deadly, Van Dorn had taught him the fine art of investigation.

Clay still mourned the day they parted company.

Van Dorn had refused to make him a partner on the grounds that Clay was more interested in currying favor with industrialists than imprisoning criminals. Van Dorn, as bitterly disappointed in his choice of protégé as any man could be with this first failure, had also suspected – but could never prove – that the brilliant Henry Clay had thrown the bomb that set off the deadly Haymarket Riot.

Clay had not seen Van Dorn in many years. But he was aware, and he knew Van Dorn was, too, of the other's presence in the detective line: Van Dorn, chief of an outfit extending its reach from regional to national; the younger Clay yet to make a bigger mark than a lucrative one-man outfit courting a clientele of rich and powerful financiers.

Back from the coalfields, Henry Clay locked the door to his private office. He kept a brass telescope in the window, a powerful instrument made for a harbormaster, which he swept across the fronts of the office-building headquarters of Wall Street tycoons. An expert lip-reader, he fleshed out their conversations with information he had acquired by bribing the engineers and mechanicians who installed their voice tubes, telephones and private telegraph lines to reroute them through his.

This morning he focused his spyglass on a one-hundred-thousand-dollar, life-size white marble sculpture – Auguste Rodin's *The Kiss* – which decorated the private office of a steel magnate that Wall Street men rated more cold-blooded than robber baron Frick at his worst. He was the financial titan who forged the old empires of Carnegie and Frick into the United States Steel Corporation – Judge James Congdon.

Judge Congdon was unyielding in his opposition to union labor. As Clay focused on the old man's lips, Congdon was haranguing a visitor, a rich owner of coal mines, who was listening attentively.

'Labor's victory will be *not* to labor when modern machines work for them. Until then, they'll accept their place in God's estate, if I have anything to do with it. And I do. After machines replace them, God knows how they'll spend their time.' He whirled abruptly to his desk, moving with startling speed for a man his age, and wrote a note in a flowing hand:

There will be great profit in providing them games.

Congdon's visitor nodded obsequiously.

Clay focused his spyglass on the mineowner's face and took pleasure in watching him squirm. 'Black Jack Gleason,' he whispered. 'Not such a big man here in Wall Street, are you?'

Gleason was standing in Congdon's office, literally hat in hand, worrying the brim of his homburg with anxious fingers, while James Congdon bullied him. Even lip-reading only parts of their conversation, as Congdon occasionally turned his face from the window, it was clear to Clay that the financier was calling the tune. The biggest coal baron in West Virginia was no match for a Wall Street titan hell-bent on consolidating the industry. Congdon's money controlled the steel mills, and the coking plants that bought coal, and the railroads that not only burned it in their locomotives but also set the rates to ship it.

'Have you read Darwin?' Congdon asked contemptuously.

'I don't believe so, Mr Congdon.'

'The weak perish, the fittest survive.'

'Oh yes, sir. I know who you mean.'

'Mr Darwin knows his business. Wouldn't you agree?'

'Yes. The weak die – perish. We'll always have the poor. It's the way of the world.'

'The way of the world,' said Congdon, 'brings us to the business of digging coal less expensively than the next man. Wouldn't you agree?'

Henry Clay, a painter like his mother though not as gifted, likened Congdon's craggy face to a sunless, cold north slope gullied by storm water. It was no surprise, looking at that face, that Judge Congdon was the most powerful man in Wall Street, and Henry Clay's chest filled with hope in the knowledge that he was about to hitch his wagon to an element as mighty as fire.

Judge James Congdon listened with a cold smile as the now thoroughly cowed Black Jack Gleason turned to flattery to try to shift the subject from the price of coal.

'Some members of the Duquesne Club were wondering out loud at lunch the other day whether you would consider a run at public office?'

'The "people" won't elect a banker president,' Congdon replied.

'I'll bet you could change their minds.'

'No, they won't vote for a Wall Street man. I know. I ran for governor and I lost. They beat the pants off me.'

'There's always a next time.'

Congdon shrugged his broad and bony shoulders. 'Who knows what the future holds?' he asked modestly while thinking to himself, *I do. Next time, I know how to win*.

'First thing you ought to do,' said Gleason, 'is get the damned newspapers to stop complaining about your senators.'

'If only it were that simple, Gleason. The papers can howl their heads off about bribing congressmen and buying senators. People don't give a hang. Oh no. People expect it. People admire a president who controls Congress.'

'So you would consider running for president?'

'Who knows what the future holds?' Congdon repeated. 'Other than that in the immediate future, starting this afternoon, my mills will pay twenty cents a ton less than you've gotten used to, and my roads and barges will increase our shipping rates by five per cent.'

Gleason turned pale.

'How am I to make a profit?'

'Rob Peter to pay Paul.'

'How do you mean?'

'You may think of me as Paul. Labor is Peter. After you meet my terms and get your coal on the market, you can keep whatever you can hold on to. In other words, pay labor less.'

'I'm doing everything I can, but, I warn you, labor is fighting back.'

Judge James Congdon stood to his full height. 'I warn *you*: I will not subsidize any mine operator's failure to bring labor to heel.'

10

Heading out to meet Isaac Bell, Joseph Van Dorn swaggered proudly from the high-class Cadillac Hotel on Broadway, where he had just signed the lease on a suite of rooms for his brand-new New York field office. He was not one to throw money around, but a client clapping eyes on its fine limestone façade would not be inclined to quibble over fees. And having passed through its marble lobby – under the watchful eye of top-notch house detectives supplied by Van Dorn in exchange for a break on the rent – and been wafted upstairs in its gilded elevator, the client would count himself lucky that the Van Dorn Detective Agency agreed to take his case.

At Forty-fourth Street, a redheaded gentleman stopped dead in his tracks and stared at him. Van Dorn stared back. Faint scars on the man's brow indicated some experience with fisticuffs, though hardly in the professional prize ring, for the fellow looked prosperous, in a tasteful tweed suit and a bowler and with a heavy gold watch chain. Van Dorn saw anguish in his expression and a tear forming in his eye.

'Are you quite all right, sir?'

The answer came in a lilting Irish brogue, 'Och, aye, forgive me, sir. I could not help but notice . . .' He swallowed hard.

'What is it, young fellow?' The accent of Van Dorn's

Dublin childhood was almost too faint to be heard over the harder layers of his Chicago years.

'Begod, sir, if you're not the spitting image of me old dad.'

'Your father?'

'Is it not as if he rose from his grave to parade big as life down Broadway?' He caught himself. 'Oye, I mean no harm.'

'No, no, no. Not to worry, young fellow.'

'The splendid whiskers – scarlet as new dawn – the piercing eyes, the high brow.' He shook his head in amazement and in sorrow.

'When did he leave us?' Van Dorn asked gently.

'Only at Easter. I thought I had reckoned with it, and there you were. You're kind to stop, sir. Don't be putting yourself out a moment longer.' The young man bowed, his expression still troubled, and turned away.

Joseph Van Dorn was a sharp detective and a shrewd businessman, but he was a kindly soul and he called after him, 'I experienced the like when mine passed. I'll not promise it gets easier, but gradually, you won't dwell every day.'

'I will cherish that thought . . . You've been very kind – Sir, it would give me great pleasure to stand you to a wee dram.'

Van Dorn hesitated. He was already late to meet Isaac Bell, but the young fellow looked to be in desperate need, and a brother Irishman in need was not to be ignored. 'Of course.'

'There's a friendly snug just around the corner,' said the redhead, extending his hand. 'Finnerty. Jack Finnerty.'

They shook hands and found the bar. The bartender greeted Finnerty with a warm 'Welcome back' and poured Bushmills.

Van Dorn waited a decent interval to let Finnerty speak about his father before, in hopes of changing the subject to one less morbid, he asked, 'What line are you in, Mr Finnerty?'

'Coal,' said Finnerty. 'Or, I should say, *supercoal.*'

'What is supercoal?'

'Something of a modern miracle. Scientists have developed a means of releasing the excess power hidden inside coal – burning a bucket of supercoal produces the heat of a carload. Imagine a locomotive crossing the continent on one full tender, or the city dweller snug in his apartment with his entire winter supply in a single cupboard.'

'I have never heard of it.'

'You'll be hearing of it soon –'

All of a sudden, Finnerty jerked his watch chain and looked at the time. 'Begor! I must run. I promised the investors I'd attend their board meeting. I've not ten minutes to get to Wall Street. Thanks be to God for the El – though they'll not finish digging the Rapid Transit Subway soon enough for me. What good fortune to meet you, Mr Van Dorn! You were kind when kindnesses made a difference.'

Van Dorn shook his hand and held tight a moment to ask, 'At what stage of development is this invention?'

Finnerty glanced around and lowered his voice. 'I would not be surprised to see customers lined up for supercoal next winter. Particularly if the miners strike.'

'How are you making out with investors?'

'Near fully subscribed – I must run, but here's my card. Perhaps we'll meet again.'

Finnerty handed Van Dorn his card and was out the door.

Isaac Bell was pacing in the front hall when Van Dorn bustled into the Yale Club at Forty-fourth Street. Even impatiently pacing, Van Dorn thought, the young detective glided like a panther – precision-cocked to spring.

'Sorry, Isaac. Tied up in a meeting.'

Bell led the way to a pair of wing chairs in a quiet corner of the lounge. He related in detail what had happened at the Gleason jail and laid out his suspicions. Van Dorn listened attentively, intrigued again by Bell's speculation about a provocateur but still dubious about the evidence.

'I'm hoping you can spare me some men to get to the bottom of this, sir.'

'Your own squad?'

'It's too big for one detective.'

'Not possible,' said Van Dorn. 'We are stretched to breaking. Prince Henry is dragging us around the country like the tail of a kite and now he's threatening to extend his visit. They love him everywhere he goes and he's having a ball.'

Bell spoke urgently. 'Before I went down in the mine, I did as you suggested and learned everything I could about the coal business. The mines employ half a million men. Hundreds of thousands more work on the railroads and barge tows that transport it. In a nutshell, coal is the most important business in America.'

'That nutshell does not alter the fact that the Van Dorn Detective Agency has other fish to fry,' Van Dorn growled back.

Isaac Bell did not appear to hear him. 'Coal is indispensable for heat, for coke to make steel, for smelting ore, for electricity generation for lights, pumps, elevators and agriculture wells, and for fuel where wood is scarce. Coal powers ocean liners, battleships and railroad trains.'

Van Dorn nodded impatiently, thinking, *All the more reason to invest some part of my savings in Jack Finnerty's supercoal.* He said, 'I am aware that the wealth coal underpins is unimaginably immense, and the benefit to the entire nation is incalculable, as is ensuring a steady supply.'

'But such wealth has the potential to stir the worst in men of all stripes,' Bell persisted, 'be they labor, owner, or financier.' He took a deep breath. 'I could begin my investigation with Wally Kisley and Mack Fulton, and Wish Clarke.'

Van Dorn could not conceal his surprise. 'Only them?'

'Kisley is expert in explosives. Fulton's been working labor cases since the Haymarket Riot. And the boys all say that Wish Clarke is the toughest fighting man in the agency, which I observed to be true when you let me work with him in Wyoming and again in New Orleans.'

'You would be the youngest squad leader in the history of the agency.'

'No, sir. You were younger when you led your first squad.'

'Times were simpler back then . . .'

'Coincidentally,' said Isaac Bell, 'your first squad consisted of Kisley and Fulton and an apprentice named Wish, for "Aloysius," Clarke.'

It was Van Dorn's turn to take a deep breath.

'OK, you can have Weber and Fields,' he said, using the agency nickname for Kisley and Fulton whose jokes reminded everyone of the vaudeville comics. 'They're in Chicago. God knows where Wish Clarke is.'

'I can find him.'

'If you can find him, you can have him.'

'Could I also have Mr Bronson?'

Joseph Van Dorn's bushy eyebrows would have shot no higher if Isaac Bell had demanded the combined services of heavyweight champion Jim Jeffries, President Roosevelt and half his Rough Riders.

'Horace Bronson,' the Boss answered coldly, 'is engaged in San Francisco.'

Bell was not surprised, but it had been worth a try. He asked, 'Is there anyone else currently at large you could spare, sir?'

'You'll have to make do with what I've given you,' Van Dorn said sternly. 'You'll be thin on the ground, so don't get cocky. Weber and Fields are old hands but no longer spry, to put it mildly. They're of the years when men age quickly. And Wish . . . well, enough said.'

'You've always said he's a crack sleuth.'

'When sober,' Van Dorn shot back.

Bell said, 'You are right, sir. I will be thin on the ground. Would you consider hiring a particular friend of mine as an apprentice? He's a handy fellow with his fists – when I met him, he was captain of Princeton's boxing team.'

'That will stand him in good stead against college men who've taken up crime.'

'He's a whiz at disguises. He wanted to be an actor.'

'If he wanted to be, why isn't he?'

'His mother forbade it.'

'Obedience to mothers,' Van Dorn responded drily, 'is an admirable trait, but not the sort that spawns detectives with the requisite moxie.'

'He's got plenty of moxie, and Kisley and Fulton will show him what to do with it. Sir, I could really use the extra hand.'

Van Dorn looked dubious. 'I'd have to speak with him, size him up.'

'But you already have spoken with him.'

'What? When?'

'I believe you have his card in your vest pocket.'

Van Dorn reached into his vest. 'Jack Finnerty?'

Isaac Bell kept a straight face. 'Based on all I've learned about coal for this case, Mr Van Dorn, I wouldn't bet the farm on supercoal.'

Van Dorn flushed red as his whiskers. His eyes narrowed to pinpricks of blue flame, and his mighty chest filled like a bull's. Isaac Bell braced for the explosion. But, at last, the Boss laughed.

'*Flimflammed!* You flimflammed me.'

'I had to demonstrate his moxie.'

'You did that, all right. Really had me going there – Well, at least I was flimflammed by a brother Irishman.'

Bell could no longer hide his smile.

'Now what are you smirking about?'

'Sorry to disillusion you, sir, but your "Irish brother" is

a direct descendant of the English and Dutch founders of New York – Archibald Angel Abbott IV, listed first in Society's Four Hundred.'

The Congdon building was more secure than most in Wall Street, tight as a bank.

Henry Clay entered by the basement service entrance, dressed in steamfitter's overalls and carrying a ball-peen hammer, a pipe wrench, a measuring tape, and an inspection gauge with its thin metal gap gauges modified to pick locks. He knew the guards' routine and eluded them easily. He picked open a lock, bounded up twelve flights of stairs without sweating or breathing hard, removed his overalls, picked two more locks in utter silence, and stepped suddenly through the back door of Judge James Congdon's private office.

Clay saw immediate confirmation of the wisdom of his plan. The tough old bird glanced up from his desk startled but not one bit frightened. He had chosen well.

I I

James Congdon was intrigued by the intruder.

He could summon help in an instant with a shout into the speaking tube or one of several candlestick telephones on his desk. Better yet, simply shoot him with a revolver from his desk. Or, best of all, he could activate his 'lunatic stopper.' But for the moment, Congdon was curious. Why would such an elegant, well-dressed gentleman break in his back door?

As if to prove that he was as cultured as he looked, the intruder complimented the marble sculpture that dominated Congdon's office with a connoisseur's appreciation. 'I commend your knowledge of antiquities.'

Judge Congdon uncapped the speaking tube. 'Antiquities? You're showing off your ignorance. Auguste Rodin carved that statue two years ago.'

'But unlike the prudish original, this superior copy of *Le Baiser* that you commissioned depicts the male form complete – in the classical Greek style – rather than draped, as it were, under a modest limb.'

Congdon snorted, 'That's a big-sounding way of saying he's showing his tackle.'

The intruder flushed and lost his composure for an instant. 'In the presence of such beauty,' he said stiffly, 'I would consider an expression less crude.'

Congdon pulled a gun from his desk. 'While I consider whether to have you beaten to a pulp or shoot you myself.'

'That is a privilege of wealth,' said Henry Clay. 'But you would miss the greatest opportunity of your life. I will make an offer you will find irresistible.'

'I am rarely tempted.'

'But when you are, sir, you seize the opportunity.'

Clay cast a significant glance at Rodin's passionate lovers. Then he nodded appreciatively at the bronze statuette on Congdon's desk, which depicted the most recent of Congdon's shapely young wives *au naturel.*

'My name is Henry Clay. I am a painter's son by birth and a private detective by profession. I offer no threat, only promise. And I do it at great risk because you *could* have me beaten or killed.'

'So you're a betting man?'

'Yes, sir. I am betting my life that you'll see this opportunity for what it is.'

'What opportunity?'

'The opportunity to destroy the miners' unions: the United Mine Workers in the east and the Western Federation of Miners in the west. Stop them dead, once and for all. It will be twenty years before another miner dares start a union, much less call a strike, anywhere on the continent. And here's a sugarplum bonus for you. You will profit mightily knowing ahead of time to invest in businesses that will flourish when you destroy the unions.'

'By what means?'

'Every means. No holds barred.'

Congdon shook his head. 'No. I risk everything if you are caught and turn blab-mouthed.'

'What would the word of a lowly detective be against the great Judge Congdon?'

Congdon fixed him with a gimlet eye. '"The great Judge Congdon" intends to be president of the United States. Unfortunately, that means convincing the ignorant people that he is above suspicion.'

'What could I blab? You can seal our deal with a nod. No signature, no contract. There is no way to record a nod.'

'Without a contract, you are betting on the groundless hope that I will reward you. What if I don't?'

'I don't need your reward.'

'Then why —'

'Here is all I need from you,' said Clay, and ticked items off on fastidiously manicured fingers. 'Unlimited operating funds to do the job. Certain information that only you possess. Rail passes on all lines, and special trains to help me travel quickly about the continent. Permission to send and receive messages over the private closed telegraph wires leased by your brokers.'

Congdon interrupted with a sarcastic comment that the Interstate Commerce Commission forbade outsiders sending messages over leased wires.

Clay laughed. Brokers of stocks, bonds and commodities bent that law day and night. 'Speed and privacy are a matter of business.' He knew that he did not have to remind Congdon that owners and lessees of private wires got a jump on competitors who had to rely on Western Union's slower public wires.

'In every city I operate, we will communicate swiftly and secretly through your branch offices.'

'Branch offices untraceable to me,' Congdon said sharply.

'Doesn't a financier of your stature hold secret controlling interests in firms that lease private wires?'

Congdon ignored the flattery and demanded, 'But what do *you* get out of this scheme?'

'Reputation. By rights, you will pay me handsomely when I succeed. But if you don't – if you cheat me – it will not matter. I will be a made man.'

'How?'

'Henry Clay Investigations will become the detective agency to presidents and kings when the men who run this country learn who smashed the unions. When you are president, I, too, will be very big in Washington.'

Congdon mulled over Clay's proposal. He was a famous judge of character. The detective, a robust physical specimen, possessed the steady gaze of a valuable man capable of finishing what he started. 'What makes you so sure that this would appeal to me?'

'I have studied you, Judge Congdon. I understand you. I am a very good detective. I am the best.'

'You think you know me, do you? Have another look at my statue. Look close at *The Kiss*. Do you see anything unusual?'

Henry Clay did as Congdon ordered. He leaned close to the marble and let his eyes roam over the man and woman in passionate embrace. 'I see a magnificent statue.'

'It draws you closer, doesn't it?'

'It does. I am actually standing closer to it than I was a moment ago. But what is it you want me to see?'

'Look up.'

The skylight that illuminated the marble was ringed by a plaster frieze studded with tiny holes one-tenth the diameter of a dime.

'I see holes in the frieze. They're barely visible.'

'Now look down.'

'I don't understand, sir.'

'Look down.'

In the pattern of the marble circle on which he was standing were dozens of similar holes. 'I still don't understand.'

'I will teach you two things about wealth, Mr Best Detective. Wealth attracts lunatics. My old enemy Frick was shot and nearly killed in his own office by a lunatic ten years ago, which set me to thinking of my own safety. Do you understand what I'm telling you?'

'You said *two* things about wealth.'

'Common wisdom holds that coal is the source of all wealth. Like most common wisdom, that's dead wrong. Coal is only fuel. It happens to be the best fuel at the moment, but it will be replaced by a better fuel. Oil is the coming fuel until the scientists come up with something even better, which they will. The *real* source of wealth for the past hundred years, and hundreds more to follow, is steam – hot steam made by boiling water with the cheapest and most efficient fuel available – wood, coal, oil, and whatever science dreams up next. Steam pushes pistons that drive locomotives. Steam whirls turbines to spin electricity. Steam storms through pipes under city streets to heat modern buildings like mine.'

Congdon reached for the bronze statuette of his current wife. He stroked it with his gnarled fingers.

'Steam scalds flesh. Steam from a mere teakettle will sear your hand with the most painful burn imaginable. Shortly after the attack on Frick, a six-inch steam riser in a building like this one ruptured. Escaping steam blasted through the walls as if they were made of paper. Every man and woman in the office died in an instant. They were found still seated at their desks, scalded head to toe, horribly disfigured, cooked to death inside and out. That set me to thinking about the lunatic attack on Mr Frick. What he should have installed in his office — and what I have installed in mine — is a steam-powered lunatic stopper.'

Congdon tightened his grip on the bronze statuette.

'Do you notice anything peculiar about this statue of my new wife?'

Clay looked more closely and saw what he had missed earlier. The bronze was hinged to the top of the desk. 'I see a hinge.'

'The hinge makes it a lever. When I move this lever, it will open a valve that will deliver a scalding hot three-hundred-and-fifty-degree blast of steam straight from the central boiler plant on Cortlandt Street to your skin, Best Detective Clay.'

Henry Clay eyed the holes in the floor and the ceiling.

'Scalding jets of high-pressure steam will cook you to death in seconds. The longest and worst, most painful seconds of your life.'

'It will kill you, too.'

'I'll be unscathed. The jet holes are calculated to deliver just enough for you.'

'OK,' said Clay, 'you caught me flat-footed. If you throw that lever, I'm dead.'

'Painfully dead.'

'Painfully dead.'

Hand firmly on the lever, James Congdon recognized a certain unique quality in Henry Clay: if the fellow felt fear, Congdon could not see it. In fact, it appeared that if Clay had one strength above all others, it was the strength to recognize the inevitable and accept it without complaint. A controlling interest in such a man could be a solid investment.

'If I were to give you unlimited operating funds, private information, rail passes, and specials, how would you use them?'

'The details are mine alone to know.'

Congdon frowned. 'You're a brave man to stand your ground in your precarious situation. Or a fool.'

'A determined man,' Clay shot back. 'The only thing you can count on in this world is determination. I'm offering determination. I repeat: the details are mine alone to know.'

'Assume, for the moment, that *tactics* are up to you,' Congdon conceded. 'What is your strategy?'

'You need a story to destroy the unions. The newspapers are already on your side. They will tell your story. I will give you your story.'

'What story?'

'The owners upon whom God has seen fit to bestow property will protect property and liberty from murderous agitators.'

'How will you tell it?'

'By starting a war in the coalfields.'

'How?'

'Are you familiar with the accident at Gleason Mine No. 1?'

'Runaway coal train, some hands killed, and production interrupted for four days. Are you telling me you started that?'

'And finished it. Before the miners returned to work, they burned down Gleason's jail and the courthouse. I'd call that a war.'

'I'd call it a good beginning,' Congdon conceded. 'A veritable Harry O'Hagan one-man triple play.'

'A quadruple play, counting the fire.'

'Yes indeed you outdid O'Hagan. But I am deeply disappointed.'

'Why, sir?'

James Congdon answered with a wistful sigh. 'My lunatic stopper will have to wait for another lunatic.'

He let go the steam lever and gestured for Henry Clay to take a seat beside him.

12

'Crackerjack army Mr Van Dorn gave you, kid: two spavined geezers and an amiable drunk.'

Isaac Bell defended his friend. 'Wish goes long stretches when he never touches a drop.'

Wally Kisley, who looked less like a private detective than an aging harness salesman in a sack suit patterned bright as a checkerboard, grinned at his old partner, ice-eyed Mack Fulton. Fulton, somber in gray and black, looked the deadly sort that no sensible man would inquire about his business.

'Say, Mack, what is the difference between a drinking man and a drowning man?'

'Beats me, Wally. Didn't know there *was* a difference between a drinking man and a drowning man.'

'The drowning man sinks in water. The drinking man sinks in whiskey.'

'Say, Wally,' asked Mack, 'here comes a passerby, strolling by the sea, what does the drowning man yell?'

'Throw me a rope.'

'What does the drinking man yell?'

'Throw me a bottle.'

They looked to Bell for a laugh.

Stone-faced, Isaac Bell said, 'I worked with Wish Clarke in Wyoming and New Orleans. He's sharp as they come.'

'So's a busted bottle.'

'I also remember when you "spavined geezers" took over my apprenticeship from Mr Van Dorn, you taught me plenty. And you weren't so spavined that you couldn't clear a saloon of Harry Frost's boys.'

'Your *recent* apprenticeship,' Kisley and Fulton chorused.

Bell saw that the old detectives were not joking but deadly serious and with a purpose. Kisley stared hard at him. Mack Fulton got down to brass tacks.

'Who's ramrodding this outfit?'

'It's my case,' said Isaac Bell. 'I am.'

Kisley said, 'It was not long ago we was changing your diapers in Chicago.'

'I've got the hang of it since.'

The partners shot back obstinate glowers and Mack said, flatly, 'The man bossing an outfit has to change everyone's diapers and still stay on top of the case.'

'You're looking at him.'

'I'm looking at a kid who started shaving yesterday,' Fulton shot back.

'Spouting highfalutin French,' Kisley piled on. '*Provocateur?* Whatever happened to good old *agitator?*'

'Or *provoker?*'

'Or *instigator?*'

Isaac Bell was constitutionally incapable of punching a man twice his age, but he was getting tempted.

Suddenly, Aloysius Clarke was standing in the doorway. He was a big, red-faced fellow who moved quietly.

Bell said, 'Hello, Wish.'

Clarke nodded. 'Kid.'

'We was just discussin' who ramrods this outfit,' said Mack Fulton.

Wish Clarke stood silent. He had small blue eyes buried so deeply in drink-swollen, purple-veined cheeks that observers who associated whiskey with dulled wits and melancholy would miss the glow of intelligence and laughter. He smiled unexpectedly and answered the question on all minds. How long had Wish Clarke been standing there and how much had he overheard?

'It's Isaac's case. The kid's the boss.'

Wally Kisley shook his head. 'Them coal miners ain't the only ones who need a union.'

'And to close another subject,' said Wish Clarke, a self-educated man who revered the English language, '*Provoker* is too general a word, *agitator* is a misspelling of *adjutator*, which means "a representative," and *instigator* is vague. But *provocateur*, short for *agent provocateur*, describes exactly what Isaac suspects we're up against – a smart fellow who's hoodwinking not-so-smart fellows into committing crimes that will discredit them.'

'For what reason?'

'For reasons,' said Wish Clarke, 'we have not yet detected, Detective Kisley.'

Isaac Bell raised his voice. 'Saddle up, gents!'

He pulled tickets from his vest and passed them out.

'Train's leaving for West Virginia. All aboard!'

Locomotive headlamp blazing through the night, a train of sixty ore cars steamed from the Cripple Creek gold mines on Pikes Peak down the Colorado Front Range into the smoke-shrouded city of Denver. Pinkerton detectives boarded the locomotive in the Auraria rail yard.

Three thousand smelter workers had walked off the

job – the opening gun in a united strike led by the Western Federation of Miners to win an eight-hour workday for every union with which it was affiliated. The Pinkertons posted riflemen on the engine pilot and took command of the heavily laden train to escort it to the Nyren Smelter.

Jim Higgins stood arm in arm with a thousand strikers blocking the tracks. In his opinion – not that the hotheads were asking for it – ruining the Nyren furnaces had been a mistake, and the strike, which could have blossomed into a general strike the breadth of the continent, was going nowhere, stuck in Denver, mired in bitterness.

Old Man Nyren – a cantankerous bully detested equally by labor and the Rocky Mountain smelter owners he had driven out of business with his giant plant fired by cheap coal – was in no mood to bargain. The strikers had drawn the fires from under his furnaces. The molten ore had frozen into a solid mass from the charge hoppers on top to the crucible drains below, rendering them useless until the hardened mass of ore, slag and gold could be cut out. Nyren ordered the ore train parked in the smelter's elevated yard, ready to tip its load into his furnaces the instant that cutting was done by scab labor.

The Pinkertons ordered the train to run the strikers off the tracks.

'Go to hell!' said the locomotive engineer. 'I ain't killing those fellers.'

'Me neither,' said the fireman, crossing his massive arms.

The detectives clubbed both men to the floor of the cab. A hard-bitten engineer they had brought with them took the controls. 'Can't see what's behind the bastards,' he said. 'For all we know, they could have pried up the rails.'

'Clear 'em,' ordered the detective in charge.

They tied down the whistle. Blowing an unbroken, ungodly shriek, the train accelerated, and the riflemen on front opened fire.

Union men scattered, dragging their wounded with them.

The riflemen kept firing until the track ahead was empty but for fallen bodies. The train increased speed. Unable to stop it, the outraged, frightened strikers roared their anger. Stones scooped up from the ballast clanged against the sides of the locomotive, shattered the headlamp, and knocked one of the shooters off the engine pilot.

'Don't slow down 'til we're inside the gates or they'll mob us.'

The gates were just beyond an iron girder bridge that carried the rails above the workers' slum that encircled the smelter, and it looked to the Pinkertons as if they would make it. Suddenly, from the helplessly raging, stone-throwing mob of strikers, a hero darted – a slight figure, no bigger than a boy – dragging a heavy ore rake.

'Where the hell – *Stop him! Don't let him move that switch!*'

No one had to tell the remaining gunman riding on front of the danger to the locomotive. His Winchester leaped to his shoulder and he snapped a shot at the running figure. The bullet missed but slammed the rake out of the boy's hands. The boy picked it up and kept running toward the switch. The rifleman took careful aim. He squeezed the trigger slowly and gently. Three stones struck at once, hitting his shoulder, hand, and knee. He dropped his rifle, fell off the engine pilot, and rolled, screaming, under the wheels.

His bullet missed the boy, ricocheted off the girdered overpass, and pierced a window in the Nyren Smelter gate tower.

The boy ran in front of the train and jammed the rake into the switch.

One hundred yards from the safety of the smelter gates, the locomotive's pilot wheels were derailed by the rake. The massive drivers right behind them sliced the steel rake like a length of sausage. But the forces squeezing that extra piece of steel crammed between the movable switch point and the fixed rail spread the rail a single inch out of line. With nothing for their flanges to grip, the drive wheels slipped off the rails.

The locomotive jumped the track and tumbled off the overpass into the slum streets below, dragging its coal-laden tender and ten full ore cars on to the roof of the building that housed the Nyren company store.

'What's troubling you, Jim? We did all right today.'

Jim Higgins looked up bleakly from his desk in the union hall. The local's secretary and vice president had returned with celebrants' beers under their belts. 'Not counting eight in the hospital and two men dead?' he asked, although the victims were not his only source of concern.

'They died like heroes.'

'Speaking of heroes, wasn't that little guy something?'

'Has anyone seen him since?' asked Higgins.

'Neither hide nor hair. Too bad. He deserves a medal.'

'He's smart to lay low – better yet, light the heck out of Denver.'

'Halfway to San Francisco, if he's got a brain in his head,' agreed Higgins, hoping against hope. From the first instant he had seen the slight figure with the rake he had an awful feeling that the 'little guy' was neither a man nor a boy but instead a slim young woman in trousers named Mary Higgins.

He had sent telegrams to friends in Chicago and Pittsburgh, where she should have gone after West Virginia. So far, no one reported seeing her. Times like this, he wished he wasn't an atheist. Times like this when there was nothing left to do but pray.

'Brother!'

In she walked, not in trousers and cap, thank God, but in a bedraggled skirt and a lady's hat with a perfunctory feather decorating it.

'Mary,' he said, rising, 'how wonderful to see you. When did you get into town?'

Mary took note of the red-faced vice president and secretary and replied, 'I just got off the train. I had a feeling I'd find you here. How is it going?'

'Gentlemen, my sister Mary.'

The secretary and vice president nearly broke their arms whipping off their hats, reminding Jim Higgins how attractive men found his sister. They told her that the strike was going wonderfully and that they would surely win. Higgins waited until he and Mary were alone in his rented room before he told her the truth. 'It's not working,' he said. 'The strike is stuck in Denver. It won't spread far.'

'I saw Mother Jones in Chicago,' said Mary, referring to a brave old labor leader who was an inspiration to them both. 'She was hoping you would convince the Western Federation to join with eastern miners back in Pennsylvania and West Virginia.'

'So was I.'

'She said that since all the mines are owned by Wall Street operators, the unions should strike simultaneously. The operators are national. We should be national.'

'Did you say you just got into Denver this evening?'

Mary looked him straight in the face. 'What do you want me to say?'

'I want you to say that wasn't you who derailed the ore train.'

'Why?'

'You could have been killed.'

'You could have been killed in Gleasonburg.'

'I would have been if that young miner hadn't come to my rescue, but that is not the point.'

'Miner hell!' said Mary. 'Isaac Bell is a Pinkerton.'

Jim Higgins could not believe his ears. 'He can't be. That's not possible.'

'I saw with my own eyes.'

'Did he say he's a Pinkerton?'

'Well, not in so many words. He claimed to be a Van Dorn.'

'There's a big difference,' Jim argued. 'Pinkertons provide strikebreakers to break unionist heads and protect scabs. I've never seen Van Dorns doing that. They are a cut above.'

'Have you ever heard of a Van Dorn working for the union?' Mary fired back.

'Bell helped you get out of West Virginia, didn't he?'

'Bell was spying, brother. Bell tricked us. He's no better than the rest of them.'

13

'Last stop, gents,' said Isaac Bell as the trolley from Morgantown bounced into Gleasonburg. 'Round up what you can before dark. Meet back here. Mr Van Dorn will buy us supper in that saloon,' he added, indicating Reilly's, where Mary had wangled coffee.

'What I most enjoy about detecting work is the opportunity to travel,' said Mack Fulton, gazing upon Main Street's unpainted company houses, goats chewing bark from dying trees, piles of broken rock and coal dust, and muddy hillsides logged to ragged stumps for propping timber.

'To see new sights,' said Wally Kisley.

'Broadening our horizons – get the bags, Archie.'

Wish Clarke passed their bags to the redheaded apprentice but held on to the heaviest, an unusually long, reinforced carpetbag that made a muted clank when he set it on the ground.

'Looks like they burned down the jail.' He winked at Isaac Bell. 'Most of the courthouse, too. Is that how you cut loose of the lynch mob?'

'I had some help from a lady – OK, gents, let's get moving.'

Mack Fulton asked, 'Who gets Archie?'

'You two,' answered Bell, and said to Archie, 'Help them up stairs and crossing streets.'

Wish Clarke headed for the company store.

Isaac Bell went to the mouth of Gleason Mine No 1. No longer disguised as a miner, he presented the Pinkerton in charge of the guards a letter of introduction he had not yet used that identified him as a Van Dorn Agency detective working for Gleason.

'What the hell is this supposed to mean? We don't need no detectives. We're the detectives.'

'It's signed by Black Jack himself, and it means you're ordered to give any Van Dorn who asks for one a safety light and get out of his way. I'm asking for one.'

They brought him the light. They were edgy, he thought, less cock of the walk, less inclined to bully. 'Where you going with this?'

'A walk,' said Bell. 'Come along if you like,' knowing the Pinkerton would never enter the mine.

'The miners are talking strike.'

'When did that start?' Bell asked, recalling Jim Higgins's promise *There's more where I came from.*

'Damned fools are takin' the bit in their teeth. Whole town's about to blow sky-high. Wouldn't be surprised if some of them took a swing at you.'

'I'll run the risk,' said Bell. He carried the light through the timbered portal and hurried straight down the haulageway.

The ventilators were running, and he could hear the clatter of hundreds of miners picking in the galleries, the muffled screech of electric drills, and the occasional heavy crump of dynamite tearing open the seam. He recognized the doorboy he had helped out after the wreck and waved. The child did not know Bell in his sack suit and fedora and looked frightened that he had drawn the attention of a detective.

Bell stopped and pressed a small gold piece into the boy's grimy hand. He stared at it with a combination of disbelief and terror. 'It's OK,' Bell assured him. 'My grandfather left me a few bucks. You can keep it or give it to your mother and father.'

'I don't got no father.'

'Give it to your mother.'

He started down. The boy called after him, 'Are you a Pinkerton, mister?'

'No. I'm a Van Dorn.'

'Wow,' said the boy, willing, Bell noted ruefully, to accept a distinction that Mary Higgins had not.

He continued down the sloping passage to the end. The wrecked train had been removed and the tunnel dug deeper into the seam. Bell worked his way back up to the lowest gallery, then counted up four props and felt behind the fourth for the crack where he had hidden the broken bridle link.

Wally Kisley was deep in conversation with a miner for whom he had bought a schooner of beer in the dirtiest saloon he could recall when the man suddenly clammed up. Young Archie, who was doing a good job of standing around not appearing to be on lookout, rapped a warning on the bar, and Kisley looked up to see a pair of Gleason company cops sashay in like they owned the place.

They walked straight up to him, said 'Get out of here' to the miner, who scooted away without finishing his beer. Then one said to Kisley, 'That's the ugliest suit of clothes I ever seen on a man.'

Wally Kisley studied his checkerboard coat sleeve as if seeing it for the first time.

The second cop said, 'Looks like a clown suit.'

Wally Kisley remained silent. The first cop noticed Archie Abbott and said, 'What the hell are you looking at?'

The tall, young redhead answered slowly and distinctly, 'I am looking at absolutely nothing.'

'What did you say to me?'

'Let me revise that, if I may,' said Archie, staring back. 'If it were possible to look at less than nothing, then you would provide the opportunity to look at less than nothing.'

Wally Kisley laughed. 'Kid, you're a blessing in disguise.'

'What?' said the cop.

The barkeep, who had been listening anxiously, left the room.

Wally replied conversationally, 'My young redheaded friend sees the joke in the fact that a man who is so ugly his face would stop a clock would criticize the appearance of my garb.'

The cop pulled a blackjack, and his partner pulled his.

'Enough,' said Mack Fulton, materializing from a chair in a dark corner with a Smith & Wesson rock-steady in his hand. 'Vamoose!'

Four Gleason cops and two Pinkerton detectives caught up with the Van Dorns in Reilly's Saloon.

Kisley and Fulton and Wish Clarke and Archie Abbott were sharing a bottle while waiting for Isaac Bell. Archie was playing the piano, a dusty upright not too badly out of tune, and Mack and Wally were harmonizing in full-blown Weber-and-Fields style on the new Chicago hit, 'If Money Talks, It Ain't On Speaking Terms With Me.'

The cops and detectives walked in with pistols drawn.

Reilly vanished into his back office. The miners at the plank-and-barrel bar, who had been talking boldly about rumors of a strike, tossed back their whiskeys and hurried out the door.

Wally and Mack kept singing: 'If money talks, it ain't on speaking terms with me . . .'

Wish Clarke said, 'If you boys are waving those fire-arms at us, you seem to be forgetting that the Van Dorn Agency is working for the Gleason Consolidated Coal & Coke Company, hired personally by Black Jack Gleason, who feared, with ample evidence to back him, that you boys were not up to detecting saboteurs.'

'Not for long,' a beefy West Virginia company cop drawled back. 'Word is, company's fixing to fire you all soon as Mr Gleason returns from New York City.'

Kisley sipped whiskey and glanced at Fulton.

Fulton sipped whiskey and glanced at Wish Clarke.

Wish Clarke drained his glass, refilled it, and said, 'When and if Mr Gleason decides to terminate our employment, we may go home. Or, we may continue to enjoy the pleasures of fair Gleasonburg like the free citizens of America we are. In the meantime, we're girding our loins for what this establishment claims will be supper. So if you boys care to gird with us, pull up a chair. If not, trundle on, and we'll commence to eating.'

'You're all under arrest.'

Wish Clarke said, 'You can't arrest us.'

'Why not?'

'Your jail burned down.'

Archie Abbott spewed a mouthful of whiskey in the sawdust.

The Pinkerton said, 'We got temporary hoosegows lined up on a siding in case the miners take it in their damned fool heads to strike – old reefer cars for refrigerating meat. There's one reserved for you boys 'til the judge gets around to filling out the papers. If you're packing firearms, drop them while you can.'

Kisley, Fulton and Clarke spread apart slightly, which neither the Pinkertons nor the Gleasons appeared to notice.

'You, too, Red. On your feet.'

Kisley said, 'Do what he says, Archie.'

Archie rose from the piano stool, looking confused by the turn of events.

'Guns, Red. Drop 'em.'

'He doesn't have any,' said Kisley. 'He's an apprentice. Van Dorns are not allowed to carry guns when they apprentice.'

The company cops snickered. 'I bet *none* of you have guns, seeing as how you're all looking like apprentices.'

14

'I have a gun.'

Isaac Bell glided out of the night with a double-barreled, sawed-off twelve-gauge shotgun cocked in each hand. 'In fact, I have two. Elevate, boys. Paws in the air.'

The Pinkerton said, 'Fire those twelve-gauges one-handed, sonny, and you'll make a comic sight kicked tail over teakettle.'

'You,' said Isaac Bell, 'will be waiting in Hell for the next batch to come down and tell you who was laughing. *Drop 'em and elevate!*'

The wiser Pinkertons observed winter in the young detective's eyes. They dropped their pistols and raised their hands. The Gleasons glowered and shrugged their shoulders.

'Drop 'em,' snapped a Pinkerton.

They obeyed reluctantly, and all six shuffled out of the saloon.

Mack Fulton gestured for Archie to pick up their guns. 'Here's your first lesson, Apprentice Archie. You know you're close to something when they threaten to poke you in the snoot.'

'Close to what?' asked Wish Clarke. 'Every miner I talked to – twenty at least – thinks that chain bridle broke of natural causes. They also indicated that if that poor union fellow walked in, they would hang him from the rafters. On the other hand, I noted a certain electricity in the air.'

'Fired up to strike?' asked Bell.

'Fired up for something, just not sure what. I think your courthouse conflagration strengthened their self-esteem.'

Fulton said, 'They hate Gleason – taking particular umbrage at his steam yacht – and hate the cops, but they don't blame either for the runaway. My impression is, they'll strike only when they find someone to lead them.'

Wally Kisley said, 'Pretty much what I heard, too. They think the wreck was an accident. Though a few men told me they blamed the company for double-jobbing what's his name, Higgins. But Wish is right, Isaac burning down the courthouse seemed to give 'em guts.'

'I didn't really burn it down,' said Bell.

'Well, you held the lady's coat.'

Archie Abbott said, 'A mechanician told me those chain bridles never break.'

'Probably the same feller who rigged it up,' said Mack Fulton, and the others laughed.

Isaac Bell tossed the broken bridle link on the table. It landed with a heavy thunk and did not bounce far. 'What do you say, Wally? What do you think broke that?'

Wally inspected it carefully. He ran his finger along the edge. 'I'll be.'

'What?'

'Looks like someone smacked it with a cold chisel. You see where the blade cut half through it?'

Isaac Bell said, 'I thought it was chiseled, too.'

'OK. Now what?'

'It broke in plain sight of a hundred men who would have noticed a guy whacking it with a chisel.'

'I recall you saying that back in Pittsburgh. But look. It looks like it was cut with a chisel.'

'How?'

Kisley sat back and stroked his chin as if he were grooming a beard. 'Several ways to drive a cold chisel through steel spring to mind. Whack it with a hammer.'

'Which didn't happen,' said Mack Fulton.

'Persuade an eagle to drop the chisel from a hundred feet in the air.'

'Which didn't happen.'

'Drive it with an explosive charge.'

Isaac watched a rare smile cross Mack Fulton's grim face. 'Which could have happened.'

'Isaac,' said Wish Clarke. 'Do you recall hearing a charge explode?'

'I heard a heck of a bang. But how would you detonate it?'

'Fulminate of mercury blasting cap.'

'How would you attach the cap?'

Wally Kisley poked the link. Then he picked it up and smelled it. 'Could have stuck it on with tar, I suppose.'

'Maybe just a short length of chisel.'

'Molded in a ball of tar – mighty cumbersome, though. Mighty cumbersome . . .'

Wally Kisley stared silently out the saloon door into the dark street. Isaac Bell observed that the explosives expert was falling less and less in love with the concept of a dynamite-driven chisel.

Archie Abbott glanced at Bell and raised an eyebrow to ask what was going on. Bell motioned for Archie to join him at the bar. He explained quietly, 'They've seen it all. They're just trying to remember which applies.'

'How the heck old are they?'

'Who knows? Wally was already a top agent when he investigated the bomb that set off the Haymarket Riot. They've got to be over fifty.'

'Amazing,' Archie marveled.

Finally, slowly, like a newly lighted oil lamp gathering kerosene up into its wick, Wally's face began to glow. He turned to Mack Fulton. 'Mack, you know what's on my mind?'

'Dynamite.'

'A great improvement over black powder, patented in 1867 by Alfred Nobel.'

'From which Alfred Nobel made so much dough – and felt so guilty for making it easier to kill people – that last year he handed out prizes of money to the best physicist, the best pacifist, the best poet, even the guy who invented X-rays.'

'You know who else should have won a prize last year?'

'Rosania,' said Fulton.

'Laurence Rosania.'

Isaac Bell and Wish Clarke exchanged a look.

Archie asked, 'Who's that?'

'Chicago safecracker,' answered Bell. 'Jewel man.'

'Best dynamite man in the business,' said Kisley, his smile growing.

'Aces across the continent, too,' said Fulton, 'since he's taken up travel. If those other guys deserved that Nobel Prize and all that dough, so does he.'

Bell called from the bar, 'What about Rosania? Do you see his hand in this?'

'No, no, no. He's a jewel thief. Too fastidious a dude to muck around coal mines even if he was sabotage-minded, which he ain't. But I am thinking about a job he pulled last year. Remember, Mack?'

'Shaped charge.'

'Sometimes called hollow charge.'

Bell and Archie rejoined the others at the table.

Mack said, 'This politician bought himself a big safe with six-inch walls made of plates of iron and steel.'

'In the event,' Wally explained to Archie, 'that a city contractor or a police chief or a sporting house proprietor had a sudden need to safeguard some cash and it was after banking hours, this politician would help out by holding it for them in his safe.'

Archie nodded.

'Performing a public service.'

'Some safecracker,' Mack continued, 'tried to blow it. Seeing six-inch walls, the yegg applied enough dynamite to blast the roof off the politician's house. Which it did, but only dented the safe. Barely scratched it. A while later, along comes Rosania. He's caught wind that the politician purchased diamonds for his girl. Rosania blows a hole in the six-inch walls big enough to stick his hand in. Like it was made of cardboard. And no one even heard the explosion.'

'How'd he do it?' asked Bell.

'Rosania's one of those fellows who's always got his nose in a book,' said Fulton.

Kisley said, 'He read about this scientist at the Naval

Torpedo Station up in Newport, Rhode Island, who came up with this big idea called a hollow charge. Sometimes they call it a shaped charge 'cause where you make it hollow, the direction its hollow points is the direction where the explosion goes. Instead of blowing off the politician's new roof, Rosania drove all that dynamite in the exact direction he wanted, straight through the wall of the safe. Quiet little poof. Four-inch hole.'

'Did he get the diamonds?' asked Archie Abbott.

Mack Fulton looked at the apprentice incredulously. 'What? No, he got diamond dust and diamond flakes.'

'I thought diamonds were indestructible.'

'So did Rosania,' said Mack Fulton.

Wally Kisley laughed. 'Clearly, the safecracking classes have some experimenting still to do. But, Isaac, if your saboteur found a way to stick a hollow charge to the chain bridle, he wouldn't need a big bunch of sticks of dynamite you'd spot a mile off. Fact is, I don't think he used a cold chisel at all. I think that hollow charge did the job all by itself. What you heard, Isaac, was a small charge of dynamite blowing all in one direction straight at this link – so concentrated that it sheared the chain like a chisel.'

'But how long would the charge stick to the chain? Jerking around like it does.'

Kisley shrugged. 'Not long. Maybe he wired it on. You said you never found that shackle. I bet he packed the entire charge inside the shackle.'

Mack Fulton said, 'Maybe you couldn't find the shackle because all that was left was shackle chips and shackle dust.'

Bell stared at Fulton. For a second he felt the floor shift

under him. Like a dream remembered days later, he could almost see a pair of golden eyes, wolf eyes, from which exploded a fist. The white-damp dream in which he thought he had seen the shackle he never found. He shook his head, wondering how to unscramble tangled memory, and pressed on. 'It doesn't take much shaking to explode fulminate of mercury. How long before the winch jerking the wire set off the detonator?'

'Minutes at most.'

'Which meant the saboteur was in the mine when he attached the explosive.'

'Had to be. Slapped it on with a wad of tar last minute as the train went by.'

'A cool customer, knowing the train might come crashing back at him before he could get out.'

'Mighty cool,' Wish Clarke agreed. 'Knowing it was coming gave him a certain leg up to get out of the way. Still, you gotta hand it to him. A cool customer.'

'Who knows his business,' said Wally Kisley.

'All of which supports young Isaac's contention,' said Wish Clarke. 'With the timing of the explosion unpredictable, what union man would perpetrate such an act knowing it could kill his brother miners?'

'It does make you wonder what he'll think of next time.'

'This calls for a drink,' said Wish Clarke, emptying the bottle into his glass. 'Wally's right, we are on to something.'

'Until Gleason fires us.'

'When Gleason fires us,' said Bell, 'I'll try and talk Mr Van Dorn into letting us stay on.'

'I wouldn't count on that.'

The food arrived, and Isaac Bell's squad began debating what it had been before the cook got ahold of it. Wish Clarke took his glass to the bar. He motioned for Bell to join him.

'If you want us to keep looking for your provocateur, steer clear of the telegraph office.'

'Why?'

'And if you see a boy coming your way with a telegram, run like hell. The Boss can't order you to stop if he can't find you.'

Bell grinned. 'Thanks, Wish. Good advice.'

'Want some more?'

'What?'

'Next time you shave, why not leave off the region encompassed by your lip and nose?'

'Grow a mustache?'

'You'll look a mite older with a mustache. Make the opposition take you seriously.'

Bell grinned again proudly. 'Those Pinkertons took me seriously. They dropped their guns like they were red-hot.'

'Indeed they did,' said Wish, draining his glass. 'Although it could be argued that what they took seriously was a brace of double-barreled twelve-gauges.'

'You always told me, the sure way to win a knife fight is bring a gun. They had so many pistols, I reckoned I needed scatterguns.'

'You reckoned correctly, no doubt about it, Isaac. But speaking for the group, I can assure you that we're all mightily pleased we didn't end up with hides full of buckshot, which is always a possibility with so much firepower on the property ... Mr Reilly probably feels the same about his piano ... At any rate, it's worth considering whether a thick old mustache might obviate the need for brandishing artillery in the first place.'

He signaled the barkeep for another bottle.

'Thirsty today?' asked Bell.

Wish Clarke smiled, amiably. 'How observant you are, Isaac. You'd make a good detective.'

'Hey, mister? *Mister?*'

A boy was whispering from the door.

'Get out of here!' bellowed Reilly. 'No kids in my saloon.'

Isaac Bell recognized the doorboy he'd given a coin to. 'It's OK, Reilly. I'll look out for him. Come in, son. What's going on?'

The boy glanced fearfully behind him and slunk inside. He had a cloth sack clutched to his chest. The sight of four Van Dorns glowering at their supper plates stopped him in his tracks. Bell shepherded him to a corner table. 'Reilly, would you have a sarsaparilla back there?'

'The only thing I got that ain't booze is coffee.'

'Do you like coffee?'

The boy nodded. 'Yes, sir.'

'OK, we'll take coffee. Lots of sugar. Make it two. What's your name, son?'

'Luke.'

'I'm Isaac, Luke.' He offered his hand and the boy took it politely. 'What can I do for you?'

'Are you really a Van Dorn?'

'Yes, I am. So are those gents at the table.'

'All of 'em?'

'Any particular reason you ask, Luke?'

The boy nodded. 'I didn't tell you the truth about my father.'

'You said you don't have a father.'

'I do have a father.'

'Good. Where is he?'

Luke looked around and whispered, 'Hiding from the cops.'

'Why's that?'

'The union sent more organizers from Pennsylvania.'

Bell nodded, recalling, again, Jim Higgins's promise that union men would replace him.

'The cops caught one and beat names out of him.' Luke's lips started trembling, and Bell saw him stare at the table as if imagining his father smashed to his knees in a hail of fists and blackjacks.

'Whose names, Luke? Your father's?'

'Somebody warned him. He got away.'

'What's that smell?' called Wally Kisley.

'That's your supper,' said Mack Fulton.

'Not these buffalo chips. I smell something good. Hey, boy, what's in that sack?'

Luke clutched his bag tighter.

Bell whispered, 'Is that for your dad?'

'Yes, sir,' Luke whispered back. 'From my mother.'

'Why'd you come here?'

'I thought if you're private detectives, maybe . . .'

His voice trailed off.

'Maybe what, Luke?'

'Maybe I could hire you to protect him from the cops. Or at least help him get away?'

'Detectives cost a lot of money,' Bell said gently.

'I don't have any money – excepting what you gave me. But I'm wondering if maybe I could trade something.'

'Like what?'

'Like things I heard.'

'Things you heard where?'

'Jake's Saloon, where the cops hang out . . .'

'Does Jake allow boys in his saloon?'

'We climb up from the river, under the cellar, and we can hear 'em yelling upstairs.'

Wally called, 'What do you have in that sack, boy?'

'Fatback and biscuits and baked taters, sir.'

The Van Dorns looked at their plates, then at Luke's sack.

'I have an idea,' said Wally Kisley.

'No,' said Isaac Bell. 'Luke's got a job to do, delivering supper. And we're going to help him.'

Truculent expressions on the faces of his men told Bell that he had a rebellion on his hands if he didn't think quick. 'Gents: Wally and Mack and Archie are going to the company store to buy fatback and flour and lard and coffee and sugar and milk and butter and potatoes, which they will carry to Luke's mother and pay her five dollars to rustle up a couple of days' worth of fatback, biscuits and baked taters.'

'What are you and Wish doing while all that shopping and cooking and waiting is going on? Eating the kid's?'

'Wish and I will provide Luke with an escort.'

James Congdon's secretary carried a single sheet of paper into his office and laid it on his desk. 'I'm sorry for the delay, sir. Detective Clay's code is complicated.'

Congdon read it, twice.

'Are you sure you deciphered it correctly?'

'Absolutely, sir. It is complicated but consistent.'

Congdon read it again.

'Shall I take down your reply, sir?'

'No reply.'

'Yes, Judge Congdon. Is there anything else?'

'Yes.' Congdon named three stockbrokers who regularly bid for him in secret. 'Tell them to buy up every share of Gleason Consolidated as they become available.'

The secretary, a sly co-conspirator with an encyclopedic knowledge of Wall Street, had been privy to Judge Congdon's schemes long before the financier hammered together US Steel. 'I was not aware that Black Jack is selling.'

'His heirs are building mansions and buying yachts and private cars. They're deep in debt, greedy and impatient.'

'But are they in a position to sell? Gleason keeps a tight rein on his stock.'

Congdon read Henry Clay's wire, again to be absolutely sure what the private detective was promising in veiled language. He said, 'His heirs will be in a position to sell. What do we know about Gleason's lawyers?'

As they were discussing heirs and inheritance, Congdon's secretary said, 'There was the incident concerning the probate engrossment of the Widow O'Leary's supposed will – yet to be resolved – which weighs heavily on their firm.'

'To be resolved by whom?'

'It is still in probate court.'

'Perfect. Resolve it for them.'

'That should make the lawyers grateful,' said Congdon's secretary — understanding in a flash that they were discussing the expeditious execution of Black Jack Gleason's will when he finally shuffled off to that heavenly coalfield in the sky. Understanding, too, that that voyage to the other side might commence sooner than Gleason expected, the secretary calculated to the penny the bribe that the probate judge would accept.

'Is there anything else, Judge Congdon?'

'Transfer all Gleason stock to a holding company with no traceable connection to my interests.'

'What do you want done with Gleason's managers?'

'They can keep their jobs so long as every last bushel of Gleason coal is barged to my Amalgamated Coal Terminal.'

15

'Hold on, Isaac,' said Wish. 'Are you sure you want to be taking sides in this dustup?'

The cave where Luke's father was hiding in the woods up the mountain had been chosen for its view of the approach up the logged slopes, and when Bell asked whether his father was armed, Luke said he had a squirrel rifle, so he had sent the boy ahead to alert him that they were coming.

'We're not taking sides,' he told Wish. 'Mr Van Dorn stressed that point when we spoke. But he also warned me not to get caught in the middle, and the best way to do that is stay ahead of both sides. Wouldn't you say?'

'Couldn't have put it better myself.'

'Here comes the boy.'

Luke led them the final hundred yards up the logged slope and into the cave, which Bell surmised, by its timber propping, was actually an old mining hole cut into the side of the hill by backwoodsmen digging for fuel to heat their cabins long before the Gleason Consolidated Coal & Coke Company commenced its commercial venture. Zeke, Luke's father, could not risk lighting a fire. He had a thin blanket for the cold, and he tore hungrily into the biscuits, after first asking whether Bell and Wish had eaten and they answered that they had. Between bites he explained that union men were coming from Pennsylvania and that he and scores of others were going to join them and call a strike.

Sounds drifted faintly up the mountain – the chug of a locomotive across the river, a steamboat whistle, bursts of raucous laughter from the saloons, and, once, the clang of the trolley. The ill-lit Gleasonburg itself appeared as a distant glow, softer than the thin moonlight filtered by river mists.

Bell said, 'Luke, maybe you ought to tell your father what you told me you overheard.'

'What's that, boy?'

'The cops said the scabs are coming.'

'What scabs? From where?'

'Italians and Poles.'

'Then we'll block the trolley. Maybe even get the Brotherhoods to stop the trains.'

'I'm afraid it won't be that easy,' said Bell. 'What Luke heard suggests that the company will barge them up the river from Pittsburgh.'

'That's not possible.'

'That's what they said.'

'Well, that just plain ain't possible. We haven't even begun to strike. What would give them the idea to bring scabs? How could they know our plans? We just made 'em. Now, what are you Van Dorn fellows doing here?'

Isaac Bell said, 'Do you need our help?'

'What kind of help? Fighting strikebreakers? We can barely feed ourselves. How we gonna pay your fees?'

Luke said, 'Pa, I asked them to help you get away.'

'I can't go away, son. I gotta stay here. The fight is here.'

'But –'

'No buts.'

'But the Pinkertons said they're calling up militia if you strike.'

'I hope that's not true.'

Isaac Bell cocked his ear. He heard a strange sound and stepped out of the cave to hear better. Wish followed. 'What the heck is that?'

'Sounds like music.'

It grew slightly louder, as if climbing on the vapors from far below.

'I'll be,' said Wish. 'Recognize that?'

Bell picked up the tune and sang softly.

> *'You can hear them sigh and wish to die,*
> *You can see them wink the other eye*
> *At the man who broke the bank at Monte Carlo.'*

The source was a mystery. None of the plank-and-barrel saloons had the means to hire orchestras. It certainly was not Reilly's upright. Bell heard violins and horns, in addition to a piano, clarinets and a double bass. And while there was no denying there were brothels in Gleasonburg, no one had the money to support a dance hall.

'There,' he said. 'Look on the water.'

A steam yacht rounded a bend in the river. It was lighted end to end by electricity, its windows and portholes casting more light than the town and the moon combined. Bell recognized the clean and graceful lines of a Herreshoff, a magnificent boat built in Rhode Island. He was too far away to see the orchestra, but he could hear the musicians finish playing 'The Man Who Broke the Bank at Monte Carlo' and then jump smoothly into Joplin's 'Easy Winners.'

'I'll bet that's Gleason's steam yacht. The *Monongahela*.'

'I wouldn't mind being at that party,' said Wish.

'What's that following it?' asked Bell.

A dark form, much longer than the steam yacht and four times as wide, crept after it. Only when it had completely rounded the bend could they see the lights of a towboat pushing a score of barges lashed together.

The orchestra bounced to the new hit 'Bill Bailey, Won't You Please Come Home?'

A loud steam whistle drowned out the music. The tow turned ponderously across the current and headed toward the barge dock.

Luke and his father had followed them out of the cave. 'Barge tow,' said Zeke. 'Empties coming back from Pittsburgh.'

Bell focused his keen eyes on the tow as it neared the barge dock. It was difficult to see for sure, but he sensed curious ripples of motion within the barges, like cattle boats landing for slaughter. 'They're not empty.'

'Who the heck barges coal *up* the river?'

'They're not carrying coal . . . They're full of men.'

Bell looked at Wish and the two detectives shook their heads in amazement. The strikers would have their hands full. While they were still getting organized, Black Jack Gleason's yacht had escorted scab labor straight to their back door.

Luke said, 'Oh, Pa, I'm powerful sorry.'

Zeke stood there, shoulders bowed, and felt blindly for his son's hand.

The *Monongahela* stationed herself in the middle of the river. The steamboat pushed the barges against the dock, and soon Bell saw lanterns bobbing as the Gleason police began herding the men off the barges and up Dock Street.

'What –'

A white flash in the middle of the river lit the water from shore to shore and etched the surrounding hills as stark as snow. It cast a diamond brilliance on the tipple that towered over the shantytown, on a tow of laden coal barges moored to the tipple pier, and on the scabs shuffling ashore – a thousand workmen clutching bundles – their startled faces whipped to the sudden burst of light.

Isaac Bell fixed on its source and saw the *Monongahela*'s superstructure jump straight up in the air. Cabins, navigation bridge and smokestack parted from the steam yacht's sleek hull. For half a second, they appeared to float.

16

A thunderous double salvo roared like battleship guns.

Isaac Bell, high above the river, felt the heat of the explosion on his face.

Then silence and darkness settled on the water, the town, and the hills. The music had stopped. Jagged flames pierced the dark. The yacht's hull was burning.

'What happened?' cried Luke.

'Her boiler blew,' said Zeke. 'The Good Lord has intervened! He has struck that Satan dead.'

Isaac Bell exchanged dubious glances with Wish Clarke.

The younger detective spoke first. 'That one-two punch sounded like someone lent the Good Lord a hand with a hundred pounds of dynamite. First the dynamite, then the boiler.'

'Isaac, old son,' said Aloysius Clarke. 'I do believe you're getting the hang of your line.'

'We better get down there and lend a hand.'

Bell discovered as he and Wish pushed their way on to the dock that the Polish and Italian scabs had not been imported from their home countries. Nor had the numerous black men come directly from the South. They had been rounded up from the coalfields of eastern Pennsylvania, where an anthracite strike had shut down the hard-coal mines. Those he talked to were stunned by the explosion, bewildered and afraid.

'They didn't tell us nothing about the union.'

'They just said there was jobs.'

In the middle of the river, the steamboat that had brought the scab tow was circling the burning remains of the *Monongahela*, playing lights on the water, looking for survivors. Suddenly, her whistle shrieked an alarm.

'Now what?' asked Wish.

Bell pointed upstream where the tipple loomed darkly against the night sky. 'Coal barges adrift.'

The entire tow that had been moored to the tipple pier – a fleet of twenty loaded barges lashed together – wheeled ponderously into the river and picked up speed as the powerful current dragged it downstream.

'How in heck did they break loose?'

'First thing I'll ask, come morning,' said Isaac Bell.

Wish said, 'Amazing how many things went wrong at once.'

Isaac Bell's eyes shot from the drifting tow to the burning yacht to the bewildered scabs milling on the dock to the steamboat, whose captain had stopped his engine to let the current sweep him away from the wreck.

'Too many things. And I have a bad hunch it isn't over.'

When the boat was a safe distance from any possible survivors still in the water, her big stern wheel churned, and she raced to capture the drifting coal barges. Deckhands scrambled with lines and the steamboat tied on. Stern wheel thrashing the water, she swung the lead barges into the current to master the tow.

'He's got her,' said Wish. 'Captain's a man to ride the river with.'

Just as he spoke, the big steamboat exploded with a colossal double roar that toppled her chimneys and wheelhouse into the river. To Bell's ear, the double roar echoed the one-two that destroyed the *Monongahela*.

But unlike the yacht, which was still drifting and on fire, the big steamboat sank straight to the bottom, leaving the wreckage of her upper decks exposed. The current slammed the coal barges against her, ripping their wooden hulls. Within minutes, twenty had sunk, blocking the channel to Pittsburgh.

'My provocateur,' said Isaac Bell, 'is getting the hang of his line, too.'

17

A pipe organ dominated the front room of Bloom House, the finest mansion in Pittsburgh. The dining room, ablaze in candle- and electric light, seated thirty-six comfortably. Livery servants glided in with silver trays from a distant kitchen. But R. Kenneth Bloom, the father of Isaac Bell's school friend Kenny, did not look happy. Nor, Bell observed, did his dinner guests, Bloom's fellow coal barons, railroad magnates and steel tycoons, whose evening clothes glittered with diamond studs and cuff links.

Bloom Sr, red-faced and carrying too much weight to be healthy, planted both hands on the snow-white cloth in order to stand up from his chair. He raised his glass.

'I won't say I liked him. But he was one of ours. Gentlemen, I give you Black Jack Gleason – struck down by the union! May he rest in peace.'

'Rest in peace!' thundered up and down the long table.

'And may the unionists burn in Hell!' echoed back.

Isaac Bell touched water to his lips.

Kenny Bloom, in line to inherit half the anthracite coal in Pennsylvania from his mother, and control of the Reading Railroad and vast bituminous fields from his father, winked at Bell. 'We shouldn't speak ill of the dead,' he muttered. 'But, if we did, the things we could say.' He drank deeply. 'I'm so glad you came, Isaac. These dinners get mighty grim.'

'Thank you for inviting me.'

Kenny grinned, 'Didn't give me much choice, did you, Mr Make-Believe Insurance Man?'

'I do appreciate it.'

Halfway up the table, Pennsylvania's attorney general raised his voice. 'The union will pay for this outrage. Steamboats dynamited. Innocent workingmen, attempting to travel to Gleasonburg to get an honest job, injured. River blocked. Coal traffic at a standstill.'

'And Gleason murdered.'

'That, too. Yes, sir, the rabid dogs will pay.'

Kenny said to Bell, 'They should, and they will, but he's talking through his hat because West Virginia's attorney general gets first crack, seeing as how they killed Black Jack in their state.'

'I'm not convinced,' said Bell, 'that the union had anything to do with it.'

The military precision of back-to-back dynamitings simultaneous with the barge tow set adrift seemed to him far beyond the capability of the union organizers, who were scrambling to keep one step ahead of the Pinkertons. Inspections of the steamboat boiler rooms had increased his skepticism.

But Kenny, who had been hitting the whiskey before dinner, didn't hear him. He was boasting instead to everyone at their end of the table about events in the anthracite fields. 'So we mounted a Gatling gun on the back of a Mercedes Simplex and welded on steel plates to protect the driver.'

'Did it work?'

'Did it work? I'll say it worked,' Kenny snickered. 'The strikers call it the Death Special.'

At the top of the table, Bloom Sr was addressing the strikers' demands.

'The eight-hour workday will be the ruination of the coal business.'

'Hear! Hear!'

'And I've heard more than enough nonsense about safety. The miner has only himself to blame if he doesn't keep his workplace in safe condition.'

Another baron agreed. 'It's not my fault if he refuses to mine his coal properly, scrape down dangerous slate, and install proper timbering.'

'Risk is naturally attached to the trade. Fact is, with prices tumbling, we'll be lucky to stay in business.'

Bell noticed a perplexed expression on the face of an older mine operator, who called up table, 'The iniquitous price we're paying to ship coal isn't helping either.'

Bloom Sr returned a tight smile. 'The railroad's hands are tied, Mr Morrison.'

'By whom, sir? Surely not the government?'

'Them, too, but it's not like we don't report to our investors.'

'There you go blaming Wall Street again. Didn't used to, in my day. We called our own tune. If the banks wanted to make money, they were welcome to invest with us. But they did not presume to tell us how to dig coal or how to ship it.'

'Well, sir, these are different days.'

Isaac Bell noticed Kenny observing his father with a thoughtful, if not troubled, expression. 'Sounds like you'll have your work cut out for you when it's your turn to run the railroad.'

'What makes you think I will run the railroad?'

'You're his son, his only son, and you've been working with him since you left Brown.'

'I'd like nothing better,' said Kenny. 'And I'm trying my darnedest to learn as fast as I can. But it may not be my choice.'

'Surely your father prefers you.'

'Of course he does. That was settled the day I graduated. But what if they don't?'

'They?' asked Bell, though he suspected the answer already.

'The banks.'

Bell glanced up the table at Mr Bloom. Behind the boasts and the bluster, even the rich and powerful railroad president R. Kenneth Bloom, Sr, was not in command of coal.

'Which banks?' he asked.

'The New York banks.'

'Which ones?'

Kenny shrugged.

'You don't know?'

'I'm not at liberty to say.'

Bell leveled a stern gaze at the railroad heir. '*Not at liberty?* You sound like a cautious lawyer instead of the pal who ran off to the circus with me.'

'That almost got us killed.'

'Did you have a good time?'

'Yes.'

'Which banks?'

Kenny Bloom grinned. He looked, Bell thought, drunk, embarrassed, and a little scared. 'Let me answer your nosy question this way – in a question back at you. Do you believe that the formation of the US Steel Corporation is an end or a beginning?'

'End or beginning of what?'

'We're dodo birds out here, Isaac. The self-determined Pittsburgh operator is going extinct. So's the independent railroad that hauls coal. Wall Street is killing us off. Black Jack Gleason was a dodo. So's every man at this table. Some of them just don't know it yet.'

'Not you. You're young. You're like me. It's 1902. We're just starting out.'

Kenny Bloom stuck out his hand. 'Shake hands with the son of a dodo.'

Bell formed a grin as lopsided as Kenny's and shook his hand.

Kenny said, 'If you're so fired up to know which banks, look in the newspapers who made Carnegie and Frick into US Steel.'

Bell's father was a banker, a Boston banker. Boston was a long way from New York, and the two cities banked differently. But some things were the same. And if there was one thing Isaac Bell had learned from his father, and his grandfather, about banks, it was those who called the tune lay low.

He said, 'It won't be in the newspapers. Those who ran the show stayed backstage.'

Kenny pulled an embossed card from his pocket and pressed it into Bell's hand. 'Here's a rail pass, good anywhere in the country. Go to Boston. Ask your father which banks.'

'We are not on speaking terms,' said Bell.

'Because you're a detective?'

'He wants me in the bank.'

'What are you going to do?'

'Be a detective.'

'That is too bad. He is a good fellow.'

'I know,' said Bell. 'He is the best.' He held up the pass. 'OK if I keep this?'

'Your grandfather left you plenty. You can afford to buy a ticket.'

'I would like to keep it,' said Bell. 'Money talks. But a railroad pass from the son of a dodo shouts.'

The servants removed the oyster shells and the soup bowls and brought caviar, herring, and pâté. Bell switched from champagne to a Sauternes. Kenny stayed with his whiskey.

'Are you going to buy Gleason's mines?' Bell asked him.

'Somebody beat us to it. Snapped up the entire Gleason Consolidated Coal & Coke Company, lock, stock and barrel.'

'Who?'

'I haven't the vaguest idea.'

'But not a Pittsburgh dodo,' said Isaac Bell.

BOOK TWO

Fire

18

'Brother,' said Mary Higgins. 'I am going back to Pittsburgh.'

Jim had been worrying about this and here it was. Back in West Virginia, a thousand miners had been evicted from their Gleason company shanties. Some were huddling in a tent city, their usual fate while a strike dragged on and scabs dug the coal. Some, however, had begun a march to Pittsburgh in hopes that newspaper stories about men, women and children marching in cold rain would raise the nation's sympathy. It might. It might even give President Roosevelt courage to intervene.

A thousand marching up the coal-rich Monongahela Valley stood a good chance of doubling their ranks and doubling them again and again as workers struck the hundreds of mines along the way to join the march. Ten thousand, twenty thousand, fifty thousand arriving in Pittsburgh might well spark the general strike Higgins dreamed of. But he hesitated to join it.

The murder of Black Jack Gleason had turned the mood violent. Governors were threatening to call up troops. Prosecutors were staging trials. And the coal mine owners had dropped even pretenses of restraint.

'There's plenty to keep us busy here. Plenty. The smelters' strike is a disaster.'

'Read this!' She thrust the *Denver Post* in his face and

pulled a carpetbag from under her cot. Jim read quickly. 'What is this? We know Gleason got blown up.'

'Keep reading. Do you see what happened next?'

Jim read to the end where it was reported that the barges that sank at Gleasonburg had blocked the river for four days.

Mary asked, 'The rivers are not deep at Pittsburgh, are they?'

'Not very. The Mon's about eight or ten feet. Shallower in many places, depending on rain. About the same for the Allegheny.'

'And the Ohio?'

'About the same . . . Why?'

Mary's eyes were burning.

'Why?' Jim repeated sharply.

'Even scab coal has to reach Pittsburgh to be shipped by trains to the eastern cities and by barge to the west.'

'I don't understand,' said Jim. He understood fully, but he didn't want to hear it.

Mary said, 'The barges that sunk at Gleasonburg blocked the river for four days. One tow's worth of barges, brother, a single fleet. What would happen at Pittsburgh if many, many, many barges sank and blocked the river?'

'No coal would move,' said Jim Higgins.

'No coal to the Pittsburgh mills,' said Mary. 'No coal trained east to the cities. No coal barged west down the Ohio.'

'But the miners are already marching. What about the march? A peaceful march.'

'The marchers will need all the help they can get. This will help them.'

'Sabotage is war, Mary.'

'Coal is the lifeblood of the capitalist class.'

'War means death.'

'Precisely, brother. Without coal, the capitalist class will die.'

Isaac Bell headed to New York to get a handle on the new owners of Gleason Consolidated Coal & Coke. He wangled the last seat on the Pennsylvania Special by flourishing Kenny Bloom's rail pass. Ten thousand buyers from out-of-town firms were flocking to the city to purchase merchandise for the fall and winter, and the eastbound trains were packed.

'Don't let the Boss catch sight of you before you can prove what's driving your provocateur,' Wish Clarke warned as they parted in Pittsburgh. Wish was heading out to Chicago to ask Laurence Rosania who, in a safecracker's opinion, might practise the esoteric and extremely rare art of shaping explosives. 'He'll pepper you with questions: Who is he? Who's behind him? What do they want? Better have a clear idea or he'll switch you to another case.'

But Bell had been far from forming clear ideas, even before the explosions on the Monongahela. Was a saboteur provoking violence for profit or to win the war between labor and operators? Whoever bought Gleason Consolidated Coal & Coke could be angling for both.

'I can't dodge Mr Van Dorn. I have to go to the office to tap the new research man.'

'Tap him in a bar around the corner. I was in New York *last* September when the buyers came. The Broadway hotels were putting up cots and turning people away. If only a small portion of them encounter New York sharpers, our new field office will be doing a land-office business. And you will get shanghaied into interviewing waiters, bartenders, cabbies, ushers, maître d's and chambermaids on behalf of a ladies' unmentionables buyer from Peoria who, having celebrated a morning of wholesaler haggling with drinks in a club, lunch at a café, an automobile ride around Central Park, dinner in a roadhouse, a show at the vaudeville, and late supper and a cold bottle on a roof garden, woke up minus his wallet – which he will finally recall he saw last in the company of a respectable, refined young lady he met in one of those establishments.'

The Pennsylvania Special's last stop was at the Hudson River's edge in Jersey City. Bell rode a ferry to Manhattan and the El uptown and walked to the Cadillac Hotel on Broadway. Avoiding the front door and the sharp-eyed house detectives recruited personally by Mr Van Dorn, he found a bellboy smoking a cigarette outside the service entrance and tipped him to pass a private message to Grady Forrer in the Van Dorn suite.

Then Bell retreated five blocks down Broadway to the bar of the Hotel Normandie, which was loud with jobbers and wholesalers entertaining buyers. He watched from a corner table, guessing who among the customers streaming through the door was the big brain that the Boss had hired to establish the Van Dorn Detective Agency's division of research.

Was it the guy with his hat cocked like a newspaperman? Reporters were trained in research. But, no, he did not appear to be meeting anyone as he went straight to the lunch bar. Was it the stern academic with a waxed mustache? No, he clapped a salesman on the back and was greeted like an old friend. Nor was it the long-haired fellow who looked like a scientist.

Suddenly, the bar grew quiet, conversations ceasing, as an immense shadow filled the door. It was certainly not this guy, large of shoulder and substantial of belly. As young as Bell, he had his hair slicked down and parted in the middle like a high-class floor manager who could keep a saloon orderly with a glance. He churned across the room, parting the crowd like a steamboat, straight at Bell. Then he placed wire-rimmed glasses on his nose and inspected the young detective closely.

His voice rumbled from deep in his chest. 'I'm Grady Forrer, Mr Bell. Your note described a fair-haired gent with a mustache. I'm going to venture that it's a mustache you have just begun to encourage.'

'I'm hoping it will be worth the wait,' said Bell, thrusting out his hand. 'Thanks for coming.'

'Glad to. It's a madhouse up there. More business than you can shake a stick at.'

'Flimflammed buyers?'

'Flimflammed buyers by the gross, yard, bolt, ream, karat, bale, peck, dram, grain, pennyweight, each according to his measure. So many beating at the door that Mr Van Dorn stripped my office of assistants to interview victims. Let's have a drink.'

Bell hailed a waiter, and when the waiter ran with their order, he asked, 'Do you have experts in Wall Street?'

'I have access to experts. And a certain rudimentary knowledge as I apprenticed down there before I became interested in this *library work*, and I've maintained friendships. What do you need to know?'

Bell told him about the sudden purchase of a controlling interest in Gleason Consolidated. 'I've pored through newspapers and buttonholed a banker at a dinner in Pittsburgh, but I got no further than the name of a trust that no one's heard of.'

'How quickly did they buy it up?' asked Forrer.

'Days.'

'Astonishing. Buying up a controlling interest takes time, particularly when trying to mask your intention. And buying from grieving heirs who are battling each other for the spoils takes even longer. Even if the deceased's will was rammed through probate. Which is not impossible. If there is a more corrupt breed of judge than probate, I've never heard of them. Interesting, though, unless it was already in the works. Has it occurred to you that whoever bought Gleason had advance notice the shares would come to market?'

'I wondered if you would ask,' said Bell. 'Fact is, whoever blew up Gleason's yacht would know precisely when.'

After an hour, during which time Isaac Bell concluded that the Boss had made a brilliant decision to invest in a research department, and doubly brilliant to hire Grady Forrer, a weedy young man sidled into the Normandie Bar and spoke urgently to Forrer.

'Himself has gone to supper and won't return 'til morning. Our boys are back at work.'

'Come on, Isaac! Now's our chance.'

Forrer's office was a collection of shabby rooms that connected by a narrow hall to the lavish Van Dorn suite. It was a windowless warren, unlike the agency's big open front office. Cabinets, chairs and tables were stacked with newspapers from towns and cities around the country, and, as Bell and Grady entered, a mailman staggered in under a canvas sack, which contained, he announced, three hundred subscription newspapers, none more than a week old. Clattering ceaselessly in one corner was the research division's own telegraph key, presided over by an operator sending and receiving the Morse alphabet with a lightning-fast fist. A telephonist with a listening piece pressed to his ear was taking notes in another corner. A typewriter banged away, printing catalog cards, and the rooms echoed with shouts of 'Boy!' as file boys were sent scampering to the ever-growing stacks.

Forrer explained that at this early stage he was devoting all his energy to collecting a library of information. He had hired students part-time from Columbia College and the seminaries to clip stories from the thousands of newspapers published around the country.

Bell asked, 'How will you keep track?'

'I'm adapting the Dewey decimal system to Van Dorn requirements,' Grady explained. 'All the information in the world is worth nothing if we can't find it.'

Isaac Bell worked at a desk deep in clippings of newspaper headlines, features, cartoons and pen-and-ink sketches about coal interests in Wall Street. The railroads had a powerful hand in the mineral, as he had seen in Pittsburgh. But Kenny's father was only one of several line presidents depicted as grasping for controlling interests in the transport and sale of coal.

The western railroad builder Osgood Hennessy had

attracted far more cartoonists' ire than Mr Bloom. Bell found the titan drawn in the images of an anaconda, an octopus and a spider, all with more teeth than such creatures possessed in their natural state. Wall Street financiers – especially Judge James Congdon, founder of US Steel; John Pierpont Morgan, consolidator of General Electric and lender of gold to the US Treasury; and the lamp oil magnate John D. Rockefeller – received similar treatment, portrayed as sharks and alligators and rampaging grizzly bears.

In contrast, on the Society pages, Congdon and Hennessy and Rockefeller assumed human form in staff-artist sketches, Congdon with young brides on his arm, Rockefeller attending his Fifth Avenue church, the widowed Hennessy escorting a pretty daughter of thirteen. Much attention was paid to Congdon's art collection, much more to Hennessy's private train.

Black Jack Gleason's obituaries touted the coal combine he had put together, mansions he had built in West Virginia, and the shooting estate he had bought in Ireland. Bell read an editorial written before his death that lauded Gleason's oft-stated opinion that labor organizers were 'vampires that fatten on the honest labor of the coal miners of the country.'

The *New York World* charged Gleason with exacting tribute from the people by illegally banding the Coal Trust into 'the most powerful, grasping and grinding trusts in existence, beyond any question, not even second to J. P. Morgan's Great Fuel Octopus that limits supply and fixes prices.' A Nebraska paper excoriated Gleason as 'a coal baron who got fat on the honest labor of the coal miners, and rich through overcharging the coal consumers of the country.'

Grady Forrer arrived with a pot of coffee.

'You've been here all night.'

'Grady, you know many things.'

'I know how to *find* many things.'

'Have you ever seen amber-colored eyes?'

'They are unusual,' said Grady. 'Very rare. And amber is something of a misnomer. I would describe them as solid yellow or gold. Except in sunlight they will likely appear coppery, even orange. Why do you ask?'

'My provocateur might have them. Or might not.'

Grady looked troubled. 'Based on the enmity already existing between labor and owners, you wouldn't necessarily need a provocateur to provoke a war in the coalfields.'

'I would only agree that you would not need a provocateur to merely foment *violence* in the coalfields. There's plenty of bitterness for that. But you would need a provocateur to set off a real, ongoing war.'

'To what purpose?!' roared a voice in Bell's ear.

'*Mr Van Dorn!*' cried Grady Forrer. The telegrapher, the telephonist, the typist shot to their feet, and the file boys froze in their tracks.

Isaac Bell stood up and offered his hand.

'Good morning, sir,' he greeted Van Dorn and answered the Boss with the main thought on his mind. 'To the purpose of drawing attention.'

Joseph Van Dorn said, 'Come with me!'

Bell winked reassuringly at Grady Forrer and glided alongside Van Dorn, confident he had discovered the answer.

Van Dorn's private office was fitted out with up-to-date telephones, speaking tubes, and its own telegraph key. He sat at a mahogany desk and indicated a tufted leather chair for Bell.

'Whose attention?'

'The President's, the Congress's and, most important, the nation's.'

Van Dorn nodded. 'I've been watching Prince Henry operate and I've been thinking along the same lines you are. By the time the Prince completes his tour, half the continent will be in love with him and all things German – despite his brother the Kaiser's dismal record as a bloodthirsty despot. It's a new world, Isaac. If you get in the newspapers, people will love you as long as the reporters spell your name right.'

'Or hate you,' said Bell.

'Tell me who wants to be loved.'

'They all do. But I don't see the union having the talent for it.'

'How can you say that? The papers are on their side. The front pages are full of cartoons of tycoons in top hats abusing workingmen.'

'Not all,' said Bell. 'Half I saw in the train stations depicted fresh-faced soldiers set upon by unshaven mobs. The same with those I read last night.'

'So it could be either side, could it not?'

Bell hesitated.

Van Dorn said, 'Let me remind you that taking sides is no way to keep a clear eye.'

'But the unionists aren't capable of a precision attack like the one I saw on the Monongahela. The timing was exquisite – two vessels dynamited within ten minutes and the barge fleet set adrift at the right moment to do the most damage. The union fellows I've encountered are brave men, but not all that practical, nor disciplined. Nor, frankly, trained in the dark arts. What I saw demanded military precision by someone who's devoted his life to destruction.'

'How many men do you reckon it took to blow up the two vessels and set the barges adrift?'

'No more than three.'

'Only three?'

'It could have been one.'

'Impossible. One could not be in all three places at once.'

Bell said, 'He wouldn't have to be. The yacht and the steamboat both burned coal in sizable furnaces. A knowledgeable saboteur could have hidden dynamite and detonators fashioned to look like large chunks of coal in their bunkers.'

'But what would persuade the fireman – who was bound to die in the explosion – to shovel it into the furnace at just the right moment?'

Isaac Bell said, 'I went aboard two of the steamboats that were clearing the channel. I took a good look at their boilers and I talked to their firemen.'

Joseph Van Dorn sat back in his chair and smiled. 'Did you? What did you learn?'

'The coal is shifted in wheelbarrows from bunker to bunker, closer and closer to the furnace, in a logical manner. And the steamboats burn it at a consistent rate, depending on the speed they're making and the current.'

'To calculate the timing, your provocateur must know all about steamboats, perhaps been employed on them.'

'No, sir. I figured it out, and I'm only a detective.'

Van Dorn looked out his window, cogitated in silence, then mused, 'He sounds like quite an operator . . . quite an operator . . . provided he exists . . . but "fashioning" dynamite and detonators to look like coal could be rather more difficult than you suggest.'

'Wally Kisley reckons that the runaway mine train was sabotaged with a so-called hollow or shaped charge. May I ask are you aware –'

'I know what a shaped charge is, thank you. Though, admittedly, the average farmer dynamiting stumps does not.'

'Nor the average coal miner dynamiting the seam,' said Bell.

'You are postulating a fellow with an extraordinary skill with explosives. I *know* what a shaped charge is, but I would likely blow my head off trying to fashion one. Particularly disguised as coal that would fool an experienced fireman. Extraordinary knowledge.'

'I've got Wish Clarke tracking down Laurence Rosania.'

'Rosania?' Van Dorn stroked his red whiskers. 'Morally, I would put nothing past Rosania of course. But why would a successful safecracker with his refined tastes stoop to blowing up coal mines and steamboats? It wouldn't be worth his trouble or the risk. He's made a splendid career of not getting caught. Yet.'

'I'm betting that Rosania can point us toward other experts in what must be a small field of inquiry. And I've asked Grady Forrer to research who among the military are experimenting with hollow charges, other than the fellows at the Torpedo Station.'

Van Dorn asked, 'What's your next move?' and Isaac Bell realized with a swell of pride that the Boss was treating him more like a fellow detective than a new man on the job.

'My next move is to find out who bought a controlling interest in Black Jack Gleason's coal mines and coking plants within a week of his death.'

'But if all this sabotage is in aid of a crime of profit, your provocateur theory falls into a cocked hat.'

'Except for one thing.'

'What's that?'

'You told me not to take sides.'

'I meant between the operators and the union.'

'Your same advice could apply to *evidence* this early in my case.'

19

'There's a lady to see you, Isaac.'

'Lady?' Bell yawned. He looked up blearily from a fresh stack of newspaper cuttings. 'What kind of lady?'

Grady Forrer removed his spectacles, polished them on his shirtfront, and considered. 'I would characterize her as the beautiful kind of lady with a snowy complexion and glossy black locks.'

Isaac Bell jumped to his feet. 'Gray eyes?'

'Like pearls in moonlight.'

'Send her in — no, wait! I'd better see her in the main office. Where is she now?'

'Reception room.'

Bell buttoned his coat over his shoulder holster, smoothed his mustache, and rushed into the main offices. Off-duty detectives were jostling for turns at the peephole that afforded an advance look at customers waiting in the reception room. Bell burst through the door.

Mary Higgins turned from the window. A sunbeam slanted through her eyes.

Diamond dust and diamond flakes, thought Isaac Bell. *I'm a goner.*

Her voice was even prettier than he remembered.

'I will not apologize for slapping you.'

'The first slap or the second?'

'Both,' she said. 'I'm not sorry for either.'

'My jaw's still sore,' said Bell. 'But I'm not.'

'Why not?'

'I deserved it. I misled you.'

'You surely did.'

'I apologize.'

Mary looked him in the eye. 'No. That is not necessary. You were doing the job your bosses demanded and you got stuck in it.'

'I insist,' said Bell. 'I'm sorry.'

'I don't want your apology. I won't accept it.'

'What would you accept?'

'We could try again for tea,' she smiled.

'How about breakfast? Which we missed last time.'

'Breakfast would be appropriate.'

'I hear the restaurant downstairs is a good one. Do you mind eating with capitalists?'

'I will take it as an opportunity.'

'For what?'

'To observe the enemy up close,' she replied.

'You're smiling,' said Bell. 'But I can't tell if you're joking.'

'Not while miners walk the Monongahela Valley.'

'You were there?'

Mary nodded. 'Their spirits are high. But rain is forecast.'

The Cadillac Hotel's breakfast room was packed with out-of-town buyers. A bribe to the headwaiter got them the last table. Mary noticed the money pass hands and said, after they were seated and she had spread her napkin on her lap, 'Do I assume correctly that, in truth, your father did not lose his mansion in the Panic of '93?'

'He did not. Nor is it in the Back Bay. I was born in Louisburg Square.'

Mary took a folded newspaper page from her purse, laid it beside her.

'That would make you a Bell of the American States Bank.'

'That is my father's bank. How is it that you know Boston?'

'Why do you work as a detective?'

'Because I want to.'

Mary returned his even gaze with a searching one of her own. Before she could ask a question, they were interrupted by a loud man at the next table, a wholesaler entertaining buyers. 'The shirtwaist and skirt will be replaced next year by a full-costume combination – a single piece of garment. How do I know? Paris declares such combinations plebeian, particularly in different texture or color. New York will lead the change, and your ladies in Chicago will take the same view.'

Mary looked down at her gray shirtwaist and blue skirt and smiled. 'So I'm to be plebeian?'

'You look lovely,' said Bell. 'I mean, stylish and attractive.'

'Do you really believe that Van Dorns are different than Pinkertons?'

'I know they are. How is it that you know Boston?'

'How are Van Dorns different?'

'We believe that the innocent are sacred.'

'Those are pretty words.'

'Words to live by. But before we debate further, our waiter is headed this way, the restaurant is busy, and we should order before they run out. What would you like for breakfast?'

'What are you having?'

'Everything that can't run away. I've been up all night and I am starving.'

'I walked from the ferry. I'm starving, too. I'll have what you're having.'

Bell picked up the menu. 'Good morning,' he said to the waiter. 'We both want coffee, buckwheat pancakes with cranberries, fried bananas, omelets with mushrooms, and calf's liver.' Mary was nodding approvingly. Bell asked, 'With onions?'

'And bacon.'

'You heard the lady. And may we have our coffee as soon as humanly possible?' Of Mary he asked, again, 'How is it that you know Boston?'

'I am by occupation a schoolteacher. I graduated from the Girls' Latin School.'

'So you were born in Boston.'

'No. My parents moved us there so my brother and I could attend the Latin Schools. Father found work as a tugboat captain and we lived on the boat.' She smiled. 'Yes, I know what you're thinking. The saloon was another time in another city. Father was always changing jobs.'

'A jack-of-all-trades?'

'He could *master* anything. Except people. He was like Jim. It broke his heart when he couldn't deny that evil people exist. That's when he gave up on the tugboat.'

'What changed his mind?'

'Too many deckhands shanghaied by knockout drops.'

'But tug captains must be used to freighters kidnapping

able seamen. And no experienced deckhand would be surprised to wake up miles from land with a splitting headache. Spiked booze mans ships.'

'Father was surprised.'

The coffee arrived. Bell sought her eyes over their cups and asked, 'What's in that newspaper?'

'The reason I'm here.'

'I thought you came to not apologize.'

Mary Higgins did not smile back but thrust the clipping across the table. 'Read this.'

Bell glanced at the headline and handed it back.

'I read it last night,' he said and recited the last paragraph from memory:

'It is understood that a great amount of evidence of the Coal Trust's existence, and proof that the railroads are large owners in the coal mines, and that they combine to regulate the price of coal to the seaboard and in every important city not only by setting carrying charges but also by naming the price at which retailers shall put the coal on the market, is in possession of Jim Higgins, president of the Strike Committee. Higgins will probably be called upon by the attorney general in the course of the investigations to be commenced.'

Mary was staring at him.

Bell said, 'I have a photographic memory.'

'I thought so. I have one, too. I always wondered if my eyes move while I'm remembering. Now I know.'

'How did your brother become president of the Strike Committee?'

'By having the guts to stand up for it.'

'How did he get ahold of the evidence?'

'He carried it out the back door of a Denver union hall while the Pinkertons were breaking in the front door.'

'How did that evidence get all the way to Denver?'

'They moved it from Pittsburgh and Chicago to keep it safe.'

'Well, I guess that didn't work . . . Does your brother realize the danger he's in by holding that stuff?'

'He doesn't think about it.'

'But you do,' said Bell, guessing what was coming next.

Mary said, 'It will get him murdered. They will kill him and burn the evidence before the attorney general gets around to calling him. Unless . . .'

'Unless?'

'Unless he is protected by a detective who claims to believe that the innocent are sacred.'

Bell nodded eagerly. It was as he had supposed and hoped. Safeguarding Jim Higgins would be an opportunity for a closer, inside look at the unions and their top organizers. That might shed light on the identity of the provocateur if he happened to be a former labor organizer. But that meant that Bell would need more men in his squad.

'We'd better go see the Boss.'

Upstairs in his office, Joseph Van Dorn listened to Mary Higgins's request. He questioned her closely about the documents and elicited that Jim, too, had been born with a powerful memory and that even if the evidence was locked in a safe the fact that it resided complete in his mind put him at great risk of being murdered to prevent him from testifying. He asked if Mary had read the documents.

'Jim wouldn't let me.'

'Of course not,' Van Dorn nodded. 'Was this your sole reason for coming to New York City?'

She hesitated only a heartbeat. 'Yes.'

Joseph Van Dorn nodded. 'Of course . . .'. He cast a shrewd eye on his young detective, noted how avidly Isaac Bell was watching Mary, and made up his mind.

'Your request for protection for your brother comes at a propitious moment, Miss Higgins. I have just started a new division of the Van Dorn Detective Agency, which will be named Van Dorn Protective Services.'

'You have?' asked Bell. 'I hadn't heard.'

'Because you were concentrating on your own case. Van Dorn Protective Services will provide valuables escorts, hotel house detectives, night watchmen, and, of course, bodyguards. Protecting Jim Higgins will be right up their alley.'

'Will Mr Bell be one of them?' asked Mary.

'Mr Bell is a detective, not a bodyguard. For your brother, we will provide men especially skilled at ensuring the personal safety of our clients.'

Mary said, 'But Mr Bell did an admirable job of protecting my brother from a lynch mob.'

Van Dorn smiled at the beautiful young woman gracing his office. It was easy to see how Bell had fallen for her; nor was it hard to imagine how she could cloud a younger man's judgment.

'We expect Van Dorns to rise to every occasion. On

156

this occasion, however, Mr Bell is already engaged on an important case in the coalfields that requires his full attention.'

He turned to Bell. 'Thank you for bringing this situation to me, Isaac. There's no reason for you to expend any more of your valuable time in my office while Miss Higgins and I conclude our business. Suffice it to say that I guarantee she will find her brother in excellent hands.'

Bell stood up. 'Yes, sir.' To Mary he said, 'Mr Van Dorn is a man of his word. Jim will be safe.'

'Thank you for introducing me.'

'It was wonderful to see you again.'

'I look forward to seeing you, again.'

They reached awkwardly to shake hands.

Joseph Van Dorn cleared his throat – a noise that reminded Bell of a water-cooled, belt-fed Maxim gun that he and Wish Clarke had drawn fire from in Wyoming – and, with that, the young detective beat a retreat. His head was spinning. What a girl! What a wonderful girl!

'There is, of course, the matter of our fee.'

'The Strike Committee is prepared to pay the going rate,' said Mary Higgins, 'asking, however, that you take into account the small fortunes of workingmen.'

'We are a new, struggling business,' said Van Dorn. 'Nonetheless, we are not heartless and can offer a rate somewhat lower than we expect from bankers and jewelers. Where is your brother at this moment?'

'Chicago.'

'I have good men in Chicago. We'll get right on it before your brother leaves for Pittsburgh.'

'What makes you think he's going to Pittsburgh?'

'Union organizers are descending on Pittsburgh like . . .'

'Flies, Mr Van Dorn?'

Van Dorn's cheeks flushed redder than his whiskers. 'I did not mean it that way. What I do mean is that I understand by reliable information that a general strike is brewing there – inspired by the Monongahela march – and any union organizer worth his salt will be heading to Pittsburgh as we speak. I have no doubt that Jim Higgins will be in the lead.'

'He is.'

'Let us be clear on one important issue, Miss Higgins. The Van Dorn Agency will not take sides. We will move Heaven and Earth to keep your brother from harm. But we will not help him pull down the institutions of law, order, property and justice.'

'There can be no order without justice, Mr Van Dorn. No justice without equality.'

'We are all entitled to our opinions, Miss Higgins. I would be surprised if you and I agree on much, if anything, but when the Van Dorn Agency takes the job to protect your brother we are honor-bound to keep him safe – fair enough?'

'Fair enough.' Mary Higgins stuck out her hand, and they shook on it.

Instead of descending the Cadillac Hotel's grand staircase that curved into the lobby, Mary Higgins waited by the elevator without pressing the call button. She needed time to collect her spirit for she was deeply disturbed by her encounter with the Van Dorn Agency's chief investigator.

Joseph Van Dorn's piercing gaze had seemed to penetrate her skull and burrow into her deepest thoughts. It was as if he knew better than she how confused she was. Van Dorn could not see why, of course. Or maybe he could. Some of it. He could not know her grand plan to block the river at Pittsburgh. She had told only her brother, and Jim would never tell anyone because he hated the idea. But Van Dorn, the renowned scourge of criminals, had suspected that something was up.

She was not a criminal. Although she had scheming in common with criminals, and the chief investigator seemed to sense that she was scheming something. That was disturbing enough – to succeed, her plan to block the river depended on secrecy and surprise – but it wasn't all that troubled her.

Waiting by the elevator did not help one bit. She pressed the button. When the runner bowed and guided her into the gilded car, she thought instantly, predictably, of the silly ballad they were singing everywhere:

> *But she married for wealth, not for love he cried,*
> *Though she lives in a mansion grand.*
> *She's only a bird in a gilded cage.*

Van Dorn had seen right through her. He had guessed her confusion about Isaac Bell. What if a woman had pledged her heart, her soul, and her entire life to eliminate *mansions grand*, and then, just as she wound up to throw a brick at a window, she saw love smiling through the glass?

20

'Shadow her!'

'What?' Isaac Bell had just bent over a fresh pile of clippings when Van Dorn rushed into the research offices.

'Find out what the devil she is up to.'

'Mary? What do you mean?'

'If I knew, I would not be impelled to send you after her. I have a hunch she is up to something big and I don't like it.'

'What about her brother?'

'I suspect it has nothing to do with him.'

'But will you look out for him?'

'Of course. We gave our word. Go! Don't let her get away. And do not let her see you.'

Mary Higgins burst from the gilded elevator. A hotel detective stared, suspicion aroused by the incongruous sight of such a tall, attractive woman in a drab costume and plain cloth hat that sported neither a ruffle nor a feather. What was such a poorly attired creature doing in such a fine establishment? An actress? Or something worse?

Mary froze the detective with a stern glare, brushed past him, passed the bowing doormen, and set a fast pace down Broadway, which veered southerly and easterly across the Tenderloin District. She walked fast, block after block, oblivious to fine hotels and theaters on the wide thoroughfare, and saloons and gambling halls along the dark and narrow cross streets, her destination a settlement house in the East Side slums where she could find shelter with the girls and women who had founded the Shirtwaist Makers' Union.

She tried to outpace the storm in her mind. But walking didn't help any more than stalling by the elevator. She was too confused, her brain swirling with questions about her brother and their cause of equality and justice, his vague dreams of a general strike, her sharp plan to block the river. How different Isaac Bell was than any other man she had ever met: strong, but tender; ferocious in a fight, but able to be gentle; privileged, but not obliviously; quick to laugh, but just as quick to comfort. Had she believed in some vague way that she could use Isaac to help her grand plan? Or had she really only wished they could somehow repeat a cold night on a freight train?

Drowning in doubt, she revisited her scheme: at Pittsburgh, the Monongahela River was lined with coal barges tied ten deep on either shore. They narrowed the channel. When the river was crowded with tows five and six wide, there was scarcely room for two to slip past each other. Plus, six bridges crossed the Mon. The piers that supported the six narrowed the waterway, dicing it into narrow channels. She envisioned drifting barges piling up against them like ice floes. If half the river was carpeted with barge fleets, how many would have to sink before they blocked traffic? Would they cause a flood? And now she could hear her brother asking, *How many will be injured? How many will die? None? Guarantee it?* She couldn't. The Mon washed along the Point, the river-girded stretch of land that formed Pittsburgh's rich Golden Triangle. Thousands lived and worked there.

The sky turned gray and it began to drizzle. She walked. The drizzle quickened to rain. And still she walked, ignoring streetcars she could ride downtown, ignoring the Els that would whisk her there in a flash, noticing nothing ahead of her or behind her, seeing neither the young detective shadowing her nor the steamfitter in the slouch hat trailing them both.

21

Isaac Bell followed Mary Higgins at a distance that varied from a half to a full block, depending upon how crowded the sidewalks were. He endeavored to keep numerous pedestrians between them, and repeatedly donned and removed his dark coat and his broad-brimmed hat to change his silhouette.

Joseph Van Dorn's orders were ringing in his ears – *Find out what the devil she is up to.* If he hadn't seen her throw the lantern that burned down the Gleasonburg court-house, he might have protested her innocence, or at least taken the accusation with a grain of salt. But he had seen her hurl it and had seen the look of triumph on her beau-tiful face. So he followed, intensely curious, and pleased to be near her, even though it took him off his own case.

She was easy to follow, taller than most people thronging the busy sidewalks, and plunging along single-mindedly, never looking back. It started to rain. She bought a red scarf from a peddler on Twenty-third Street.

She stopped on Fourteenth Street where Broadway and Fourth Avenue joined at Union Square and listened to a speaker haranguing a crowd about the coal strikes and the United States war against the Philippine insurgents.

'Three cheers for anarchy!' he roared, and the crowd took up the cry.

Mary Higgins put money in the hat when passed and

hurried on. South of Houston Street, she cut east into the crowded Jewish district, and Bell drew closer to keep her in sight.

'Don't buy beef!'

Groups of women were mobbing Kosher butcher shops and yelling at housewives who emerged with bundles: 'Boycott the Beef Trust!'

Cops gathered on the corners, big men in blue coats and tall helmets.

Bell almost lost sight of Mary in a mob of women screaming at one another.

'My babies are sick. They must eat.'

Isaac wedged through and ran after Mary. He was no longer afraid of Mary seeing him. There was a grim electricity in the air – the same threat of imminent, mindless violence that he had felt in the miners' mob at Gleasonburg. The women and the butchers and the glowering cops were all about to lose the last vestiges of reason, and Mary Higgins was caught in the middle.

A hundred feet ahead of Isaac Bell, half a city block, Mary Higgins followed her ears to the exciting roar of a mass meeting that was spilling from the new Irving Hall and packing Broome Street sidewalk to sidewalk. She was thrilled that the bold immigrant Jewish women leading New York's needle-trades union battle were exerting their newly won power against the Beef Trust's extortionate prices.

'The Hebrews are rioting!' roared a red-faced Irishman.

Whistles shrieked and the police advanced.

'Break it up!'

The women screamed back at the cops. 'Who do you work for? The trusts? Or the people?'

'Move along, sister.'

'Cossacks!' screamed a woman, and her sisters combined to chant.

'Cossacks! Cossacks! Cossacks!'

'Break it up! Break it up!'

Then a girl screamed at the top of her lungs, 'What's a penny made of?'

'Dirty copper!'

A big cop shoved a woman. She fell on the rain-slicked cobblestones.

Mary Higgins jumped to help and pulled her to her feet before she was trampled.

Another woman sprawled and her bundles went flying. Something soft landed on Mary's boots – blood-soaked butcher paper had torn open, spilling a slab of liver. A fat cop with a handlebar mustache and bushy eyebrows knocked Mary to her knees. Terrified of being trampled, she tried to stand.

The cop held her down and roared in her face, 'What's a pretty Irish lass doing with a bunch of dirty Yids?'

In that eruption of hatred, Mary Higgins felt her doubts evaporate. There was a huge difference between right and wrong, and what she had to do in Pittsburgh was right. She picked up the liver, hauled back, and slapped the cop's face with it. The soft red flesh splattered on his eyebrows and mustache and stuck to his skin. Blinded, he reeled away, shouting in anger and confusion.

The other cops saw him pawing at his bloodstained face.

Thirty charged up Broome Street, swinging clubs.

The women's screams of anger turned to shrieks of fear. They stumbled back and tried to run, surging into those behind, slipping on the wet cobblestones. Mary yanked a wild-eyed girl to her feet only to fall herself, crushed by the pack. A shoe mashed her hand against a cobblestone, another slammed into her back. The sky turned black with bodies tumbling on top of her. Struggling with all her strength, she could not rise. She could hardly breathe under the weight of the bodies. Suddenly, a powerful hand closed around her arm.

'I've got you,' a strong voice cut through the shouts and screams. 'Stick close.'

The hand lifted her effortlessly up and out of the crush and set her on her feet and pulled her through the mob as if its owner was a mighty sword cleaving a path through the melee and around a corner.

More cops were coming on the run.

'Don't look at them. Walk fast. Don't run.'

She finally got a glimpse of her rescuer at Canal Street when he let go of her arm and turned to her. A broad-shouldered workman in a loose coat and overalls. He had a red scarf knotted at his throat, a battered felt hat with the brim slung over his eyes.

'Are you all right?' he asked her.

'You saved my life.'

'Someone had to. I just happened to be close enough.'

She offered her hand. 'Thank you. I'm Mary Higgins.'

'Pleased to meet you, Mary Higgins. I'm John Claggart.'

22

'Those poor women. They were right. The cops attacked like Cossacks.'

John Claggart had led her into an eatery that catered to the workers digging the ditch for the Rapid Transit Subway and pressed a hot cup of coffee into her trembling hands. 'If you give cops the Devil's task,' he answered, 'they'll use the Devil's methods.'

'It should make every American cheek tingle with shame.'

'This is a bum government,' said Claggart. 'Rotten to the core.'

'Three cheers for anarchy,' Mary said bitterly.

Claggart shook his head. 'Anarchy's a joke. It gets you nowhere. You have to do something. Something the bloodsucking capitalists will feel like a body blow. Something that will knock them flat.'

He was, Mary thought, very intelligent-looking. Though of similar build to the sturdy ditchdiggers downing their knockwurst and pea soup, he had an air of refinement about him that reminded her of Isaac. Also, like Isaac, he possessed the unflappable gaze of a man accustomed to success, which was rare in workmen beaten down by the struggle to put bread on the table. He was not, of course, as handsome as Isaac. Nor, she realized, was he as warm.

She could see a remoteness in his eyes, almost an

emptiness. She had thought at first glance that they were hazel-colored, but they were actually that rarest of colors, amber. They looked golden in the smoky light of the eatery. But they did not glow like gold. They were opaque like copper. If, as she suspected, John Claggart was a man who harbored secrets, his eyes would never give them up. But whatever secrets he harbored, she did not care. She did not need warmth.

'I know a way,' she said, 'to knock them flat.'

Isaac Bell searched for Mary Higgins at the Tombs, the damp and gloomy city prison, still under construction, where the police had booked nearly a hundred women. He had last seen her half a block away in a crush of cops and boycotters, but before he fought his way to the spot she had vanished. A telephone call to the Cadillac Hotel had produced a messenger with a letter of introduction signed by Joseph Van Dorn. The Boss had already made enough friends in New York to get special treatment – as did Mary's Irish name. But it didn't help. The Halls of Justice had no record of a Mary Higgins being arrested.

'You might check the Emergency Hospital for Women on East Twenty-sixth,' said a sympathetic sergeant. 'God forbid Miss Higgins may have fallen in the melee. Those Hebrew women are ferocious.'

'No hospitals closer?'

'Brooklyn?'

It was raining hard when he stepped out, and he stood sheltered under the portico while he looked for a horse cab or a streetcar. He spotted a cab and ran for it. A workman in a loose-fitting coat and slouch hat got to it first.

A dirty bandage masked his nose and cheeks, and folds of a red neckerchief muffled his chin.

'Take it,' said Bell. Blood had soaked the bandage, and he guessed the poor devil had been caught in the riot.

'No, you take it,' the man said and turned away.

Bell had glimpsed the eyes under the brim of the hat, and his dream in the coal mine was suddenly as real as the rain pelting down. The man glanced back and headed around the corner. Bell hurried after him.

'Wait!'

The man walked faster.

'Wait. You, sir!'

Bell broke into a run.

The man he was following darted to the demolition site where the thick granite walls of the old Tombs were being leveled and slipped between two remaining columns. Maybe he had been injured working on the demolition, thought Bell.

'Hold on, there!'

The man looked back again. When he saw Bell still following, he ran down an exposed flight of stairs. Bell followed him, deep down, into an enormous cellar that reeked of decay. The little light there came from holes in the ceiling.

The man stopped suddenly.

'Are you following me?'

'Yes,' said Bell. 'Didn't you hear me shouting?' He peered at features obscured by bandage and neckerchief and shadowed by the hat. 'Have we met, sir?'

'Not that I recall,' he answered through the folds of his neckerchief. 'Where are you from?'

'West Virginia,' said Bell.

'Nope. Never been there.'

'Where are *you* from?'

'Mister, you've got cop written all over you, and I ain't done nothing that gives no cop call to ask questions.'

'Shrewd eye,' said Bell, thinking that fear of cops could explain him running. 'But not entirely accurate. I'm not a cop. I'm a private detective.'

'Dicks, cops, bulls, strikebreakers, you're all the same to me. Back away, mister.'

'I'm asking you civilly,' said Bell. 'Where are you from?'

'Don't try and stop me.'

'I met you somewhere. I want to know where.'

The man moved fast, feinting like a heavyweight, with his left hand to jab and set Bell up for a knockout right. Isaac Bell was equally quick. His left flew to block the right, and his right cocked to counterpunch. But instead of swinging his fist, the amber-eyed man plunged his right hand into his coat and whipped out a revolver. The cold click of a hammer thumbed back to fire told the young detective he had been duped by a master.

'You look surprised.'

Bell peered past the gun into his eyes. Grady Forrer was right. In this dim light, they were gold. Equally odd was a tone of pride in the voice. Almost as if he expected Bell to express admiration for getting the drop on him. But what in blazes was going on? They had not ended up in this cellar by accident. The man had laid a trap, and Bell had obligingly walked right into it. He felt like a fool. But at least this proved that his dream in the mine had been no dream.

'Remove your pistol from your shoulder holster. Thumb and forefinger on the butt. If I don't see your other three fingers, you're dead.'

Bell reached slowly, opening his coat, gripping the butt of his single-action Colt Army with his thumb and forefinger and slowly pulling the revolver from his holster. The man reached for it. Bell placed it in his palm and he slipped it into his shoulder holster.

'Now your sleeve gun.'

Bell shook his two-shot derringer from his sleeve and handed it over.

'And your other one.'

'I don't have another sleeve gun.'

'It's in your coat pocket.' He snapped his fingers.

Bell pulled a single-shot derringer from his coat pocket. It was small and unusually lightweight – a 'graduation' gift from Joe Van Dorn – and he had thought after repeated inspections that it did not bulge the pocket or tug the cloth.

'Sharp eyes,' he said.

'I've seen it before, sonny.'

Bell heard the pride he had hoped to elicit. Not a world-weary *I've seen it before* but a boast. Again the man seemed to be expecting applause. Bell *was* impressed. The man knew his business. But he was not about to clap. Not yet. Instead he said, 'Seen it before? Or tracking me? Who are you?'

'The knife in your boot.'

He pointed the derringer he had taken from Bell in Bell's face and swiveled his revolver down at Bell's feet. It looked like a Colt, thought Bell, but the hammer was unusually wide, the frame's top strap was flat, and the front sight had been removed, undoubtedly to smooth his fast draw.

'Which boot?'

'I can shoot a hole in one of them. Or you can show me – slowly!'

Bell pulled a throwing knife from his right boot. 'Your hands are full. Where do you want it?'

'Stick it in that doorjamb, if you think you can hit it.'

The doorjamb, all that remained of the cellar wood-work not yet demolished, was twenty feet away. Bell raised his arm. The gun stayed pointed at his head. His blade flew across the cellar and stuck in the narrow strip of wood a quarter inch off dead center.

The man with amber eyes shrugged dismissively. 'Your overhand throw wastes time.'

He dropped the derringer in his pocket, reached down under his trouser leg, and pulled out a flat sliver of steel identical to Bell's.

'Here's a better way.'

His hand flipped outward, with an underhand twist of his wrist. The knife hissed through the air and thudded beside Bell's, dead center, in the jamb.

Bell was betting the man would repeat that self-congratulatory lapse of attention, and it happened. He gazed proudly, as if inviting Bell to express awe. It lasted only a fraction of a second but long enough to kick, Bell sinking the point of his boot into the man's wrist.

His hand convulsed, his fingers splayed open.

Bell was already reaching to catch the gun when it dropped.

Too late. Moving with speed Bell would not have believed if he didn't see it, the man caught the falling gun in his left hand, sidestepped Bell's rush, and swung hard, raking Bell's temple with the barrel. The young detective saw stars, pinwheeled across the cellar, and slammed into a wall.

He sprang to his feet and was trying to shake sense into his head and launch a counterattack when a trio of workmen thundered down the stairs to resume demolition of the cellar.

'What in hell —'

The man in the long coat brushed past them and bounded up the steps with his gun and all three of Bell's.

Bell, scattering the trio with a bellowed 'Gangway!' yanked both throwing knives from the doorjamb and tore after him.

23

The rain had intensified to a deluge, and Isaac Bell could not see a full block. But the downpour had cleared the streets and sidewalks surrounding the Tombs of cops and pedestrians, and across that empty expanse he thought he saw on the farthest edge of his vision a single figure. The man's long, loose coat was flapping as he headed west toward Elm Street.

Bell ran after him. Tall and long-legged, Bell halved the distance, when suddenly the man disappeared into a hole in the sidewalk. Isaac Bell jumped into the same hole and landed on a wooden scaffolding a few feet below grade. He saw a wooden ladder and climbed down it into a seemingly endless tunnel lit by electric lights. He found himself on the concrete floor of the covered ditch they were digging for the Rapid Transit Subway.

It resembled an orderly and much larger coal mine. It was ten times as wide as a mine and five times as high, and brightly lighted. Instead of rickety timber props, ranks of steel columns marched into the distance, holding up massive girders that spanned the tunnel to support the trolley line on Elm Street above and the stoop lines of the buildings along the sidewalks. Huge water pipes and sewer mains – from around which the ground had been painstakingly dug – were suspended from the girders with chains.

Bell looked downtown, where the lights were brightest,

then uptown, where they faded. Far, far ahead in the up-town direction, he saw the man in the long coat weaving through the construction site, dodging workmen, steam hoists and wheelbarrows. He stopped suddenly, handed something to a man pushing a wheelbarrow on a plank track, and broke into a run again. Bell raced after him. When he reached the point where he had seen him, the man with the barrow, and another burly workman who had dropped his barrow, blocked his path. Clutched in their fists were the dollars the man had given them.

'No cops allowed.'

'Don't believe what he told you,' Bell shouted. 'Get out of my way.'

'Why should we believe you?'

Bell hit the first high and low, kicked the legs out from under the second, and ran after the man in the long coat. He had a two-block lead. The concrete floor stopped abruptly. Ahead, they were digging through raw earth. Rainwater muddied the floor of the ditch. The space narrowed and grew crowded with workers with picks and shovels. Where steel columns had held the city above, here were temporary wooden beams, a rough-plank roof, and openings to the sky through which poured the rain and fading daylight.

Bell ran for what felt like miles, city block after city block, until he thought he could not run another step, nor lift his boots once more from the grasping mud. And still the man kept running, covering the broken ground at a strong pace, brushing past startled workmen, smashing aside those who got in his way and leaving Bell to dodge the angry ones still standing.

Bell heard thunder, and the ground shook. Streetcars rumbled overhead, high above, on temporary timbers. Lights flickered. The water pipes swayed in their chains. On he ran, ignoring shaken fists and shouts of foremen, air storming through his lungs. The tunnel changed abruptly. Gone in an instant was the muddy floor; gone the men shoveling and picking. The floors, the walls, the ceiling, had turned to stone. The builders had hit Manhattan Schist in their drive north to Grand Central Station. The bedrock beneath the city had risen to the surface, and the tunnel was boring into it. The space felt more like a mine, with jagged walls and low ceiling and the whining rumble of steam drills.

Free of the mud, Isaac Bell poured on the speed. The man ahead of him was tiring, stumbling occasionally, and Bell was catching up. Better yet, Bell thought, the tunnel would soon come to an end. It looked like the only way out would be up one of the shafts where steel buckets were hoisting excavated rock by steam derrick. That his quarry had at least four guns and he had only knives did not slow him.

Suddenly, the man scrambled up the side of the tunnel, where it opened into an exposed gallery, and ducked under ropes that had been stretched to block off the area. Light spilled down from above. It looked like there was an opening to the street. A foreman came running from the other direction.

'Get out of there, you damned fool,' he shouted. 'That chunk of work is loose.'

A shaft of daylight fell on the man Bell was chasing and Bell saw his face was still covered by the bloody bandage and the hat. But his eyes were gleaming as if in triumph, and Bell knew that he had seen something to his advantage. Bell ran harder. The man scrambled up the slanting side of the gallery where a section of bedrock had broken loose from the wall and slid down on the floor.

Bell could see that layers of the bedrock slanted at a steep angle. An immense chunk was propelled like a toboggan about to slide down an icy slope. He caught up with the foreman, who was shouting, 'That'll kill you! Get down from there, you idiot! Hey, what are you doing? Don't do that. You'll kill us all.'

The man had found a heavy pick and was using it to dig into the crumbling rock and pull himself higher up the slope.

'He'll start another slide!' the foreman wailed in despair. 'Run, boys! Run for it.'

Bell scrambled up on to the slope. The man had reached the opening and was flailing away with the pick, trying to make it wide enough to fit through. Broken rock rolled down at Bell. The hole suddenly opened wider, and the man started scrambling up through it. Bell took one of the throwing knives and hurled it overhand.

The blade flew true to its target and stuck in the heel of the man's boot as he disappeared up the hole. Bell scrambled after him. Then the rock around the hole separated in a giant sheet of stone that slid down the slope, hurtled past Bell, and crashed to the tunnel floor. The impact shook Bell loose and sent him sliding after it. He hit bottom and barely had time to move aside as a slab of rock half a block long broke off and thundered into the tunnel.

It left in its wake a jagged slope that Bell climbed as

easily as a flight of stairs. He emerged at the corner of Fourth Avenue and Thirty-seventh Street just in time to see a full block of brownstone mansions shaking as if in an earthquake. A chasm opened in the sidewalk. The front walls separated from the brownstones and plunged into the subway tunnel.

Isaac Bell could see into the front rooms of the mansions as if he were at the theater watching a play on a stage. The occupants ran like actors who were exiting upstage as fast as they could. Bell ran to help. Motion caught his eye a short block across Thirty-seventh Street. A train on the tracks elevated above Third Avenue was accelerating downtown. Clinging to the back of the rear car was the man in the long coat, and as the El disappeared behind the buildings, he waved good-bye to Isaac Bell.

'He got away,' Bell reported to Joseph Van Dorn.

The Boss was seething.

'What happened to the young lady I ordered you to follow?'

'I lost sight of Mary in a riot. I was looking for her at the Tombs when I ran into him.'

'Was she arrested?'

'The police arrested a hundred women, so I thought I might find her there. But she was not among them.'

'The police,' growled Van Dorn. 'Speaking of the police, I just had an unpleasant conversation by telephone with a deputy commissioner who informed me that his patrolmen received reports from the subway contractor that you were present at the street collapse. Apparently, there is speculation that you caused it.'

'I did not,' said Bell. 'But I did ask the engineers to explain what happened. They refer to that section of the tunnel between Thirty-fourth Street and Grand Central Terminal as the hoodoo part. All sorts of terrible things have gone wrong with its construction – a deadly explosion of blasting powder, rockfalls, a contractor killed. What happened today was the result of an unforeseen geological fault. The man I was chasing precipitated the slide – either by accident as he tried to escape or deliberately if he had knowledge of mine engineering and recognized the flaw in the rock.'

Van Dorn spoke in a voice that rose. 'Rest assured, I do not believe that any of my detectives would *deliberately* precipitate the collapse of a city block, but I would hope that at future such events you would not stick around to allow the police to link the name of the Van Dorn Agency to a natural disaster.'

'I had to help some people out of the buildings.'

'You're sure you'd seen this man before?'

'I'm not sure,' Bell said, because he was not yet able to explain, to the Boss's satisfaction, his strange, dreamlike memory of the man with amber eyes who had to be the provocateur. 'But I am convinced that he was looking for me. He lured me into that cellar.'

'*Lured?*' echoed Van Dorn. '*Lured* is what penny-dreadful villains do to unsuspecting maidens.'

'What I mean to say is, I feel like a darn fool.'

Van Dorn nodded agreement. 'I think you could do with a night's rest.'

'Yes, sir,' said Isaac Bell. But instead of going home to his room in the Yale Club, he went straight to a gunsmith that Wish Clarke patronized on Forty-third Street. It was after hours, but the gunsmith lived above his shop, and Wish's name got Bell in the door.

He bought a two-shot derringer, a tiny one-shot, and a Colt Army to replace the weapons taken by the amber-eyed man. Then he described the man's revolver to the smith.

'It was a .45. And I would have thought it was a Colt. But it had no front sight. And the hammer was much wider than this,' he added, hefting the gun. 'I was wondering, do you know a smith who might modify a Colt that way?'

'Folks do all sorts of things to six-shooters. Did you notice the top strap?'

'It was flat,' said Bell. 'Not beveled like this. And the hammer had a graceful little curl to it.'

'Was the front sight cut off or ground down?'

Bell considered for a moment. 'No. There seemed to be a notch you could slip one into.'

'How long was the barrel?'

'Not so long it couldn't come out of his holster real quick.'

'And it had a slot for the front sight? . . . Did you get a look at the trigger?'

'No. His finger was curled around it.'

'How big was the grip?'

'Let me think . . . The man had large hands, but I could see the butt – it was longer than most.'

'I think you were looking at a Bisley.'

'The target pistol?'

'Yes, that flat top is for mounting a rear windage sight. Fine, fine weapon. Very accurate.'

'It is, in my experience,' said Bell, remembering how close two pistol shots had come to killing him at extreme range in Gleasonburg.

'But it is more than a target pistol,' said the smith. 'It makes an excellent close-in fighting gun with that long grip and wide hammer.'

'Do you have one?'

'I'd have to order it special.'

'Send it to the Van Dorn office at the Cadillac. They'll forward it to me.'

Bell paid for the guns, dropped the one-shot in his pocket, and put the Army in his shoulder holster. Then, as he started to slide the two-shot up his coat sleeve, he weighed it speculatively in his hand, wondering. Had the amber-eyed provocateur assumed or guessed he had a derringer in his sleeve? Or had he been sharp enough to spot that the sleeve was tailored extra-wide? Or had he just been covering all the places a man might hide a gun?

'I'd like another of these, please. But a lighter one, if you've got it.'

'I've got a real beaut I made myself. Weighs half that. Fires a .22 long. But it won't pack quite the punch.'

'Some punch beats no punch,' said Bell. 'I'll take it.'

The gunsmith brought out a miniature two-shot over-under derringer. 'Always happy to make a sale,' he said. 'But you're running out of places to put them.'

'Can you recommend a good hatmaker?'

The hatmaker was working late and eager to please the gunsmith, who was a source of clients who paid top dollar for custom-made. At midnight, Bell hurried back to the Cadillac Hotel to check for wires that had come in on the Van Dorn private telegraph.

Grady Forrer, who never seemed to sleep, said, 'Excellent chapeau!'

Bell touched the wide brim in salute and looked for telegrams in his box.

Weber and Fields had not reported in, and he could only guess whether they were keeping tabs on the strikers heading for Pittsburgh or holed up in a saloon; he made a mental note to instruct Archie to report to him independently. But two wires had just come in from Chicago, both sent in the money-saving shorthand that the parsimonious Joseph Van Dorn demanded.

Wish Clarke reported,

R LAMING
LIKELY JOB.

In other words, Wish could not find Laurence Rosania in any of his usual haunts to question him about fellow experimenters with shaped explosives, but the detective had caught wind of rumors in the Chicago underworld that a wealthy dowager or an industrialist's girlfriend was about to be separated from jewelry locked in her safe.

Bell sat up straight when he read the second wire. It was from Claiborne Hancock, who Joseph Van Dorn had coaxed out of early retirement to manage Protective Services.

CLIENT'S SISTER HERE
A LOOKER.
GLAD TO PROTECT TOO.

A looker and *glad to* equaled four excess words, but Hancock had done Van Dorn a favor and could take liberties.

Bell wired back.

UNTIL I ARRIVE.

24

'You're looking mighty full of yourself,' said James Congdon.

Henry Clay took dead aim at *The Kiss* and sailed his hat across Congdon's office. 'I have every right to,' he exulted. 'Our coalfields' war is exploding.'

'From what I read in the newspapers, it would be exploding regardless of your expensive efforts to shove a chunk under the corner.'

Clay was not to be denied his victory. His grand joust with Isaac Bell had been deeply satisfying. He had duped, disarmed, and humbled Joseph Van Dorn's new young champion. Better yet, the fact that Bell had been shadowing Mary Higgins proved that Clay had chosen Mary brilliantly. Bell – or, more likely, Van Dorn – suspected what Clay had already learned from his spies in the union about her derailing a train in Denver. Mary Higgins was a dangerous radical because she was imaginative and supremely capable. That Joe Van Dorn sensed her powers made Clay's plans for the unionist even more gratifying.

'Don't believe anything in the newspapers.'

'You promised me we'll win this war in the newspapers,' Congdon shot back.

'We will win, I promise. The newspapers will destroy the unions when they convince their readers that only the owners can stop murderous agitators.'

'When, dammit? Winter's coming, and the miners have struck. What are you waiting for?'

'An earthshaking event.'

'Earthshaking requires an earthquake.'

'I have recruited an earthquake.'

'What the hell are you talking about? Stop playing games with me, Clay. What kind of earthquake?'

Henry Clay smiled, supremely confident of Judge James Congdon's approval. 'A lovely earthquake. In fact,' he boasted, 'an earthshakingly beautiful earthquake.'

'A *woman*?'

'A lovely woman with a big idea. And who happens to be smarter, braver and tougher than any unionist in the country. Her only weakness is that she's so dedicated to "the good fight" that she can't see straight.'

'I want to meet her,' said Congdon.

'I told you at the start,' Clay objected coldly, 'the details are mine.'

'Tactics are yours. Strategy is mine. An earthquake falls in the category of strategy. I will meet her.'

Isaac Bell paid extra for the biggest private stateroom on the Pennsylvania Special and tipped the porter to bring his meals on a tray. The train to Chicago, which steamed from the ferry head in Jersey City, ran on a twenty-hour schedule, and he intended to use every waking hour teaching himself how to draw his derringer from his new hat.

There was a mirror on the door to his private bath. He faced his reflection. He raised his hands in the air as if already disarmed of his Colt, his sleeve gun and his pocket pistol. Moving in slow motion, he experimented, devising a series of steps to get the gun out of the hat and cocked to fire.

The special rocketed across New Jersey, stopped in Philadelphia briefly, and sped into Pennsylvania. Bell worked at the draw with an athlete's hands and eyes and let his mind chew on the few facts he knew about the amber-eyed man who had gotten the drop on him and had taken away his weapons.

It was strange how they had almost identical throwing knives. And strange how he knew that Bell's was in his boot. Some men hid it behind their coat collar. Some in the small of their back.

He also knew where Bell hid his derringer, knew it was in his sleeve instead of his belt or his boot. And he had spotted the tiny one-shot in his coat pocket, which no one ever noticed.

What else do I know about him? thought Bell.

He no longer doubted that his memory of being slugged unconscious in the coal mine was real and not a hallucination conjured by the damps. Nor did he doubt that the coalfield provocateur who shot him in Gleasonburg was the same man who had taken his weapons and run circles around him in New York. But other than that, he had more questions than answers. *Why did he follow me all the way to New York? How did he find me outside the Tombs? Had he followed me down Broadway while I was shadowing Mary?*

The train was two hours west of Philadelphia, climbing the foothills of the Allegheny Mountains, when the tall young detective felt he had choreographed a series of movements to draw the gun swiftly using both hands, one for the hat, one for the gun. Now he had to master the sequence. That meant practice, drilling over and over and over again, until the steps were automatic. Hour after hour. Day after day. Starting now.

They stopped in Altoona to change engines and pick up a dining car. Bell jumped down to the ballast and walked briskly back and forth the length of the train to work out the kinks in his arms and legs. The cold air felt good, but it was beginning to rain. By the time the yard crew had the old Atlantic off and a fresh 4-4-2 coupled on, rainwater was streaming down the sides of the train.

Bell swung aboard as the special resumed rolling, asked the porter for a sandwich and coffee, and returned to his stateroom to practise, barely aware that the rain was lashing the window.

Eight hours after leaving Jersey City, the Pennsylvania Special slowed to a sedate forty miles an hour, and the conductors began announcing Pittsburgh. Bell sat on his berth and tore hungrily into the sandwich he had yet to eat and washed it down with cold coffee. Night and cloud had closed in. Through the window he noticed dots of red fire. He turned out the lights to see better in the dark beyond the rails.

Bonfires were burning in the rain, lighting the haggard faces of men and women huddled around them. The porter came for the tray. 'Strikers,' he said.

'Hard night to be outdoors,' said Bell, and the porter felt free to say, 'Poor devils. They got nothing and nowhere to go. Militia won't let 'em into Pittsburgh.'

'Where are their tents?'

'Folks say the police impounded them. Took 'em off a train and stuck 'em in a warehouse.'

The bonfires vanished at the city limits, and the special glided into Union Station.

He knew me, thought Bell. *My provocateur knows me.*

25

Isaac Bell saw Wish Clarke waiting for him on the platform at Chicago's Union Depot. His face was red, his eyes bright blue pinpricks nearly buried in puffy flesh.

Bell jumped off before the train stopped rolling. 'Do we have Laurence Rosania?'

'Chicago's leading fencer of stolen property reports that the son of a gun is so sure of himself, he's negotiating terms for jewels he hasn't even stolen yet.'

'How'd you learn that?' asked Bell, deeply impressed. Wish stank like a distillery this morning, but how many detectives could pry such gold out of a fence?

'He owes me a favor,' Wish answered.

'Big one.'

'It was. I didn't shoot him when I have every right to and he knows it. Also, he was irritated that a jewel thief had the nerve to compare prices with his chief competitor. I reminded him that Mr Rosania is in a class by himself, but he was not in a charitable mood.'

'Did he tell you what Rosania is planning to steal?'

'A necklace comprised of a fifteen-carat, heart-shaped pink diamond on a string of two-carat gems.'

'That should narrow it down to the very rich.'

'No one ever called Rosania a piker. At any rate, we'll watch the fence, and his competitor, and when our safecracker shows up with the loot we'll grab him.'

'When?'

'Soon, was my man's impression.'

'No,' said Bell. 'We don't have time to sit around waiting for him.'

'A few days.'

'But what if Rosania decides to lay low – do the smart thing, let the dust settle before he shops them? It could take weeks. We don't have weeks.'

'I'm open to better ideas,' said Wish Clarke. 'Got any?'

'Wire Grady Forrer in the New York field office.'

'Who's that?'

'The new fellow I told you about who Mr Van Dorn made chief of the research division.'

'Research *division*? When did that happen?'

'About a month ago,' said Bell. Wish looked perplexed, and Bell recalled Van Dorn saying, *God knows where Wish Clarke is*. 'The Boss is moving quickly,' he explained, 'adding on all sorts of things.'

'What modernity will he dream up next?' Wish pretended to marvel. 'OK. So what do I wire this Furrier?'

'*Forrer*. Grady Forrer. He's a sharp one. See what he's got in his newspaper files on prominent Chicagoans shopping for jewels in New York.'

'They're not going to print in the paper that Mrs Thickneck bought a pink diamond necklace.'

'We can read between the lines. Particularly in the Society sections. Match Chicago buyers in New York to upcoming balls in Chicago and get a jump on Mr Rosania's shopping plans.'

'Interrupt him in the middle of the job?'

'I'd rather grab him as he comes out.'

'Fine plan, Isaac – two birds with one stone.'

'Put him in a mood to talk.'

'And a mighty modern idea about Mr Forrer keeping up to date on the Society page. Old-fashioned I, meantime, will visit Black's Social and Little's Exchange.'

'For what purpose?' Bell asked warily. Ed Black's Social and Wes Little's Exchange were both saloons.

'There's Little's,' said Wish, nodding as they stepped out of Union Depot at a brightly lighted bar on the corner. 'Black's is a similar stone's throw from the LaSalle Street Station where the Twentieth Century comes in.'

'So?'

'When their trains arrive from New York and it's "quittin' time," Pennsylvania Special express messengers hightail it around the corner to Little's. And Twentieth Century Limited boys hoist a glass at Black's. Don't you reckon those heavily armed agents protecting valuables might recall which passengers coming home from New York stashed jewelry in their express car safes?'

Isaac Bell conceded that Wish's was the more savvy tactic.

'Don't waste time berating yourself, old son. You thought of catching the thief in the act. I just came up with a quainter way of anticipating it.'

Bell grinned at his old partner. 'I keep telling Mr Van Dorn you're the sharpest operator in his outfit.'

'How delighted he must be to hear it.'

'Hold it right there, Mister!'

Two big men blocked Isaac Bell's path into the Mine Workers' union hall, which was on a street of saloons in

191

the First Ward. Ragtime music clattered from player pianos on either side. The miners had installed steel shutters on their windows and a rifleman on the roof.

'Hello, Mike. Terry. How are you?'

The Van Dorn Protective Services agents looked more closely. 'Isaac! Haven't seen you since you apprenticed.'

Mike Flannery and Terry Fein were a pair of handsome bruisers who made excellent hotel dicks at the Palmer House but laid no claim to the mental machinery required of an investigator.

'Your mustache threw me off,' said Mike.

'Mighty becoming,' said Terry. 'The ladies'll love it.'

'Let's hope you're right. Is Mary Higgins in there with her brother?'

'Showed up yesterday,' said Terry, adding a broad wink as he escorted Bell into the front room. 'Amazing how many unionists suddenly have pressing business with her brother since she hit this town.'

'Is Mary all right?'

'Of course I'm all right!' Mary said, striding into the front room.

She was buttoning a coat over her shirtwaist and trumpet skirt. A plain red hat, with neither ribbons nor feathers, was pinned to the portion of her hair swept up to the top of her head. The rest tumbled, glossy black, to her shoulders. Her eyes were as gray and unfathomable as a winter sky.

'Why wouldn't I be?'

Isaac Bell could not say, *Because you vanished in the middle of a riot while I was shadowing you – orders of Mr Van Dorn, who thinks you're up to something.* Nor could he blurt out in front of her brother and the Protective Services boys, *You are even more beautiful than I remembered.*

'I'm glad to see you, again,' he said. 'You, too, Jim.'

Jim Higgins took his hand. 'Welcome to Chicago,' he said warmly.

Mary did not offer her hand, and her smile was as remote as a nod to a casual acquaintance seen across a busy train station. 'Brother, I'm going out. Nice to see you, Isaac.'

'I hope to see you again.'

'Are you in Chicago long?'

'Hard to tell.'

'Same here.'

She swept out the door and was gone.

'Who's watching out for her?' Bell asked Mike and Terry.

'No one.'

'What? Why not?'

'She won't let us.'

'But if Jim's in danger, surely his sister is, too.'

'We've already had the argument,' said Jim Higgins.

'And lost,' chorused the Protective Services agents.

'Don't worry, Isaac,' said Jim, 'I'm taking her to Pittsburgh. The boys are watching me, and we'll all stick close.'

Henry Clay made absolutely sure that none of the Van Dorns had shadowed her before he followed Mary Higgins inside a nickelodeon in a long, narrow converted storefront on Halsted Street. A coin piano banged away in a corner, and the audience was howling at a comedy on the screen, *Appointment by Telephone*, in which a couple drinking champagne at lunch was spotted through the restaurant window by the man's wife.

Clay located Mary in the back row, where he had instructed her to sit. His heart took him by surprise, soaring when the projection light jumped from the screen to her beautiful face. She was the only person in the theater not laughing.

Before he could reach her, a man stood up and moved a few seats over to sit next to her. Suspecting one of the mashers who preyed on women who sat alone in nickelodeons, Clay rushed to the seat next to him. He had guessed right. The man was already laying a hand on Mary's leg. She slapped it away. The masher whispered, 'Don't play hard to get.'

Clay took the masher's hand in his right, clamped his left over his mouth to muffle his scream, and broke his finger. 'Leave quietly,' he whispered in his ear. 'If I hear a peep out of you or ever see you again, I'll break the other nine.'

The masher stumbled away, moaning, and Clay slipped into the seat he had vacated. Loud laughter and the coin piano allowed them to speak in low tones without fear of being overheard.

'I've lined up fifty barges and a couple of towboats.'

Nothing in her manner suggested whether she had noticed what he had done to the masher, and he could not tell whether that was because he had done it smoothly or because she didn't care. Her reply was all business.

'Mr Claggart, where did the money come from? Fifty barges and two towboats must cost a fortune.'

'Empty barges are going cheap at the moment. What with the operators fearing the strike will diminish production. Pittsburgh is awash in empties.'

'Fifty barges and the services of two steamboats still must cost money.'

'Don't you read the papers?'

'What do you mean?'

'There's been a slew of bank and payroll robberies in the Chicago area, out toward Evanston and Cicero and all the way down to Hammond and Gary.'

'What do bank robberies have to do with the coal strike?'

'Not every bank robber is in it for personal gain,' Clay answered. 'Some support worthy causes.'

The idea of labor radicals raising money by robbing banks had a ring of truth, he thought. And regardless of her scruples, if any, about robbing capitalist banks, they would be nothing compared to her scruples about financing her brilliant barge scheme with Judge James Congdon's Wall Street money.

He glanced at her to see how the lie registered.

She was staring straight ahead at the show on the screen. The wife stalked into the restaurant. Crockery flew. Tables were overturned. The woman scorned procured a horsewhip from somewhere and flailed away, and the audience roared as she chased her husband and his girlfriend around the restaurant. Henry Clay feasted on Mary's compelling profile, waiting, thinking, She's got to laugh. She's not made of stone.

*

Mary Higgins had been troubled from the first by the money. It seemed that whatever Claggart needed, he had access to limitless funds. But she found it difficult to believe that the bank robbers, who had inspired all sorts of lurid reporting in the newspapers, were nobler than common criminals. Albeit skillful ones who had managed enough successful robberies to inflame so much attention. With the Spanish War long gone from the headlines, and a reluctance on the part of many newspapers to lend the mine strike credence by writing about it, their editors were probably getting desperate.

But none of that guaranteed the robbers were supporting the strike.

She felt as she had since she first met Claggart in New York. She could not entirely trust the man. Despite his radical talk, his underlying motive was a mystery. But she hadn't thought through how much money it would take to accomplish blocking the river, and she had little choice but to subscribe to the old saying, *Don't look a gift horse in the mouth*. What if it was a trick by the owners? What kind of trick, she had no idea.

All she knew for sure was that she had thrown her lot in with someone she knew nothing about. She had seen a man of action when he saved her from the cops. And now she had just observed a vicious streak, brutalizing the masher, who would think twice about molesting other women. And she had to admit that Claggart's reaction could have been inflamed by the fact that he was falling for her.

She wondered what she would think and what she would do if the bank robbers were suddenly caught by the police. If they turned out to be ordinary criminals, then Mr Claggart would have a lot of explaining to do. Until then, she resolved to keep her wits about her and watch him closely.

26

Isaac Bell found Wish Clarke drunk in Little's Exchange. He walked him out of the saloon, heaved him into a hansom cab, and gave the driver an enormous five-dollar tip to deliver him to the inexpensive hotel around the corner from the Palmer House, where Van Dorns rented rooms in Chicago.

Wish grabbed his arm as Bell tried to shut the cab's door. 'No jewels of note aboard the Pennshulvania Speshule.'

'I'll check the Twentieth Century messengers at Black's.'

'Shorry I let you down, Ishick. It cashes up wish me now and again.'

'Make me a promise, Aloysius.'

'Anythin'.'

'Go straight to bed. I'll need you in the morning.'

The driver flicked his reins and the cab clattered off.

Bell hurried on foot down Clarke, over the rail yards on Harrison Street, and waited for a tall-masted schooner to pass before he could cross the South Branch of the Chicago River on an ancient cast-iron jackknife bridge. It took a long time to creak back down, and he recalled that when he apprenticed in Chicago there were cries to replace it with a modern bascule bridge. But Chicago's corrupt aldermen could not agree who would do the work and who would pay for it.

Black's Social, like Little's Exchange, was a cut above the ordinary workingman's saloon, being near the LaSalle Street terminus for New York Central passenger trains. Drinks were not cheap, and the free lunch was correspondingly lavish, served by a chef in white who presided over the newest of innovations, a stainless steel steam table. The customers were businessmen, clerks and drummers dressed in sack suits and sporting vests, watch chains and a variety of head- and neckwear.

The express messengers were easy to spot if you knew what to look for. While dressed like businessmen or clerks or drummers, they had the steadier gaze of men who worked at a profession with a high mortality rate. Protecting gold, cash, bearer bonds and jewels locked in their fortified express cars, they routinely encountered masked robbers whose methods of attack ranged from derailing trains to blasting open cars with dynamite and shooting the survivors. They were famous for shooting back.

Bell, like every Van Dorn, often caught free train rides in their express cars as the messengers enjoyed the company of gun-toting detectives who knew their business. He greeted some he knew, bought drinks, and established who was currently working on the 20th Century Limited, the New York Central train most likely patronized by passengers who could afford fifteen-carat diamonds.

Bell had been at it several hours when Wish walked in in a clean suit and went straight to the coffee urn at the lunch table. He downed a cup black, poured another, and wandered over to join Bell. 'How are we doing?'

'The Twentieth Century is running five consists,' Bell answered, meaning that five separate trains carried the

20th drumhead to accommodate demand. 'I found messengers from four of them, no luck. The fifth is coming in any minute. How are *you* doing?'

'Tip-top,' said Wish, observing the crowded saloon through slitted eyes. He was swaying slightly on his feet but looked otherwise indestructible. 'There's your fellow walking in now. Ben Lent. I've ridden with him. He's all right.'

Ben Lent was short and powerfully built. The scars on his cheeks looked more likely from bullets than fists. He greeted Wish warmly, kidded him about the coffee cup, 'Where a glass ought to be,' and shook hands hello with Bell. And with Ben Lent, just off the last train of the day, they hit the jackpot. Bell described the necklace that Laurence Rosania was supposedly intending to steal.

'Mrs Stambaugh.'

Isaac Bell and Wish Clarke exchanged glances.

'Mrs *Stambaugh*?'

'*Rose* Stambaugh?'

'The lady herself. And still quite a looker, I don't mind saying. She stopped personally in the car to ask me to keep a special eye on it.'

Wish grinned at Isaac Bell. 'Doubt your Society page Furrier would have tumbled to Mrs Stambaugh.'

Bell agreed. Mrs Stambaugh's jewelry-shopping expedition to New York would never make the Society pages of either city. She could easily afford the expensive necklace that attracted Rosania, but her vast fortune was neither inherited nor earned in the conventional manner, as Rose Stambaugh had been for forty years the greatly admired proprietress of the finest brothel in Chicago.

'That must be some necklace for Rosania to risk a lynching if he's caught,' said Wish. 'Everyone loves Mrs Stambaugh – cops, judges, politicians, even the Cardinal. You remember, Isaac. I took you to meet her once.'

'I sure do.' Bell recalled a shapely little blonde of uncertain years with an hourglass figure, an arresting smile and a welcoming glint in her fiery blue eyes.

'When was this?' Bell asked Lent.

'Last week.'

Bell said to Wish Clarke, 'There's a charity ball for the news boys tomorrow night at the Palmer House. Do you think the bluenoses will let her into that?'

'They'll take her money anywhere since she retired.'

'Does she still live on Dearborn?'

'Moved to a mansion on the North Shore.'

The two detectives rented a Baker Electric Runabout and found the new Stambaugh mansion just as night fell. It was enormous, fenced by heavy wrought iron on three sides and open to Lake Michigan on the fourth. Golden light streamed from many windows, and music wafted on the wind blowing off the lake. They parked the Baker on the darkest stretch of the street in a space between an Aultman Steamer and a long five-passenger Apperson Tonneau and watched from the shadows of the leather top. Every half hour, one of them took a walk around the neighborhood.

A policeman came along and peered in the car.

'Van Dorn,' Wish told him and slipped him three dollars.

Buggies clip-clopped past, and occasionally a grand

carriage rolled behind a team of four. Another cop stopped and peered in. Wish gave him three dollars. More carriages passed, stopping at parties at other mansions along the street. Wish expressed the concern that Rose Stambaugh was wearing her new necklace to host a party, but Bell assured him, judging by the Aultman and the Apperson, that her gathering tonight was not big enough to rate the display and it would be locked in her safe, awaiting Rosania.

'She'll save it for the Palmer House.'

A third cop came along. Wish gave him three dollars. Bell worried that the bribe seekers would scare Rosania off. When a fourth appeared soon after, he said, 'I'll do this one.' He plunged his hand deep in his pocket, sprang from the Baker.

'What do we have here?' asked the cop, a tall, jowly man with a walrus mustache hung like a Christmas ornament on a bad-tempered face.

'A twenty-dollar gold piece,' said Isaac Bell, holding it up. 'What's your name?'

'Muldoon,' the cop lied.

'Keep ten, Muldoon. Share the rest with the boys and save them the trip.' He held on to it until the cop nodded, agreeing that he would be the last, and left.

At midnight, the music stopped. Musicians filed out of the Stambaugh service entrance. Three men in dinner jackets exited the front gate, laughing, and piled into the Apperson. A couple left the mansion holding hands, raised steam on the Aultman, and drove away. Lights began going out.

'This is looking like a bust,' Wish muttered.

'I'll take another look around.'

Bell made sure no one was coming and got out of the Baker. The wind was picking up, getting brisk, and it carried a sound that it took him a moment to place, as it was not a noise he associated with a city street. He darted around the fence and stared at the lake, which was dark but for shipping lights and channel markers. He raced back to the car.

Wish saw him coming and stepped down.

'He came on a boat. I heard the sails flapping.'

Bell and Wish Clarke rounded the corner of the fence and ran along it to the water. The mansion had a dock, and Bell could see a small sloop tied to it with its mast bare.

'He dropped the sails. He's in the house.'

'That son of gun is quick,' said Wish. 'He'll be in and out while most safecrackers would still be building their nerve.'

They climbed the iron fence and found a spot in the shrubbery from where they could watch both the house and the boat. Thirty minutes passed. Bell began to get anxious. 'Wish, cover the front door in case he leaves on foot.'

Wish hurried to the street.

Bell kept watching. Moments later, a shadow emerged from a second-storey window and descended the back wall of the mansion.

Hand over hand, Laurence Rosania went down a drainpipe as agilely as a spider. Ducking low, he crossed the lawn and on to the dock and knelt to untie the little sailboat's bowline. Suddenly, he froze, his eyes locking on the front deck where he had lowered the foresail. The sail was gone.

Before the safecracker could stand, darkness closed in on him. Wet, mildewed canvas covered his head and wrapped his arms and legs, pinning them. The next thing he knew, a very strong man was picking him up and carrying him somewhere.

Despite fifteen years away in New York, Henry Clay had Chicago roots that still ran deep. Friendly with corrupt cops and gangsters who had moved up the ranks, and generous with Judge Congdon's money, he had kept tabs on Isaac Bell since Joe Van Dorn's favorite stepped off the train at Union Depot. The seasoned men working for him recognized trouble in the formidable Wish Clarke and operated with appropriate caution. So far, at least, neither Van Dorn had spotted them.

Clay had expected Bell would visit Jim Higgins's union hall, if only as an excuse to call on Mary. But the reports of Clarke and Bell standing drinks for express car messengers was a puzzle. Train robbers were known to try that gambit, but the detectives' motives were not as obvious.

Clay had paid a savvy plainclothes police detective to nose around Little's Exchange, where Wish Clarke spent much of the day. The police dick coaxed one messenger into revealing that Clarke had been inquiring about jewelry purchases in New York. Clay racked his brain.

What in hell? Were the Van Dorns looking to steal jewels? Of course not. That was ludicrous. Were they tracing contraband? No. United States Customs had their own investigators, and, besides, Isaac Bell was still working on his coalfield case.

Clay had still been pondering the jewel connection when a shadow he had set on Bell and Clarke reported that they had driven an auto up to the North Shore and parked outside Rose Stambaugh's new mansion. A moment later it had struck him: *Newport.* The Van Dorns were even sharper than he gave them credit for and he was suddenly at risk of being exposed.

He had summoned the highest-ranking policeman in his pay.

27

Unwrapped from the sail, Laurence Rosania had recovered his equilibrium quickly, brushed off his dinner jacket and straightened his collar. He looked about the windowless room Bell and Wish Clarke had taken him to and concluded there was no escape until they were ready to let him go. That the Van Dorns wanted something from him was very good news, and he had high hopes of getting out of this mess without going to prison. That Wish Clarke was one of them meant he would be treated fairly as long as he did not make the mistake of underestimating Clarke's intelligence. The handsome young fellow with him who explained what they wanted conducted himself like a gentleman, and soon all three were on a first-name basis.

'Thank you for that clear explanation, Isaac. And thank you, Aloysius. Always a treat to run into you. Now, here's the deal as I understand it. I will tell you what you need to know and you let me go.'

'No,' said Isaac Bell. 'You will tell us what we need to know. We will return what's in your pockets to the lady who owns it and let you go.'

'Or,' said Wish Clarke, 'you won't tell us what we want to know. We return what's in your pockets to the lady who owns it and give you to the cops. Take a moment to think on it.'

'I've reached a decision,' said Rosania. 'What do you need to know?'

'Everyone you know who's experimenting with shaped charges.'

Rosania had dark brown eyes. They opened wide. 'Are you asking me to betray every thief I know who's experimenting with shaped charges?'

'There can't be that many,' said Wish.

'It's rather an exclusive club,' Rosania agreed. 'And the membership has been reduced drastically by experiments that went *Poof!* before they cleared the room. In fact, believe it or not, I'm the last man standing. Hollow charges are more complicated than anyone imagined.'

Isaac Bell's face grew wintry. 'Laurence. You are trying our patience.'

'And putting unwarranted faith in our good nature,' Wish added.

'What if I tell you what you need to know and I keep half the contents of my pockets and give you half and we go our separate ways?'

Bell tugged the thick gold chain draped across his vest and pulled out his watch. 'Ten seconds.'

'If you insist, there are two safecrackers I can name who've not only survived but are getting quite good at it.' He named them.

Bell looked at Wish.

Wish shook his head. 'Those guys are like you, Laurence, professionals happy in their work and not about to go to the trouble of wrecking coal mines.'

'Coal mines?' echoed Rosania. 'What are you suggesting?'

'*Everyone*,' said Isaac Bell. 'Not only thieves. Everyone experimenting with shaped explosives.'

For the first time since they waylaid Rosania, the jewel thief looked worried. 'How would I know someone *not* a thief?'

'For your sake, you'd better.'

'You're not going to love my answer.'

Wish nodded to Bell that it was his turn to be unpleasant, and Bell said, 'In which case, you're not going to love our reaction.'

'No, I'm serious. I can tell you something about him, but I can't tell you his name because I don't know his name.'

'Tell us what you know.'

'He's a big fellow – as tall as you, Isaac, and wider than you, Wish. He is very intelligent. He is very quick on his feet and quick with his hands. He talks like he's from Chicago, but I've never seen him around. So I think he's probably a bit older than me and left town before I took up my calling. He wears a slouch hat that covers his hair, and he pulls it down low over his eyes. He's clean-shaven. The bit of hair that shows below his hat is brown.'

So far, thought Bell, Rosania could be describing the man he had confronted in the Tombs and chased through the subway.

'What color are his eyes?'

'Hard to tell, the light was poor.'

Wish Clarke said, 'Laurence, you are usually more observant than that, knowing that the alert safecracker is the free safecracker. Poor light would have prompted you to redouble your efforts to inspect his eyes.'

'You're forgetting that I was attempting to learn the finer points of blowing holes in safes – not identify strangers.'

'Blue?'

'No, not blue. Some shade of brown.'

'Amber?'

'Amber is rare,' said Rosania. 'But they could be amber.'

'How do you know he's not a thief?' asked Wish.

'Good question. There's something about him that's more like a cop.'

'What about him was like a cop?'

'It's hard to say. He had something of the authoritative air about him. Like you gentlemen. I mean, you could pretend to be police.'

'How?' asked Bell.

'I wouldn't want you to take this the wrong way,' said Rosania, 'but words like *convincing, confident, cocksure, swaggering* and *arrogant* spring to mind.'

'I'm working hard at not taking it the wrong way,' said Wish Clarke.

Bell asked, 'And you're saying he came all the way to Chicago to study shaped explosives?'

'No, no, no. I didn't say that. I met him in Newport.'

'Rhode Island, Virginia, or California?' asked Wish.

'Rhode Island,' said Bell. 'The Naval Torpedo Station.'

'Where else? The fellow I'm talking about was standing drinks in the nearest bar and so was I. We both ended up talking to the same torpedo scientist. One of these big brains who doesn't know anything except one thing. Of the three of us, he was the only one who didn't know why we were asking all our questions. Good thing we weren't foreign spies.'

'Are you sure the other fellow wasn't a spy?'

'He was a safecracker through and through. Knew all the right questions. In fact, it went through my mind to exchange business cards. Team up for a big job.'

'But you said earlier he wasn't a thief.'

'Did I? I suppose what I am trying to tell you is, he asked all the questions a safecracker would ask but he conducted himself more like a policeman.'

'A cop with amber eyes,' said Bell.

'Possibly amber. Very likely a cop.'

'Was he armed?' asked Bell.

'Brother, was he! Big revolver in his coat, and his wrist banged on the table like he had a cannon in his sleeve.'

'Any knives?'

'Why do you ask?'

'Curiosity.'

'He had a blade in his boot.'

'How'd you happen to see that?' asked Wish Clarke.

'He cut a cigar he gave to Wheeler.'

'Who's Wheeler?'

'The big brain. And, by the way, his arsenal was another reason I figured he was not a thief. No self-respecting thief packs weapons. He was armed like you two.'

Isaac Bell exchanged glances with Wish Clarke, who looked like he agreed that they had gotten all they were going to. 'Thank you, Mr Rosania. You've been very helpful.'

'My pleasure. And with that, I will bid you gentlemen good evening.'

Rosania started for the door. He stopped abruptly at the sound of two Van Dorns cocking firearms.

'Don't forgot to empty your pockets.'

*

'Like cops?' asked Wish as the detectives exited the Stambaugh mansion, having returned the lady's necklace and been rewarded with snifters of forty-year-old brandy, memorable embraces, and an invitation to come back anytime they were in the neighborhood.

Wish drove. Bell was silent all the way into Chicago. They returned the auto to the stable where they had rented it and walked toward Black's Social to get some late-night breakfast.

'Did you ever pretend to be a cop?' asked Bell, aware that Van Dorn regulations forbid it.

Wish shrugged. 'Only when necessary.'

'What's the trick?'

'In the words of the safecracker, act cocksure, swaggering and arrogant.'

'Did you find it difficult?'

Wish grinned. 'Would I be immodest to claim that arrogance did not come natural?'

'Otherwise you acted yourself?'

'I focused on cocksure. Any cop, good, bad or indifferent, has to be cocksure to be taken seriously.'

'Like us,' said Bell.

'Except when we disguise ourselves as someone with a lower profile than a cop.'

'A detective,' said Bell.

'Beg pardon?'

'Ten-to-one, our provocateur is a private detective.'

'Why not a cop?'

'What cop could operate days apart in Gleasonburg, New York and Chicago? Policemen can't travel. They're locked in their jurisdiction. But we can go anywhere in the country. That's why Joe Van Dorn is opening field offices. Cops are stuck at home. We're not, and neither is this guy. He's a private detective.'

Wish Clarke nodded thoughtfully. 'Son, I keep saying you're getting the hang of this detecting line and you keep proving me right. He could most certainly be a detective. In fact, I'd bet on it.'

Bell asked, 'Have you noticed we have three fellows sticking close behind us?'

'If you're referring to the short, fat, and tall gents in bowler hats, they latched on to us where we left the auto.'

'The short ugly one was hanging around Black's.'

They started across the Harrison Street jackknife bridge. Wish pretended to admire the elaborate ironwork of the lift towers and glanced back. 'The fat ugly one was stuffing his face at Little's lunch.'

'Do you happen to have your coach gun in your bag?' Bell asked.

'Right on top.'

'How about you stop to tie your shoelace?'

Wish knelt and opened his carpetbag. 'Move a hair behind me, Isaac. She spreads wide.'

'Cops,' said Bell.

Three in blue coats and tall helmets coming up behind the men following them. The tallest had a handlebar mustache.

Wish Clarke had worked Chicago long enough to ask, 'Whose team?'

Bell said, 'That's Officer "Muldoon" in the middle. Looks like they were freelancing earlier.'

'And finishing the job here.'

Wish counted heads. 'Six of them, two of us. We have to pull off a couple of triple plays, Isaac. Or is that Harry O'Hagan I hear galloping to our rescue?'

The answer came in the thunder of iron-shod hooves, and it was not the first baseman but two gigantic horses dragging a paddy wagon around the corner on the far side of the bridge.

28

The men in bowlers followed Isaac Bell and Wish Clarke on to the bridge. Moving in unison like a drill team, they drew press-button knives and released the blades with a simultaneous click that the detectives heard twenty feet away.

The cops led by Muldoon stopped under the lift towers, blocking that side.

The paddy wagon driver wheeled his horses across Harrison Street, barricading the other side.

Wish left his coach gun in his bag.

'It appears that the forces of the law have come to watch a knife fight.'

'Neutral observers,' said Bell.

'Unless we introduce firearms.'

'In which case,' said Bell, 'the cops will shoot us.'

'How you fixed for knives?'

'A little throwing steel in my boot.'

'I'd hold on to that as a last resort,' said Wish, rummaging in his bag. 'Well, look here. Would you like a Bowie knife?' He pulled a twelve-inch blade sharpened on both sides from its fancy worked-leather sheath.

'How many do you have?'

'Just the one. Flip a coin?'

'Keep it,' said Isaac Bell. 'I'll borrow one of theirs.'

He went straight at them at full speed, eyes locked like

binoculars on the tall man in the middle. Five feet away, Bell feinted a kick at the fat man on the right, launched off his left foot and pivoted a half circle away from him. His right boot grazed the nose of the man in the middle and smashed the face of the short man on the left, who dropped as if poleaxed.

Isaac Bell snatched his knife off the deck. 'Thank you.'

Wish was beside him in a rush, Bowie knife slashing the air like a saber. 'Run for it, boys, while you still have faces.'

Fat & Ugly lunged with startling speed and skill. His blade plunged into the space where Wish Clarke had been an instant earlier. The razor edge of the Bowie knife parted his coat sleeve and tore the flesh of his forearm from his elbow to his hand. He dropped his knife, screamed, clutched his arm, and ran.

That left the tall man in the middle. His eyes flicked from Bell's slim blade to the blood dripping from Wish's Bowie. He shoved his blade at Wish. Isaac Bell chopped down with all his strength. The knife he had taken pierced the attacker's hand and stuck there as the man reeled away.

Wish Clarke gave a harsh laugh. 'Now all we have is to reason with the police – *Look out, Isaac!*'

29

The blade came out of nowhere.

The first man down, the man on the left whom Isaac Bell had kicked unconscious, awakened in a flash and lurched to his feet, gripping the knife that had fallen beside him and driving it toward the young detective's ribs.

Bell tried to twist aside, but the blade kept coming and there was nothing he could do to avoid it. Just as suddenly as it had blazed at him, it disappeared, blocked by Wish Clarke, who grunted and staggered back, clutching his side.

Isaac Bell slammed a fist that started at his knees up against the attacker's jaw, tumbling him over the side of the bridge and into the river. He caught his friend as he fell. 'Wish!'

'I'm OK. I'm OK.'

But he was not. Bell could feel his big body go slack.

He made sure no arteries were cut. Thank God, there was no blood pumping from the wounded side. Then he slung Wish over his shoulder, picked up his carpetbag, and stalked to the paddy wagon blocking the bridge.

The driver and the officer riding shotgun stared down at him.

Isaac Bell said, 'Odds are, your precinct captain is an old pal of our boss, Joe Van Dorn. You sure as hell don't want him to hear you're freelancing tonight.'

The driver looked across the bridge. Muldoon and company were shuffling their feet but not coming to help. 'You're right about that.'

'Drive us direct to the hospital and we'll be square.'

'Jake,' the driver told his shotgun, 'hop down and make the gentlemen comfortable in back.'

Bell laid Wish on a long bench and knelt beside it to keep him from rolling off. The driver whipped up his team, and the paddy wagon lurched through the city.

'Stop trying to talk,' Bell told Wish.

Wish beckoned him closer.

'I said, that mustache is working like I said it would.'

Aloysius Clarke woke up at dawn and looked around the private room Isaac Bell had paid for. 'What are you doing here?' he asked Bell.

'Wish, what do you mean what am I doing here? You saved my life.'

'Heck, you did the same for me in New Orleans.'

'I didn't step in front of a knife.'

Wish shrugged, which made him wince. 'You're making a mountain out of a molehill.' Then he winked. 'Fact is, I enjoy the occasional wound. Nobody complains when I take a little something for the pain.'

Bell passed him his flask.

'How bad am I?'

'Doc says a couple of weeks in bed ought to do you.'

'Sorry, Isaac. I'll catch up as soon as I can. You going to Pittsburgh?'

'Just stopping at Union Station to see Mack and Wally and Archie on my way to New York.'

'Why New York?'

'Report to the Boss.'

'What happened to the telegraph?'

'I want to see his face when I tell him what I'm thinking.'

Mary Higgins felt like she was falling backwards in her nightmare.

But she knew for sure that she was not dreaming. And she certainly was not sleeping. She was too cold and wet to sleep. Besides, who could sleep standing up, much less slogging along a road that had turned to mud?

Suddenly, screams pierced the dark, worse than any nightmare.

'They're coming!'

'They're coming!'

A glaring white light almost as bright as a locomotive raced straight at them. Men and women scurried off the road, dragging their children into the ditches and shoving them through the hedges. Eight huge white firehorses galloped up the road towing a freight wagon on which the Coal and Iron Police mounted a gasoline dynamo and an electric searchlight. Its only purpose was to terrorize. The miners' wives had named it the Cyclops.

Their march was twenty miles short of Pittsburgh, and they were pressing on through the night, hoping to reach a farm where philanthropists and progressive church people were erecting a tent city. In this place, they dreamed, they would find hot food and dry blankets.

When the Cyclops had gone and Mary was helping people to their feet, a deep despair descended upon her. The cause seemed hopeless. But worse than her fear that the march and the strikes would achieve nothing was the bleak realization there existed in the world a brand of human being that wanted to attack with something as diabolically cruel as the Cyclops. *A tiny, tiny minority*, her brother always said, but he was wrong. It had taken many to dream up such a monstrosity, many to build it, and many, many more to allow it.

'*Cyclops!*'

Again it roared, blazing through the night, and again they jumped. From the ditch, Mary Higgins caught a fleeting glimpse of the horses as they galloped ahead of the light, nostrils flaring, eyes bulging, heads thrashing against their harness, terrified by the whip, the dark and the screaming.

It was still raining when the last of the marchers straggled into the tent city at dawn. Mary was last, carrying a child in one arm and propping up the mother, a woman with a racking cough. She was surprised when church ladies, who looked like they had never missed a meal or ironed their own linen, rushed to help. They took the child and the mother to a makeshift infirmary and directed Mary to a soup kitchen under a stretched tarpaulin. Hundreds of people had lined up to eat, and she had just found the tail end when John Claggart appeared out of nowhere and pressed into her cold hands a mug of hot coffee that smelled better than seemed possible.

Claggart had men with him. They were dressed like miners. But none, she noticed, looked like they worked with their hands, and she recognized the flash operators who hung around prize rings, pool halls and racetracks. She saw in their eyes their contempt for the miners.

'Who are those men?' she asked.

'Not choirboys,' Claggart replied boldly. 'But they'll get the job done.'

The word *accomplices* wormed its way into her mind.

'Criminals?' she asked.

Claggart shrugged. 'It's not for me to judge. But I'll bet that you and your brother know plenty of men who have been railroaded into prison for fighting the good fight.'

'Those I know,' she said, 'don't resemble criminals.'

Claggart said, 'Give me a brave man, quick on his feet, and I don't care what you call him as long as he knows that the bosses are the real bums. Now, listen carefully. I have more barges tied along the banks and more boats to move them into the channel.'

'Missed your spittoon. Sorry, Chief.'

Henry Clay recognized the brown trail of tobacco juice that soiled his pale blue Aubusson carpet for what it was, a challenge by a thug who had never lost a fight and was too stupid to imagine that he ever would. A dozen of them – all blood-oath members of the Hudson Dusters, a West Side New York docks gang – had crowded into his front office through the back hall. He would never permit these scum in his private rooms. Most didn't know him from Adam. All they knew was their boss had ordered them to appear for a special job. But now, instead of quietly listening to Clay's orders, they were snickering at the mess on his carpet.

The spitter's second mistake was to underestimate a Wall Street swell just because he wore a splendid suit of clothes. Clay stood up. The Dusters' boss and his enforcer exchanged expectant glances. Pain was about to be suffered.

'What's your name?' Clay asked.

'What's it to you?'

'Tell him your name,' said the boss, signaling Clay that he had no desire to get in the middle.

'Albert,' said the thug, watching with amusement as Clay walked closer.

'Not to worry about missing the spittoon, Albert. Just lick it up.'

'What?'

'Lick it up.'

'Go –'

Clay hit him high, low and in between, then put him in a hammerlock, slammed him face-down on the floor, and jerked his pinioned arm higher and higher until the gangster screamed. Eventually, his screams turned to pleas. Clay jerked harder. Pleas dissolved into sobs.

Clay let go.

'Don't bother licking it up, Albert. We know you would, and that's all that matters.'

Eleven Hudson Dusters laughed.

'All right, boyos, you're here because I have a strong feeling that I am going to have an angry caller bursting into my office. When he arrives, I want you to beat him slowly to a pulp. Make what happened to Albert here seem like a friendly wrestling match.'

'When's he coming?'

'Soon. Meantime, there's a spread laid out in the back room and cots where you can nap. Don't get drunk, don't molest my staff, and don't spit on the carpet. Is that clear?'

'Yes, sir.'

After they had trooped out, Clay unlocked his private office and focused his telescope on Judge Congdon's window. The Judge was hard at work, bullying someone on the telephone. Clay put on his hat, bid his staff farewell, went down to the street, entered the Congdon Building and rode the elevator to the top floor.

Congdon kept him waiting half an hour. When he did allow him into his office, he said, 'I'm busy. Make this quick.'

'This may be my last report in person for a while,' said Clay.

Somehow, Isaac Bell had survived. Clay blamed himself. He had made a rare mistake sending assassins instead of doing the job himself and he had no option but to pay the price.

'What's wrong?' Congdon demanded.

'Suffice it to say that events are on schedule.'

30

Isaac Bell reported to Joseph Van Dorn in Van Dorn's office twenty minutes after the Pennsylvania Railroad ferry landed at Twenty-third Street.

'I'm afraid Wish got stabbed. The blade missed his vitals, but it was a shock to his system, and he's out of commission for weeks.'

'Stabbing Aloysius Clarke used to be near impossible. I've warned the man a hundred times that drink would slow him down.'

'Not drink,' Bell answered coldly. 'He took a knife meant for me.'

Van Dorn lowered his gaze. 'Sorry, Isaac. I should not have said that. He'll be OK?'

'I found him the best doctor in Chicago.'

'The agency will pay for it.'

'I already have.'

They sat silent for a moment, Bell biding his time until Van Dorn felt impelled to speak.

'How'd you make out with Rosania?'

'As I hoped. He is indeed studying shaped charges. And so is our provocateur.'

'Is that so?'

'Rosania actually ran into him up in Newport outside the Torpedo Station.'

'You're sure Rosania wasn't having you on?'

223

'Positive. He described a man who looked very much like the one I've seen. He thought he had a Chicago accent, but he swore he'd never seen him before.'

'So if he was from Chicago, he was gone before Rosania went into business.'

'Judging by what Wish and I ran up against, he's stayed on speaking terms with the Chicago police.'

Van Dorn shrugged. 'Money talks to Chicago cops.'

'You're friends with some, sir. Could you ask around?'

'We won't stay friends if I just go fishing. Do you happen to have a name I could lay on them?'

'His name is a bit of a dead end so far,' Bell admitted and fell silent again.

At length, Van Dorn asked, 'Where's the rest of your gang?'

'Weber and Fields are in Pittsburgh with Archie. Mack discovered a county sheriff is making secret arrangements to extradite union leaders back to West Virginia for the murder of Black Jack Gleason.'

Van Dorn gave an admiring whistle. 'Mack must have burrowed mighty deep into the sheriff's office to find that.'

'Wally claims that the sheriff's girlfriend took a shine to Mack.'

'I'd have thought Mack's seducing days were over.'

'And Wally's collected rumors of a radical attack on the railroads.'

'What sort?'

'Trestle bombings, Wally thinks.'

Van Dorn shook his head. 'Lunatics.'

'Plenty of lunacy to go around. Pittsburgh is bracing for the marchers. Half the Monongahela Valley is joining up along the route. So the Pinkertons and the Coal and Iron Police are offering a bounty for city prisoners released early to fight the strikers.'

'Good God! How'd your squad find that out?'

'Archie infiltrated the Coal and Iron Police.'

'He's only an apprentice.'

'Archie convinced them he's on the lam from Idaho for beating a miner to death with his fists. They welcomed him like a brother.'

'That is very dangerous for an apprentice to be alone inside. Too dangerous. What if they tumble to him? He doesn't have the experience to see it coming, and with no one to back him up, God knows what will happen.'

'Anyone who challenges Archie Abbott's boxing skills will quickly cease to doubt his story.'

'I'll shake Archie's hand, but I want you to take him off that job.'

'Don't worry. I've already shifted Archie from the Coal and Iron Police to shadow someone slightly less dangerous.'

'Who?'

'You want to know what Mary Higgins is up to. Well, so do I.'

'Any hint?'

'She's back in Pittsburgh. And she still refuses Van Dorn protection. That's why I put Archie on her.'

Van Dorn gave a faint smile. 'You must trust your friend immensely to let him shadow a girl you're sweet on – don't bother denying that.'

Bell grinned back. 'I'm hoping that Archie recalls the only boxing match he lost.'

'Back to business. What's your next step?'

The mirth left the young detective's face. He looked the Boss in the eye. 'I am about to identify the provocateur.'

'You are?'

'With your help.'

'Me? How?'

'Start by looking at this.'

Bell's hand flicked to his boot. He laid his throwing knife on Van Dorn's desk.

'I'm looking at it. What about it?'

'You gave it to me.'

'I give one to all my apprentices.'

'The man who got the drop on me in the Tombs cellar was packing the same knife.'

'Shows he knows his business. It's a good one.'

'It was identical.'

'I get them from a cutler in Connecticut. His craftsmen turn out thousands. What are you up to, Isaac?'

Bell said, 'This man knows a lot about me. He knew about my sleeve gun.'

Joseph Van Dorn looked amused. 'Isaac, if you were a stranger and I ran up against you in a dark cellar, I'd check for a sleeve gun so quick it would make your head spin.'

'He also knew about the one-shot in my pocket.'

'You can bet I'd look for one of those, too. Though, first, I'd inspect your shoulder holster – remove the heavy artillery.'

'He did that, too. First.'

'Like I say, everything you reported about him suggests a fellow who can handle himself.'

Bell picked up his throwing knife. He balanced it on

one finger and flicked it gently with another to make the light play on it.

'Mr Van Dorn, do you remember who taught me how to throw a knife?'

Van Dorn laughed. 'I tried. But you were so damned bullheaded, you insisted on that overhand throw they taught you in the circus.'

'It's got more power. The knife travels farther and hits harder.'

'Overhand looks fancy,' Van Dorn shot back. 'But it's slower and not as accurate.'

'Than what?'

'*Than what?* You know what. What are you talking about?'

'Say it, please.'

Van Dorn gave him a puzzled look. At length, quizzical wrinkles furrowed his brow as it dawned on him that his young detective was asking for a reason. 'Sidearm. Overhand is slower than a sidearm. And, in my experience, less accurate.'

'Speaking of accurate, his main artillery is a Colt Bisley.'

A peculiar look flickered across Van Dorn's face. He tugged reflexively at his beard.

'Yes,' he said slowly. 'As I said, a professional through and through.'

'Mr Van Dorn, you know this man.'

'If I know him, I'll get him. Who is he?'

'I don't know his name.'

'What does he look like?'

'Big fellow. Broad in the shoulders. Light on his feet.'

'What color hair?'

'I don't know.'

'Eyes?'

'He's got yellow eyes.'

Van Dorn stared. 'Are you sure?'

'I saw them.'

'Did Rosania?'

'Rosania was not quite as sure. But I saw them twice. In the coal mine. And in the Tombs. Yellow and gold, almost like a wolf.'

Van Dorn surged to his feet and grabbed his hat.

'Where are you going?'

'I'll take care of this.'

'I'll come with you.'

'Stay where you are!' Van Dorn shouted. 'I'll take care of it myself.'

He pushed so hard out the door that it banged against the wall of the detectives' bull pen, knocking street maps and wanted posters askew. When he shoved through the hall door, frosted glass shattered. Then he was gone, storming down the hotel's grand stairs, barreling across the lobby, and shouting on Broadway, 'Cab! You there. Stop now!'

He leaped aboard, next to the driver.

'Wall Street!'

By the time Bell reached the sidewalk, the cab careened around the corner on one wheel, and the horse broke into a gallop.

'Wall Street!' the hotel doormen told Isaac Bell Mr Van Dorn had bellowed at the cabbie.

Bell ran full tilt to Sixth Avenue, climbed the steep covered stairs to the Elevated three at a time, and reached the platform just as a downtown train pulled away. The next seemed like it would never come.

31

Isaac Bell jumped off the El at the Rector Street stop, pounded down the stairs and across Rector, cut through Trinity Church's cemetery, and bolted across Broadway, dodging six lanes of streetcars, wagons, autos, freight vans and carriages. He stopped at the head of Wall Street, praying he had gotten there before Joe Van Dorn. He had never seen the Boss so disturbed and knew his rage would make him reckless, which was a dangerous state in which to confront the provocateur.

But now that he was here, how to find him?

Wall Street stretched nearly half a mile between the soot-blackened graves in Trinity's cemetery to the East River docks and was lined on both sides by innumerable buildings. The cab Van Dorn had hailed was one of thousands of identical black horse-drawn two-wheelers, and all that Bell had seen of the driver was a wizened man in a black coat and a flat cap.

Many cabbies wore a tall black stovepipe. He could eliminate them as he ran down Wall Street. But his best clue would be an exhausted horse with its coat lathered from galloping top speed from Forty-third Street. He found one in the second block, forelegs spread wide, head down, flanks heaving.

'Ready in a jiff, sir,' the driver called. 'He's not so bad as he looks. Just catching his breath.' He jerked the reins to pull its head up.

Bell kept running. The driver was wearing a top hat.

A block down, a crowd had gathered in the street, blocking traffic. Bell pushed through it. He saw a hansom cab with its traces empty. A horse was in the street, down on the cobblestones. A wizened man in a flat cap knelt beside it, stroking its face.

Bell pushed beside him and pressed ten dollars into his hand. 'For the vet. Where did your fare go?'

The cabbie pointed mutely at a small, well-kept office building.

Bell ran to it, shouted to the doorman, 'Big fellow, red hair and beard?'

'Blew past me like a maddened grizzly.'

Bell ran into the lobby and grabbed the elevator runner. 'Big man. Red beard. What floor?'

The runner hesitated and looked away.

Bell seized his tunic in his fist. 'That man is valuable to me. *What floor?*'

'Tenth.'

'Take me.'

'Mister, I don't think you ought to go up there.'

Bell shoved him out of the car, slammed the gate shut, and rammed the control to rise at full speed. He overshot the tenth, brought it back down, threw the door open, and leaped out into the shambles of a business office. Chairs and desks were tumbled everywhere, glass was shattered, and five men in colorful gangster garb lay still on the carpet.

Five more were gripping Joseph Van Dorn by his arms

and legs. A sixth was swinging wildly at his face. The man's fists had already blackened his eye and split his lip, but Van Dorn had not seemed to notice as he battled to free his arms.

Bell pulled his Army and fired two shots into the ceiling. 'Next are in your bellies,' he roared. 'Let that man go.'

The gangsters were not easily intimidated. None moved, except the man who had been punching Van Dorn. He reached into his pocket. Bell fired instantly. The heavy .45 slug threw the gangster into a wall.

'Let him loose.'

'Mister, if we let him loose, he'll start up again.'

'Count on it,' Van Dorn bellowed.

Bell fired, dropping a man who pulled a revolver from his belt. The others let go. Van Dorn slugged two, as he barreled across the wrecked office, and kicked a fallen man who was starting to rise with a knife. Shoulder to shoulder with Isaac Bell, Van Dorn drew a heavy automatic pistol from his coat.

'Louses started swinging the second I came in the door.'

'Where's our man?'

'Not with these street scum. All right, boyos. You were waiting for me, weren't you?'

No one answered.

'Where is he?' Van Dorn shouted. 'Where is that son of a bitch?'

A weaselly little man with a swollen eye and no teeth whined, 'Mister, we're just doing a job. We didn't mean no harm.'

'Eleven men ganging one?' Isaac Bell asked incredulously. 'No harm?'

'We was just supposed to beat him up.'

'Shut up, Marvyn.'

A gangster, a little older than the rest and clearly the boss, stepped forward and said, 'If you know what's good for you, you two, you'll just turn around and leave like nothing happened.'

'Cover them.' Van Dorn passed Bell his automatic. Bell leveled both guns at the gangsters. Van Dorn picked up a telephone off the floor.

'Central? Get me the police.'

'Hey, what are you doing?'

'Pressing charges.'

'That's not how it's done.'

'I'll promise you this,' Van Dorn retorted coldly. 'Next time you try to beat up a Van Dorn, we *won't* press charges. We'll throw you in the river.'

'But—'

'Answer this! Where did Clay go?'

'I don't know. He doesn't tell me where he goes.'

'Where's the people who worked in his office?'

'Ran for it when this rumpus started.'

'How long have you worked for Clay?'

'Years.'

Joseph Van Dorn was still holding the telephone and still breathing hard. 'How long were you waiting for me?'

'Two days – Mister, you ain't gonna call the cops, are youse?'

Van Dorn said, 'You'll owe?'

'Sure.'

'Make no mistake. If you give me your marker, I'll collect.'

'I ain't a welsher.'

'OK, I'll take you at your word. You pick up your boys and leave quietly. Got a man who does bullet wounds?'

'Sure.'

'All right. You owe me.'

'Me, too,' growled Isaac Bell.

'Hear that?' Van Dorn pointed at Bell. 'Him, too. Whenever we come to you with a question, you'll give us a straight answer. Square?'

'Square,' said the gangster. 'Want to shake on it?'

'Get out of here!'

The Hudson Dusters carried their fallen down the back stairs.

Joseph Van Dorn gave Isaac Bell a tight grin. 'Heck of a scrap. Thanks, Isaac. Saved my bacon.'

'Who is Clay?'

'Henry Clay. A private detective.' Van Dorn pointed at a brass wall plaque that was smeared with the blood of a gangster Bell had shot. 'Henry Clay Investigations Agency.'

'What is he to you?'

'My first apprentice,' said Van Dorn.

Bell glanced around the demolished office. 'Turned out to be a disappointment?'

'In spades.'

'How did he know you were coming?'

'Henry Clay is about the most intelligent man I have ever met. I am not surprised he knew I was coming. He has an uncanny ability to see the future.'

'A psychic?'

'Not in any mystical way. But he is so alert – sees much

more clearly than ordinary men in the present – that it gives him a leg up on the future. Darned-near clairvoyant.'

Van Dorn looked over the wreckage of what had been a first-class office and shook his head in what seemed to Isaac Bell to be sadness. 'So gifted,' he mused. 'So intelligent. Henry Clay could have been the best detective in America.'

'I'm not sure how intelligent,' said Bell. 'He disguised nothing about his past. He practically handed it to me on a silver platter.'

Van Dorn nodded. 'Almost like he wanted to be caught.'

'Or noticed.'

'Yes, that was always his flaw. He was so hungry for applause – but Isaac?' Van Dorn gripped Bell's arm for emphasis. 'Never, ever underestimate him.'

Bell wove through an obstacle course of broken furniture and tried a door marked *Private*. It was locked. He knelt in front of the knob and applied his picks, then stepped aside abruptly.

'What's the matter?'

'Too easy.'

Van Dorn handed him a broken table leg. They stood on either side of the door, and Bell shoved it with the leg. The door flew inward. A twelve-gauge shotgun thundered, and buckshot screeched where he would have been standing as he pushed it open.

Bell glanced inside. Blue smoke swirled around a wood-paneled office. The shotgun was clamped to a desk, aimed at the doorway. Rope, pulleys and a deadweight had triggered the weapon.

'Heck of a parting shot.'

'Told you not to underestimate him.'

'That was on my mind.'

They went through Clay's desk and inspected his files carefully.

Not a word or a piece of paper applied to current cases.

'I've never seen so many telephone and telegraph lines in one office,' said Bell. 'It's a virtual central exchange station.'

Closer inspection showed every wire had been cut.

'He did not run in haste.'

'No, sir. He took his own sweet time. I doubt he's out of commission.'

Van Dorn said, 'I cannot imagine Clay out of commission until he wants to be. He'll regard having to flee as a minor setback.'

Bell put his eye to a handsome brass telescope that was mounted on a tripod in the window. It angled upward and focused on a penthouse office atop the tallest building on the block. A storklike figure was pacing back and forth, dictating, apparently to a secretary seated below the sight line. As the man turned, his face filled the glass, and Isaac Bell recognized the financier Judge James Congdon from scores of newspaper sketches.

'Clay spied on his neighbors.'

Van Dorn took a look. 'Who's that?'

'Congdon.'

'Oh yes, of course.' Van Dorn pivoted the telescope, sweeping it side to side. 'I'll be. You can see into twenty offices. You know, Clay's a heck of a lip-reader. Probably how he paid for these digs. A man could make a pretty penny knowing what Wall Street's got on its mind.'

'You know him, sir. What will he do next?'

'I told you, I don't see him throwing in the towel.'

'Is he the sort of man who would take pleasure in provoking bloodshed?'

'Only for profit.'

'Profit or acclaim?'

'Smart question, Isaac. Acclaim.' Van Dorn swung the telescope at the Wall Street buildings. 'He wants to be one of them.'

'Which of them do you suppose he's working for?'

'A man wise enough to take account of Henry Clay's talents and greedy enough to employ them.'

BOOK THREE
Steam

32

Isaac Bell rejoined his squad in Pittsburgh. After he had filled in Wally Kisley, Mack Fulton and Archie Abbott on events in New York, Archie parroted a favorite Weber and Fields saying:

'A poke in the snoot means you're getting close.'

'If we were close,' said Bell, 'we would know what Henry Clay is going to do next. But we don't have a clue. Nor do we know who gives him his orders. All we know is, we have a bloody-minded provocateur serving a ruthless boss.'

Dressed like a wealthy Southern banker, in a white suit, a straw planter's hat and rose-tinted glasses, Henry Clay pretended to admire the launchways of the bankrupt Held & Court Shipyard of Cincinnati. Scores of rails ran side by side down a muddy slope into the Ohio River, and the owner of the yard – foppish young Mr Court Held, who was anxious to borrow money or sell out, or both – boasted that his family had been launching side-paddle steamers and stern-wheelers down those rails for sixty years.

'Ah suppose you-all have the hang of it by now?' said Clay, laying a Deep South drawl on thick as he pleased. Not only was Court Held desperate, but repeated inter-marriage among the founding families had bequeathed his generation the brainpower of a gnat.

'Yes, sir. In fact, crane your neck around that bend and you'll see fine examples of our product.'

Henry Clay had already looked around that bend.

'I would like very much to see a large steamboat.'

Held & Court had two of the biggest paddleboats left over from the steamboat age that ended when fast, modern railroads rendered leisurely travel passé. Nimbler Cincinnati shipyards still boomed, launching by the hundreds utilitarian stern-wheelers that pushed coal barge tows. Numerous such workboats were churning the river white as Clay and the yard owner walked across the yard for a look around the bend. But Held & Court had persisted in building giant floating palaces until the last grand Mississippi riverboat companies went under.

'Behold, sir. *Vulcan King* and *White Lady*.'

They towered over their wharf. Four tall decks of painted wood, polished metal and cut glass were heaped upon broad, flat hulls three hundred feet long. Topping their decks were glass pilothouses near the front, and soaring about the pilothouses were twin black chimneys with flaring tops. Each boat was propelled by a giant stern wheel forty feet in diameter and fifty feet wide.

'We installed the latest triple expansion engines.'

The *White Lady* was appropriately white.

'She's the prettier one, don't you think? A brag boat, sure as shootin'.'

The *Vulcan King* was painted a dull blue-gray color. It was this more somber of the vessels that had brought Henry Clay to Cincinnati.

'Which has the reinforced decks?'

'Where'd you hear about reinforced decks?' the owner demanded. 'That's a government secret.'

Henry Clay returned a smile much colder than his drawl. 'Ah believe a United States senatah acquaintance confided War Department plans to dispatch a shallow-water gunboat to Cuba. Although it could have been my friend the admiral who told me about the cannon and the Maxim gun.'

'Well, then, you know the sad story,' said the shipyard owner. 'A darn shame that the Spanish War ended too soon. We were just fixing to mount the cannon when the War Department canceled the order.'

'Which boat?'

'*Vulcan King*. The Navy said she couldn't be white, so we found this gray paint.'

'How much are you asking for her?'

The young heir blinked. No one had offered to buy a steamboat from Held & Court since the aborted gunboat scheme and that was four years past. 'Are you saying you want to *buy* her?'

'Ah'd consider it if the price is right.'

'Well, now. The *Vulcan King* cost the better part of four hundred thousand dollars to build.' He glanced at Clay and appeared to decide that this banker with friends in high places knew too much of her history to be fleeced. 'We would accept a rock-bottom price of seventy-five thousand.'

Clay asked, 'Can you have her coaled by morning and steam up?'

'I could certainly try.'

'Try?' Clay asked with a wintry scowl.

'Yes, sir! I'm sure I can do that. Coaled and steam up tomorrow morning.'

'Throw in the cannon and the Maxim, and you've got a deal.'

'What do you want her guns for?'

'Scrap steel,' said Henry Clay with a straight face. 'Defray the cost of a paint job.'

'Mighty fine idea. She'll look her best in white.'

Black, thought Henry Clay. Her gigantic stern wheel would thrash the river white. But while she steamed up the Ohio River to Pittsburgh, his crew would paint the *Vulcan King* black as the coal that fired her boilers.

The strikers who marched down the Monongahela River had cursed the cruel and heartless owners for abusing them with Clay's Cyclops. Terror bred anger. Hotheads shouted down the moderates, and the miners' Defense Committee had armed themselves, spending their meager treasury on repeating rifles. How rabidly would they rage at the grim sight of an evil-looking *Vulcan King* steaming up their river? How angrily would they seize the gauntlet thrown in their faces? How violently would they defend their tent city?

So violently – Henry Clay had promised Judge James Congdon, who had balked initially at buying a steamboat – so rabidly, that law-abiding Americans would offer grateful prayers in their church pews: God bless the mineowners for mounting Maxim guns and cannon to protect them from the mob. And newspapers would thunder, commanding the defenders of property to pull out all stops to crush the socialists before labor tore the nation asunder with a second civil war.

Court Held cleared his throat.

'As "steam up" implies, you intend to leave Cincinnati tomorrow. May I ask how do you intend to pay for her?'

Other than having satchels bulging with cash, it was always difficult to pony up an enormous sum of money in a distant city. It was even harder to do it quickly and anonymously. But there was a way. 'Obviously, I don't expect you to accept a check that would not clear until after I steam away. I can offer railroad bearer bonds in denominations of twenty-five thousand dollars.'

The shipbuilder looked uncomfortable. Bearer bonds were, in theory, negotiable as ready cash and a lot less cumbersome, but the holder had to hope that they were neither forgeries nor issued by an entity no longer in business.

'Would the issuing agent happen to have a branch office here in Cincinnati?'

Clay would prefer not to appear in that office, but he had no choice. 'Thibodeau & Marzen have a branch in Cincinnati. Why don't we go there now? They'll guarantee the good faith of the issuer, and you can get the bonds locked up safely in your bank.'

'Would Thibodeau & Marzen redeem them immediately?'

'I don't see why not. If you prefer to cash in, they will accommodate you.'

33

Mary Higgins walked fast from her Ross Street rooming house, down Fourth Avenue and across Smithfield, toward the waterfront. She was easy to track in the red scarf Isaac Bell had seen her buy from a peddler in New York. Even without it, how could he miss her erect carriage and determined stride?

In a factory town like Pittsburgh, workingman's clothing was the simplest disguise, and Wish Clarke always said, *Keep it simple*. To shadow Mary, Bell donned overcoat, overalls and boots, and covered his distinctive blond hair with a knitted watch cap.

Archie Abbott trailed Bell, alternately hanging behind and sprinting to catch up when he signaled. The streets were crowded with men and women pouring out of offices and banks and hurrying home from work, and Bell was teaching Archie what Wish Clarke had taught him: alternating their profile between one figure and two made them less conspicuous when Mary peered over her shoulder, which she did repeatedly as they neared the river.

She crossed First Avenue into a district of small factories and machine shops.

'So far, she's headed for the same place,' said Archie.

The soot-blacked trusses of the Smithfield Street Bridge spread graceful curves against the grimy sky. Instead of boarding a trolley to cross the Monongahela on the bridge or walking the footpath, Mary Higgins followed a street that circled alongside its stone piers and down to the riverbank.

'Just like yesterday,' Archie whispered in his ear. 'Now, watch.'

Barges were rafted ten deep into the channel and appeared to extend down the shore as far as the bridge at the Point – the tip of Pittsburgh where the Mon joined the Allegheny. They were empty, riding high on the water. Across the river, all but the lowest reaches of Mount Washington and the Duquesne Heights were lost in smoke. The sun had disappeared, and night was settling in quickly.

Mary Higgins took another look around.

'Down,' said Bell, and they ducked behind a wooden staircase that ran up the side of a building. When they raised their heads, Mary had climbed a ladder on to a barge and was walking on planks laid barge to barge toward the middle of the river.

'She has amazing balance,' said Archie.

'Her father was a tug captain. They lived on the boat.'

'I thought it was those long, long legs.'

Bell gave his friend a cold, dark look, and Archie shut up.

Mary crossed ten rows of barges and stepped down on to a workboat moored at the edge of the fleet. 'Was that boat there yesterday?' Bell asked.

'Right there. That's where she went.'

'How long did she stay on it?'

'An hour and four minutes.'

Bell nodded approvingly. Mack and Wally were teaching Archie to be precise in observation and report.

'Were these same barges here?'

'Yes.'

'How can you be sure? They all look alike.'

'You see the barge right smack in the middle with the white cookhouse sitting on it?' The apprentice detective indicated a painted shack with a stovepipe poking through the roof. 'Exactly where it was yesterday.'

Bell thought it strange that on such a busy river the empty barges had not been moved. He would expect them to be swarming with deckhands preparing for towboats to push them back up the Monongahela to move the coal being mined by scab labor. Even as he watched, a tow of empties bustled up the river from the harbor pool between the Point and Davis Island Dam, and an oversize towboat was pushing a loaded fleet of Amalgamated Coal's big Ohio River barges downstream.

'I tried to get closer,' said Archie. 'A watchman spotted me halfway across, and I thought I better run for it.'

'I'll take a shot at it,' Bell said. 'Give me a whistle if you see the watchman.'

He crossed the barges several rows down from the route Mary had taken, loping gunnel to gunnel as his eyes adjusted to the failing light. At the outside row, he drew close to the workboat, keeping an eye peeled for Mary and its crew. Its decks were empty. A thin wisp of smoke curled from its stack, indicating that steam was being kept up, but the boat wasn't going anywhere immediately. He smelled coffee.

Bell stayed on the barge and worked his way alongside the boat. A round port was open, spilling light from the cabin, and he could hear voices. He eased closer silently until he was perched beside the cabin. Mary was talking. She sounded angry.

'How much longer are we going to just sit here?'

'Until he gets back.'

'We should at least move the barges upstream. They're too far downriver to sink here. There's only one bridge below us.'

'Like I said, miss,' a man answered, 'we're not going anywhere without the boss's say-so.'

'Where *is* Mr Claggart?'

'Didn't say.'

'Did he say when he would return?'

'Nope.'

'Then I think we should begin on our own.'

'Sister,' another man interrupted with a smirk in his voice, '*we* ain't beginning nothing without the boss.'

'But there's more rain forecast. The water's rising. Soon it will be too deep. We can't just sit here doing nothing.'

'Nothing?' said the smirker. 'I'm not doing nothing. I might have a drink. In fact, maybe I'll have one right now.'

Bell heard the pop of a cork pulled from a bottle.

Mary said, 'You wouldn't dare in front of Mr Claggart.'

'Like you say, Mr Claggart ain't here – Hey!'

Bell heard a bottle smash.

'What the hell do you –' the smirker roared angrily.

Bell started to go to Mary's defense, then ducked as the cabin door flew open and she stalked out and climbed on to the nearest barge. Inside, he heard the first man shouting, 'Are you nuts? Let her go! If you touch her, Claggart'll kill you . . . Miss! Miss!'

A head popped out the door. Bell glimpsed the slick

hair and pinchback vest worn by a cardsharper or a race-track tout. 'He'll be back in two or three days. I wasn't supposed to tell you, but come back then. Don't you worry, we'll start sinking them the second he's here.'

Mary threw an icy, 'After you move them upriver' over her shoulder and kept going.

Bell pressed his face to the porthole. The second man, the smirker, was staring morosely at the broken bottle at his feet. He looked like a saloon bouncer who had seen better days. The gambler stepped back inside and shut the door. 'That is one angry woman.'

'I wouldn't want to be in Claggart's shoes when he gets back.'

'He can handle her.'

'Not if he changes his mind about sinking them barges.'

'You can bet your bottom dollar he won't change his mind.'

'What makes you so sure?'

'He's got a big plan. The barges are just a small piece of it.'

'Does she know that?'

'No.'

Mack and Wally set up shop in separate waterfront saloons near the Smithfield Bridge. Nowhere near as drunk as they looked, the detectives quickly made names for themselves as exceedingly generous, treating Monongahela towboat pilots and captains to round after round. Archie Abbott acted as runner, shuttling between them to exchange information and passing it on to Isaac Bell, who was glued to the front door of Mary Higgins's rooming house.

Bell weighed the value of confronting her to find out what exactly the talk of sinking barges meant. What did 'too far downriver' mean? And 'only one bridge'? Or would he learn more by waiting until 'Mr Claggart' returned? Waiting meant he would have to move in a flash to stop whatever they were up to. In the meantime, as he watched and waited, he tried to imagine what they thought they would accomplish by sinking barges.

Mack Fulton spelled him so he could catch some sleep.

Back in four hours, he found Wally Kisley there, too. Wally had just come from the Allegheny County sheriff's office. He had bad news about Jim Higgins.

Isaac Bell went looking for the union man.

The Van Dorn Protective Services agents reported that Higgins had gone missing.

34

'We're real sorry, Mr Bell. We turned our backs for one second, and he lit out like a rocket.'

Mike Flannery and Terry Fein had promoted him to 'Mr Bell,' he noted wryly, now that they had bungled the job of protecting a client being stalked by the Pinkertons, the Coal and Iron Police, and possibly an assassin hired by the Coal Trust to keep Higgins from testifying for the attorney general. Flattery would come next.

'Where did you see him last?'

'Amalgamated Coal Terminal.'

'What the heck was he doing up there?'

The Amalgamated transfer operation was three miles upriver from the Golden Triangle, Pittsburgh's business district, where Higgins and the Strike Committee had rented their union hall in a storefront under an old warehouse. It was fully seven miles downriver from the tent city where the Monongahela march had ground to a halt in a trolley park, shuttered since summer ended, on the outskirts of McKeesport.

'We don't know, Mr Bell. We went with him twice yesterday. He just stands and stares at it.'

'Why don't you look for him there?'

'He'll dodge us if he sees us coming,' said Mike.

Terry explained, 'When the march ran into trouble, he blamed us for getting in his way.'

'When all we're trying to do is make sure no one shoots the poor devil or shoves a knife in his ribs.'

'But he's always rattling on about what a fine fellow you are, Mr Bell, and we thought maybe if he saw you coming, he wouldn't run.'

Well-rehearsed flattery. 'OK, Mike, you watch his room. Terry, you watch the union hall. I'll go out and look for him.'

'Try the toast rack.'

The toast-rack trolley – an open-sided electric streetcar that Bell rode out from the Golden Triangle – ran on tracks that paralleled those of the Amalgamated Coal trains. Passing Amalgamated from the inland side, the trolley offered views of locomotives pushing empties under the tipple and snaking them out full, and occasional distant glimpses of the barge wharves that ringed the Point. The operation seemed to Bell to be mechanically perfect, as if each barge and railroad was a minute cog in an immense and smooth-running wheel. He jumped down when he saw Jim Higgins standing at a trolley stop with his hands in his pockets.

'How you getting on, pardner?'

'Not good, Isaac. Not good at all.'

'What's wrong?'

'The mineowners armed every bum with a gun. Then they let the jailbirds out and gave them ax handles. They're blocking the march, and the hotheads are yelling, "Let the working people take guns and shoot down the dogs who shoot them!"'

Bell said, 'If they do, the governor will call up militia with rifles and Gatling guns.'

'I know that. In fact, he's already put them on alert. But the hotheads are talking each other out of the good sense to be afraid.'

'Mike and Terry told me you gave 'em the slip.'

'I need solitude to think.'

'They also told me you find something attractive about this Amalgamated operation.'

'It's about as up-to-date as can be,' Higgins answered vaguely. He glanced away from the tall detective's probing gaze and changed the subject. 'Somehow, I've got to convince the Strike Committee to stand up to the hotheads.'

'I'm afraid I've got bad news on that score,' said Bell.

'Now what?'

'The Strike Committee was just rousted on to a special train headed for Morgantown, West Virginia.'

'What?'

'The Allegheny County sheriff extradited them to stand trial for the murder of Black Jack Gleason.'

Jim Higgins's shoulders sagged. 'They didn't blow up Gleason's yacht.'

'I'm sure they didn't,' said Bell, 'since they were in Chicago at the time. But proving that will take months.'

Higgins looked around for a place to sit, saw none, and stared helplessly at Isaac Bell. 'Now it's all on me,' he said. 'But they've got me blocked at every turn.'

'Maybe Mary can help.'

Higgins shook his head. 'I don't think so.'

'Do you know what she's up to?' Bell asked bluntly.

'She's gone her own way.'

Bell asked, 'Is she in danger?'

'If I believed in God, I'd say, God knows.' Jim Higgins

lifted his eyes to the giant tipple. Suddenly, to Bell's astonishment, he straightened his shoulders and stood tall. A
thin smile crossed his face, expressing, Isaac Bell thought,
a sad farewell to hope or a final good-bye to illusions.

'Whoever built this tipple knows his business. He's got
himself the center of coal distribution, east, west, north
and south.'

'It's efficient,' said Bell. 'I hear he's putting the smaller
coal yards out of business.'

'This point of land would have made a beautiful park.'

'I beg pardon, Jim?'

'Water on three sides, the way the river snakes around
it. Just a short trolley ride from town. Imagine a great big
Ferris wheel where the tipple is. Picnic grounds. Swimming pool. Carousel. Baseball diamonds. A racecourse.
You could hold revival meetings. And Chautauqua assem-
blies.'

Isaac Bell looked up at the coal smoke matting the sky.
'You would need a lot of imagination.'

'But imagine our tent city here instead of down in
McKeesport. Winter's coming. If we could occupy this
place, we could shut it down. Industry's furnaces will
starve for fuel, and city dwellers freeze in their homes.'

'You sound like your sister,' said Bell.

'Maybe they'll listen to us then . . .' He turned eagerly to
Bell. 'We wouldn't have to shut it down. Once we were
here and *could* shut it down, they would see our position
and have to bargain. If we could threaten that shutdown,
we'd settle a fair agreement and all go back to work.'

'That could happen,' Bell said neutrally. An Army general might see a certain raw genius to Higgins's idea:

surrounded by water on three sides, the Amalgamated Coal Terminal's point of land would be easier than most encampments to defend. A Navy admiral would see a trap, sitting ducks exposed to gunfire on three sides.

'But how do I move ten thousand miners from McKeesport to here with strikebreakers, company cops and militia blocking the way?'

Bell was mindful of his orders not to take sides but concerned that Jim Higgins was turning a blind eye to the danger. He asked, 'Would the men leave their families behind?'

Jim Higgins shook his head. 'No . . . but, Isaac, this must be done. I have to find a way to move them here.'

'The risks are enormous. Women. Children.'

'It's more risky leaving them where they are. The camp is a shambles at McKeesport. It's just a trolley park. A bunch of picnic tables, a swimming hole and some shuttered-up amusement rides. You know, for working people to ride out on Sunday and have fun in good weather.'

Bell nodded. All around the country, trolley companies were building parks at the ends of their lines to get paying passengers on their day off. 'But how did the marchers get in?'

'McKeesport cops looked the other way. They were glad to keep us out of the city. But now the trolley company is threatening to shut off the water and electricity. It's a mess – too many people, more and more every day, no sanitation and no way to care for the sick. But here, we would be inside Pittsburgh's city limits. There are hospitals and doctors and food and clean water nearby.

Churches and charities to help and newspaper reporters to witness. Wouldn't they temper the actions of the strike-breakers?'

'But to get here, you have to run the gauntlet of militia and those "bums" and "jailbirds." You could set off a massacre.'

'That's a chance we'll have to take,' Higgins fired back. His jaw set, his spine stiffened, and Isaac Bell saw that the mild-mannered union man had made up his mind to fight a fight he shouldn't – a pitched battle with strikebreaking thugs and company police backed up by state militia.

Overriding his own better judgment and ignoring Joseph Van Dorn's direct orders, the young detective said, 'I know a better way.'

'What way?'

'Black Jack Gleason's way.'

35

'Me and Mack is too old for the Boss to fire,' said Wally Kisley. 'Even for backing you in a stunt like you're proposing. And Joe Van Dorn won't fire Archie, he's just a dumb apprentice – no offense, Archie.'

'None taken. My classics professor at Princeton expressed a similar opinion in heroic hexameter.'

'But you, Isaac, you're just starting out. You can't afford to be fired – I know you're rich, and *you* know I'm not talking about money. If you want to continue working as a private detective, there ain't a better outfit for a young fellow to learn his business than Van Dorn. But, make no mistake: if he catches you in the middle of this, he'll fire you.'

Isaac Bell rose to his full height, bumping his hat on the low wooden ceiling of the workboat cabin. The others were hunched over a galley table that was covered with oilcloth. A cookstove smelled of grease and coffee. It was dark outside. The porthole was open to the pungent odors of the river and coal smoke.

'I appreciate the thought, Wally. And you, Mack. But this "stunt" is the right thing to do. I can only hope Mr Van Dorn will see it's right, too.'

'I wouldn't bet on that.'

'I'm not betting on it. I'm taking my chances.'

Archie ventured a sunnier scenario. 'Maybe Mr Van

Dorn will regard moving all those families into the safety of the city as a humanitarian act.'

'Maybe President Roosevelt will give the coal mines to the miners,' Mack Fulton said.

'And while he's at it,' Wally added, 'declare the United States Socialist Republic of the Big Rock Candy Mountain.'

'We're agreed,' said Bell. 'Jim, how many towboat pilots did you round up?'

'I've got five committed.'

Bell multiplied boats and barges in his head. He had hoped for more boats so the barges would not be too big and unwieldy. Five towboats pushing twenty barges apiece, one hundred people in each barge, crammed in tighter than sardines. Ten thousand people, if they all made it aboard before the Pinkertons noticed. God help them if any sank. 'What about engineers?'

'Towboat engineers are like hermit crabs. They never leave the boat.'

'Deckhands?'

'A few, plus as many miners as we slip out of the camp.'

'Pretending to be deckhands,' growled Mack Fulton.

'They're no strangers to hard work,' said Jim Higgins. 'And they've spent their lives wrestling things heavier than they are.'

'They'll do,' said Bell, knowing they would have to.

Wally and Mack exhaled loud stage sighs. 'OK, Isaac,' said Mack. 'When do we do it?'

Isaac Bell looked at Jim Higgins.

Jim Higgins said, 'The pilots predict another black fog tonight.'

'Tonight,' said Isaac Bell. 'We move them tonight.'

'Cheese it!' hissed Wally Kisley. 'The cops.'

It was not, of course, the Pittsburgh police, or even the Coal and Iron Police, but Mary Higgins, who the Protective Services boys had warned was heading their way. She stormed into the workboat's cabin with color high in her cheeks. She glared at her brother, the others, and Bell.

'Where are the men who were here?'

'They left town for their health,' said Mack Fulton.

'Taking the waters at the Greenbrier,' said Wally.

'What are you doing here?' she shouted, turning all her fury on Bell.

'We are borrowing your barges,' he said. 'And you're lucky we found out instead of the police or the Pinkertons or the militia.'

'Are you asking me to be grateful?'

'You can thank us by staying out of our way.'

She whirled on her brother. 'Did you tell him?'

'I only confirmed what they figured out on their own.'

'Why?'

'So you don't get killed or thrown in prison.'

'Go to hell, brother. You, too, Isaac Bell.'

Isaac Bell followed Mary out on deck. She was staring at the fogbound river, blinking back tears. 'You ruined it.'

'Mary?'

'Leave me be.'

'Good will come of what you did. These barges will save the miners' march and save lives.'

'How?'

'Your brother has the idea to move their tents to the

260

Amalgamated Coal Terminal. The hope is, we can transport the miners and their families in these barges. Once there, he thinks, they will hold a safer and stronger position.'

'Do you believe that?' she asked.

'I believe that at this moment their position could not be worse.'

Mary nodded and said quietly, 'I saw the trolley park this afternoon. They can't stay there . . . Was it true what my brother said?'

'Jim did not betray you. He only confirmed what I guessed.'

'You're quite the clever guesser, Isaac Bell.'

'It was quite guessable,' Bell replied. 'There's no reason to sink a hundred barges in the channel other than to block the shipment of coal.'

'But how did you know I intended to sink them?'

'I shadowed you, Mary. I followed you here. To this boat. I listened to you argue with those men.'

'But I looked behind me. I made sure I wasn't followed. The Pinkertons are everywhere.'

Bell smiled and said gently, 'I told you Van Dorns are different.'

'Sneakier?' she asked with the faintest of smiles back.

Bell took her hands, and when she did not resist he said, 'Mary, you once told me that knowing what is right is not enough. If you know what's right, you have to do right.'

'Who are you to judge what's right?'

'I have eyes and I have ears. The marchers are stranded. Your brother was so discouraged that he was willing to fight their way out of McKeesport. It would be a blood-bath. These barges – your barges – can save them. We couldn't even try this if you hadn't gathered them all here.' He pointed out in the dark where the barges carpeted the river. 'But I have to tell you that this is a far, far better use than what you intended.'

Mary Higgins turned to Bell again. 'I hate to give it up. Hate to lose it. It was a good scheme, wasn't it?'

'Good,' said Bell, 'is not the first word that comes to mind. But it was very clever.'

'Let's hope your scheme is as clever,' she replied.

'I am praying it is,' said Bell. 'There are so many people.'

'I wish them luck.'

'Who is Mr Claggart?'

The instant the words were out of Bell's mouth, he knew he should have waited.

Mary stiffened. 'Once a detective, always a detective?'

'I'm afraid I'm not "sneaky" enough to be a good one.'

'You'll get better at it very soon at the rate you're prac-tising.' She pulled away from him.

There was no getting out of it now. Bell had to know if Claggart was Henry Clay, and there was one very quick way to find out. 'Does he have yellow eyes?'

'Why do you ask?'

'Because if he does, he is using you.'

'Go to hell.'

That answered that, thought Bell. 'Do you know that he happens to be a detective?'

'Good-bye, Isaac.' She stepped on to the ladder to the barge.

'His real name is Henry Clay,' said Bell. 'He is a provocateur. He is instigating violence, setting labor against owners and owners against labor. And he is using you for his game. If you sank those barges, Clay would get exactly what he wants. Workers will be blamed.'

'It's not his game.'

'What?'

Mary shook her head violently. 'Nothing.'

Bell grabbed her arm. 'What did you mean it's not his game?'

'Let go of me.'

'Who's game is it? Is someone else giving orders?'

'I have no idea.'

'But you do know that Clay answers to someone, don't you?' She shook her head. It was too dark to see her eyes, much less read her expression. He tried again to force an honest answer. 'Who paid for a hundred barges?'

'That was the first thing I asked,' she said.

'Did he answer?'

'Bank robberies. They raised the money with bank robberies.'

'Where?'

'Chicago.'

'What would you say if I told you that those robberies were committed by several different gangs, half of whom have been caught this week?'

'I'd say you're practising again.'

Mack stepped out of the cabin, calling urgently. 'Isaac! If you insist on trying this tonight, there isn't a moment to lose.'

A towboat loomed out of the fog, paddles thrashing, and banged against the barges. Miners clambered on to them with ropes and looked around uncertainly, waiting for someone to tell them what to do.

'Now or never, Isaac.'

'Mary, I will talk to you tomorrow.'

She climbed the ladder on to the barge and started toward the shore.

'Where are you going?'

'You're not the only one who has "right" to do, Isaac.'

'Will you be careful?' Bell called after her.

'Why should I be careful? You'll be following me.'

'Not tonight. I can't tonight.' He gestured helplessly at the steamboat and the barges.

'Then tonight I'll take my chances.'

'Clay is deadly.'

Mary Higgins stopped, turned around and looked back at him. Spark and flame erupted from the towboat's stacks, illuminating her pale skin. Eyes aglow, chin high, she looked, Bell thought, utterly beautiful and supremely confident. He wondered how she could be so sure of herself in the face of her disappointment. The answer came like an icicle in his heart.

'He is not deadly to me.'

36

Pittsburgh's infamous 'black fog' was a grimy mix of the natural fog that rose from the rivers and the coal smoke and soot that tumbled out of mills, foundries, power-houses, locomotives and steamboats. Black fog was dense and oily, painful to breathe, and nearly impossible to see through. When the pilot of the lead tow shined his electric carbon arc searchlight ahead to inspect the empty barges he was pushing, the beam bounced back into the pilothouse as if reflected by a mirror.

'The barges are up there somewhere,' the pilot joked to Isaac Bell, who was standing at his shoulder. He was Captain Jennings, an old-timer with a tobacco-stained swallow-tailed beard. His boat was the *Camilla*, a low-slung, two-deck ninety-footer with a stern paddle wheel as wide as she was. The glass pilothouse, which reminded Bell of a New England sea captain's widow's walk, was perched on the second deck behind the chimneys and let them view the murk ahead, behind and to both sides.

'You can feel it different in the wheel if the tow breaks up and you and the boat are out all by your lonesome while they're drifting every which way. We're doing fine, don't you worry none. I don't have to see what I know.' He spat tobacco juice into a box filled with sawdust. 'Heck, most of what I can't see I can feel in the floor or whether the paddle wheel turns sluggish. Feeling the river shoals tells me where I am. What I can't see or feel, I have stashed in my memory machine.'

Bell wondered how the pilot saw other tows on a collision course with his. Jennings's white beard suggested he had survived decades on the river, but it seemed worth asking.

'If in doubt, I ring the stopping bell,' came the laconic reply.

Bell looked back and saw a dim light that might be the barge fleet behind them. Jennings's son was driving it. The three tows behind it were invisible. Bell had stationed the levelheaded Archie Abbott, who like he had grown up around sailboats and steam yachts, on the rearmost. He put Wally Kisley on the next, then Mack Fulton. And if there was anything to be grateful for, it was the blinding black fog.

Ahead, an eerie reddish luminescence began to spread in the dark. It grew steadily in size and intensity. 'What's that red light?'

'Jones & Laughlin blast furnaces . . . Watch close, you'll see something you'll never forget. There!'

A procession of red balls appeared to float in the air as they moved across the river, high above the water. Bell was mystified at first until his keen eyes distinguished the girders of trusswork. 'Is that a bridge?'

'The Hot Metal Bridge.'

As the forward barges in their tow pushed under it, Bell could see a locomotive pulling flatcars through the trusses. On each car was a glowing red mass of fire.

'What are those railcars carrying?'

266

'J & L crucibles of molten steel from the furnaces across to the rolling mill. Ain't that something?'

After clearing the bridge, the pilot nudged his big wooden wheel, which was as tall as he was, and coaxed the tow into a broad turn. There was a white glow to the left. A gust of wind shredded the fog momentarily, and Bell glimpsed the point of the Amalgamated Coal Terminal. It was ablaze in electric work lights as the conveyors lifted coal from barges to the tipple. Seven miles of dark river to go. At least an hour. Load the people, and seven miles back. The black fog thickened.

Suddenly, Bell sensed movement alongside. *Camilla*'s searchlight played on a masonry bridge pier. They passed close enough to see the cement between the stones. 'Brown's Bridge,' said the pilot. 'We're on our way.'

Below the Homestead Works, as the smoke thinned, the black fog dissipated slightly, just in time to see a fully laden twenty-barge tow coming downriver straight at them – a fast-moving two-acre island of coal.

'Shoot!' growled Bell's pilot. 'That's Captain Andy. Of all the boats to run into tonight.'

'What's the matter?'

Jennings spat at the box of sawdust. 'Captain Andy owns three steamers, inclining him toward the capitalist camp. Allowing what we're up to for our friends in labor would be like dipping an oar in a nest of water moccasins.'

He blew his whistle. The oncoming tow's whistle answered. As they passed, the pilots played their searchlights on each other's tow and stepped out of their houses to exchange hellos.

'Where you headed?' the downriver-bound Captain Andy shouted.

'Gleasonburg!' Bell's pilot bawled back.

'Look out for that pack of strikers at McKeesport. I heard they're getting a cannon to shoot at our tows.'

'Where they going to get a cannon, Captain Andy?'

'Steal it. They's strikers, ain't they?'

Jennings waved good-bye and said to Bell, 'Just hope the boys behind us tell him the same.'

They passed beneath another hot metal bridge, over which ran the fiery juices of the Carrie Furnace and, soon after, a trolley bridge. A streetcar with gaily lighted windows thundered the wooden deck as the tow steamed under it.

'West Braddock Bridge,' said the pilot. 'Smooth sailing from here to McKeesport. Just some railroad bridges with real wide spans. And a bunch of dredges crowding the channel.' His searchlight flashed on a big white diamond board on the bank that marked another bend in the river.

The black fog continued to thin. Bell could see the tow behind theirs and the lights of two behind it. 'Hope nobody's looking for us,' said Captain Jennings. 'We're becoming mighty apparent.'

Bell was not that worried about being seen. As long as they kept moving, who ashore would take notice? They had peeled the tows loose from the riverbank under cover of the fog. Now they were indistinguishable from the other river traffic. Nor did Bell fear, even for a moment, that Mary Higgins would betray them. His main worry was that 'Claggart' had returned in time to see the last tow leave the Smithfield Bridge. But, so far, there was no pursuit.

He left the pilothouse and went down a flight of stairs to the galley where a grizzled deckhand was telling a dozen coal miners about the alligators that swarmed when novice deckhands fell overboard. 'And I reckon you boys noticed how low the main deck is to the water. Sometimes them critters just walk on. Prowl about, looking for something to eat.'

'Been in West Virginia my whole life. Never seen no alligators in the Mon.'

'They congregate at Pittsburgh.' He winked at Bell.

Bell addressed the miners. 'We're almost at the trolley park. There'll be a lot of folks milling around when we land. I'm hoping you boys can help keep order while we get them into the barges. You'll see your own people and –'

'Ah wouldn't bother your head too much about that,' drawled the West Virginian. 'The Strike Committee organized committees for everything from Drinking Water Committee to the Cooking Committee to the No Cusswords Committee to the Defense Committee. You can bet by now there's a Barge Gittin' On Committee and a Barge Gittin' Off Committee.'

Camilla's tall-tale-telling deckhand stood up. 'Right now, I'm organizing a Mooring Line Committee. The captain'll do most of the work driving us alongside, but I want every man of you ready to jump with a rope.'

Twenty minutes later, steaming at nearly eight knots against the current, *Camilla* squeezed her tow past a string of dredges that Captain Jennings said were building locks and a dam at Braddock. 'About damned time, too. Above here, in a dry spell, the Mon drops so low you can plow it.'

269

The dredges were working through the night. A lucky break, thought Bell, as their lights might provide cover for the towboats' lights.

'There's the park,' said Jennings.

Bell had already spotted the tall circle of the Ferris wheel. It was silhouetted against the electric-light glow of the outskirts of McKeesport. If he had any doubts about the wisdom of this 'stunt,' they evaporated when he saw the mass of men, women and children crowding the riverbank with their bundles in their hands.

'Where's the Defense Committee?' Isaac Bell called down from *Camilla*'s top deck as Captain Jennings flanked his barges back against the riverbank.

'At the gates.'

'Holding off the Pinkertons.'

Jennings's searchlight swept inland, and Bell saw a sight he would never forget. Mary Higgins had estimated that ten thousand had joined the ranks since the march began at Gleasonburg. It was a number hard to imagine until the light swept over the rippling mass of people – men and women, and children sitting on their shoulders – all with their faces turned to the river.

'Soon as your barges are full, head back down,' he told Captain Jennings. 'If I'm not back, leave without me.'

Bell hurried down the two flights to the main deck, jumped on to the muddy riverbank. Miners were dismantling a shuttered cold-drinks stand and spreading the boards across the mud. Bell walked inland, through acres of people carrying their belongings and loads of canvas wrapped around tent poles. He walked under the Ferris wheel and circled a swimming lake. A carousel stood still, with canvas tied over the horses. A freak show was boarded up for the winter. When at last the crowd thinned, he arrived at the fence that separated the park from the trolley barns.

Miners with lever-action rifles guarded the gates, which they had barricaded with planks, crossties, and lengths of track pried up from the station. The riflemen had their backs toward the retreating crowd and the towboat searchlights piercing the sky, concentrating on what was outside the gate.

'Where's Fortis?'

The miner in charge of the detail, a hard-eyed man in his forties, was in the ticket booth. He looked like he had not slept in a long time.

'Mr Fortis? I'm Bell. Jim Higgins said you were covering the retreat.'

'Not a minute too soon. Look at those boys.'

Bell peered through a crack between the planks. The lights were on in the trolley barns and the huge doors open. Inside, scores of strikebreakers armed with pick handles had sheltered from the rain. A streetcar parked outside the barn drew his eye. Twenty men with Winchesters sat inside it.

'Pinkertons?'

'In that one. Coal and Iron cops in another behind the barn.'

'Where's the militia?'

'So far, the government's holding them in reserve in McKeesport. But one of our spies says those jailbirds are waiting to attack about four in the morning. I'm worried they'll jump the gun when they cotton to your barges.'

'They must have spies, too.'

'We caught three tonight. A triple play. They won't be telling nobody.'

'What did you do to them?'

'Bought us some time,' came the opaque reply.

Bell said, 'I want to be sure you boys make the last boat.'

'We're loaded and ready to run.'

Bell had already noticed the wheelbarrows lined up and covered with canvas.

'What's in those barrows?'

'Rifles, ammunition and dynamite.'

Wondering whether he had led the Van Dorn Detective Agency into a shooting war, Bell asked, 'Sure you need explosives?'

'Sure we won't get caught short.'

'I'll come for you when we've got the last of your people loaded.'

Back at the river Bell found the loading going slowly. When *Camilla* finally swung her barges away from the bank and started down the Monongahela, and Captain Jennings's son maneuvered the second fleet alongside, the tall detective opened his pocket watch. At the rate this was going, they would be lucky to land the last tow at Amalgamated before the morning fog lifted ten hours from then.

37

Henry Clay spotted a junior stockbroker waiting under a light where the *Vulcan King* landed for coal in Wheeling, West Virginia. He recognized the type employed by Midwestern branch offices of the brokerage that Judge Congdon controlled with his secret interest. Hair short and combed, suit pressed, collar freshly starched despite the late hour, smile hopeful, the young man was hungry to please anyone from New York headquarters.

'Mr Claggart?' he asked, his eyes wide at the spectacle of the biggest steamboat he had ever seen hulking over the wharf, broad as a steel mill and twice as black.

'You from the office?'

Gone was Clay's Southern banker costume and his drawl. He was brusque – his dark frock coat as severe as the freshly painted *Vulcan King*, his costly homburg fixed at a sober angle – a valuable man obliged to journey from the great city to direct enterprises too lofty to be trusted to ordinary mortals.

'Telegram for you, sir. On the private wire.'

The young fellow handed him an envelope and emphasized its importance with a breathless, 'It's in cipher.'

'Cipher means private,' snapped Clay. 'Private means don't shout about it in a public place.'

It was nearly midnight. The wharf was remote, chosen for its distance from the public wharf, and deserted except for *Vulcan King*'s firemen wheeling fresh coal up the steamboat's landing stage. The junior broker stammered apologies.

'Lesson learned,' was Clay's magnanimous reply. 'Wait over there until I give you an answer to wire back.'

He sent the broker scurrying with a cold nod and moved under the light, slit open the envelope, and immediately began grinding his teeth. Inside the envelope was the standard printed company message blank:

Form A-14

Private Wire Telegram Received

Thibodeau & Marzen, Brokers

Wheeling, West Virginia Office

In the space after **The following message received at Time**: they had written '8:48 pm.'

After **By telegraph from**: they had written 'New York.'

And, incredibly, after **To**: they had written 'John Claggart' in letters big enough to advertise a circus.

'Young man!'

'Sir?'

He beckoned him close and muttered grimly, 'Inform your office that if fate ever drags me back to Wheeling not to use your standard form for my private wires but enter the cipher on a blank sheet with no names attached.'

He had gone through this at every branch office, even Chicago, where they should know better. The only reason none of the morons had written 'Judge James Congdon' after **from** was that no one knew that Congdon owned Thibodeau & Marzen.

The message itself, written by hand, contained several strings of four-digit numbers. He read quickly, deciphering the figures in his head. Then he balled the paper in his fist.

'Cast off!'

He bolted up the boarding stage.

'Any reply, sir?' called the junior broker.

'Send immediately in cipher. "The Point. Nine hours."'

Judge Congdon was in a rage. His spies in Pittsburgh had seen the miners moving camp from the McKeesport trolley park. About to hurl the crumpled telegram into the water, Clay remembered the lesson he had just taught about privacy, smoothed the paper, folded it repeatedly, and slid it deep in an inside pocket reserved for business cards.

'Cast off, I said! Take in the stage!'

The firemen raced aboard. Deckhands threw off lines. The steam winch lifted the boarding stage from the wharf and swung it inboard, and the *Vulcan King* backed slowly into the river.

Clay ran up the four flights of stairs to the pilothouse.

'Go! What are you waiting for? Full speed!'

The pilot was dithering with the engine room telegram. 'Where?'

'Pittsburgh!'

'I don't know if we took on enough fuel.'

Clay crossed the lavish pilothouse in three strides and slammed both engine levers to *Ahead Full*.

'Burn the furniture if you have to. Get us there.'

It had taken a full day and a half to steam three hundred and eighty miles from Cincinnati. Ninety more to Pittsburgh. 'What speed can you make?'

The pilot wrestled the brass-bound wheel, and the

steamboat surged from the bank. 'River's running hard, all this rain,' he said. 'Nine knots.'

Clay smoothed out the telegram and read it again. Foolishness. It hadn't changed. How could it? He stuffed it back in his pocket.

Ninety miles to Pittsburgh would take ten hours at nine knots. 'Make it ten knots.'

'I don't know –'

'Lower the water in your boilers. Jump your pressure. You'll get hot steam easier with little water.'

'Blow up easier, too.'

'Hot steam! Do what it takes. Ten knots!'

Congdon had every right to rage. The strikers were moving in barges. *Clay's* barges. God knows where they were going next, but it couldn't be good. Had Mary Higgins changed her mind? Not likely. Not at all. No, this reeked of Isaac Bell.

The steamboat had modern voice pipes. Clay shouted down for the boat's carpenter, who came quickly, rubbing sleep from his eyes.

'Mount the cannon.'

'Now?'

'And the Gatling.'

Mary Higgins knew that Isaac Bell was right. John Claggart – the man Isaac called Henry Clay – was no friend. Not to the strikers betrayed by slogans they had wanted to hear – *Bum government* and *bloodsucking capitalists*. Not to her, fooled so cunningly. What could be more seductive to a woman determined to build a new world than to hear anarchy dubbed a joke?

But Claggart was not the enemy.

Mary felt no comfort that she had suspected correctly from early on that another man was paying for the barges. She had not been surprised when Isaac told her that bank robbers were not stealing for the workers' cause. She had never fully believed Claggart's story. But she had hoped and acted like a drunkard – drunk on the cause, drunk on hope, drunk on passionate belief. Like any drunkard, blind to truth.

She swore that she would never let hope and belief blind her again.

Anger at Claggart was useless, worse than useless. Anger would derail her hunt for the man who paid Claggart. *He* was the enemy. He was the provocateur sowing violence to give the owners and the government the excuse to destroy the union. He was the enemy of justice served by equality.

The furtive Claggart was not the enemy. A detective no less, and a shrewd one at that. Deadly, as Isaac said? No doubt deadly. She had seen what he was capable of. But never deadly to her. That she knew in her heart. He would never hurt her. He was not the enemy. He wanted to be her friend. She would let him be. A helpful friend who would lead her to the enemy.

38

When the fourth barge fleet steamed into the dark with two thousand striking miners, their wives and their children, Isaac Bell stepped into the beam of towboat *Sadie*'s searchlight and signaled to Archie to land. Captain Jennings had claimed that *Sadie* was the oldest of the riverboats, a Civil War relic that had run the Confederate gauntlet at Vicksburg, and Archie reported, as he stepped from her low hull on to the planks the miners had laid to stabilize the bank, her pumps were running full blast to keep up with leaks in her bottom.

'Don't let anyone on that barge,' Bell told him, indicating the lead barge touching the shore farthest from the towboat. 'I'm reserving it for the Defense Committee's dynamite.'

Bell ran through the dark and now deserted trolley park to the gates.

Fortis, the head of the Defense Committee, was reeling with exhaustion. 'I hope you're ready for us. The jailbirds are fixing to bust in.'

Bell looked through a crack in the gate. Twenty strikebreakers were carrying a battering ram fashioned from lengths of trolley track. Fifty, at least, were arrayed behind them, each with a pick handle. And the Pinkertons were dismounting from their streetcar and spreading out, taking up positions with their rifles.

'Where are the Coal and Iron Police?'

'Look at the roof.'

Now Bell spotted them, dimly silhouetted against the McKeesport glow. They were crouching behind the ridgeline of the trolley barn roofs, rifle barrels leveled at the gates. 'We,' he said, realizing as he spoke how totally he had cast his lot with the striking miners, 'have to do something better than a running gun battle to cover our retreat.'

Fortis's answer was a stark reminder that Bell had entered a war that was already well under way. 'We've arranged a reception for the battering ram that'll buy us some time – wait! Now what are they up to?'

A trolley car glided from the mouth of one of the barns and stopped where a curve in the rails pointed it straight at the gate. If the rails continued to the gate, the car would have been an electrified battering ram, but the rails turned away. Puzzled, Bell looked more closely and suddenly realized that the front windows of the car had been removed. In their place, the strikebreakers had jury-rigged headlamps cannibalized from other cars.

Bell turned his back on the gate just as all the headlamps lighted at once. The men who had their faces pressed to the cracks in the gate cried out, temporarily blinded. Bell snatched a rifle from the nearest miner, shut his left eye, slitted his right, scrambled to the top of the barricade, and fired repeatedly into the blazing-white glare. The rifle magazine held five bullets. When it was empty, two headlamps still glared. He whipped out his Colt Army, steadied the barrel on the top of the gate, and squeezed the trigger twice.

The trolley yard was dark again. Shadows rose from the

ground, and the strikebreakers who had dropped their battering ram when they ducked for cover picked it up again.

'Run!' Isaac Bell shouted. 'Run!'

They started toward the barges, twenty miners trundling wheelbarrows, ten firing wild shots behind them, as the strikebreakers charged the gate. Bell, taking up the rear, gun in hand, heard the battering ram thunder against the gate. Once. Twice. Running backwards, he waited for the third blow to burst the gate open.

An orange flash lit the dark, followed by a loud explosion and the shouts of dismayed strikebreakers. When the fleeing miners cheered, Bell realized that the Defense Committee had mined the gate with dynamite, set off when the battering ram smashed into a detonator.

'That'll fix the sons of bitches!' Fortis yelled.

And give the militia the excuse to attack, thought Bell.

The towboat *Sadie* blew her whistle as the running men drew near. The Defense Committee fought to shove their wheelbarrows through the mud to the barges, from which came shouts of encouragement.

Isaac ran ahead of them. 'Stow all your dynamite in that lead barge, away from these people.'

The wheels were sticking in the muddy bank, and that barge was distant.

'Here's fine,' yelled Fortis. 'There's room in this one. Dump it here, boys!'

'Dynamite deteriorates in damp and becomes volatile,' Bell protested. 'You've been carrying it in the rain.'

'Are you telling a coal miner how to handle explosives?'

Bell seized the older man's arm in an iron grip. 'Volatile

means *boom*, it goes off by itself. Get it away from these people.'

'I won't abide some whippersnapper –'

Isaac Bell held his Army high. 'I'll blow the head off the first man who puts dynamite anywhere but that front barge.'

Isaac Bell stood watch outside the pilothouse on towboat *Sadie*'s hurricane deck, wishing that the river fog was thicker. *Sadie* wheezed slowly past the Homestead Works, and the Amalgamated tipple rose against a sky that was turning bright.

He heard shouts.

Pursuit, he thought, looking for a fast police launch packed with riflemen. But the shouts were coming from the lead barge, where some miners had elected to ride with the dynamite, and it sounded like a drunken fight. Bell ran down to the main deck and on to the barges, intending to run to the front of the tow to break it up before they accidentally set off an explosion.

A muffled boom told him he was too late.

Smoke pillared from the lead barge. A geyser of water shot into the sky. It sounded to Bell as if a single stick of dynamite had blown a hole in her hull. Would the rest blow before the water rushing in smothered the detonators?

The dynamite barge was sinking. Three men clambered off drunkenly on to the barge behind it. As the stricken dynamite barge sunk deeper, it pulled hard against the lines holding it to the other barges in the tow. All at once, they snapped, parting with a loud bang. The dynamite barge broke from the pack. The tow pushed it ahead as it sank, dashing it to pieces. The next barges ran over planks, timbers and crates of dynamite. Bell waited, heart in his throat, for the rest of the dynamite to explode under the barges loaded with people. As each barge rumbled over the debris, bottom planks were staved, water rushed in, and the people in them tried frantically to plug the holes.

Bell felt it crunch under the barge he was on. Then the towboat ran over it. Bell saw the pilot turning his wheel to force the tow out of the deep channel.

'She's sinking!' a deckhand howled. 'Ripped her bottom out.'

For a second, Bell stood frozen. I led these people into this, he thought. All their lives are in mortal danger. This was why Joseph Van Dorn had warned not to take sides. Two thousand were about to drown in the bitter-cold river, and what in the name of God could he do to save them?

Bell ran back and leaped to the towboat's main deck. Archie was peering down into the engine room. The water was knee-deep and rising. When it drowned the engine, the current would sweep the people past Amalgamated while the damaged barges sank.

Bell jumped into the hold and waded toward a surge of current that marked the breach in the planks. The water clamped around his legs like ice. Archie peeled off his coat and threw it to Bell and ran, shouting he would get blankets. Bell waded to the breach, stomped Archie's coat in it, pulled off his own and stuffed it in. His shirt went next. Archie returned with blankets, towels and people's precious coats.

Isaac Bell stuffed garments and blankets into the broken seam.

The leak slowed, but not enough. The water kept rising. He heard steam roar. The rising water had reached the furnace and was beginning to drench the fire. Steam pressure was dropping. The engine slowed. Just as the stern wheel stopped turning, Bell felt the hull grounding in the mud.

Boots pounded on deck as men ran with ropes.

'OK, she's on the bottom. She can't sink any more. Save the blankets.'

'You'll need one more,' said Archie, throwing it to him. 'The ladies have suffered enough. Spare them their hero in his altogether.'

Bell slung the blanket around himself and climbed out of the hold. To his astonishment, in the time he was belowdecks, the sun had burned through the fog and was shining bright. Ashore, the gentle upward slope of the Amalgamated Terminal was dotted with white tents pitched by the people who had arrived on the first tows. He smelled bacon frying and coffee brewing. In the shadow of the coal tipple, small boys had started a pickup game of baseball.

'Happy sight, Isaac. A safer place, and no one drowned.'

'It would be a lot happier if they weren't tearing up that rail line.'

A thousand miners were uprooting track on which the coal trains entered the terminal. A thousand more were tumbling cars on their sides, blocking the trolley lines from the Golden Triangle.

'They're digging in,' said Archie. 'You can't blame them for keeping the Pinkertons out.'

'And the cops,' said Bell, directing Archie's attention to the downtown side of Amalgamated's spit of land.

A contingent of uniformed Pittsburgh police dismounted from a toast-rack trolley that had been stopped by a heap of crossties and a gap in the tracks. A second contingent was milling around blocked tracks on the Homestead side. Neither formed a line nor charged. On the river, a police steam launch flitted about agitatedly like a bird helpless to stop its nest from being invaded. The cops on land climbed back on their trolleys and rode away.

As Isaac Bell watched the miners fortify the point, he had to concede Archie was right. This place they had retreated to was vulnerable until they barricaded the approaches. But it had the grim face of war.

'At least,' he said, 'the hotheads lost their dynamite. Maybe now both sides can settle down and horse-trade.'

'What in heck is that?' said Archie. The tall redhead was staring at the river behind Bell, his expression a mix of puzzlement and awe. Bell turned to see.

Chimneys billowing smoke, stern wheel pounding foam, an enormous steamboat rounded the point. It was immensely long, and tall, and black as coal.

39

'Is that a cannon on the foredeck?' asked Archie.

Bell shielded his eyes with cupped hands and focused on the gun. 'Two-inch Hotchkiss,' he said. 'The Navy had them on a gunboat Wish and I boarded in New Orleans.'

'Where the heck did they get it?'

'More to the point,' said Bell, 'who are they and what do they want?'

'I can't quite make out her nameboard.'

'*Vulcan King.*'

The black giant came closer.

One after another, then by the hundreds, the women pitching tents and the men building barricades stopped what they were doing. Ten thousand stood stock-still, waiting for the black apparition to turn midriver and point its cannon at them. It steamed very slowly, its giant wheel barely stirring the river, closer and closer, at a pace no less menacing for its majesty.

Directly opposite the point, it stopped, holding against the current. Not a living figure showed on deck, not a deckhand, not a fireman. The boiler deck and engine doors were shut, the pilot invisible behind sun-glared glass. Ten thousand people held their breath. What, Isaac Bell asked himself again, have I led these people into?

It blasted its whistle. Everyone jumped.

Then it moved forward, slicing the current, up the river,

swung around the bend of the Homestead Works, and disappeared.

'Where's it going?' asked Archie.

'My guess is, to collect the Pinkertons,' said Bell. 'We'll have to find out. But if I'm right, then the miners hold this point of land, and the owners hold the river. And if that isn't the beginning of a war, I don't know what is.'

Dried off and clothes changed, Bell went looking for *Camilla*'s pilot.

He found Captain Jennings and his son in a Smithfield Street saloon up the slope from where their boats were docked. The two pilots congratulated him on the strikers' safe passage.

'Did you see the *Vulcan King*?' Bell asked.

'Hard to miss,' said the younger Jennings, and his father declared, 'Who in hell would paint a steamboat black?'

'Who owns her?'

Both pilots shrugged. 'Never seen her before. We was just asking ourselves, was we thrown off by the black? But even imagining her white, she does not look familiar.'

'Where do you suppose it came from?'

'She weren't built in Pittsburgh or we'd know her for sure. That leaves Louisville or Cincinnati.'

'Nowhere else?'

'It took a heck of a yard to build a boat that size. Like I say, Louisville or Cincinnati. I'd say Cincinnati, wouldn't you, Pa?'

The older Jennings agreed. 'One of the big old yards like Held & Court.'

'They still in business, Pa?'

'They're the last that make 'em like that anymore.'

'What do you think of that cannon?' asked Bell.

'Not much,' said the senior Jennings.

His son explained, 'Riverboats are made of spit-and-sawdust. The recoil will shake her to pieces.'

'Could they reinforce it to stand the recoil?'

Both Jenningses spat tobacco. 'They'd have to.'

'"Insurrection",' said Judge James Congdon, casting a stony gaze about the Duquesne Club's paneled dining room. 'When first offered the privilege of addressing the august membership, I intended to call my speech "New Economies in the Coal, Iron, Coking and Steelmaking Industries." But for reasons apparent to anyone in your besieged city, my topic is changed to "Insurrection."'

He raised a glass of mineral water to his wrinkled lips, threw back his head, and drained it.

'By coincidence, I happen to be your guest speaker on the very day that the criminal forces of radicalism and mindless anarchy seized a modern enterprise in which I hold an interest, the Amalgamated Coal Terminal. Amalgamated is a center of coal distribution, east, west, north and south. Winter looms. City dwellers will freeze in their homes, locomotives will come to a standstill, and industry's furnaces will be starved for fuel. Insurrection, you will agree, is a subject if not dear to my heart, extremely close by.'

The members laughed nervously.

'Were this attack to occur in New York City, where I conduct business, I have no doubt that government would respond with force and alacrity. Not blessed with residency in Pittsburgh, I can only guess your city fathers' answer to this challenge. For the moment, I will leave that to them, trusting in their Americanism, their decency, their principles, and their courage to stand up to labor, which wields far too much influence in the state of Pennsylvania.

'But to you – those who have built this great city by transforming the minerals that God deposited in Pennsylvania's mountains into the mightiest industry the world has ever seen, producing more iron and steel and coal than Great Britain and Germany could dream of – to you titans I say, labor must be brought to heel.

'Labor must be brought to heel or they will destroy everything you have worked to build. If we fail to master labor, future enlightened civilizations will look back on us in pity. "What did they fail to do?" The answer will be, "They failed to fight. Good men failed to fight evil!"'

Judge Congdon slammed his fist down on the podium, glared one by one at every face gaping back at him, then turned his back and stalked off the stage.

Stunned silence ensued. It was followed by a roar of applause.

'Come back!' they shouted, pounding their palms together. 'Come back! Come back!'

Congdon returned to the podium with a wintry smile.

'I hope,' he said, 'that the men of Pittsburgh know who the enemy is and have the courage to face him. To those who don't, to those who would appease, to those who would restrain the forces of order, I say, Get out of the way and let us do our job.'

James Congdon's special was waiting for him at a Union Station platform reserved for private trains. His Atlantic

4-4-2 locomotive, which had just rolled, gleaming, from the roundhouse, had steam up, and his conductor was arranging to clear tracks with a Pennsylvania Railroad division boss. The cook was shucking oysters from Delaware Bay, a steward was chilling champagne, and the actress who had come along for the ride to New York was luxuriating in a hot bath.

Congdon himself raised a brandy in the paneled library that served as his mobile office and said, 'Nothing becomes Pittsburgh like the leaving of it.'

'You seem mighty cheerful for a man whose business has been seized by radicals,' answered Henry Clay.

'Bless them!' Congdon laughed. 'They've outdone themselves. And outdone you, for that matter, Clay. You could not have planned it better.'

'They exceeded my expectations,' Clay admitted. 'Even my imagination. But I will take full credit for creating the atmosphere that stimulated them.'

'Credit granted. What's next?'

'Exploding steamboats and burning union halls.'

'In that order?'

'Simultaneous.'

Congdon eyed the younger man closely. 'I don't mind telling you that you're doing an excellent job.'

'I was hoping you would say that.'

Of course you were, thought Congdon, saying only, 'You deserve it.'

He checked the gilded clock on the wall and opened the louvers of the rosewood shutters. The railcar's window overlooked the train yard and the sidings that snaked into the private platforms.

'Is there any more archetypical symbol of rampant capitalism than the special train?' he asked.

'None. Yachts pale by them.'

'Have you considered having the vicious strikers wreck a special?'

Clay sat straighter, alert as a terrier.

Congdon said, 'The governor would have no choice but to call out the militia and hang strikers from lampposts.'

'Do you have a particular one in mind?'

'You see through me as if I were made of glass.' Congdon smiled, thinking, as Clay lit up like limelight, My oh my, does that make you preen. 'Any special would do.'

As he spoke a locomotive glided into view, drawing a beautiful train of four cars painted in Reading Railroad green livery, with the yellow trim done in gold as befitted the president of the line.

'Look! Here comes one now.'

'That looks like R. Kenneth Bloom's,' said Clay.

'I believe it is.'

'Two birds with one stone?'

'What do you mean by that?' Congdon demanded.

'President Bloom has been resisting your takeover of his Reading Line.'

'You presume too much, Clay. Be careful.'

'Forgive me,' Clay said contritely. 'I've been up several days. I'm not thinking clearly.'

'Get some sleep,' said Congdon. And then, to put Clay deeper in his thrall, he warmed up a friendly smile and said, 'Three birds, actually.'

'I beg your pardon, Mr Congdon?'

'It so happens that young Bloom, who's been goading his father to fight back and has given him spine where there was only jelly, is making a quick round-trip to Cincinnati. Four hours out, a secret meeting at the Queen City Club with some bankers, and four hours back. He'll have a guest on board. A friend of the family asked to ride along. His name is Isaac Bell.'

Henry Clay was both delighted and astonished. 'How do you know that?'

'Bloom's resistance forced me to employ spies.'

Clay surged to his feet, sleep forgotten. 'Three birds. A triple play.'

40

Isaac Bell could not find Mary Higgins. A new renter had moved into her room, and the landlady had no forwarding address.

He went next to the tent city, riding the Second Avenue trolley to the end of the line where the strikers had torn up the tracks. The expressions on the sullen Pittsburgh cops observing from a block away told Bell that they feared the obvious: the coal miners defending the tent city included Army veterans of the Spanish and Philippines wars, military men who knew their business.

They had installed an iron gate that was only wide enough to admit one man at a time. Bell showed a pass signed by Jim Higgins. Only then was he allowed through. And while approaching and entering, he was under the watchful gaze of strategically posted riflemen. Lookouts were stationed on top of the coal tipple with views of the city in three directions. Any movement of cops or militia would be spotted a mile away before they reached the gates. And in the shallows beside the riverbank, the strikers had sunk the barges that had floated them there, creating a crude breakwater like a crenellated castle wall, which would make it difficult to land police launches.

Two thousand tents pitched in neat rows with straight walks between them further conveyed the atmosphere of a military camp. By contrast, well-dressed women of means from Pittsburgh's churches and charities swept by in long skirts, directing the placement of kitchen tents and water taps. The ladies' presence, Bell thought, must be constraining the cops as much as the miners' riflemen. Not to mention the city fathers who were their husbands, and it was amusing to imagine how many Pittsburgh bigwigs were sleeping at their clubs until the strike was settled. But despite strong defenses and capable administration and charity, the coal miners' tent city had a precariousness, which was expressed by one stern matron whom Bell overheard:

'This is all well and good until it snows.'

He found a harried Jim Higgins directing the operation from under a tent's open canvas fly. Mary's brother said he had not seen her since the night they took her barges. He had no idea where she was. He admitted that he was worried, and he asked Bell to pass on the message, if he found her, that he could use her help desperately.

As Bell was leaving to head back downtown, he looked up and suddenly had to smile. A painter with a sense of humor was changing one word of the Amalgamated Coal Terminal sign on top of the tipple to read

AMALGAMATED COAL MINERS

The downtown union hall was deserted but for an elderly functionary left in charge. He had not seen Mary Higgins nor had he heard anything about her.

Bell found Mike and Terry in the back, sitting around a cookstove, drinking coffee.

'I'll give you a choice, boys. Now that Jim Higgins is

holed up in Amalgamated, you can go back to Chicago as Protective Services agents or you can work for my squad.'

'Is it OK with Mr Hancock and Mr Van Dorn?'

'I'll clear it with them,' said Bell. He would pay them out of his own pocket if he had to. He could use the manpower.

'What do you want us to do?'

'Find out where that big black boat went. I have a feeling you should start looking at McKeesport. But wherever it went, I want to know who they are and where they are going next because I do not believe that thing arrived here by coincidence.'

Bell waited for them to put down their coffee cups and stand up. But they just sat there. 'Is something the matter, gents?'

'Not really, Isaac.'

'Then get going.'

'Sure.' They exchanged heavy looks and portentous headshakes. 'There's just one thing.'

'What?'

'We heard you asking about Miss Mary.'

'Have you seen her?'

'Yes. That is, well . . .'

'When? Where?'

'Saloons. By the river.'

'Who was she with?'

'Talking with a whole bunch of fellows.'

'If you see her again, follow her. Meantime, find that black boat. I'll be back tomorrow.'

'Where you headed?'

'Cincinnati. If you need me for any emergency, wire

me care of R. Kenneth Bloom, Jr, Reading Railroad. His train has a grasshopper key.'

'How do you happen to know a fellow with his own train, Isaac?'

'We ran away to the circus together.'

Henry Clay unlocked the door of his apartment. The drapes were drawn, and it was dark. He was halfway in and reaching for the wall switch beside the door when he sensed a presence. Wrong-footed, too late to back out, he hurled himself sideways along the wall, pushing the light switch with his left hand and drawing his Bisley with his right. When the light flared on, he had the gun pointed at the figure sitting in the armchair.

'I am not armed,' said Mary Higgins, raising her hands to show they were empty.

'How did you find me?'

'When I learned that you were a detective,' she said calmly, 'I wondered how I would ever track you down on my own, much less shadow you, without you seeing me. I thought of hiring another professional to find you.'

'Bell!'

'Not Bell. Don't be ridiculous. Although I did consider my brother's bodyguards. The Van Dorn Protective Services pride themselves on being more than bodyguards.'

'Stumblebums. They couldn't find me.'

'That's what I thought. Besides, they might run straight home to tell Bell.'

'Then how did you find me?'

'I remembered that the old fellows in Bell's squad told me that those flash men you put in charge of the barges had fled the city. But that didn't seem likely. Why would they let a couple of Van Dorns chase them out of their hometown? So I went looking for familiar faces.'

'Where?'

'Casinos and concert saloons by the river.'

'My God, Mary, you could have been killed, or worse.'

'Not killed,' she said. 'Not even compromised.'

'You were lucky. People in those places would not hesitate to slip chloral powder into an innocent girl's drink.'

'I would recognize the odor of knockout drops in my tea,' she said drily.

'It is not as easily detected as people think. There are ways of compounding it that mask taste and smell.'

'You would know more about that than I,' she replied pointedly. 'But, in actual fact, I met more gentlemanly sorts – including one of your flash men. He directed me to the man I suspected had not fled Pittsburgh. *He* recommended I look for you in this street of apartment buildings. I smiled at many janitors.'

'But I am not known to the landlord as Claggart.'

'Oh, I didn't give them your name. I wouldn't betray you that way. I only described you.'

'How did you unlock my door?'

'I didn't. I climbed the fire escape.'

Clay holstered the Bisley, greatly relieved. It was one thing for an intelligent girl to make inquiries – particularly with a winsome smile. But the extremely rare ability to pick locks would make her far less innocent than he thought she was. He was still troubled, however, that she had been alone in his apartment. He was vigilant about not leaving evidence behind, but even the most careful man could give himself away with a small mistake.

'How long were you waiting for me?'

'Long enough to look around. You live well. It's an expensive apartment.'

'Who told you I was a detective? Bell?'

She nodded.

Clay said, 'Bell bent the truth. I was a detective once. I'm not any longer.'

'What are you now?'

'I am John Claggart.'

'Isaac called you Clay. Henry Clay.'

'Henry Clay no longer exists.'

'And what are you, John Claggart?'

'I am a revolutionary.'

'I found that easier to swallow when you wore work-man's duds. A smart frock coat and homburg hat make you look like a Morgan or Vanderbilt.'

'If you find it hard to swallow, then hopefully the enemy will, too.'

'Who paid for the barges?'

He was ready for this one. 'Bank robberies.'

'The bank robbers were caught.'

'Bell told you that?'

She nodded.

Clay said, 'Bell does not know as much as he thinks. They didn't catch them all. The one who wasn't caught stole the most money by far. And when he needs more, he can steal more in some other city. He walks into the bank president's office, wearing his frock coat and his costly hat, remains with the president after hours, and leaves quietly with a full satchel.'

'I want to believe you,' she said.

'It touches me deeply to hear you say that.' It was quite remarkable, he thought, but she did believe him. 'You honor me.'

'But nothing we did has amounted to a hill of beans. Our whole plan is destroyed now that the barges are lost.'

'May I ask,' said Clay, 'do you hate Isaac Bell for taking the barges?'

'Of course I hate him. He ruined everything.'

'Would you kill him?' Clay asked.

'Never,' she said fiercely.

'Why not? Revenge can be sweet.'

'I would never kill a soul. Not for any reason.'

'Do you want me to kill him?'

She did not answer immediately. He watched her gray eyes rove the room and its costly furniture. They settled back on him. 'No. It would be a waste of your energy.'

'What *do* you want?'

'What I have always wanted. I want to bring down the capitalist class. I want to stop them dead. And I still believe that the way to do that is stop coal.'

'The strike is doing a good job of that already.'

'No. Scab labor is digging more than half a million tons a week. The operators are regaining control of production. And now that the miners have a base at Amalgamated, they will negotiate, and the strike will be settled with a pittance for the miners and no recognition of the union. We must do something to shake all that loose.'

'What?'

'I don't know. I hope you might.'

Henry Clay said, 'I have disruptions in the works. All sorts of turmoil.'

'What turmoil?'

Clay took off his hat and sank into an armchair. 'Excuse me,' he said. 'I haven't shut my eyes or changed my clothes in three days. I need to sleep before I can think straight.'

'I'll come back later.'

'You don't have to leave. I'll just close my eyes in this chair.'

'It would be better if I left,' she said primly.

Clay said, 'Of course.'

He walked her to the door and shook her hand. Was it trembling? he wondered. Or was his?

A productive first step, thought Mary Higgins.

But she needed more. A search of his apartment, constrained by fear of it being noticed, had produced no clue to the identity of the man Claggart-Clay served, nothing that would bring her even one inch closer to the enemy.

She said, 'I hope you understand that I will demand more from someone with whom I join forces.'

'More what?'

'More than vague promises of "turmoil".'

Claggart surprised her. 'I need to sleep. When I wake, you will have your "more".'

'Promises?'

'Do you recall Harry O'Hagan's triple play?'

'Who doesn't?' Mary nodded impatiently. There was

more in the newspapers about the first baseman's miracle than the strike.

'I'll give you results,' he said. 'A bigger triple play than O'Hagan's.'

41

Even after a celebratory bender that went on days too long, Court Held still could not believe his luck in selling the *Vulcan King*. So it seemed beyond conception when another man dressed in white, though taller and younger, walked into his office to inquire whether he had any large steamboats on the property.

'How large were you considering, sir?'

'Floating palace size.'

'I've got one left.'

'I was told you had two.'

'I did. I just sold one.'

'To whom, may I ask?'

'I'm not at liberty to say. I am obliged to respect the buyer's privacy.'

To Held's surprise, the tall young fellow, who was about his own age, laughed out loud.

'Well, that proves that.'

'Proves what, sir? I don't know that I follow you.'

'A certain well-fixed gentleman and I engage in friendly competitions. We started in business, buying outfits out from under each other – factories, railroads, banks – and we've since moved into more pleasurable contests. We had a yacht race across the Atlantic Ocean. He won. By a nose. We had a train race from San Francisco to Chicago. I won. By fifty lengths. Now he's gone and challenged me to a steamboat race. Pittsburgh to New Orleans and back.'

'That sounds like a fine idea.'

'Yes, except he obviously planned ahead and bought the only available boat. So now you say you have one that is as good.'

Court Held winked. 'I'll tell you this, sir, he didn't buy the fastest.'

'Is that a fact?'

'Nope. Though it is the stronger, the *Vulcan King* is not as fast as *White Lady*.'

'Why's that?'

Court Held lowered his voice and looked around the empty shipyard as if to ensure they were alone. 'She's packing a lot of extra weight, seeing as how the government wanted her reinforced to carry cannon.'

'So the *Vulcan King* is much stronger?'

'Her decks are.' Court lowered his voice to a whisper. 'Between you and me, any steamboat is more an *idea* of boat than a solid boat. They have short lives. Ours are the best you could buy, but none of them lasted that long.'

Bell recalled Captain Jennings's spit-and-sawdust.

'Before I buy it, I'd like to be sure that he's already bought his. You understand, we also compete at leg-pulling. I got him good recently. He's out for revenge. So I want to be darned sure he hasn't set me up buying a steamboat I don't need.'

'You could always use her to travel.'

'How long does it take to steam from here to Pittsburgh?'

'I told you, sir, she's a fast boat. She'll make Cincinnati to Pittsburgh in two days.'

'My special just took me here in four hours. So I'm not planning any steamboat traveling, but I do intend to be in this race if it is a race. I'm asking you again, who bought your other boat?'

'His name was Smith.'

'Smith?'

'Smith. I know. I worried, too.'

'I don't think I'd take a check from an out-of-town fellow named Smith.'

'Nor would I, sir. Cash on the barrelhead from any man who calls himself Smith.'

'That's a lot of cash for an out-of-town fellow to pack with him.'

'He paid with bearer bonds.'

'Bearer bonds?' the gent in white echoed. 'They're a risky proposition. How'd he guarantee they were still good?'

'A New York broker was the issuing agent. Thibodeau & Marzen. He marched me straight to their Cincinnati branch office on East Seventh and I walked out with the cash.'

'What did he look like?'

'Not quite so tall as you. A bit wider. Dark hair, what I could see of it under his hat.'

'Beard?'

'Clean-shaven.'

Bell shook his head. 'Maybe he shaved . . . I always kidded him it made him look old. Say, what color were his eyes?'

'Strange-colored. Like copper, like a snake's. I found 'em off-putting.'

'I'll be,' said Bell. 'It's not him.'

'What do you mean?'

'His are blue.'

Bell stood up. 'I'm sorry, Mr Held. The louse tried to trick me into buying a boat I don't need.'

'But maybe he bought his down in Louisville or New Orleans.'

'Well, if I find out he did, I'll be back.'

Bell put on his hat and started out the door, feeling a mite guilty for the disappointed look on Held's face. A funny idea struck him – a scheme that could upend the situation in Pittsburgh and, with any luck, defuse it.

'Mr Held, I do know some fellows who might like a steamboat.'

'Well, send them to me and I'll cut you in with a finder's fee.'

'I couldn't take a fee among friends. But the trouble is, these fellows don't have much money.'

'I have a lot sunk into this one.'

'I understand. Would you consider renting it?'

'I might.'

'I'll tell these fellows about her. Meantime, let me pay you to coal her and get steam up by tomorrow.'

'By tomorrow?'

North Pole light flickered in Isaac Bell's eyes.

'I'm sure I could, now that I think about it,' said Held. 'She'll be raring to go in the morning.'

Bell paid Court Held for the coal and labor and hopped a trolley back to the business district. He got off at a Western Union office and sent a long telegram to Jim Higgins about the *White Lady*, recommending that he round up men who had worked on steamboats. Next, he went to East Seventh Street and found the Cincinnati branch office for Thibodeau & Marzen on the ground floor of a first-class building.

He stood outside, reading the gold leaf on the window, while he thought about how Wish Clarke, or Joseph Van Dorn, would pry information about 'Smith' from prominent brokers – the leading New York-based broker in Cincinnati, judging by the look of the office – who had every reason not to give it.

He started by presenting a business card from Dagget, Staples & Hitchcock, an old-line New England insurance company. Joseph Van Dorn had made a deal to allow select agents a business disguise in return for discreet investigations of underwriting opportunities and losses incurred. Thibodeau & Marzen's manager himself was summoned. Behind the broker's friendly salesman's smile, Bell detected a serious, no-nonsense executive, a tough nut to crack.

'Dagget, Staples & Hitchcock? Delighted to meet you, Mr Bell. What brings you all the way from Hartford, Connecticut?'

'The principals have sent me on a scouting expedition.'

'Well, as stockbrokers and insurance firms are potential partners rather than adversaries, I do believe you started scouting in the right place. May I offer a libation in my office?'

They felt each other out over bourbon whiskey, the manager probing for Bell's status at the venerable Hartford firm, Bell dropping names of school friends' fathers he had met and men he had read about in Grady Forrer's newspaper files. Turning down a hospitable refill, he said, 'I've been asked to look into some bearer bonds that went missing in Chicago.'

'Missing bearer bonds are never a happy story, as whoever possesses them can cash them and whoever lost them can't. Which, of course, I don't have to tell a man in the insurance line.'

'Dagget, Staples & Hitchcock would not dream of trying to recover them, or the losses, which as you point out would be impossible. However, we do have a strong interest in the man in whose hands they ended up.'

'If missing bearer bonds have ended up repeatedly in this man's hands as you are implying,' the branch manager said drily, 'I am not surprised you do.'

So far, thought Bell, the branch manager was holding him off adroitly, as if he had been in business long enough to guess what was coming next from this seemingly casual visitor. The young detective said, 'I would not be surprised if you have an inkling about the sort of question I am going to ask next.'

'Not one bit surprised,' the manager answered with a cool smile.

'The latest that went missing were railroad bonds. In twenty-five-thousand-dollar denominations.'

'May I ask which railroad?'

'It could have been one of many. The owner – previous owner, I guess we should say – had an affection for railroad bonds and owned a broad range, with various maturity dates and coupon rates of course.'

'Of course.'

'Of those stolen from his safe, we are particularly interested in three that were cashed within the week in a branch office of the issuing agent.'

'My branch office?' said the manager.

'Let me assure you that we are suggesting no impropriety on your part, and certainly not on the part of Mr Court Held.'

'I should think not.'

'Surely not, in your case. But we do find, rarely but occasionally, that businessmen facing hard times will do very foolish things, so I am extremely happy to say that this has nothing to do with Mr Held beyond the fact that the man who gave him the bonds in the course of a legitimate transaction might – and I emphasize *might* – be the man we have been investigating.'

The manager said nothing.

Bell said, 'His name is John Claggart.'

'That's not the man.'

'Sometimes he calls himself Henry Clay.'

'Not this time.'

'May I describe him to you?'

'Go ahead.'

Isaac described Henry Clay, ending with the eyes.

The branch manager of Thibodeau & Marzen said, 'He called himself Smith. The bonds were on the New Haven Railroad, maturing in 1908, with a coupon rate of five per cent.'

'Thank you,' said Bell, but he was disappointed. He had been half hoping that the manager would try to protect Claggart. With branches throughout the Midwest,

Thibodeau & Marzen would make a good front for a private detective, or a provocateur on the run.

'I wonder if there is anything else I should report back about Mr Smith. Is there anything he did that might help us track him down? I do hope I've made it clear that the firm regards him as a determined thief who will strike again.'

'You finally worked your way around to that, young man.'

'Anything. Anything odd?'

The manager stood up abruptly. 'No, sir. Nothing I can recall.'

Bell stood up, too. He did not believe him. He had touched a nerve. And he had probably put him in the position he didn't want to be. He said, 'A man I've worked with who taught me my trade once told me that the hardest thing in the world is to get a man to do the right thing for the wrong reason.'

'What trade is that, Mr Bell?'

'I'm actually a private detective.'

'I hope you don't think I'm shocked by your admission. What agency?'

'Van Dorn.'

'Ah. A reputable outfit . . . Well, you've been honest at last. I'll take a chance and be honest with you. Smith made me uncomfortable. For one thing, who in blazes buys a floating palace steamboat in this day and age? For another . . . Well, for another, my instincts were aroused. On the other hand, there was no legitimate reason not to cash the bonds – and, in fact, an obligation – since our firm was the issuing agent.'

'If the legitimacy of the bonds was not in doubt, what was odd?'

'While he was here, a message came in for him on our private wire.'

Isaac Bell felt an electric jolt. Pay dirt!

42

'Did you see the wire?'

Bell tried to sound casual but doubted he was fooling the manager.

'It was in cipher. Just numbers.'

'Does that imply he works for your firm?'

'No. And I'm quite sure he doesn't. If he happened to work for the firm, wouldn't he have introduced himself as such when he arrived?'

'Then how did he gain the use of your private telegraph?'

'The firm extends certain courtesies to good customers – as does any broker. Perhaps sometimes more than we should. By law, outsiders are forbidden to use leased wires. But everyone does it.'

'As I understand it,' said Bell, hoping to encourage his candor, 'it's a matter of business.' He was no stranger to private wires. The Van Dorn Detective Agency leased one. But he wanted the manager's version untarnished by his preconceptions. Something was troubling the man.

'Yes, a matter of business. To send a message on an existing private wire is less costly than the usual commercial message, quicker, and certainly more convenient.'

'And more private,' said Bell.

'Yes, the advantages of a private closed wire include economy, quickness of dispatch, and privacy.'

'Did he send a reply?'

'It was brief. An acknowledgment, I presume, but it, too, was in cipher.'

Bell asked another question to which he knew the answer. 'Are ciphers unusual?'

'Not among brokers. It's only sensible to conceal buy and sell orders just in case the telegrapher violates his oath of privacy.'

'What do you make of it?'

'He is a friend of the firm, shall I put it? A special customer. Of the New York firm, I mean. I don't know him from Adam. But he knows someone in New York.'

Isaac Bell stood up and offered his hand. 'I appreciate your candor.' What was it the manager had said earlier? *The firm extends certain courtesies . . . Perhaps sometimes more than we should.* 'May I ask you one more thing?'

'Go ahead.'

'I am curious why.'

'Why what?'

'What made you candid?'

The manager straightened his shoulders. 'Mark Twain says that he intends to move back to Cincinnati on Judgment Day because we're twenty years behind the times. Fine with me. I'm old-fashioned. I don't like stock traders who can afford private wires getting a jump on the fellow who has to use the public wire. And Thibodeau & Marzen didn't used to be the sort of outfit that liked them either.'

Bell stopped at Western Union on his way to meet Kenny Bloom at the Queen City Club and wired a telegram to Grady Forrer:

RESEARCH PRINCIPALS THIBODEAU & MARZEN.

He doubted very much that Henry Clay was communicating on private wires to get a jump on a stock sale as the Cincinnati branch manager suspected. Instead of fraudulent profits, a business with branches scattered around the continent could offer direct private communication with someone in their New York office. In the case of Smith, Claggart and Henry Clay, Isaac Bell bet that someone was the man who gave the provocateur his orders.

He found Court Held at the Queen City Club bar. The shipyard heir greeted him like an old friend and invited him and Kenny to stay for dinner. Kenny, who was on his fourth whiskey, looked like he thought that was a good idea, but Bell reminded the coal-and-railroad heir that having raced to Cincinnati to meet with his Ohio bankers, he should be racing home, which was why he had taken his father's special in the first place.

'We better eat on the train.'

'Pittsburgh in one hour,' announced the Bloom Special's conductor as they neared the Ohio border for the run across West Virginia's Northern Panhandle.

'Why so long?' Kenny demanded. He had fallen asleep on the couch in the office–sitting room car and sat up, rubbing his temples.

'Sorry, Mr Bloom, we have to stop for water outside Steubenville.'

'Why outside? Jeez, my head is aching. Can't we just go straight?'

'As I mentioned earlier, the dispatcher had to shunt us around Steubenville for a mail train. We didn't lose more than ten minutes.'

'But now we have to stop for water.'

'Or don't stop and blow up the locomotive,' said Bell, and Kenny laughed. 'All right, all right. Just get us there.'

The train slowed and stopped by a dark water siding.

The conductor, who was doubling as brakeman, jumped down to the tracks to throw the switch. His name was Bill Kux, and he'd been hankering after a job on the New York Central's 20th Century Limited – or, better yet, way out west on the Overland Limited – and this Cincinnati trip with Old Man Bloom's spoiled brat had pretty much made up his mind.

Kux threw the switch. The engineer backed the special on to the water siding. The fireman climbed up on the locomotive and jerked a chain that pulled the waterspout down to the engine. The engineer climbed down from the cab to stretch his legs. Kux said, 'You'll make all our lives easier if you can make up some time.'

The engineer swore he would do his damnedest. The fireman climbed down. Kux turned to run back to the switch and found himself staring into the twin maws of a twelve-gauge double-barreled shotgun. Gasps behind Kux told him that the engineer and fireman were peering down gun barrels, too.

'This way, boys, right behind the water tower.' There were three of them with bandannas pulled over their noses. They had brought iron manacles, which they clamped around the train crew's wrists and ankles. The fireman got the big idea to resist, which earned him a gun-butt to the head.

Conductor Kux was not entirely displeased to imagine Bloom Jr. being relieved of his watch, cuff links, stickpin and billfold. But from what he had seen of Bloom's friend Isaac Bell, the robbery would likely turn into a bloody shoot-out, so he tried to dissuade them.

'If you're fixing to rob my passengers, there's only two of 'em, you damned fools. You stopped a special.'

'We ain't robbing your passengers. We're robbing your train.'

'Kenny?' asked Isaac Bell as the train started rolling again. 'Do you know Thibodeau & Marzen in New York?'

'The brokers.'

'Right. What do you know about them?'

'I think Dad used them once or –'

The train jerked, and he spilled whiskey over his shirt. 'Dammit to hell. I will fire that engineer.'

'He's displayed a fine smooth hand up to now,' said Bell. 'I wonder what's got into him?'

Kenny Bloom dabbed his shirt with a napkin. 'Overpaid son of a bitch has probably been drinking.' The train picked up speed.

'What do you know about Thibodeau & Marzen?' Bell asked again.

'Old-fashioned old codgers.'

'Are they honest?'

Kenny dabbed his shirt some more, then poured another glass. He gestured with the bottle. Bell shook his head.

'Are they honest?'

'Honest as the day is long. Frankly, I don't know how they survive on Wall Street.'

Bell looked at their reflections in the night-blackened

glass. Lights in a farmhouse raced by. Old and honest? Had Clay and his boss somehow tapped secretly into Thibodeau & Marzen's private system?

'We're making time at last,' said Kenny. 'Running fast and hitting the curves hard. Maybe I won't fire him after all.'

'What? Oh yes.'

The train was highballing through the night, although the rate of speed was not that apparent. Their car was coupled between a stateroom car, which rode directly behind the tender, and the diner car at the back of the train. Thus anchored, it did not sway much, while thick insulating felt between the paneling and the outer walls muffled wind and track noise. Bell was surprised, as they passed a small-town train depot, how fast its lights whipped by.

A sudden chatter broke the silence.

Kenny darted to the telegraph key. They had picked up a message by grasshopper telegraphy, the signal relayed to the speeding train from the telegraph wires that paralleled the tracks through an Edison-patented electrostatic induction system. Fluent since boyhood in the Morse alphabet, Kenny cocked his ear and wrote furiously, then carried what he had written to Bell, his expression grave. Bell, who had listened intently, knew why.

'For you,' said Kenny.

'I told the boys I'd be on your train.'

He read it, his brow furrowing.

'Looks bad,' said Kenny.

'Hellish,' said Isaac Bell.

REGRET TOWBOAT CAMILLA EXPLOSION.
CAPTAIN DIED.
REGRET UNION HALL FIRE.
BODYGUARDS FRIED.
ENJOY YOUR RIDE.
TRIPLE PLAY.

43

'"Enjoy your ride?"' asked Kenny Bloom. 'What the hell kind of joke is that supposed to be?'

'A vicious joke,' said Bell, mourning Captain Jennings, murdered for helping the marchers, and Mike Flannery and Terry Fein, whom he had sent into action over their heads.

'And what does "triple play" mean?'

The floor shook and the windows reverberated as the train thundered across an iron trestle bridge. 'Where's the conductor?'

'I don't know. Back in the diner.'

'Are you sure?'

Bell strode quickly to the back of the car and threw open the door into the enclosed vestibule. The wheels were thundering on the track, and the wind was roaring past the canvas diaphragm. Bell opened the diner door and stepped into the car. It was swaying violently.

'Kux! Conductor Kux! Are you there?'

The cook stuck his head out of the kitchen. 'We're going mighty fast, Mr Bell. In fact, we're going faster than I've ever seen this train go.'

'Where's Mr Kux?'

'I haven't see him since we stopped for water.'

Bell ran forward. Kenny was pouring a fresh drink.

'We're bouncing around like a yawl in a storm. What the hell is going on?'

'First thing I'm going to ask your engineer.' Bell pushed into the front vestibule, heading for the locomotive. The door to the stateroom car was bolted shut. It was a steel express car door. There was no budging it short of dynamite.

'Locked,' he told Kenny.

'Something's nuts,' said Kenny Bloom. 'We're doing ninety miles an hour.'

The train hit a curve hard. Wheel flanges screeched on the rails.

'"Triple play,"' said Isaac Bell, 'means we're next. He shanghaied our crew and tied down the throttle.'

'I'm stopping us!' Kenny lunged for the red handle of the emergency brake on the wall at the front of the car.

Bell beat him to it and blocked his hand. 'If we slam on the air brakes at this speed we'll derail her.'

'We've got to stop her. Feel that? She's still accelerating.' Kenny, who had carried his glass with him, put it down. 'Isaac, we're heading for Pittsburgh at a hundred miles an hour.'

'How drunk are you?' Bell asked.

'I'm too scared to be drunk.'

'Good. Help me out the window.'

'Where you going?'

'Locomotive.'

Bell dropped the sash. A hundred-mile-an-hour wind blasted through the opening and sent everything not nailed down flying about the car in a tornado of cloth and paper. Bell tugged off his coat and thrust his head out the window. The rushing air hit him like a river in flood. He wormed his torso out, sat on the sash, and attempted to stand. The wind nearly knocked him off the train.

'I'll block,' yelled Kenny. He yanked down the next window and squirmed his bulky chest and belly out the opening. Bell tried again. With Kenny blocking the wind with his body, he managed to plant his feet on the windowsill. But when he stood up, it took all his strength to hold on. If he let go either hand to pull himself on to the roof of the car, he would be blown away. Kenny Bloom, hanging on for dear life, saw that and shouted, 'Wait!' Then he struggled to stand on his windowsill to shield Bell's upper body so he could reach for the roof.

'Don't!' shouted Bell. 'You'll fall.'

'I was just as good an acrobat as you,' Kenny yelled back. 'Almost.'

With a herculean effort that made his eyes roll into the back of his head, the rotund Bloom stood up. 'Go!'

Isaac Bell wasted no time pulling himself on to the roof. Kenny had been a pretty good acrobat in the circus, but that was back when they were kids and since then he had lifted nothing heavier than a glass to build his strength. The wind was even stronger on the roof. Bell slithered flat on his belly to the front of the car, over the canvas-covered frame of the vestibules and on to the stateroom car, and crawled forward into a blizzard of smoke, steam and hot cinders spewing from the engine. Reaching the front of the car at last, he found a six-foot space between its roof and the tender. Coal was heaped in the front of the tender. The back, the steel water tank, was flat, and lower than the roof of the stateroom.

The wind of their passage at one hundred miles per hour made it impossible to jump the space. Bell put his hands together and extended his arms, narrowing his body as if diving off a high board, and plunged. He cleared the back of the tender, and when his hands hit the steel tank, he tried to curl into a tight ball. He tumbled forward, skidded on the slick surface, and reached frantically for a handhold.

He found one wrapping the edge, dragged himself forward, dropped on to the coal pile, scrambled across it, and found himself peering into an empty locomotive cab lit by the roaring flames of the firebox that gleamed through a crack in the door. He climbed down a ladder on the front of the tender and jumped into the cab, a hot, dark labyrinth of levers, valves, gauges and piping.

He was generally conversant with locomotives from avid reading as a child, schoolboy engine tours hosted by Kenny's father, and leading a Yale Glee Club midnight excursion to Miss Porter's School on an Atlantic 4-4-0 'borrowed' from the New Haven Railroad train yards. He left the Johnson bar reverser in the center notch and searched for the throttle.

The throttle would not budge. He looked closely. The train wreckers had screwed a clamp on to hold it in the wide-open position. He unscrewed the clamp and notched the throttle forward to stop the flow of steam into the cylinders. Tens of thousands of pounds of steel, iron, coal and water just kept rolling. Gently, he applied the automatic air brakes on the cars behind him, reducing about eight pounds of pressure, which also set the locomotive's brakes. Screeching steel and a violent bucking told him, Too much. He put on more air pressure, easing the brake shoes on the wheels, and tried a softer touch. At last the train began to slow until there came a point at about fifty miles an hour when Isaac Bell realized to his huge relief that he, more than momentum, was in command.

Just in time. He had reduced the train's speed to a crawl when he saw a red lantern ahead. A brakeman was standing on the tracks, swinging the *Stop* signal. A passenger train had stopped for a dispatcher's signal and was blocking the tracks. 'Ran back as fast as I could,' shouted the brakeman. 'Good thing you saw me. Bumping into us at ten miles an hour, somebody might get hurt.'

'Wouldn't dream of it,' said Bell.

While he waited for the train ahead to get moving again, he checked his gauges for boiler pressure and water level and injected more water into the firebox and scooped coal into the fire. Then he followed the passenger train into Pittsburgh, tight on its tail to squeeze through the same switches. Crossing the Allegheny River, he saw a fire at the Point – the still-burning wreckage of the stern-wheeler *Camilla*. A bigger fire was shooting flames into the sky from the edge of the Golden Triangle. It looked as if the union hall fire had spread to surrounding buildings.

Wally and Mack were waiting at the specials' platform. One look at Bell's face and Wally said, 'I see you already heard what happened.'

'Henry Clay wired the news himself. Couldn't resist bragging. And I just saw the fires from the bridge. Did the boys burn to death?'

'Firemen I talked to think they had their heads bashed in first.'

'I should have sent you two. You'd have seen it coming.'

'Don't start blaming yourself,' said Mack. 'Terry and Mike were grown-ups.'

'Just so you know, Isaac, they found another body, apparently the guy who set the fire. Papers in his wallet said he was on the Strike Committee.'

'How come his wallet didn't burn up?'

'Smoke poisoning killed him, apparently,' said Wally. 'Or so the cops say.'

Mack said, 'Whatever happened, the strikers will catch hell for it. The newspapers are putting on extra editions, howling for blood.'

'What about Jennings's steamboat?'

'Similar situation,' Wally said. 'Sheriff's men shot a striker in a rowboat. It was nearby.'

Mack said, 'With all this in mind, we sent Archie to keep an eye on Jim Higgins.'

Bell said, 'But Jim Higgins is protected by armed strikers.'

'So they'll protect Archie, too.'

Bell nodded. 'Of course. You're right. Thank you for looking after Archie.'

'Now what?' asked Wally.

'Any word from Research?'

'Dead end.'

Mack handed him a telegram from Grady Forrer.

THIBODEAU & MARZEN PRINCIPALS UNNAMED, UNKNOWN, UNKNOWABLE.

Bell had been counting heavily on the broker leading him to Henry Clay's boss. He crumpled the telegram in his fist and flung it from him. Mack caught it on the fly, smoothed the paper, and handed it back. 'Put it away for later. Sometimes dead ends turn around.'

'Now what?' Wally asked again.

'Where's that black steamboat?'

'Terry and Mike saw it tied up behind a mill at McKeesport.'

'Which is probably what got them killed.'

A bell clanged. A gleaming locomotive pulled a New York-to-Chicago limited into the train shed. Bell looked around the train platforms, which were deserted at this late hour. He wondered where Mary was. But he asked, 'Where's Jim Higgins?'

'Forted up at Amalgamated,' said Mack. 'He's got trains blocked, trolleys blocked, and streets blocked. But the black boat is making them nervous.'

Wally said, 'The cops are gnashing their teeth.'

'So's the sheriff,' said Mack. 'At least, according to my sources. Rarin' to roust the strikers out of their tents.'

'That would be a bloodbath.'

Wally said, 'The operators, and the Coal and Iron cops, and the Pinkertons, and the state militia wouldn't mind a bloodbath one bit.'

'But the mayor and some of Pittsburgh's powers that be are afraid of a bloodbath,' said Mack, 'account of all the women and kids. And with church ladies and progressives breathing down their necks. They're hinting they'll negotiate.'

'At least 'til after the ball,' said Wally.

'What ball?'

'Pittsburgh Society ball. Big annual la-di-da. Industrialists looking for gentility. Swells steaming in on specials. The mayor knows the newspapers would have the real ball – tycoons dancing on workmen's graves – so he's trying to sit on the hotheads for a couple of days more. Meaning we have two days before this blows sky-high.'

Bleeding steam, the limited from New York rolled beside a platform, and a big man in a voluminous coat bounded down before it stopped.

Wally Kisley said, 'Look out, Isaac! If you think you have problems now, here comes the Boss.'

Joseph Van Dorn spotted Bell's wave from across the tracks, strode into the station building, and doubled back to the private platform where his detectives were conferring. On the way he had bought an extra edition the newsboys were hawking inside. He waved it in their faces.

'Couldn't help but notice that the city's on fire. Says here, we lost two men.'

'Terry Fein and Mike Flannery,' said Bell. 'And a steamboat captain who went out on a limb for us.'

'Us?' Van Dorn demanded. 'Who are "us"? Detectives or strikers?'

'Both,' said Isaac Bell. 'We ended up on the same side.'

Instead of remonstrating with Bell, Joseph Van Dorn asked, 'Driven there by Henry Clay?'

'Explosives and arson are Clay's hallmarks,' answered Bell. 'Captain Jennings's towboat was a dependable workhorse. Highly unlikely it would blow up without help. And even the cops say the union hall was arson.'

'But conveniently blame a dead striker,' said Wally Kisley.

Joseph Van Dorn looked Bell in the eye. 'What's your next move, Isaac?'

Wally Kisley blurted, '*Isaac's* next move? Aren't you taking over?'

Joseph Van Dorn's hard gaze never left Bell's face. He answered in a tone that invited no questions. 'Isaac got us into this mess. I'm counting on him getting us out of it. What's your next step, Detective Bell?'

Now Mack Fulton protested, exercising the privilege of the Van Dorn Agency's oldest employee. 'It's too much to put all on him, Joe.'

And Wally chimed in, 'It needs an experienced man with a bird's-eye view.'

Van Dorn asked, 'What do you say to that, Isaac?'

Van Dorn, Kisley and Fulton were staring expectantly at him, and if Isaac Bell had any doubts left about his 'bird's-eye view' of the Striker Case, they were demolished once and for all when Kenny Bloom staggered off his train arm in arm with the cook.

Both men were clutching highball glasses. Kenny raised his in salute.

'The man of the hour. Gentlemen, I give you Isaac Bell, the hero engineer who saved the lives of a worthless plutocrat and his worthy cook. Whatever you want shall be yours.'

Bell said, 'It's not all on me, I've got you gents. Here's what I want – Wally, Mack, I want you two to keep trying to track down Henry Clay.'

'I'll track Clay,' growled Joseph Van Dorn.

'No,' said Isaac Bell, 'you can do better than track Clay.'

'Clay is my fault. He's my monster. I created him. I'll kill him.'

'No. If you fail – if Clay eludes you even for a moment – ten thousand people's lives are at risk. You have to do more – you met the President.'

'TR. What about him?'

'Can you meet him again?'

'Not easily. I'd have to go to Washington. It could take a week. What for?'

'Go to Washington. We have to keep the strikers and the strikebreakers from killing each other until someone persuades cooler heads to negotiate. If we can't stop Henry Clay, the President will be the only one who can even try.'

'You want me to organize a fallback?'

'If all else fails.'

Before Van Dorn could formulate an answer, Bell whirled on Kenny and his cook.

'Cook! I want a big breakfast laid on for twenty men. Kenny! I want a fresh locomotive and train crew.'

'What for?'

'I'm highballing your special back to Cincinnati.'

'Why?'

'We have only two days. There isn't a moment to lose.'

44

Mary Higgins tipped a nickle-plated flask to her lips and tossed her head back. Her glossy black hair rippled in the thin sun that penetrated the smoke.

'I was not aware you drank,' said Henry Clay.

She was amazed how a man who could be so brutal was so prim. 'My father had a saloon. I learned how when I was young.'

'At his knee?' Clay smiled. She looked lovely, he thought, wearing a long coat she had borrowed from her new land-lady and a wide-brimmed feathered hat that he had persuaded her to accept after most of her belongings had burned in the union hall. They had ridden the cable-powered incline up Mount Washington and were sitting in a little park with a murky view of the Golden Triangle and the Monongahela, Allegheny, and Ohio rivers. He was in business attire: frock coat, homburg, and a walking stick that concealed a sword.

'Father always said a girl should learn to hold her whiskey.'

'Didn't you say he had a tugboat?'

'The saloon was another time, in another city. He was always changing jobs.'

'A jack-of-all-trades?'

'He could *master* anything. Except people. Just like my

brother, Jim. It broke his heart that evil people exist.' She touched the flask to her lips again. 'He also said, "Never drink alone." Would you like some?'

'It's barely noon.'

'Don't put off 'til tonight what you can do today. Here.'

She handed it to him with a smile. Henry Clay weighed the flask tentatively in his hand. 'Pass it back if you're not going to use it,' said Mary, her gray eyes warming as she teased him.

Clay tilted it toward her in a toast, 'Don't put off 'til tonight . . .' and raised it to his lips. He handed it back.

Mary said, 'See you on the other side,' and drank deeply.

When the flask was empty, Henry Clay said, 'I'll run and get us a refill.'

Mary Higgins pressed her fingers to her temples. 'Oh, my poor head. This was a terrible idea.'

'What do you mean?'

'I need coffee. I need gallons of coffee.' She sprang to her feet, swayed a little, and said, 'Come on, I'll make some at my place.'

They rode down on the incline and then took a horse cab across the Smithfield Bridge to her latest temporary digs. It was a small furnished apartment, more expensive than a rooming house but worth it for the extra privacy. She had begged the rent from her brother's strike fund. She brewed strong coffee in the tiny kitchen and brought it to Clay in the sitting room. She was betting that the combination of the whiskey she had persuaded him to drink and the strong, heavily sugared coffee would mask the taste of the chloral hydrate.

Not only did Clay not notice the knockout drops, he

asked for a second cup, half of which he spilled on his trousers when he suddenly passed out with a mildly incredulous expression on his face.

She searched his billfold and his pockets but found absolutely no clue about the man who paid him to provoke violence so the owners and the government could destroy the union. In disappointment and disbelief, she went through everything again. Again, nothing. She riffled through his business cards, thinking maybe he had slipped one he had been given among his own.

She found a sheet of paper that had been folded over and over until it fit between the cards. She unfolded it. It was a private-wire telegram to his John Claggart alias from a New York broker. She slammed it down on the couch. Every word of it was in cipher. Useless.

She could go to New York to the broker. But then what? Persuade them to decipher it for her? If they knew who he was, they would not tell.

Clay's hand closed around her boot.

She looked down. He had awakened and was watching her through slitted eyes.

'What are you doing?' he asked.

'Searching your pockets,' she said. What could she say, with his billfold sitting in her lap and his private wire next to her?

'Why?'

'Because you still won't tell me who is paying for everything. Did he send you this telegram?'

'Why do you care so much?'

'Because he is trying to destroy us.'

Clay mumbled, 'Oh, Mary, for God's sake,' and that was

329

when she realized that the knockout drops had put him in a half-delirious state.

She sat on the floor beside him and took his hand in both of hers.

'What is his name?'

'You don't understand.'

'I'm trying to.'

She looked into his strange eyes. The chloral had turned him inside out. The pharmacist had warned her. Reactions varied. The drug could put a man to sleep, or make him delirious, or writhing in agony. Did Clay know he was awake? Did he know his own name? He knew her. He stared, his mouth working. 'Mary, when I'm done, perhaps you and I . . . I would fund progressive impulses.'

'What do you mean?'

'Important men, men of means, do that for their wives . . .' His voice drifted.

Mary said, 'What for their wives?' She had to keep him talking.

'Reformers' husbands pay the bills. When I am done, I will do that.'

'Done with what?'

'Mary. I'm doing something very important.'

'Yes, yes, I know.'

'I want you to understand that.'

'I'm trying to . . . I do.'

'I will be a made man.'

'Of course.'

'I will have so much to offer you.'

'You do already,' she said. 'You are quite remarkable.'

For once, he ignored praise, saying, 'But I couldn't do this without him.'

In a flash of insight into his strange mind, she said, 'But he couldn't do it without you.'

'That's right. That's right. You know. As powerful as he is – the most powerful man in the country – he could not do it without me.'

'Does he know that?' she asked.

'He doesn't *want* to know it,' Clay said bitterly. 'He thinks he doesn't need me.'

'But he does!'

'Yes. Even *he* needs me. The most important man in the world. Mary, it's James Congdon. The most powerful man in Wall Street. The most powerful man in steel and coal and railroads. But he needs me.'

My God, she thought, Clay had gone straight to the top. Or bottom. Judge James Congdon made Frick look like a company store butcher overcharging for fatback.

He was watching her, waiting. She said, 'James Congdon is lucky to have you.'

'Thank you,' Clay whispered. 'Thank you for saying that.'

When Henry Clay fell asleep, again, Mary stuffed his Bisley revolver in her bag and left, shaking.

He could have killed me, she thought. But he didn't.

She went straight to Union Station and bought the cheapest coach ticket on a slow train to New York with the last of her money. On the train, she wrote a letter to her brother, and another to Isaac Bell, and posted both when the train stopped at a station in the middle of Pennsylvania and changed engines to climb the Allegheny Mountains.

The train was crowded. The seat was hard. Her reflection in the night-blackened window revealed her father's features. His favorite saying had always been, The only thing you'll ever regret is the thing you didn't do.

45

Henry Clay drove a narrow, closed wagon with two high wheels in back and two shorter wheels in front. The wagon was much heavier than it looked, particularly as the words *Hazelwood Bakery* painted on the sides and the loaves of bread heaped in the left-hand front corner behind glass implied a bulky but light load. It took the combined effort of two strong mules to pull it up the hills.

Clay walked alongside with the reins in his hands. On the driver's seat beside the loaves sat a kindly-looking middle-aged woman clutching a Bible. Her cheeks were round and pink, her hair pulled back in a modest bun, her eyes alert.

'Cops,' she said.

'Just do as I told you and everything will be fine.' He was not worried. She was levelheaded and had weathered many strikes in the coalfields.

The cops, shivering in dirty blue Pittsburgh Police Department uniforms, were manning the outside of a barricade the strikers had made of toppled streetcars to protect their tent city. They were cold and wet from the rain squalls that kept sweeping the Amalgamated point, they were bored, and they were hungry. The pink-cheeked, gray-haired woman tossed them loaves of bread that were still warm.

The cops tore off chunks and chewed on them. 'Can't let you go in, lady.'

'It's from our church. There's children in that camp and they're hungry.'

'Can't you give 'em a break?' said Henry Clay.

'We got our orders. No guns, no food.'

Clay tied his reins to the wagon, nodded for the cop in charge to step aside, and passed an almost full bottle of whiskey from his coat. He whispered, 'Don't let her see this, but I figure you guys must be cold.'

The cop took a slug of it.

Clay almost gagged from the smell. The chloral Mary had drugged him with had left him with a heaving stomach, a splitting headache, and weird dreams. But he could not for the life of him remember what had transpired between them at her apartment. All he knew for certain was that she was gone and had stolen his Colt Bisley. What she had wanted he could not guess. Had she drugged him for Bell? But she hated Bell. Besides, if she had done it for Bell, the Van Dorns would have slapped the cuffs on him while he was passed out. The cop was talking to him.

'This is the good stuff.'

'Keep it.'

'You must really love them strikers.'

Clay nodded in the direction of the woman on the driver's seat. 'She's my big sister. Took care of me when I was a kid. What am I going to do? She wants to bring 'em bread.'

'OK. OK. I don't want to starve kids, either. Go on in. But don't come back this way. Go out another side in case the sergeant comes.'

'Thanks, pal.'

The cops walked away. Henry Clay rapped on the barricade. Twenty men dragged a car aside, and the mules dug in their shoes to pull the weight over the hump in the road and through the opening. As soon as the car was pushed back, the head of the Defense Committee, Jack Fortis, greeted Henry Clay by the name John Claggart, and led the wagon into the tent city. The woman on the driver's seat threw bread to the people crouched in their tents but quickly ran out. She climbed down without a word and plodded away in the rain. The wagon continued on, through the tents and up a muddy hill to the masonry base of the coal tipple.

'Put it there,' said Fortis.

Henry Clay nodded his approval. The strikers had chosen well. The site commanded the entire bend in the river.

The mules were unhitched and led away. Carpenters and a blacksmith gathered with crowbars, hammers, wrenches and chisels and quickly dismantled the bakery wagon. Sides, roof, driver's seat, dashboard, shafts, and an improvised coupler were carried off. The front wheels were detached and rolled away.

Henry Clay watched the carpenters, the smith, and especially Fortis's picked men from the Defense Committee, all Spanish War veterans, gaze with great satisfaction at what was left – a four-foot-long cannon capable of firing an explosive shell two miles. It was a Hotchkiss Mountain Gun mounted on its own carriage, which had served as the fake bakery wagon's high back wheels. The tube and its steel wheels and ammunition weighed seven hundred pounds. Portable and accurate, the type had proved its worth for a generation, slaughtering savages in the Indian Wars and Spaniards on San Juan Hill and currently blasting Philippine insurgents with jagged shell fragments.

Fortis raised his voice. 'Thank you, John Claggart. This will even things up. You are a true friend to labor.'

Henry Clay replied, 'I wish I could have brought you more ammunition. Only thirty rounds. But once you get the *Vulcan King*'s range, you ought to blow enough holes in her to sink her before they get off too many shots. Better yet, blow up a boiler. Remember, her boilers are directly underneath her wheelhouse. If you manage to hit a boiler, the explosion will sweep away the whole forward part of the boat, from the wheelhouse down to the waterline, and bury their guns.'

'And the state militia,' said Fortis.

'And the Pinkertons,' said Clay. 'And the Coal and Iron Police. Good luck, boys. God go with all of you.'

A US Marshal boarded the railroad ferry from Jersey City to Cortlandt Street with a prisoner in handcuffs and leg irons who recognized Mary Higgins from the union. He looked away so as not to cause her trouble. She had just bought a sandwich in the terminal. She carried it over and asked the marshal, 'May I give this to your prisoner?'

A smile got him to allow it.

It was a short walk from the ferry terminal to Wall Street. She paused in Trinity Church cemetery, and paused again to stare in the tall windows of Thibodeau & Marzen. It looked like a bank.

Nearby, she found the Congdon Building, the tallest on the block. The doorman eyed her borrowed coat and the hat Henry Clay had bought her and asked politely who she had come to see. Her voice failed her. She had lost her nerve. Stammering something unintelligible, she hurried away. She rode a streetcar uptown, clutching Clay's revolver in her bag, walked a bit, and came back down on the Third Avenue El. The doormen had changed shifts. The new man was polite, too, equally impressed by her coat and hat.

'Mr James Congdon, please.'

'Top floor,' he said, indicating the elevator.

The elevator runner, a gawky kid who in a better world would still be in school, asked her what floor, and when she told him he asked, 'What's your name, please, miss? I have to call ahead to Mr Congdon's floor.'

So much for surprising the great man in his lair. 'Mary Higgins.'

He called on the intercom, spoke her name, and listened.

'He wants to know who you are.'

'A friend of Mr Clay.'

'He says bring you up.'

The elevator delivered her to a small foyer with a reception desk. A middle-aged woman at the desk pointed toward a series of rooms that spilled one into another. 'Through there. Close each door behind you, please.'

Mary Higgins went through the first door, closed it, and in through a second. Each room was quieter than the last. In the third she found a closed door and knocked.

A strong male voice shouted, 'Enter!'

337

She pushed through the door, closed it behind her, and gasped.

'My sculpture is Auguste Rodin's *The Kiss*. Do you like it?'

'It is the most beautiful thing I have ever seen.'

She tore her eyes from the white marble to look across the room at Congdon, who was standing at his desk. He looked older than in the newspaper sketches but more vigorous. He was very tall and stood well.

'Go on. You can look at it. Touch it. It feels wonderful.'

She approached reverentially. The confident way the woman's left arm pulled her lover toward her was the most erotic sight she had ever seen.

'What do you want?'

'I want a world where everyone can see this beautiful statue.'

'Not in this life,' Congdon said coldly.

His office had double windows. No sound from the street penetrated. The walls were hung with paintings, most of thinly veiled naked women in the French Academy style. On his desk Mary saw a bronze statuette, another naked woman.

'My wife,' said Congdon, stroking it. 'Go on, you can touch it, if you like. I find the marble draws me close.'

Mary laid her hand on the woman's arm.

'What else do you want?' Congdon asked. 'What did you come for?'

'I want you to stand aside and let the coal miners organize, and I want you to pay them a fair wage.'

'Higgins? Yes, of course. You're Jim Higgins's sister, aren't you? The unionist.'

Mary nodded.

Congdon said, 'Even if I wanted to, which I don't, you're talking to the wrong man. I don't own coal mines.'

'You control them by the prices you pay for the coal the miners dig and for what your railroads charge to ship it. And please don't insult my intelligence. If you don't "officially" own those railroads, you control them by their purse strings. If there is only one person in the country who can allow a union and pay the miners a fair wage, it is you.'

'Assume, for a moment, I could. What would I get out of it?'

'The well-being gained when equality spawns justice.'

'Equality spawns mediocrity at best, the mob at worst.'

'If you refuse, I will expose your scheme to foment violence in the coalfields.'

'And how will you do that?'

'I will persuade Henry Clay to confess everything you two have done and everything you plan to do next.'

James Congdon regarded her with a thoughtful smile. At last, he said, 'I'll be damned . . . You know, I have no doubt you could do that. I suspect you are an extraordinary young woman. I would not be at all surprised if you've established insights into Clay that would allow you to command his frail emotions.'

'You and I are similar,' said Mary Higgins.

'In what way?'

'Clear-eyed and quick.'

'I take that as a compliment. But we are *dissimilar* in more important ways. I would build – you would tear down. You love mankind – I can't abide it. I am old – you are young. And very, very beautiful.' He roved his eyes over her. 'Have I insulted you by observing that?'

Mary let her own eyes rove around his paintings again. They settled on the statuette. He was rubbing its breasts with his thumb.

'Well? Have I?'

Mary draped her arms around the marble couple. 'Considering your penchant for women in the altogether, I'd have been insulted if you hadn't at least noticed me.'

'Good! Let's get right to it. I will make you an offer, young lady. I won't ask you to even pretend that you find a man three times your age attractive. I don't care about being "attractive" to you or anyone. I care about possession. And I have no objection to paying for possession. It is the most tangible reward for success. In return, you will live lavishly in comparison to the vast, vast majority of other women. Whether I decide to keep you or not. If not, you will receive a generous pension, based, of course, on how long I've kept you.'

'How large a pension compared to your regular employees?'

'There's no comparison. Few receive pensions. The handful who do do not discover themselves rolling in wealth they didn't earn.'

'If you decided to keep me, how much?'

'You'll want for nothing.'

'An automobile?'

'Of course.'

'An apartment on Fifth Avenue?'

'For as long as I have the only key.'

'Could I come and see this statue?'

'Every night.'

'Could I have a yacht?'

'A yacht would require extra effort on your part.'

'I hoped you would say that.'

A broad smile uncreased Congdon's face. 'That suggests we understand each other perfectly. And let me put your mind to ease on one score. I can pretty much guarantee that when you find yourself on silk sheets, an older man might surprise you more than you imagine.'

'I've been surprised only once in my life and it wasn't on silk sheets.'

'Where was that?'

'On a freight train. Go to hell, Congdon.'

Congdon, visibly surprised, fumbled around his desk and laid a hand on the bronze statuette of his naked wife. 'But you just said you were hoping –'

'I was hoping you would say something that would give me enough courage, or enough hatred, to shoot you. And you did, thank you.' She took Henry Clay's revolver from her bag and braced it on *The Kiss*.

The veins in the back of Congdon's hand bulged as he gripped his statuette with sudden intensity. 'Did the yacht do it?'

She tried to answer but couldn't. Finally, she whispered, 'I guess we all have our limits.'

'What do you mean?'

'I cannot kill another human being, even the worst one in the world.' She lowered the gun. 'I can't do it.'

'I can,' he said, and slammed the statuette down and jumped back – just in case a twenty-foot separation was not enough – and watched from afar.

Steam roared. Hot, needle-sharp jets spewed down from the ceiling and up from the floor and enveloped Mary Higgins in a scalding white cloud. She screamed only once. Congdon was surprised. He had expected it to take longer with a strong young woman. But she had died in a flash. So much for pain, he thought. She had died in the space of a single breath. Probably never knew what hit her.

He edged back to his desk and lifted the lever gingerly. It was actually cool to the touch, so tightly focused were the jets. The steam stopped gushing. The windows were fogged, and he felt dampness on his cheeks and saw a layer of dew on his polished desk. But the cloud that had enveloped Mary and *The Kiss* had already dissipated. Congdon wished he had planned ahead. He usually did; he could usually imagine consequences. But he had not thought to keep a sheet nearby – something, anything, to throw over the corpse.

46

The *White Lady* careened through a sharp bend in the river at mile marker 25 and pounded toward Pittsburgh belching black columns from her chimneys and churning a white wake behind her.

'She smells the barn!' said the Ohio River pilot – one of two Isaac Bell had hired in Cincinnati – along with a chief engineer famously reckless in the pursuit of hotter steam.

'Faster,' said Bell, and the pilot rang the engine room.

Forced draft furnace fans roared. Jim Higgins's miners shoveled on the coal. And the engineer played fast and loose with his boiler levels, tempting eternal oblivion by pumping water on red-hot plates to jump the pressure.

At mile marker 10, Bell saw the horizon grow dark with city smoke. Thunderheads loomed. Bolts of lightning pierced them. Rain sizzled down and flattened the seething currents of the river in flood.

Soon the hills of Pittsburgh hunched into the dismal sky. Tall buildings emerged from the smoke. The *White Lady* steamed out of the Ohio River and up the Monongahela, past the Point and under the bridges of the Golden Triangle. Fifty-five minutes after mile marker 10, by Isaac Bell's watch, forty-four hours from Cincinnati, the immense steamboat backed her paddle blades.

Escape pipes blew off excess steam with a roar that drowned out the ringing of her bell, and she nosed to a

343

landing at the foot of the Amalgamated coal miners' tent city. Miners recruited as deckhands hoisted her boarding stage on to a temporary wharf that the strikers had improvised by raising one of the barges that the Defense Committee had sunk to fortify the point with a crenellated breakwater.

Coal miners, their wives and children, church ladies, reformers, and scribbling newspaper reporters stared. Isaac Bell stared back, as amazed. The last person he expected to walk up the stage lugging his long carpetbag was Aloysius Clarke, decked out in top hat and tails.

'Pretty steamboat, Isaac.'

'What are you doing out of the hospital?'

Wish dropped his bag with a clank and caught his breath. 'Couldn't miss the Duquesne Cotillion.'

'You came all the way to Pittsburgh for the ball?'

'Quite a shindig. Everybody who was anybody was there. I even met Colonel J. Philip Swigert of the Pennsylvania state militia. Talkative gent, particularly when he's had a few.'

'Well done!' Bell reached to slap Wish on the shoulder in congratulations. Wish stayed him with a gesture. 'Don't tear the stitches.'

Bell pulled up short. 'Are you OK?'

'Tip-top.'

'You don't look tip-top – what did the colonel say?'

'You got here just in time,' Wish answered gravely. 'State militia, and the Pinkertons, and the Coal and Iron Police, are marching aboard the *Vulcan King* this morning. They'll head downstream lickety-split. Reckon to round the Homestead Works two or three hours from now, depending how fast they load up. Then their cannon'll blast an opening in these barges, and their whole gang will storm ashore.'

Bell called down to the miners tending the *White Lady*'s furnaces. 'Get her coaled up and the boys fed. We're going back to work.'

The appearance of Captain Jennings, master of the exploded *Camilla*, was even more unexpected, and Isaac Bell thought for an instant he was seeing a ghost. But the old pilot was no ghost, only a grieving father. 'We swapped boats that night. They murdered my boy.'

'I am so sorry, Captain.'

'I'll run your boat. I know this stretch of the Mon better than your fellers from Cincinnati.'

'She's a lot bigger than *Camilla*.'

Jennings started up the stairs to the wheelhouse. 'Boats are the same. Rivers ain't.'

'Letter came for you,' said Wish, pulling an envelope from his vest. 'Lady's handwriting.'

He stepped aside to give Bell privacy to read it.

Bell tore it open. It was from Mary. But it contained only four lines.

My Dearest Isaac,

What I am going to do, I must do.
I hope with all my heart that we'll be together one day in a better world.

He read it over and over. At length, Wish stepped closer to him. 'You're looking mighty low for a fellow about to fight a naval battle.'

Bell showed him Mary's letter.

'Write her back.'

'I don't know what to say. I don't know where to send it.'

'Write it anyway. If you don't, you'll wish you had. You've got a moment right now before all hell breaks loose.'

Bell stood aside while the firemen wheelbarrowed coal and tried to pen an answer in his notebook. The words would not come. He stared at the crowded tent city. They'd flown a defiant red flag from the top of the tipple. But people were staring at the river, bracing for attack. He saw Archie Abbott, running down the slope, waving to get his attention, and, in that instant, he suddenly knew what to write.

Dear Mary,

When you hope we'll be together in a better world, I hope you mean a changed world on Earth so we don't have to wait until Heaven, which your words had the sound of. Wherever it is, it will be for me a better world with you by my side. If that's not enough for you, then why don't we do something here and now to fix it, together?

He paused, still grasping for clarity. Archie was almost to the stage and calling him. Bell touched his pen to the paper again.

What I'm trying to say is, come back.

All my love

'Isaac!' Archie bounded up the stage, out of breath. He spoke in a low and urgent voice. 'The miners got a cannon.'

'*What?*'

'I heard that someone – presumably, our friend Mr Clay – gave the strikers a cannon. I found it. They told me it's a 1.65 Hotchkiss Mountain Gun. Fast-firing and accurate. Look up, right at the foot of the tipple. They just pulled the canvas off it.'

Bell focused his eyes on the distant emplacement. It was a wheel-mounted gun, and largely hidden behind stacked gunnysacks of coal and thick masonry at the base of the tipple.

He said, 'The first shot the miners fire at the *Vulcan King* will give the militia all the excuse they need to pounce ashore shooting – unless the miners get lucky and sink her with their first shot, which is highly unlikely. Even if they did, it would just prolong the inevitable and make it worse.'

'What are you going to do, Isaac?'

Bell called, 'Hey, Wish, do you have a cigar?'

'Of course,' said Wish, tugging a Havana from his tail-coat. 'What dapper bon vivant attends a ball without cigars?'

Bell clamped it between his teeth.

'Want a light?'

'Not yet. You got a sawed-off in your bag for Archie?'

Wish beckoned Archie and handed him the weapon. 'Try and make sure no innocents are downwind.'

Archie said, 'I thought apprentices aren't allowed –'

'You're temporarily promoted. Stick it under your coat. Don't get close to me unless I yell for you.'

Bell strode down the boarding stage and hurried across

the point to the powder shed the miners had erected far from the tents to store the fresh dynamite they'd managed to smuggle in at night. They were guarding it closely, recalling, no doubt, the accidental explosion that nearly sank the *Sadie* and half her barges. The Powder Committee remembered, too, the tall detective, who had recommended – at gunpoint – that the dynamite ride in its own barge apart from the people, and greeted him warmly.

'That's a handsome steamboat you brought us, Mr Bell. What can we do for you?'

'I need,' said Bell, 'one stick of dynamite, a blasting cap, and a short safety fuse.'

'Want me to assemble it?'

'Appreciate it.'

He watched as the miner worked quickly but meticulously.

'How short a fuse do you want?'

'Give me ten seconds.'

The miner looked at him. 'I hope you can run fast.'

'Fast enough.' Bell slipped the greasy red stick in his coat and gestured with his cigar. 'Got a light?'

'Let's move away from the powder shed.' The miner struck a match and shielded the flame from the wind and rain until Bell got the cigar lit and glowing.

'Thank you.'

'I'd recommend keeping the business end away from that fuse.'

Puffing on the cigar, trailing aromatic smoke, Isaac Bell walked up the slope to the gun emplacement. The Hotchkiss was oiled and well cared for, not a speck of rust on the wheels or the tube, and the men serving looked like they knew their business. They had seen *White Lady* arrive and echoed the gratitude of the men at the powder shed.

Bell turned around as if to admire the steamer, which gleamed in the Pittsburgh murk as tall and long and white as the finest seaside resort. He puffed the red-hot coal at the front of his cigar, took the dynamite from his pocket, touched the cigar to the fuse, and puffed up a cloud of smoke to distract the gun crew as he faced the cannon and slid the cylinder of dynamite down the four-foot barrel.

'What did you –'

Hurrying down the hill at a fast lope, Bell called over his shoulder in a commanding voice, 'Run for it! It's dynamite. *Archie!*'

Fifty yards down, he looked back. The dynamite went off with a muffled peal. The gun jumped off its wheels, and the breech peeled open as if made of paper. The crew gathered around the shattered weapon. Angry men ran after Bell, shouting:

'*What did you do to us?*'

Bell kept walking fast, signaling Archie not to pull the shotgun until they really needed it.

'*Why?*'

'*What did you do to us?*'

'I'm hoping I saved your damned fool lives,' Bell said.

'*How can we beat 'em? How can we win?*'

The shouts died on their lips. All eyes flew to the top of the tipple. A lookout was bellowing through cupped hands:

'They're coming! The black boat is coming.'

47

'Cast off!' Isaac Bell ordered.

He and Archie raced up the boarding stage. Bell gathered Mack and Wally on the wheelhouse stairs. 'Somehow we have to keep them apart.'

The wheelhouse stood five decks above the river, and from it Bell could see much of the tent city sprawled on the Amalgamated point. On the other side of the barricades of heaped trolley cars, a rippling blue mass marked Pittsburgh police pacing in the rain.

'Itching for an opening,' muttered Mack Fulton. 'Can't wait to break heads.'

Captain Jennings stood with both hands on the six-foot-high brass-trimmed wheel, grim-faced and intent. At Bell's command, he rang the engine room for *Astern*, turned his wheel slightly to swing the stern into the stream, and flanked the three-hundred-foot hull off the improvised wharf.

A Defense Committee detail, wielding axes, surged on to the barge they had raised to make a wharf and chopped holes in the bottom, resinking it into a protective wall of barges half sunken in the mud.

Bell said, 'Put us between them and the point.'

Jennings angled the boat into the river and turned upstream. A tall Homestead Works blast furnace blocked the view beyond the next bend. For moments that seemed endless, they had the rain-spattered water to themselves.

'Did you write Mary?' Wish asked.

'I should have said it to her face – here they come!'

Vulcan King's tall chimneys showed first, swinging around the somber obstruction of the Homestead furnace. She was moving fast, flying with the current, and upon them before the *White Lady* was halfway into the river. Suddenly, with no warning, the cannon on her bow boomed.

A shell screamed, skimming the river, and exploded on one of the barges blocking the bank. Timbers flew in the air.

Isaac Bell moved closer to Captain Jennings. 'He's got a cannon and we don't. Can you ram him?'

'Saddlebag the murdering devils? You bet. Tell your boys down there to put on the blowers.'

Bell shouted the order into the engine room voice pipe.

Forced draft blowers roared in the chimneys, fanning the furnaces white-hot.

The *Vulcan King* fired again, and a second barge exploded. A third shot went high. It tore a swath through a line of tents, and the hillside seemed to quiver as hundreds of people ran, screaming.

'How can I help?' Bell asked Jennings.

'Tell me if he's got himself a Mon pilot or a Cincinnati pilot.'

'I don't know.'

'If he's from Cincinnati, when he comes around that bend he just might put himself in the wrong place. There's a crosscurrent when the river floods this high that'll kick his stern and crowd him to the bank.'

The cannon boomed. A fourth shell blasted the barges. And Isaac Bell thought, I'm supposed to be stopping a war, not losing it.

Henry Clay was beside himself. Why weren't the miners shooting back?

The Hotchkiss he gave them should be raking *Vulcan King*'s decks by now. Instead, militiamen were standing in the open, cheering each shot. And the company police and Pinkertons were clapping one another on the back like it was a baseball game.

A grinning Coal and Iron cop slapped Clay's shoulder. 'We're winning.'

But Clay's plan was to start a war – a shooting war on both sides – and keep it going, not win it. He grabbed an officer's field glasses, ignoring his protests, and focused on the Hotchkiss. The cannon was there, shielded by coal bags at the foot of the tipple, but no one was manning it. And when he looked more closely, he saw the tube was perched at an odd angle. Something had happened to it, and that something was very likely named Isaac Bell.

'Give that back or I'll have you up on charges,' shouted the officer. Clay, disguised in a private's uniform, pushed through the cheering fools and headed for the main deck where the furnaces fired the boilers. His disguise included a khaki knapsack – a US Army-issue Merriam Pack with an external frame supported by a belt. In it, he carried what at first glance appeared to be jagged chunks of coal but were actually dynamite sticks with detonators and one-inch fuses bundled in chamois leather dyed with lampblack.

Vulcan King was a ten-boiler boat, and firemen were scrambling from one to the next, shoveling coal into wide-open furnaces. Someone saw Clay's uniform and shouted, 'How's it going up there?'

'We're winning!' said Clay, and when the fireman turned to scoop more coal, Clay lobbed one of his bombs into the furnace and ran as fast as he could to the back of the boat.

The Monongahela crosscurrent that Captain Jennings had hoped for caught the *Vulcan King*'s Cincinnati pilot unawares. Generated by the Amalgamated point of land deflecting extraordinarily high water, the current grabbed the steamboat's stern and overwhelmed her thrashing paddles. Before her pilot could recover, the black boat's bow was crowding the bank. Her hull thrust across the channel directly in the path of *White Lady*, which Isaac Bell had churning Full Ahead to ram.

Vulcan King's cannon boomed.

It sounded immensely louder this time, thought Bell. Did they have a second cannon? Or had they finally unleashed the Gatling? But even as a wild shell soared over the barges and exploded in a kitchen tent, he saw it was the last shot the steamboat would ever fire at the strikers' camp.

'Her boiler burst,' Captain Jennings shouted.

The steamboat's chimneys leaned forward, tumbled off her hurricane deck, and crashed on her bow. Timbers followed. Glass and planking rained down. From her wheelhouse forward, her upper works were demolished.

'The murdering devils' boiler burst!'

'It had help,' said Isaac Bell, who had seen it happen twice at Gleasonburg. 'That was no accident.' But why would Henry Clay blow up his own boat?

'They got what they deserved!'

Captain Jennings rang for more steam.

The blowers roared.

'I'll finish the sons of bitches.'

The shock of the explosion scattered burning furnace coal. The *Vulcan King*'s forward decks took fire from the shattered wheelhouse to the waterline. Militiamen in khaki stampeded from the flames. A man in the dark uniform of the Coal and Iron Police threw himself into the river. Strikebreakers dropped their pick handles and splashed in after him, calling for help.

'Stop!' said Isaac Bell. 'Back your engines.'

48

'What are you doing, Isaac?' Wish, Wally and Mack were at his side.

'Coming alongside to get those people off. Back your engines, Captain Jennings. Wheel hard over.'

'Not 'til I saddlebag the murderers.'

'Back them!'

'You can't let 'em win.'

'Henry Clay doesn't want to win. He wants mayhem. I won't give it to him.'

Mack Fulton cocked his Smith & Wesson, told the pilot, 'Boss man says back your engines.'

A single lever in the engine room engaged the reversing gears on both engines at once. Coupled to the same shaft as the stern wheel, when the engines stopped, the wheel stopped.

Escape pipes roared behind the wheelhouse.

Bell threw an arm around the grieving pilot's shoulders. 'Right now, they're nothing more than scared fools. Like us – Hard over with your wheel, Captain. Bring us alongside. Let's get those people off.'

Bell turned to his squad.

'Shoot anyone who tries to bring a weapon. Rifle, pistol, blackjack, or brass knuckles, shoot 'em. And watch for Clay. There's more militia than anyone else, so he'll probably be wearing a uniform.'

He led them down to the main deck. Captain Jennings circled to a position upstream from the *Vulcan King*, where he could use his paddles, rudders, and the hard-running Monongahela to maneuver beside the burning steamer.

Bell stationed Wally, Mack and Archie where the boats would touch. Wish Clarke passed out shotguns and insisted on staying in the thick of it, claiming he would protect his hospital stitches with his sawed-off. Bell climbed one level to the boiler deck, where he could watch from above.

The fire was spreading, fed by dry wood and fresh paint, marching back from the *Vulcan King*'s bow, driving men toward the stern. In their chaotic, writhing mass, Bell saw that most wore khaki uniforms – short, four-button mud-colored sack coats, foraged caps on their heads, and cartridge boxes belted in back at the waist. Their weapons were a typically motley state militia collection of Spanish-American War black powder, single-shot .45-70 trapdoor rifles, improved Krag-Jørgensen magazine rifles, and even some 1895 Lee Navys – all with bayonets fixed. The Coal and Iron Police, easily identified by dark uniforms and shiny badges, had pistols and clubs. Known for brutality, they looked terrified, and many of the hard-eyed Pinkerton detectives had lost their bowlers in their panic.

The gap of water separating the boats narrowed.

The ex-prisoners drafted as strikebreakers clawed frantically to the rail.

Isaac Bell cupped his hands to shout, 'Drop your weapons!'

Rifles and pick handles clattered to the deck.

Wish Clarke tipped his shotgun skyward and triggered a thunderous round.

'Drop 'em!'

Pistols and blackjacks carpeted the deck.

A Pinkerton scooped up a fallen Colt automatic and slipped it in his coat. Mack Fulton shot him without hesitating. As he fell, men turned out pockets to show they were empty.

The two hulls neared. Men poised to jump.

'Reach for the sky!' the Van Dorns bellowed. 'Hands in the air.'

The flames bent toward them suddenly, driven by a shift in wind.

The hulls came together with a crash that nearly threw Bell from his perch on the boiler deck. Hundreds jumped, kicking and fighting to safety. Bell leaped on to a railing to see better. The Coal and Iron cops, the prisoners, and even the Pinkertons, had dissolved into a mob with a single mind – to get off the burning boat – and it was nearly impossible to distinguish individual features. Only the trained militia still held their hands in the air, trusting that if they followed orders, they would not be shot.

Henry Clay, Bell knew, was expert at melting into his surroundings, which was why Bell was positive Clay had disguised himself as a militiaman. But even they were so densely packed, as they crossed over, that every soldier in khaki looked the same. Desperate, Bell tried to concentrate on the bigger soldiers, those built more like Clay.

Here came one now, hands up to show they were empty, jumping on to *White Lady*, face inclined downward as he watched his footing. He was aboard in a flash, crowding into those ahead of him, stumbling forward when another behind him shoved his pack.

His pack. Instead of a cartridge box, he was wearing a khaki Merriam Pack big enough to hold a bomb.

'Stop that man!'

49

Wally Kisley lunged after Henry Clay.

Three men leaping madly from the flames trampled him.

Bell saw his checkerboard suit disappear in the scrum. He jumped from the rail to the deck and swung down to the main deck, landing on fallen men, kicking to his feet and running after Clay, who was racing toward the stern, straight-arming men out of his way. Suddenly, he cut across the open freight deck.

Bell veered after him.

Clay yanked a gun and fired three shots without breaking stride. Two fanned Bell's face, the third drilled the brim of his hat, whirling it from his head. Bell stopped running and took careful aim with his Colt Army and triggered it just as Clay turned to fire again. He cried out as Bell's shot, intended for his head, creased his hand instead when he raised his gun. The gun went flying. But the wound did not slow him as he leaped up the boiler deck stairs, slinging the Merriam Pack off his shoulders and clutching it by the straps.

Bell knew he was heading for the furnaces, intending to bomb a boiler.

He spotted him from the top of the stairs and again took careful aim.

The Colt roared. The shot staggered Clay. His arm dropped straight to his side, and the pack slipped from his hand. But he kept moving, ever swift and indestructible. He scooped up the fallen bag with his other hand and darted toward the nearest furnace. Bell took aim again. Firemen, panicked by gunshots and ricocheting lead, scattered for cover, blocking Bell's shot. Henry Clay ran past the open furnace and tossed the pack underhand with a softball pitcher's smooth delivery.

Bell saw a cloud of sparks as it landed in the shimmering bed of cherry red coals. In the half second he took to reach the firebox door, the canvas was burning brightly. He had to pull it out before the fire burned though the canvas and ignited the fuse.

Bell grabbed a fireman's rake, reached into the blaze, caught the strap, and yanked. The strap burned through, and it broke. He thrust the rake again, caught the wooden frame, which was drenched in flame, and pulled it out. The pack fell, smoldering, at his feet. 'Pull the fuse,' he shouted to the nearest coal miner and tore after Henry Clay, who was racing sternward on the freight deck.

Clay ran out of space where the boiler deck overlooked the *White Lady*'s fifty-foot stern wheel. Bell caught up. The wheel was throwing spray as paddle blade after paddle blade climbed out of the water behind the boat, circled through the air, and plunged down to push again. Henry Clay turned with a smile on his face and a derringer in his unwounded hand and fired. The bullet seared the heel of Bell's hand. His thumb and fingers convulsed. His gun fell to the deck and bounced into the narrow slot between the back of the boat and the stern wheel.

Clay's smile broadened in triumph. 'I've waited a long time for this.'

He squeezed the trigger. Isaac Bell was already swinging, hoping that the only thing that would slow down the rogue detective would be talking too much. Before the slug had emerged from the barrel, Isaac Bell's left fist smashed Clay's jaw.

The shot missed.

Bell feinted with his wounded right hand, punched Clay with another powerful left. It staggered Clay, and he reeled backwards to the edge of the stern.

'Give it up,' said Bell. 'It's over.'

Clay looked at him incredulously. 'It's never over.'

He flew at Bell, cocking his left hand in a powerful fist. He tried to raise the right Bell had wounded and could not. An angry light filled his amber eyes, and he glared at his arm as if it were a traitor.

'I'm taking you in,' said Bell. 'We'll recommend mercy if you reveal who paid for this. Who's the boss?'

'It's never over,' Henry Clay repeated. He swung his good arm. Bell took the punch, rolled with it, and counterpunched, rocking Clay back on his heels.

'You can't fight me with one arm. Give it up.'

'It's never over,' Clay said again. But even as he spoke, he turned away.

Bell suddenly realized that Clay was so desperate to escape that he would risk certain death by trying to dive into the narrow strait of water between the *White Lady*'s stern and her churning wheel. Without Henry Clay, he had no case against the man backing him, no way to discover the identity of the true murderer, the real provocateur.

Bell lunged for him, and as fast as Henry Clay was, Isaac Bell was faster. He seized Clay's militia tunic in his right hand and started to drag him from the edge. But this time, the young detective was the fighter betrayed by a wound. The bullet that had disarmed him had robbed his hand of too much strength. Thumb and fingers feathered apart. Clay tore loose and dived into the seething water.

Isaac Bell watched the wheel wash spewed by the slashing paddle blades. But Henry Clay's body never broke the surface of that endless rolling wave behind the boat.

50

'I wish I'd been there to watch him drown,' Joseph Van Dorn said heavily. 'I taught that man every trick I knew. It never occurred to me until it was too late that I'd created a monster.' He shook his head, rubbed his red whiskers, and looked probingly at Isaac Bell. 'It makes a man wonder, will he create another?'

'Relax, Joe,' said Mack Fulton. 'Isaac's just a detective.'

'And a pretty good one,' said Wally Kisley, 'once he masters the art of bringing criminals in alive.'

'Or at least a corpse.'

The Van Dorns were waiting for a train in a saloon close to Union Station. Prince Henry of Prussia was sailing home on the *Deutschland*, and the Boss was taking them all to New York for what threatened to be a wild scramble.

'How wide was the space between the wheel and the boat?' asked Archie.

'Three feet,' Bell answered. 'But to survive without me seeing him, he would have had to dive under the blades and then stay underwater and swim a long ways off before he surfaced.' Bell had relived Clay's dive over and over in his mind, bitterly aware that if he had captured him alive, he would be much closer to identifying the real provocateur behind Henry Clay.

'We'll get him one of these days,' Van Dorn said

magnanimously. 'There's no statute of limitations on murder. At least the strike is over. The miners aren't all that happy, but they're heading back to work, and their families will be living in houses instead of tents.'

'Company houses,' said Bell.

'Yes, of course. Did your young lady show up yet?'

'Not yet.' Bell had no idea where Mary was.

Wish Clarke walked in with his carpetbag.

'Wish looks like he lost his best friend.'

'Or dropped a bottle,' said Mack.

Wish did not sit. 'Son, do you have a moment?' he asked and walked to a table in a far corner. Bell followed.

'Sit down, Isaac.'

'What's the matter?'

'While they were dismantling the wreck of the *Vulcan King*, they found –'

'Clay's body? It drifted –'

'I'm so sorry, Isaac. They found your girl.'

'What?'

'Scalded to death when the boiler burst. Looks like she was engaged in sabotage.'

'But that can't be,' Bell gasped.

'Maybe not, son. But you showed me her letter. She might have done what she thought she had to do.'

'Where is – where do they have her?'

'Remember Mary as she was, Isaac.'

'I have to see her.'

'No, Isaac. She doesn't exist anymore. Not the girl you know. Let her be the girl you remember.'

Bell turned toward the door. Wish blocked him. Bell said, 'It's all right. I just have to tell her brother.'

'Jim knows.'

'How did he take it?'

'He refuses to believe it. He swears she wrote him that she was going to New York to confront the man staking Henry Clay.'

'*Who?*'

'She didn't put it in the letter.'

Bell said, 'I will find him if it takes every minute of my life.'

Wish Clarke laid a comforting hand on Isaac Bell's shoulder. 'Keep in mind, son, when you never give up, time's on your side.'

Epilogue

A Smoke-filled Room
1912

The Congdon Building's elevator runner reached for the intercom. 'May I have your name, sir? I gotta call ahead.'

'Don't,' said Chief Investigator Isaac Bell. He opened his coat to show his gold Van Dorn Agency badge and the butt of a Browning automatic polished by use.

It was hot and smoky in James Congdon's office, and ash-trays were deep with cigar butts. Congdon, bright-eyed and flushed with victory, recognized Bell when the detective walked in without knocking. He welcomed him warmly.

'Chief Inspector Isaac Bell. I haven't seen you since you relieved me of a carload of money playing poker on the Overland Limited back in '07.'

'If I had known then what I know now, I'd have taken more than your money.'

'I recall it as a friendly game – if expensive.'

'You're under arrest, Judge James Congdon, for murder in the coalfields.'

Congdon laughed at the tall detective.

'I have no time to be arrested. My train is taking me to the convention in Chicago with enough delegates to nom-inate me to run for vice president of the United States.'

'Then I've caught up with you just in time to save the life of your running mate.'

Congdon laughed again, and mocked him, 'Never give

up? Never? I know you've been sniffing around for years, but you'll never link me to any murders in that strike. Fact is, thanks to me intervening with the coal operators and persuading President Roosevelt to mediate, the strike ended peacefully. Everyone got something they wanted – the miners received a small raise, the producers were not forced to recognize the union – and there've been no coal strikes since.'

'Even if that lie were truth,' Bell answered quietly, 'even if you got away with every killing in the coalfields, you will die for the murder of Mary Higgins.'

'Mary Higgins died while sabotaging a company steamboat,' Congdon said. 'But I can't allow accusations to confuse gullible voters.' He raised his voice and shouted through the closed door to an adjoining office. 'Mr Potter! I need you.'

A well-built middle-aged man with a beard that was showing flecks of gray limped into the office carrying a leveled Colt Bisley.

Isaac Bell looked him over. ' "Mr Potter," you will disappoint the many who hoped that Henry Clay drowned in the Ohio River.'

Congdon said, 'Mr Clay became Mr Potter so that I could help him live in great comfort, free of the electric chair.'

'In exchange,' said Bell, 'for killing your enemies and rivals.'

Congdon said, 'I'm disappointed that you don't seem one bit surprised. I had hoped to see your jaw drop.'

'Joseph Van Dorn suspected years ago that Clay had to be your assassin. Who else, he asked, could be as cold-blooded? And he described you to a T, Congdon: a man wise enough to see Henry Clay's talents and greedy enough to employ them.'

Clay's expression turned cold at Bell's mention of Van Dorn. 'That bulge in your coat where you used to pack your Colt Army, and subsequently a Bisley, is now, I'm informed, a Browning No. 2. Put it on Mr Congdon's desk.'

Bell surrendered his favorite pistol of many years, a Belgian-made semi-automatic modified to fire an American .380 caliber cartridge.

'I presume you replaced the sleeve gun I took away from you in New York. Drop it, too.'

Bell shook the derringer out of his sleeve and handed it over.

'And the pocket pistol.'

'You have a long memory,' said Bell.

'It's kept me alive. Put it on the desk.'

Bell placed the tiny one-shot on the desk.

'And the knife in your boot.'

'Want me to throw it at anything?'

'If you still can, hit the edge of that bookshelf.'

Bell threw overhand. The knive struck like a flash of lightning.

James Congdon howled in dismay. The blade had pierced the portrait of his latest wife, depicted as a shapely goddess in silk gauze, and stood quivering in the lady's nose. Bell used the distraction to glide behind the shimmering white Rodin marble.

'Sorry, I missed.'

Clay leveled his gun.

'What if you miss me and shoot your boss's favorite statue?'

Clay started toward him, saying, 'I'll get so close, I can't miss.'

'Be careful!' Congdon shouted.

As Clay turned to assure him, Bell whipped his two-shot derringer from his hat.

'Drop it!'

Henry Clay stopped in his tracks. His startled expression seemed to shout *Where the hell did that come from?*

Bell said, 'Live and learn. Toss your gun over there, on the carpet.'

Clay shrugged with a faint knowing smile and did as Bell ordered. Then he looked at Judge Congdon. The old man caressed the bronze statuette on his desk. 'You're wrong, Chief Inspector. The statue you're hiding behind is not my favorite. This is my favorite.'

'I can't believe you prefer that little thing to this magnificent marble.'

In answer, the financier jerked the steam lever.

Isaac Bell, Henry Clay, and James Congdon all looked up at the ceiling.

Only Bell smiled.

He stuck out his hand. Warm water dripped on to his palm.

'It appears to be raining in your office. And on your parade.'

Congdon jerked the steam lever again. Nothing happened. Frantically, he tugged the statue again and again, slamming it down, jerking it upright, slamming it down.

372

Bell said, 'I thought it sensible to shut the steam-conditioning valves to your office.'

Congdon's long, thin frame sagged, and he slipped off his feet into his chair.

'But how did you know?'

Bell moved swiftly forward and swept the guns off the desk on to the floor before Congdon or Clay got any ideas. 'Judge Congdon, you are under arrest for the murder of Mary Higgins.'

Henry Clay's expression shifted from flummoxed to deeply puzzled.

'You were out of the room earlier, Clay. You didn't hear me charge your boss with murdering a young woman in 1902.'

'Are you crazy, Bell?'

'I wish I were,' Isaac Bell answered sadly. 'I would give anything to be wrong. But she died a horrible death right here in this office.'

'Mary died in Pittsburgh.'

'Mary Higgins was *found* in Pittsburgh. Many were led to believe that Mary was scalded to death helping you blow up the militia's steamboat.'

Clay shook his head. 'Mary didn't help me. I had no idea she was aboard. She must have used that boy disguise she used in Denver.'

'She was never aboard the *Vulcan King*. Not alive. She died here, in New York. Mary's brother swore that she could not have been in Pittsburgh because Mary wrote him that she was going to New York to confront the saboteur's boss – your boss. No one believed Jim Higgins. But why would he say it unless he was addled with grief or telling the truth? So I asked questions. Turns out, I was not the only man sweet on her.'

Clay was listening closely.

Bell said, 'I'll bet you boasted to her, hoping to impress her – she was the kind of girl a fellow would do most anything to impress. You did brag, didn't you? Bragged how you had partnered up with the most powerful man in Wall Street.'

'I didn't brag.'

'Maybe you got puddingheaded when she slipped you the knockout drops.'

'How do you know about that?'

'Give Van Dorns some credit. The pharmacist she bought the chloral from told me. You gave Mary Congdon's name, didn't you?'

'I must have.'

'You signed her death warrant.'

Clay looked at Congdon, who was slumped behind his desk. 'Did you hurt her?'

Congdon said, 'It's a trick, you idiot.'

Clay looked to Bell. The color of Bell's eyes had darkened to a steely blue. He directed them straight at the rogue detective. 'We never give up,' he said softly. 'You know that better than anybody. It was Mr Van Dorn's motto from the beginning, wasn't it?'

Clay stared. Then he lowered his eyes and nodded agreement. 'Yes, from the beginning.'

Isaac Bell said, 'It took me ten years to trace her steps from Pittsburgh to New York, to Wall Street, to this building, to this office. You know your business, Clay, you know how it works. A word here, a hint there, a memory, a glimpse. It's easier when it's a pretty girl who struck the eye. Ticket agents. Train conductors. Landladies. A unionist finally out of prison. Bits. Pieces. Bits of nothing. Suddenly, you get lucky with a clerk who makes change for the El. Right around the corner. A hundred feet from this building. Then back to bits of nothing. Finally, a stroke of luck.'

Bell turned to Congdon.

'The brokerage house of Thibodeau & Marzen went bankrupt in the Panic of '07. There were lawsuits by the dozen. Judge James Congdon's name surfaced in court. Turned out you owned the broker. And thanks to an old detective who once told me that sometimes dead ends turn around, I had in my files a copy of a private wire transmitted on Thibodeau & Marzen's leased telegraph line to Henry Clay's alias, John Claggart.'

Bell turned back to Henry Clay. 'But I still had no final absolute, provable connection. Until, one night, I got lucky again. An elevator runner, a temporary filling in that evening and who left town the day after, was all of a sudden back ten years later. His uncle was still the superintendent of the building. The nephew's hopes hadn't panned out. And his uncle gave him a job.'

Bell shifted his gaze to Congdon for a long moment, then back to Henry Clay.

'The lucky detective stopped by – as he had regularly – and this time found the new elevator runner and recognized him as the temporary who had been working that night ten years ago.

'"Sure, I remember that girl. She was a looker. But, boy, did she look mad."'

Bell's voice thickened. 'I asked, "When did you take her back down?"

'"Didn't," he said. "She never come down on my shift and I was on for darn near ten hours straight." And I asked again, "You ran her to what floor?"

'"Top floor. Mr Congdon's own private floor."

'"Are you sure?"

'"Sure I'm sure. Orders were, you had to call ahead to go to Mr Congdon's floor. I called ahead. Mr Congdon said, 'Bring her up.' I brought her up."

'Mary Higgins died right here in this office. Right beside your boss's statue.'

'It was self-defense!' Congdon shouted.

'What?' said Clay.

'She did not come here to "confront" me. She came to kill me.'

Isaac Bell said, 'I never doubted that Mary Higgins was a woman of the highest moral standard. You just confirmed it with your confession that you thought she intended to kill you.'

'I made no confession.'

'I just heard it from your own lips.'

'It's your word against mine.'

'And his,' said Isaac Bell.

Henry Clay, who was listening stone-faced, asked James Congdon, 'Did you kill Mary?'

Congdon pulled a pistol from his desk. Clay stared at it, his face lighting with recognition. 'She told me she could never kill anyone. I believed her. I still do.'

'She changed her mind,' said Congdon. 'A lady's prerogative.'

'Where did you get that gun?'

'I'll explain after we tend to Mr Bell.'

'That's a Colt Bisley. Mary took mine.'

Congdon heard the threat in Clay's voice and whirled with his pistol.

Clay dove to the carpet with astounding speed, scooped up the gun he had dropped, and shot first, lacing two bullets into the old man's chest. Congdon tumbled backwards, jerking his trigger as he fell. His bullet struck *The Kiss*, shattering the marble. Congdon's eyes locked in mourning on the ruin.

Clay stood over him. 'But how did you move Mary's body to the steamboat in Pittsburgh?'

James Congdon answered with his dying breath.

'You weren't the only ambitious fool who worked for me.'

Henry Clay's shoulders sagged as Congdon's had in his defeat. He shook his head in dismay. Then he turned to Isaac Bell. 'You never gave up, and you got the man who killed Mary.'

'But Judge Congdon didn't kill Terry Fein, Mike Flannery, young Captain Jennings, Black Jack Gleason, and countless others caught in your schemes. Henry Clay, you're under arrest.'

Clay's amber eyes were dead with defeat, but his pistol was rising with superhuman speed. Isaac Bell shot it out of his hand. It fell on Congdon's chest. Clay gazed at it a moment, clutching his fingers. His empty gaze shifted to Bell's derringer, and his eyes came alive.

'Looks like a .22,' he said. 'And only one shot left. Do you think you can stop Henry Clay with one bullet?'

The door behind him banged opened and a big voice boomed, 'Isaac *could* stop you with one shot between your murderous eyes. But I made him swear to me that I would get the first *seven* shots if you gave us the slightest excuse to pull the trigger.'

Henry Clay looked over his shoulder and down the barrel of Van Dorn's Colt M1911 semi-automatic pistol and raised his hands.

'Pick up that telephone and call Congdon's train,' Van Dorn ordered.

'Train?'

Isaac Bell explained, 'You've got a date with the electric chair. Sing Sing's on the way to Chicago. We'll drop you there for safekeeping until your trial.'

Marion Bell knew from experience that after her husband solved a case, he would tell her everything that had happened when he was ready to. But this time was special. When he glided across Wall Street and slipped soundlessly into the auto, she sensed that he wanted to tell her now but couldn't form the words, and might never.

She started the Marmon, pulled away from the curb into the empty street, steered around the corner, and headed up Broadway. Isaac Bell sat quietly, watching the boisterous late-night city streets. When they got to Forty-second Street, Marion turned left toward the Hudson River.

'Where are we going?' asked Bell. Archie's town house, where they stayed in New York, was up in the East Sixties.

'Home.'

Bell considered her answer for a couple of blocks.

Home was three thousand miles away in San Francisco, where they first met six years ago at the time of the Earthquake. It was a two- or three-month trip in an auto, depending on the weather and the state of the roads, and a Marmon Speedster probably wasn't up to it. Of course Marion knew that, which meant she had a plan. They had married two years ago on the *Mauretania*, and he knew her well enough by now to know she had a plan.

'Joe Van Dorn won't let me off for that long.'

'I'll bet we could make the Mississippi in ten days.'

'Depending on the roads.'

'And ten nights.'

'We'll run out of roads beyond the Mississippi.'

'Then we'll put the car on a special at St Louis. Home on the train in four days.'

Bell leaned over to read the gauges. 'You filled the gasoline tank.'

'There's a picnic basket in the trunk.'

Marion drove on to the ferry, and they went up to the passenger deck and stood at the railing, watching the lights of Manhattan. In the middle of the river she asked, 'What did Congdon say?'

'He confessed.'

'What did *you* say?'

'I said good-bye to my old friend Mary Higgins.'

Also available in the bestselling Isaac Bell series

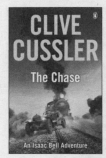

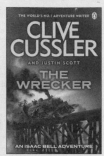

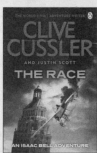

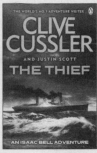

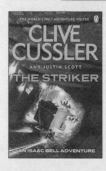

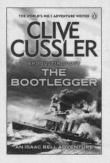

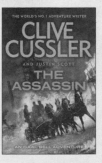

Why not try Cussler's other series?

**Dirk Pitt Adventures | NUMA Files
Fargo Adventures | Oregon Files**